OH MY GODS! II
THE FORGOTTEN MAZE

Written by Stephanie Cooke & Insha Fitzpatrick
Art by Juliana Moon

Etch
Clarion Books
Imprints of HarperCollins*Publishers*

To Lily, Andy, Maria, and Whitney.
This book wouldn't be the same without you.

Etch and Clarion Books are imprints of HarperCollins Publishers.

Oh My Gods! 2: The Forgotten Maze

For information address HarperCollins Children's Books, a division of HarperCollins Publishers, 195 Broadway, New York, NY 10007.
clarionbooks.com

Library of Congress Cataloging-in-Publication Data has been applied for.
ISBN: 978-0-358-29953-0 hardcover
ISBN: 978-0-358-29954-7 paperback

The text was set in Amescote.
Color by Whitney Cogar
Lettering by Andrea Miller
Edited by Lily Kessinger
Proofread by Susan Buckheit and Erika West
Cover and interior design by Andrea Miller

Manufactured in Spain
EST 10 9 8 7 6 5 4 3 2 1
4500840289

First Edition

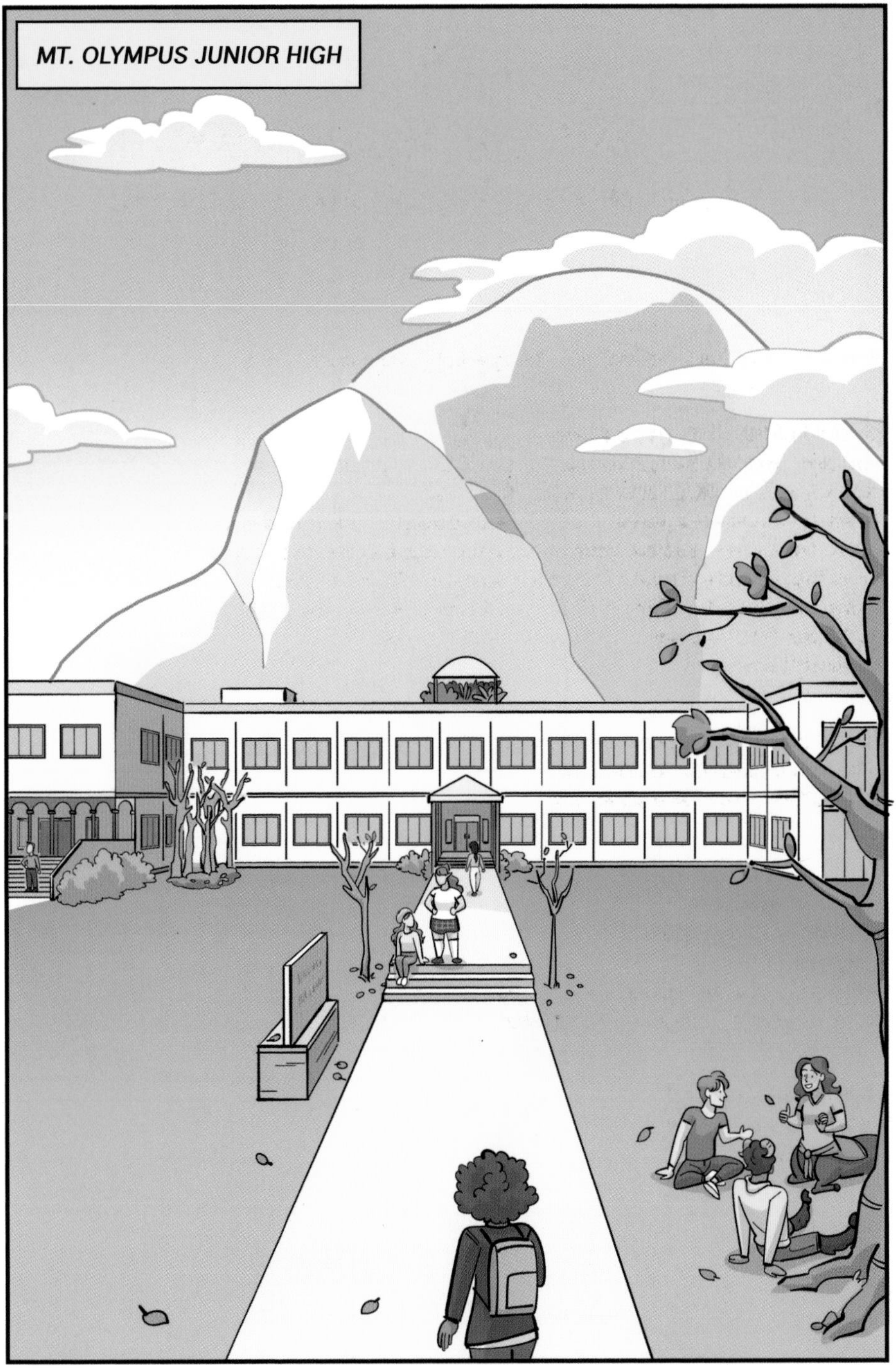
MT. OLYMPUS JUNIOR HIGH

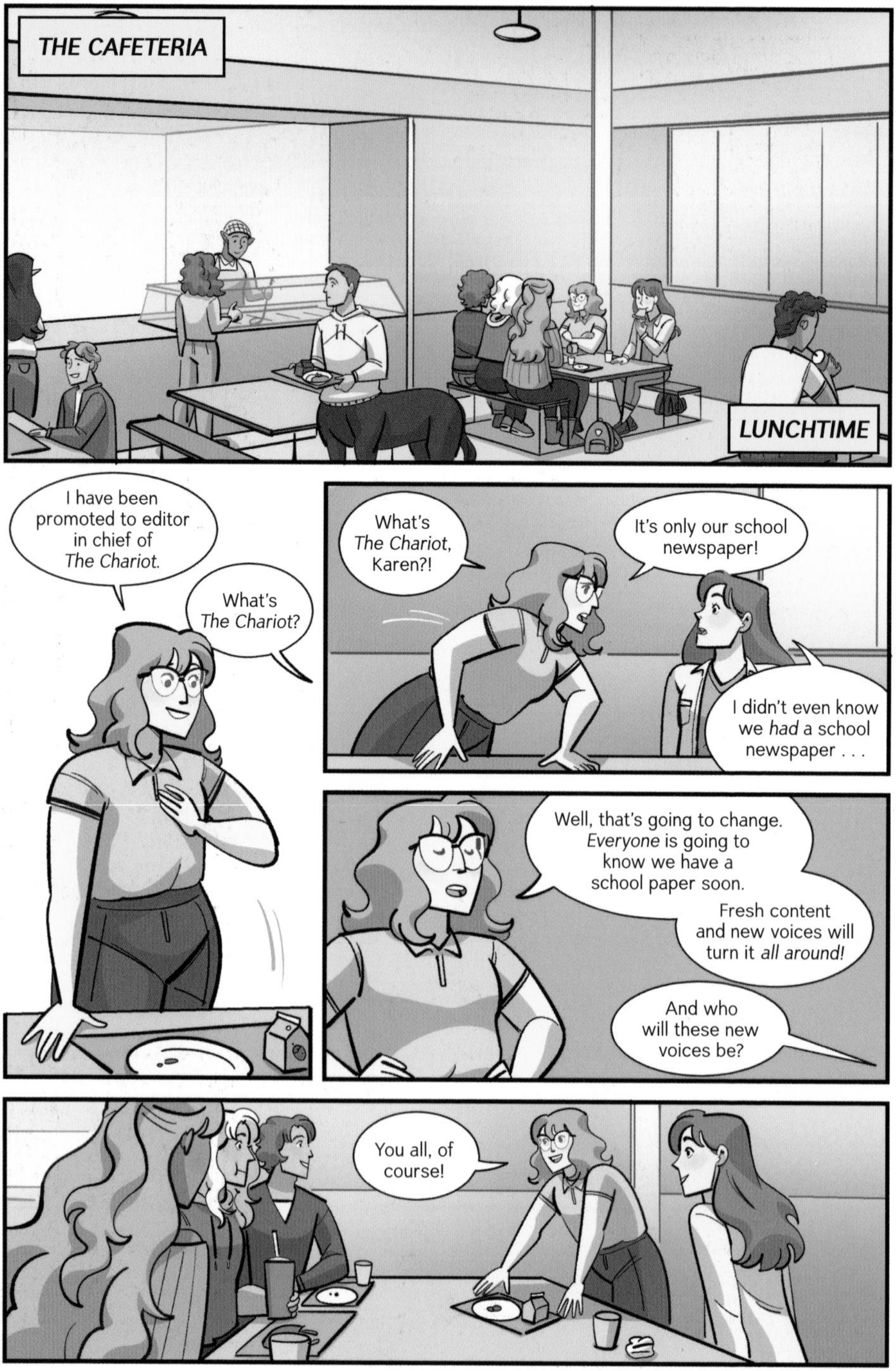
THE CAFETERIA
LUNCHTIME
I have been promoted to editor in chief of *The Chariot*.
What's *The Chariot*?
What's *The Chariot*, Karen?!
It's only our school newspaper!
I didn't even know we *had* a school newspaper . . .
Well, that's going to change. *Everyone* is going to know we have a school paper soon.
Fresh content and new voices will turn it *all around*!
And who will these new voices be?
You all, of course!

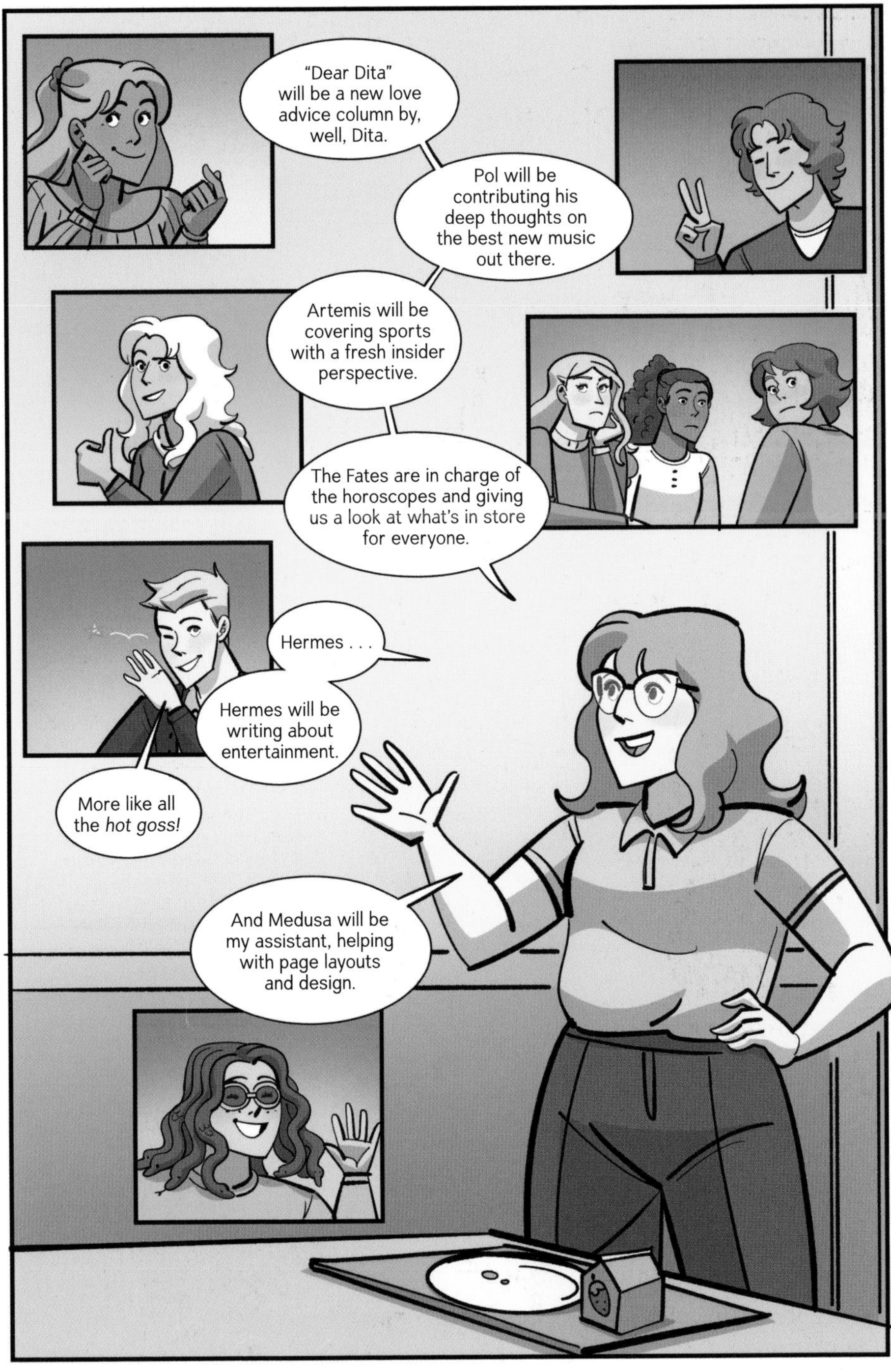
"Dear Dita" will be a new love advice column by, well, Dita.
Pol will be contributing his deep thoughts on the best new music out there.
Artemis will be covering sports with a fresh insider perspective.
The Fates are in charge of the horoscopes and giving us a look at what's in store for everyone.
Hermes . . .
Hermes will be writing about entertainment.
More like all the *hot goss!*
And Medusa will be my assistant, helping with page layouts and design.

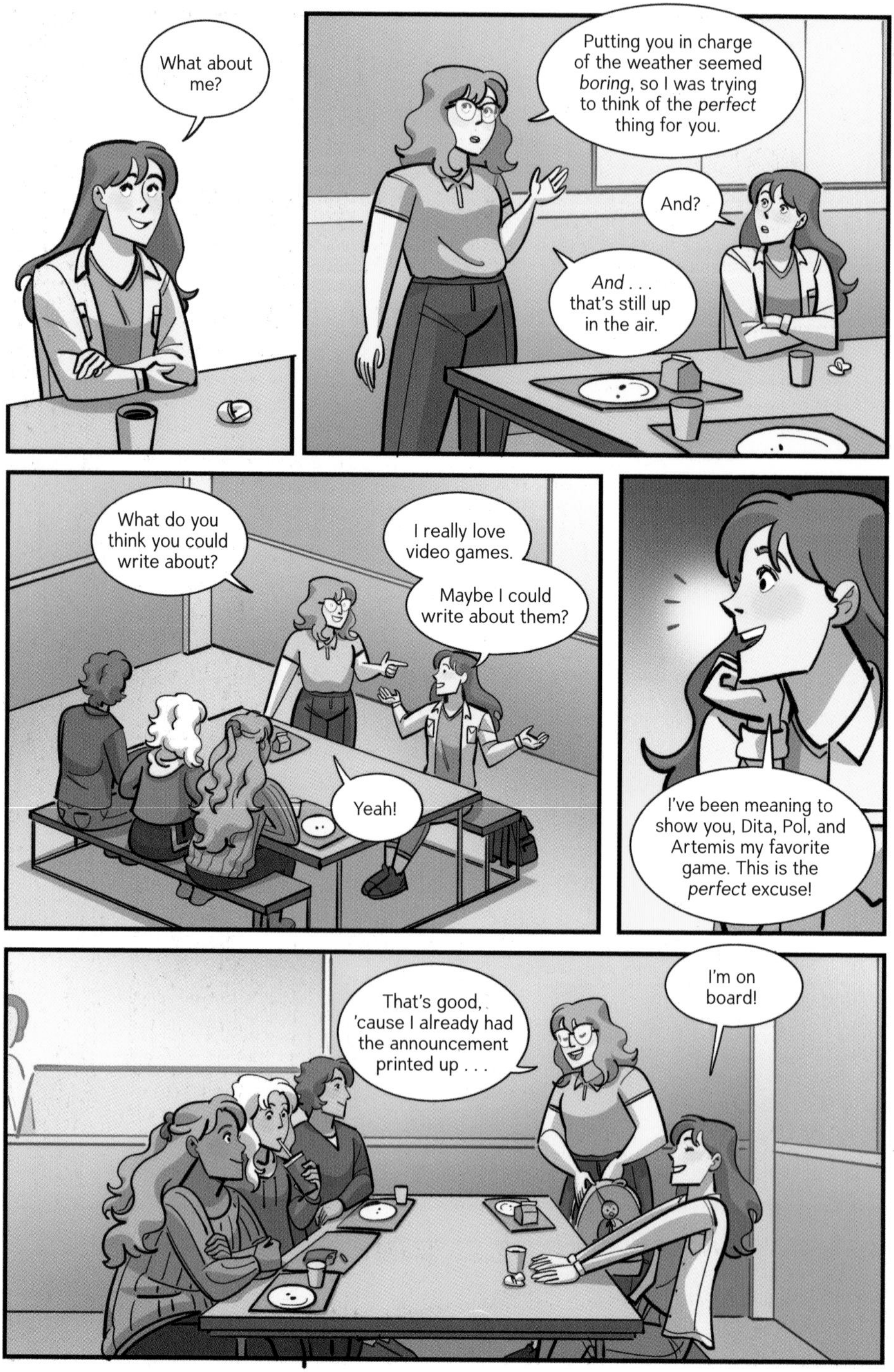
What about me?
Putting you in charge of the weather seemed *boring*, so I was trying to think of the *perfect* thing for you.
And?
And . . . that's still up in the air.
What do you think you could write about?
I really love video games.
Maybe I could write about them?
Yeah!
I've been meaning to show you, Dita, Pol, and Artemis my favorite game. This is the *perfect* excuse!
That's good, 'cause I already had the announcement printed up . . .
I'm on board!

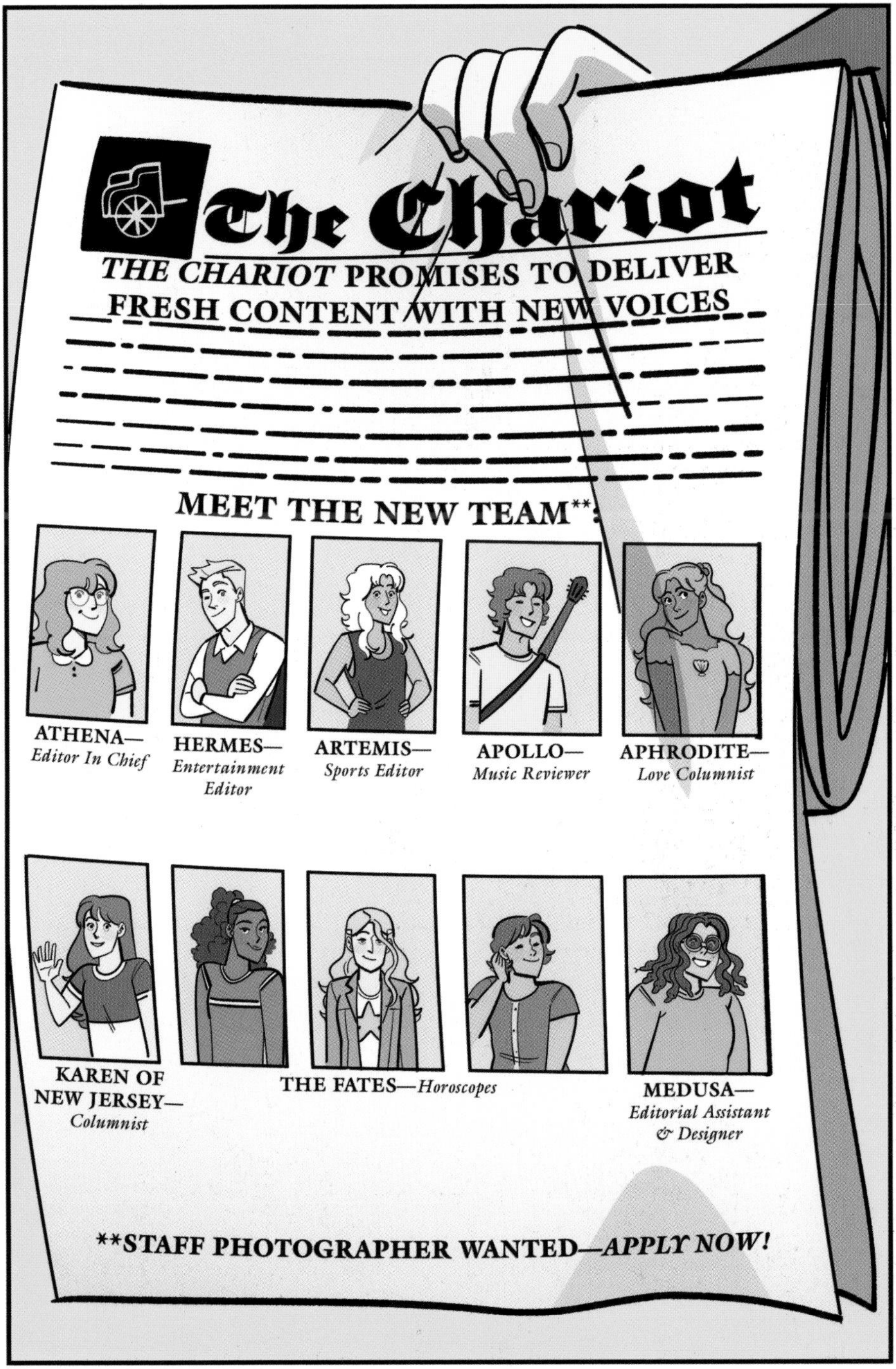
The Chariot
THE CHARIOT PROMISES TO DELIVER FRESH CONTENT WITH NEW VOICES
MEET THE NEW TEAM**:
ATHENA—Editor In Chief
HERMES—Entertainment Editor
ARTEMIS—Sports Editor
APOLLO—Music Reviewer
APHRODITE—Love Columnist
KAREN OF NEW JERSEY—Columnist
THE FATES—Horoscopes
MEDUSA—Editorial Assistant & Designer
**STAFF PHOTOGRAPHER WANTED—APPLY NOW!

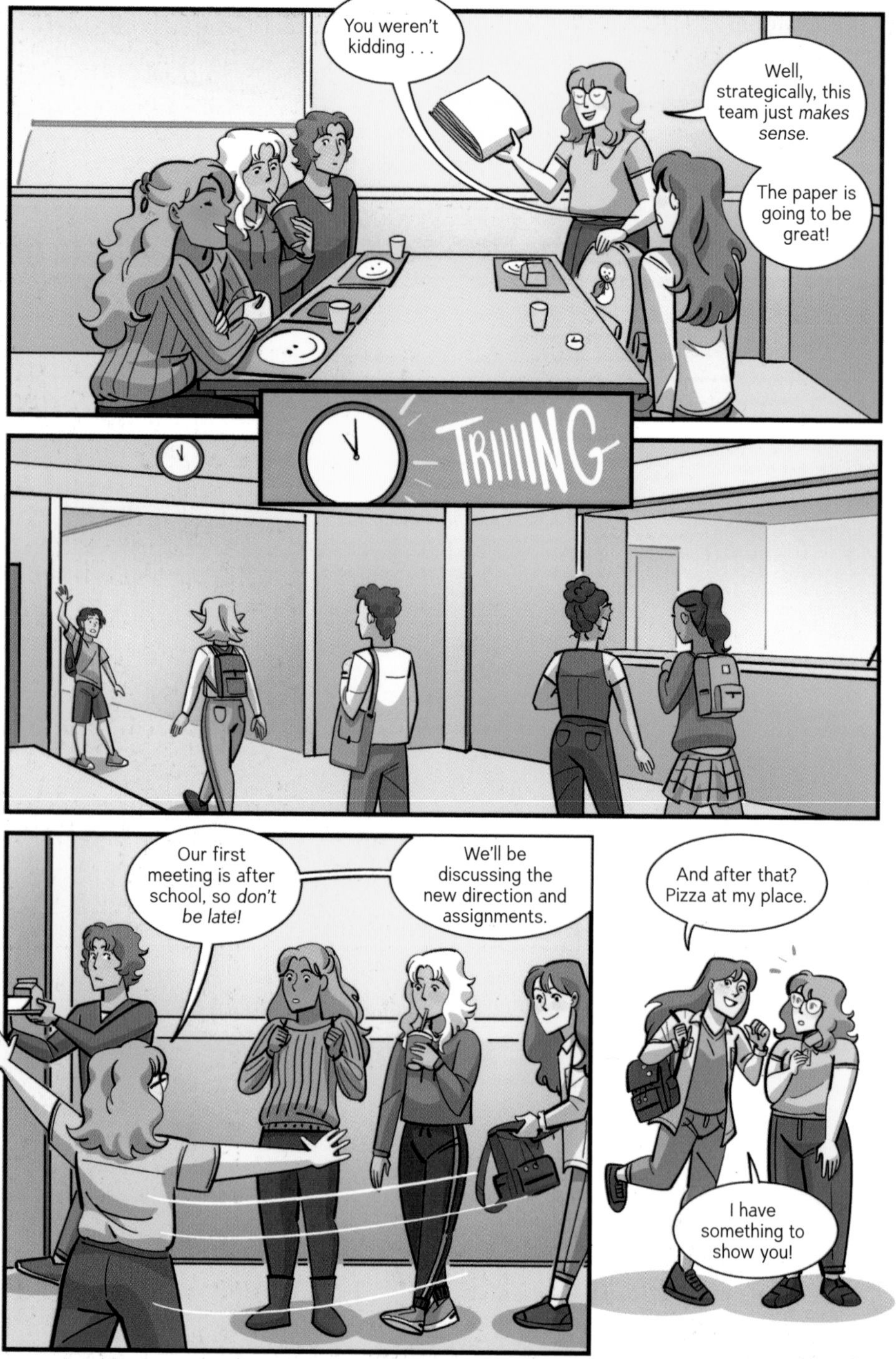
You weren't kidding . . .
Well, strategically, this team just *makes sense.*
The paper is going to be great!
TRIIIING
Our first meeting is after school, so *don't be late!*
We'll be discussing the new direction and assignments.
And after that? Pizza at my place.
I have something to show you!

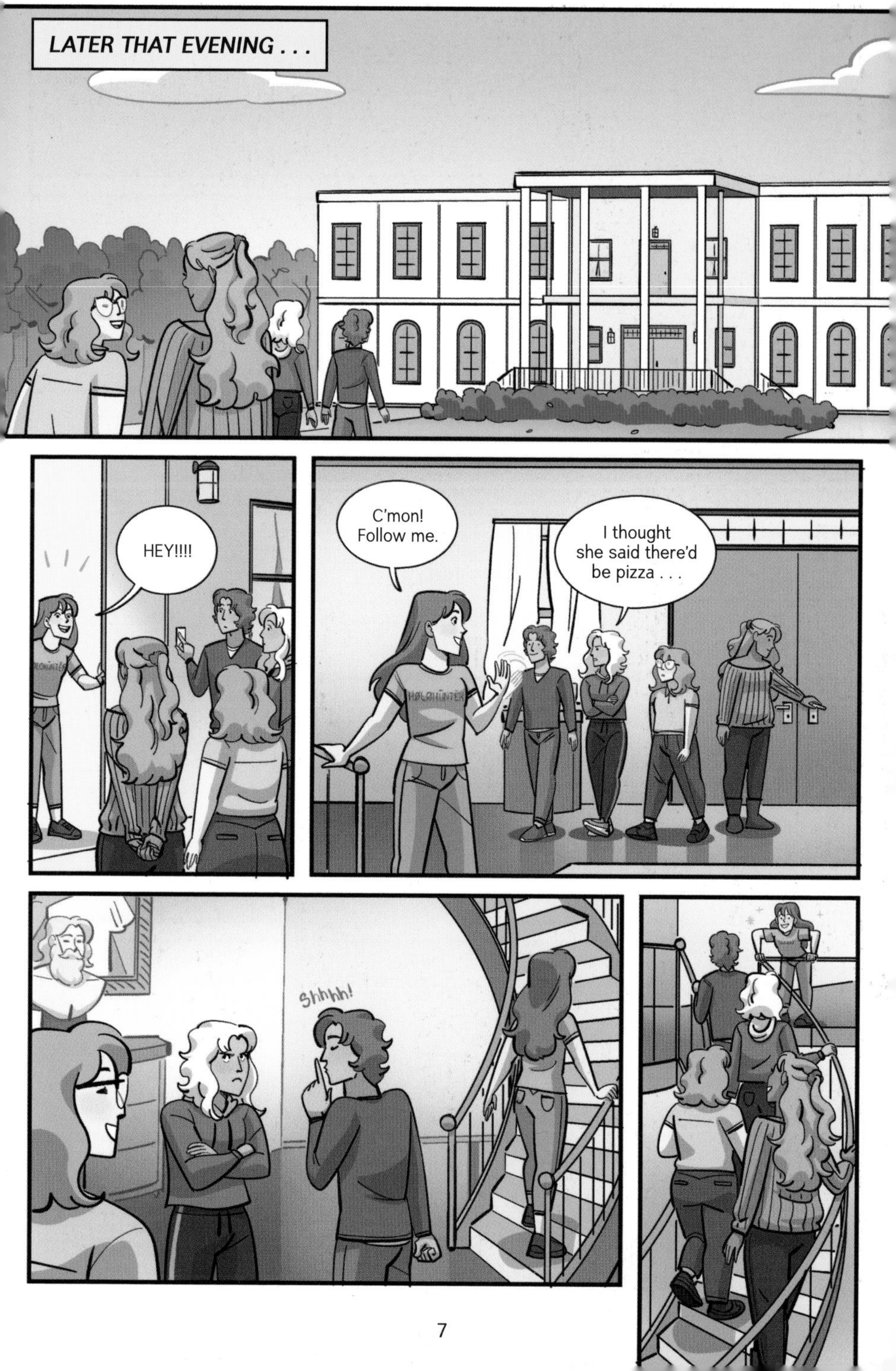
LATER THAT EVENING . . .
HEY!!!!
C'mon! Follow me.
I thought she said there'd be pizza . . .
Shhhh!

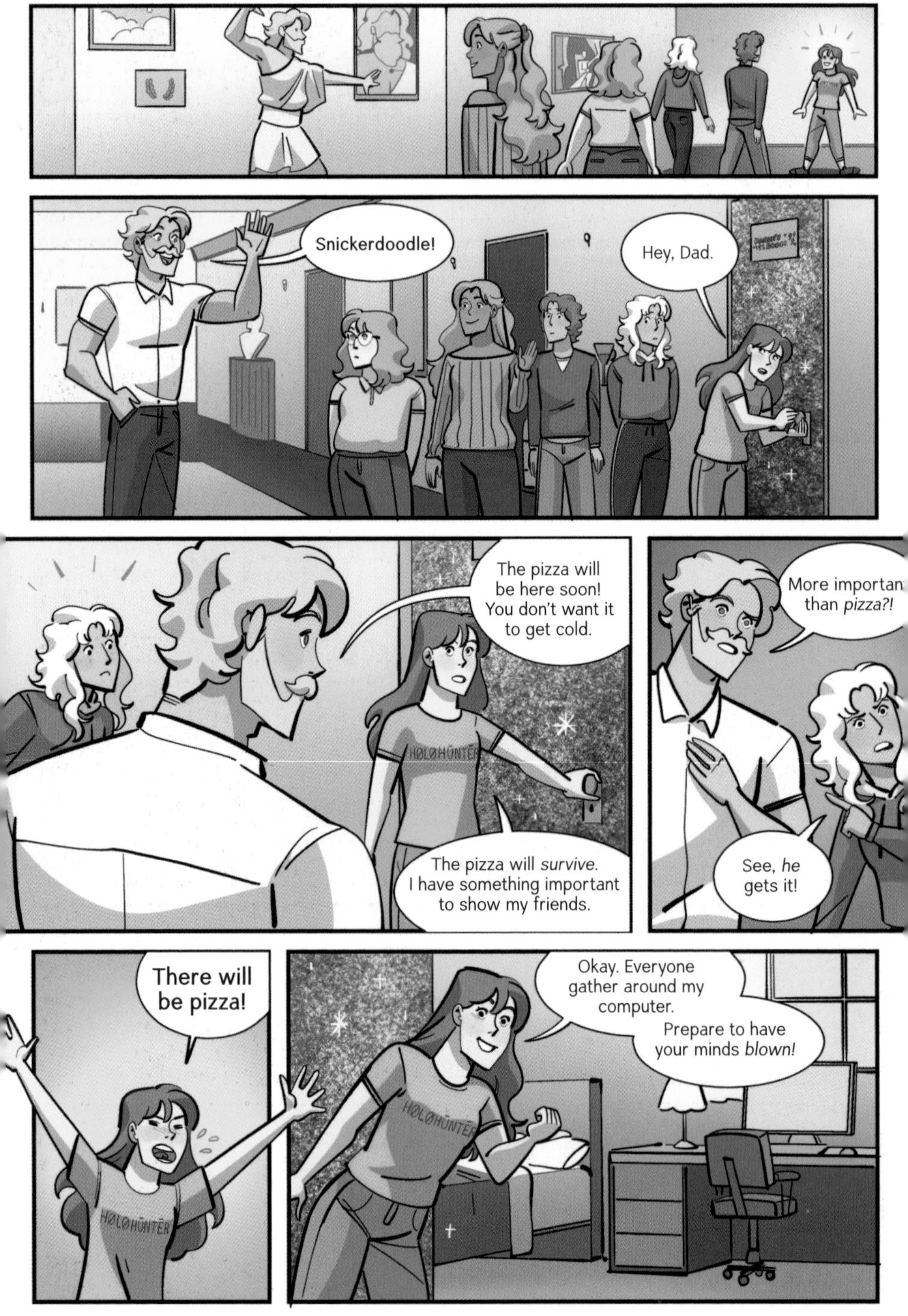

Snickerdoodle!
Hey, Dad.
The pizza will be here soon! You don't want it to get cold.
The pizza will *survive.* I have something important to show my friends.
More importan than *pizza?!*
See, *he* gets it!
There will be pizza!
Okay. Everyone gather around my computer.
Prepare to have your minds *blown!*

On a distant, remote planet . . .

. . . the fight for our galaxy is taking place.

Humans have taken the battle directly to the home planet of a fierce invading species known as the Høløs.

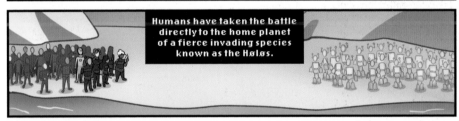

A small, elite military squadron from Earth is sent to the Hølø base to eliminate enemy leadership in what is surely a suicide mission.

But if they don't succeed, it could mean the end of the human race.

It's all up to . . .

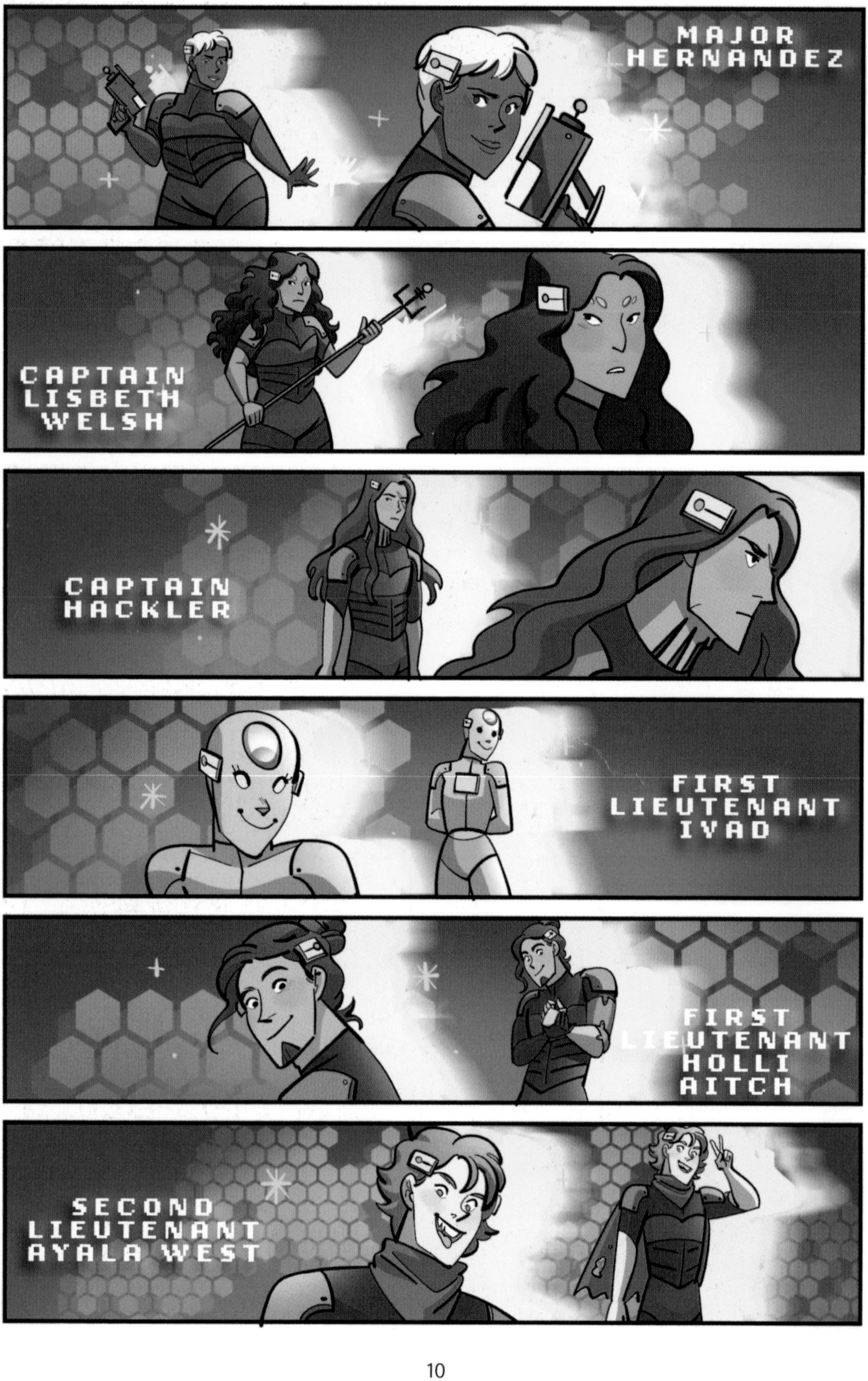
MAJOR HERNANDEZ
CAPTAIN LISBETH WELSH
CAPTAIN HACKLER
FIRST LIEUTENANT IVAD
FIRST LIEUTENANT HOLLI AITCH
SECOND LIEUTENANT AYALA WEST

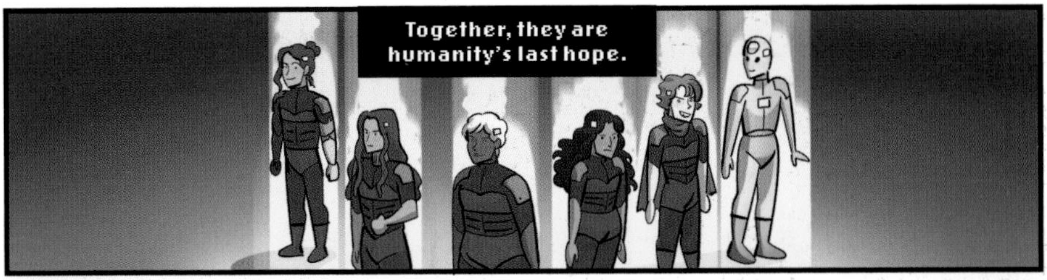
Together, they are humanity's last hope.

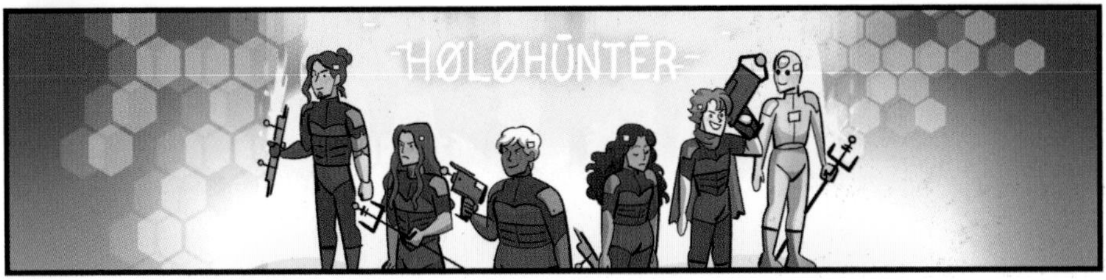
HØLØHŪNTĒR

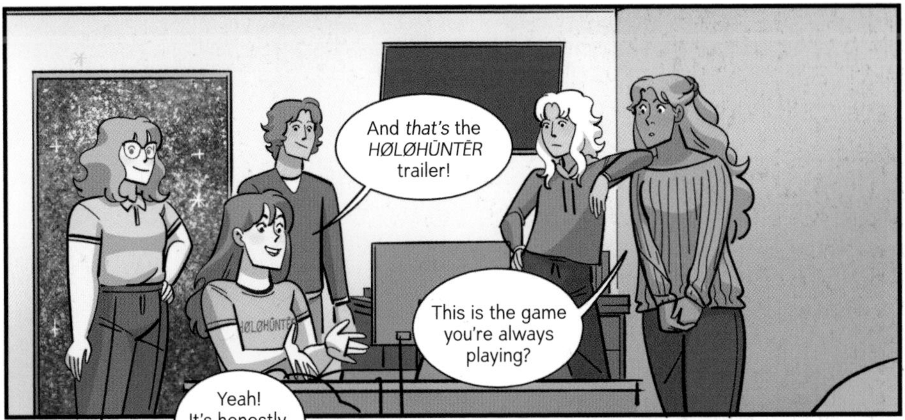
And *that's* the *HØLØHŪNTĒR* trailer!
HØLØHŪNTĒR
This is the game you're always playing?

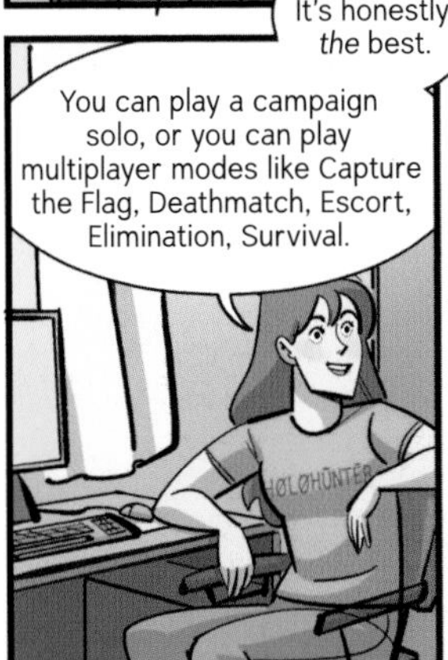
Yeah! It's honestly *the* best.
You can play a campaign solo, or you can play multiplayer modes like Capture the Flag, Deathmatch, Escort, Elimination, Survival.
HØLØHŪNTĒR

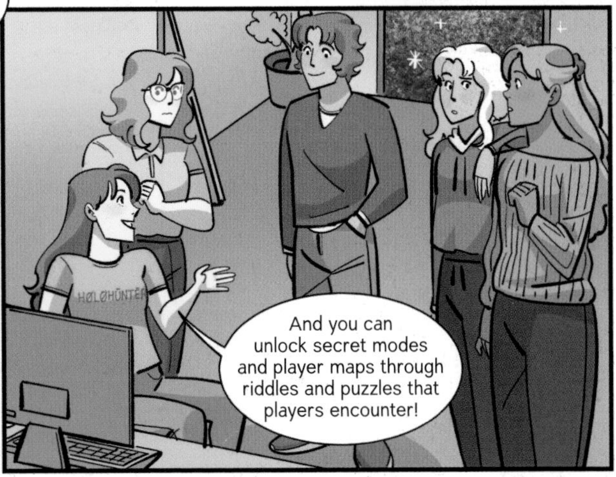
HØLØHŪNTĒR
And you can unlock secret modes and player maps through riddles and puzzles that players encounter!

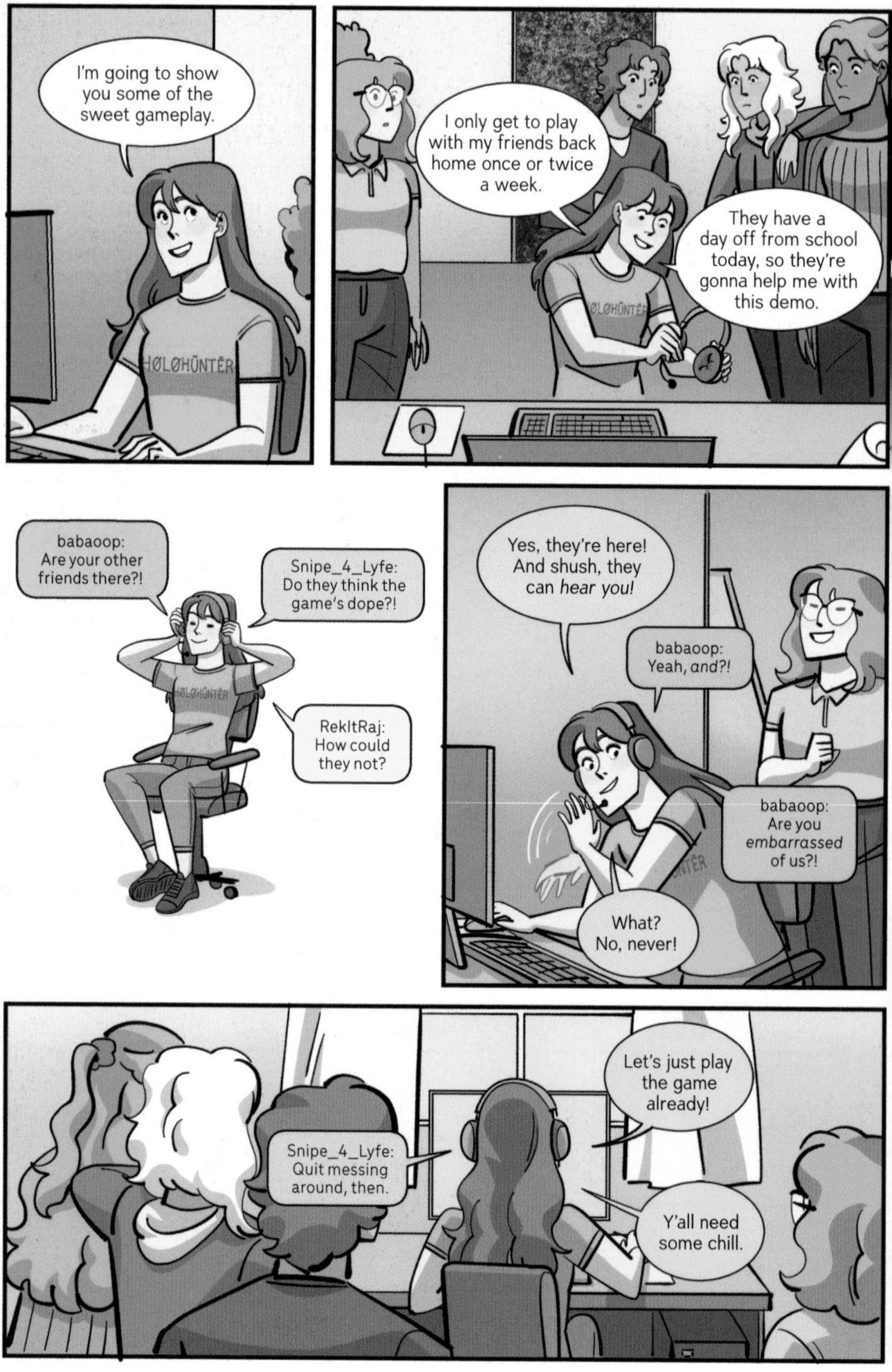
I'm going to show you some of the sweet gameplay.
HØLØHŪNTĒR
I only get to play with my friends back home once or twice a week.
They have a day off from school today, so they're gonna help me with this demo.
babaoop: Are your other friends there?!
Snipe_4_Lyfe: Do they think the game's dope?!
RekItRaj: How could they not?
Yes, they're here! And shush, they can *hear you!*
babaoop: Yeah, *and*?!
babaoop: Are you *embarrassed* of us?!
What? No, never!
Let's just play the game already!
Snipe_4_Lyfe: Quit messing around, then.
Y'all need some chill.

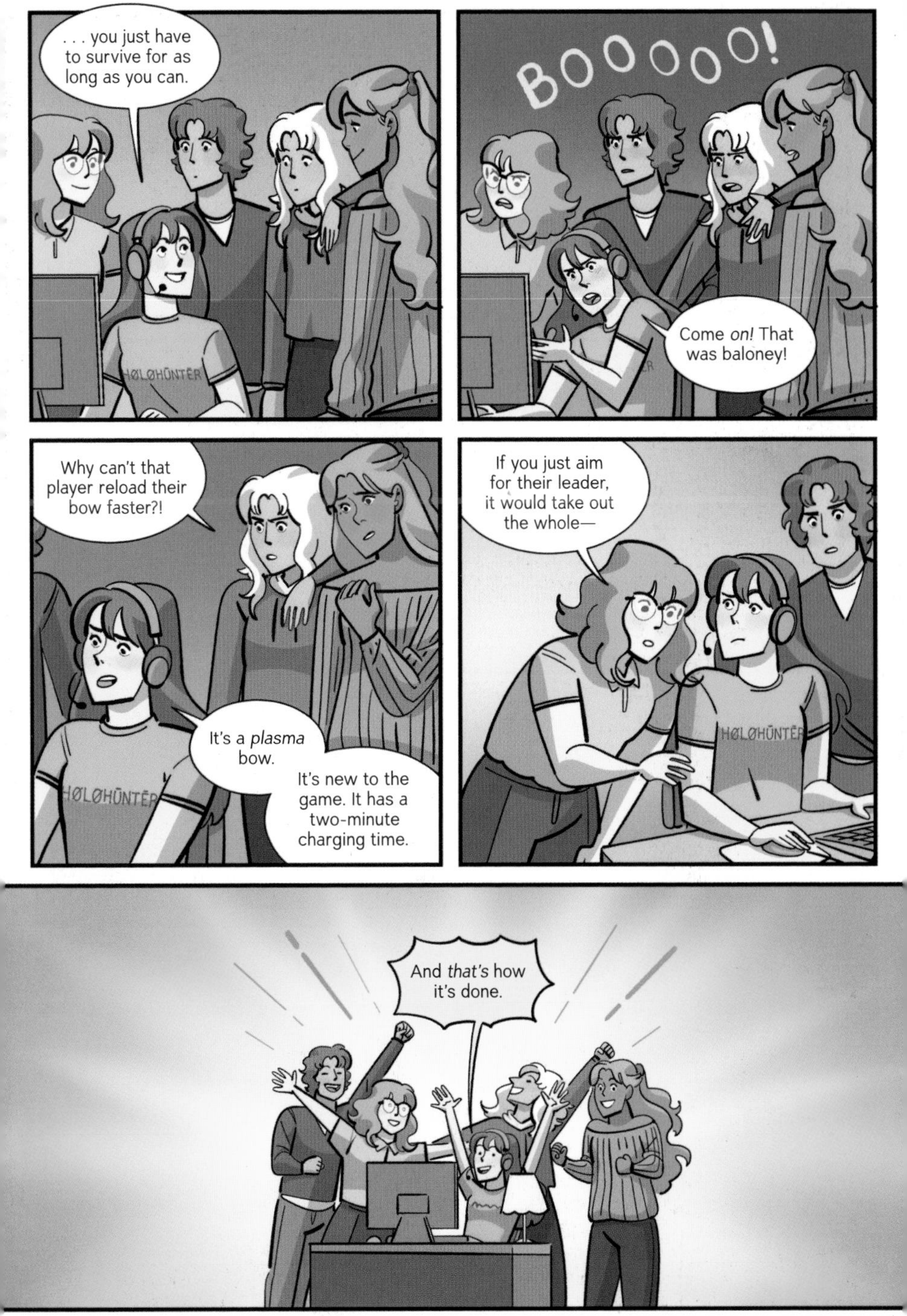

. . . you just have to survive for as long as you can.
HØLØHŪNTĒR
BOOOOO!
Come *on!* That was baloney!
Why can't that player reload their bow faster?!
It's a *plasma* bow.
It's new to the game. It has a two-minute charging time.
HØLØHŪNTĒR
If you just aim for their leader, it would take out the whole—
HØLØHŪNTĒR
And *that's* how it's done.

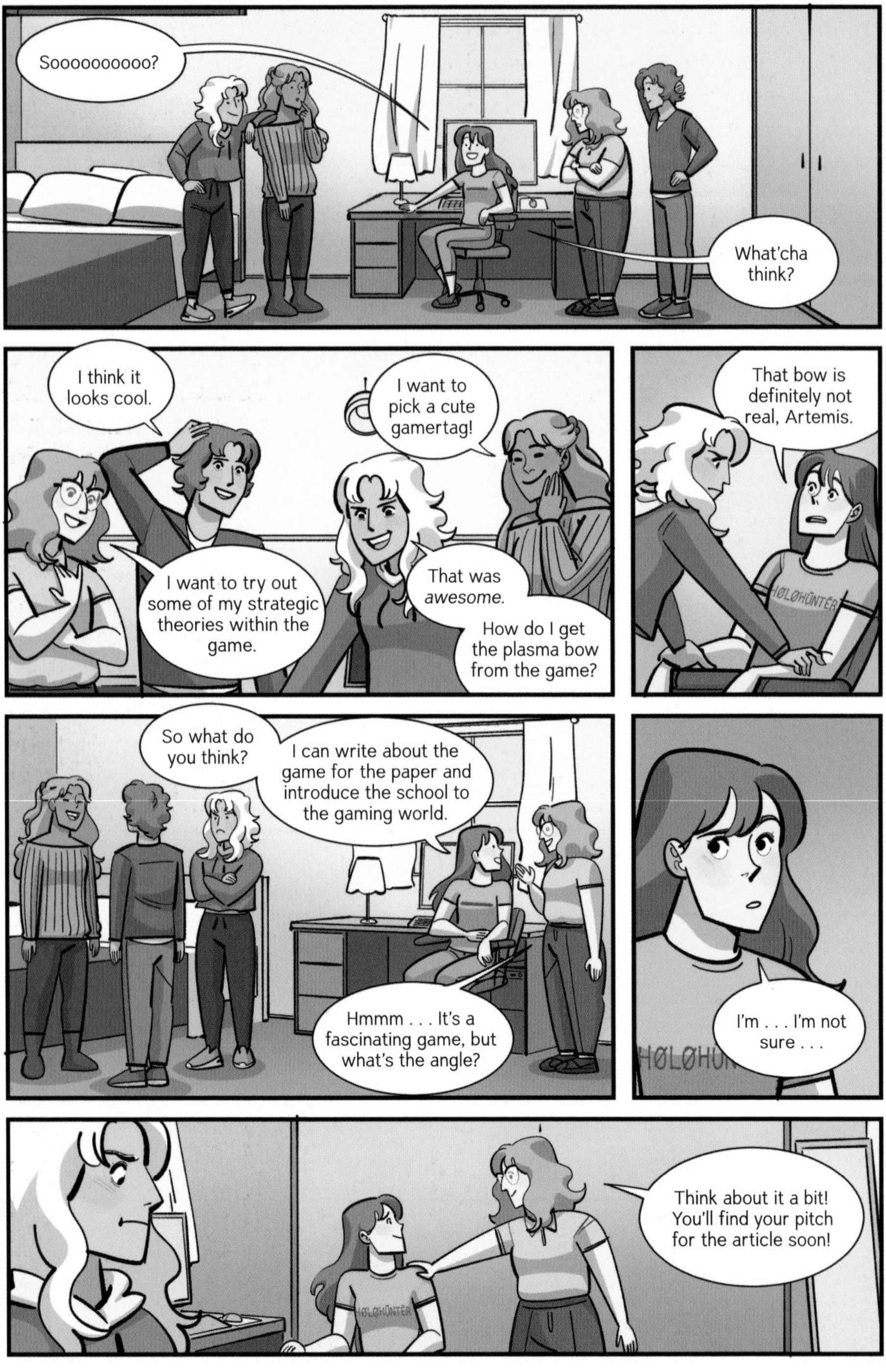
Soooooooooo?
What'cha think?
I think it looks cool.
I want to pick a cute gamertag!
I want to try out some of my strategic theories within the game.
That was *awesome.*
How do I get the plasma bow from the game?
That bow is definitely not real, Artemis.
HØLØHÜNTËR
So what do you think?
I can write about the game for the paper and introduce the school to the gaming world.
Hmmm . . . It's a fascinating game, but what's the angle?
I'm . . . I'm not sure . . .
Think about it a bit! You'll find your pitch for the article soon!
HØLØHÜNTËR

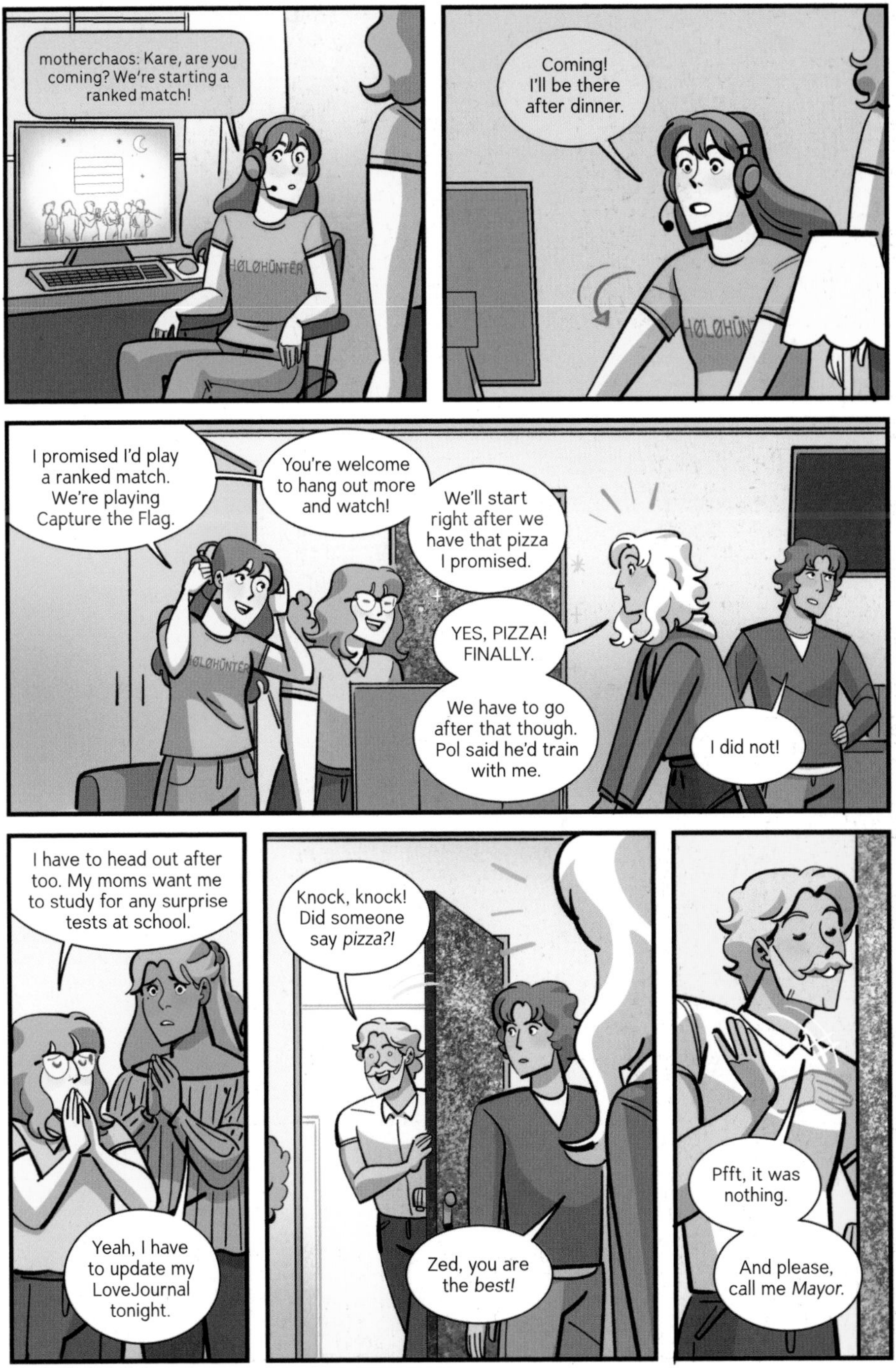
motherchaos: Kare, are you coming? We're starting a ranked match!
HØLØHŪNTĒR
Coming! I'll be there after dinner.
I promised I'd play a ranked match. We're playing Capture the Flag.
You're welcome to hang out more and watch!
We'll start right after we have that pizza I promised.
YES, PIZZA! FINALLY.
We have to go after that though. Pol said he'd train with me.
I did not!
I have to head out after too. My moms want me to study for any surprise tests at school.
Yeah, I have to update my LoveJournal tonight.
Knock, knock! Did someone say *pizza?!*
Zed, you are the *best!*
Pfft, it was nothing.
And please, call me *Mayor.*

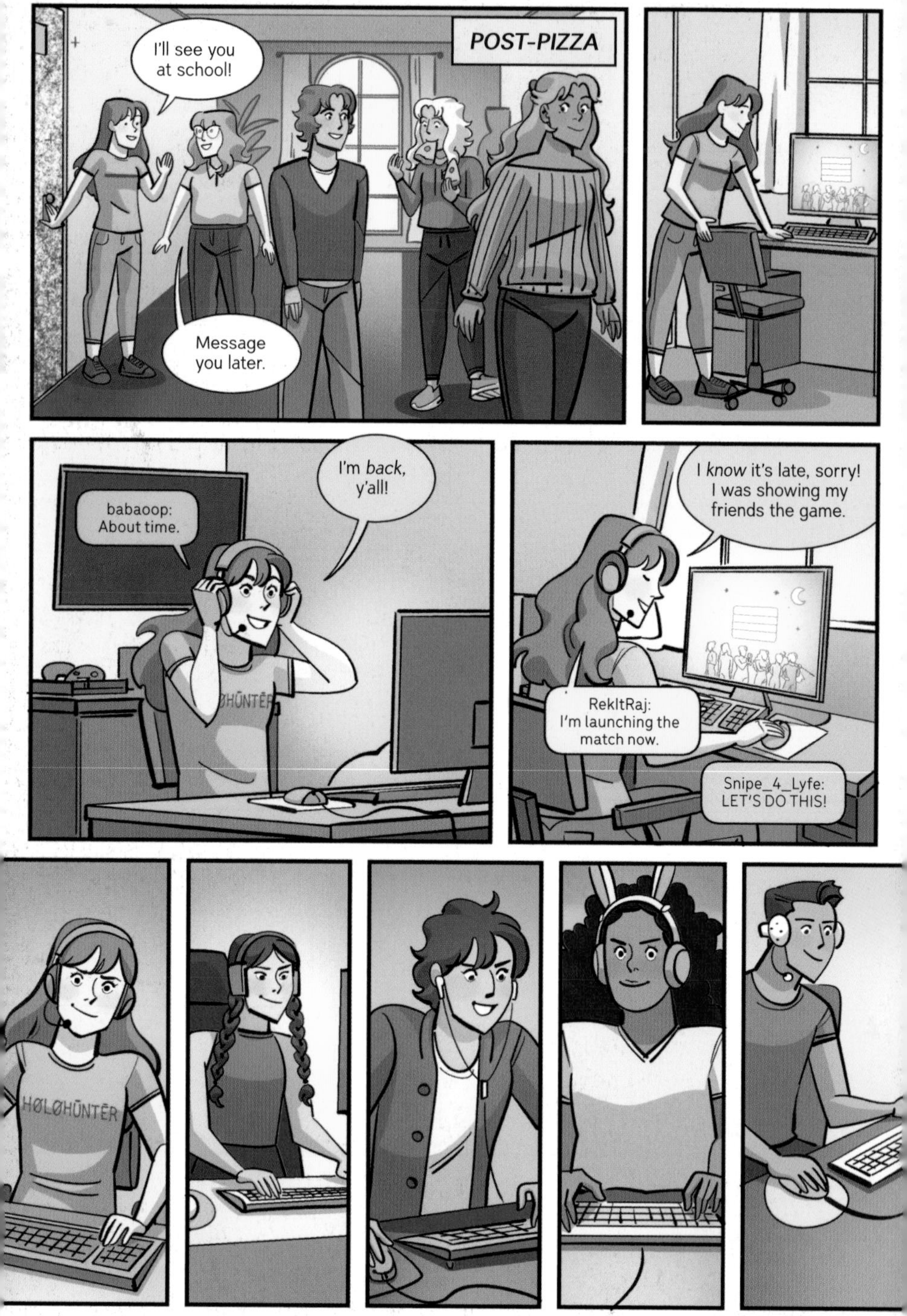
POST-PIZZA
I'll see you at school!
Message you later.
I'm *back*, y'all!
babaoop: About time.
I *know* it's late, sorry! I was showing my friends the game.
RekItRaj: I'm launching the match now.
Snipe_4_Lyfe: LET'S DO THIS!
HØLØHŪNTĒR

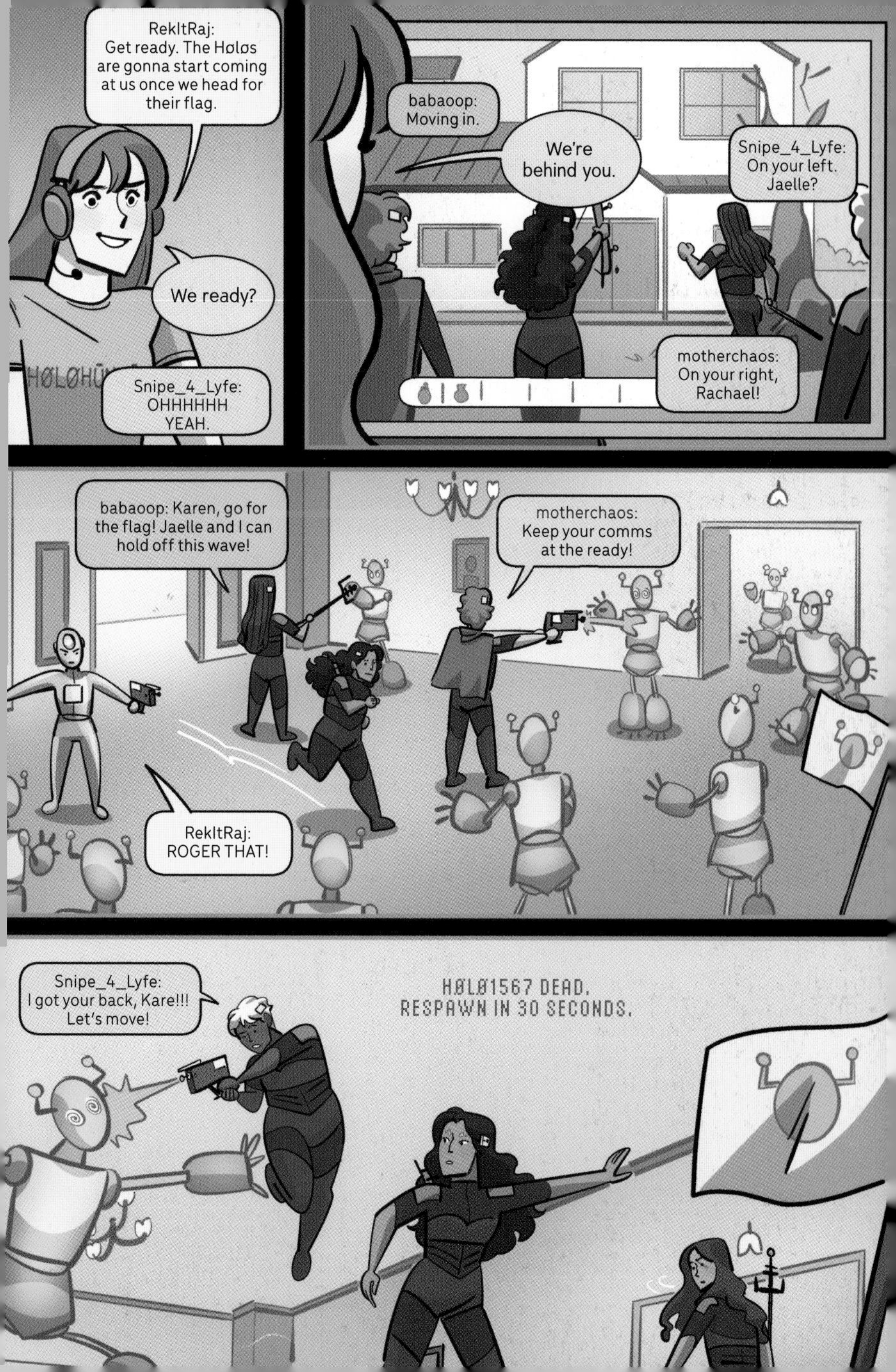
RekItRaj: Get ready. The Høløs are gonna start coming at us once we head for their flag.
We ready?
HØLØHŪ
Snipe_4_Lyfe: OHHHHHH YEAH.
babaoop: Moving in.
We're behind you.
Snipe_4_Lyfe: On your left. Jaelle?
motherchaos: On your right, Rachael!
babaoop: Karen, go for the flag! Jaelle and I can hold off this wave!
motherchaos: Keep your comms at the ready!
RekItRaj: ROGER THAT!
Snipe_4_Lyfe: I got your back, Kare!!! Let's move!
HØLØ1567 DEAD.
RESPAWN IN 30 SECONDS.

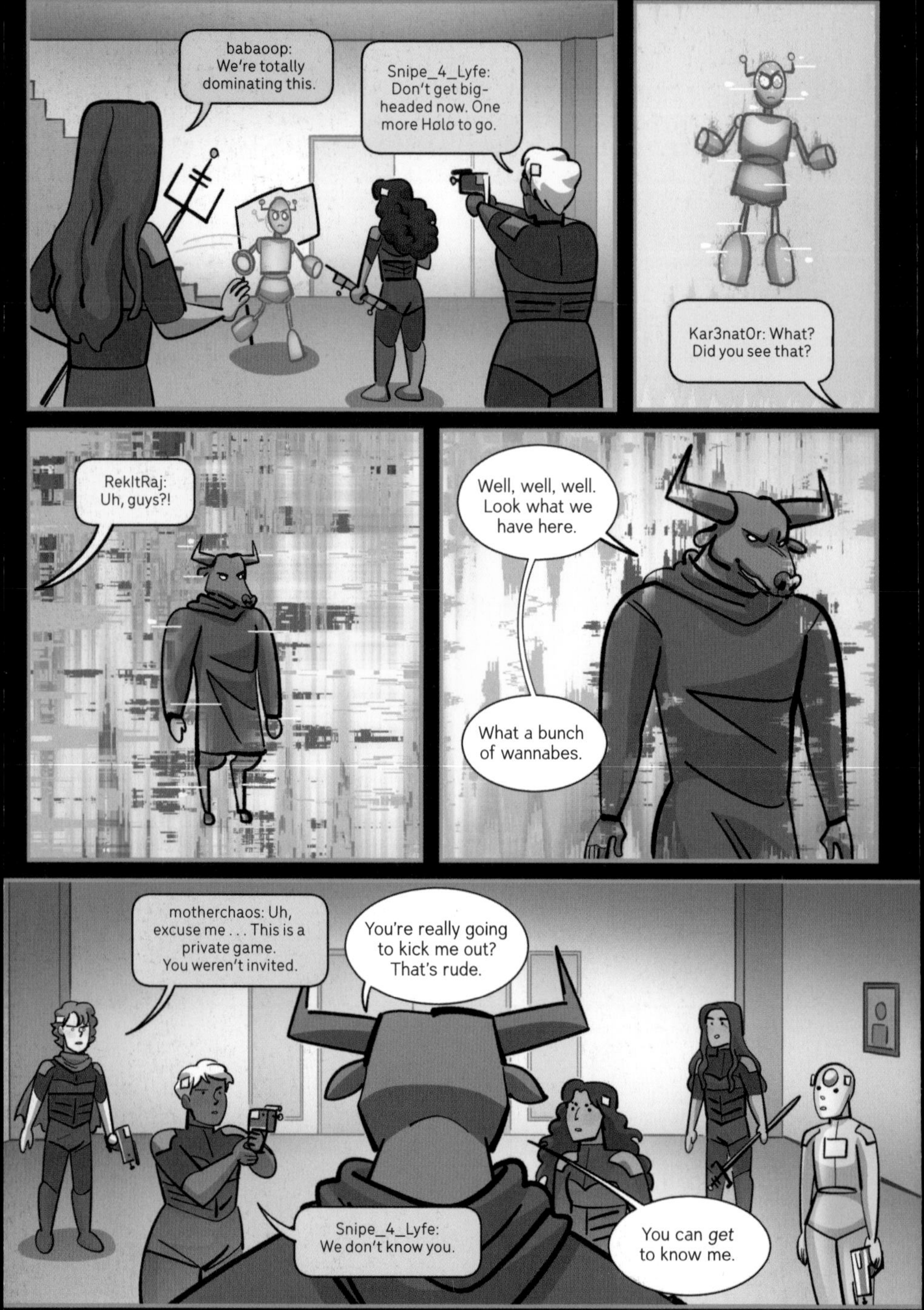
babaoop: We're totally dominating this.
Snipe_4_Lyfe: Don't get big-headed now. One more Hølø to go.
Kar3natOr: What? Did you see that?
RekltRaj: Uh, guys?!
Well, well, well. Look what we have here.
What a bunch of wannabes.
motherchaos: Uh, excuse me . . . This is a private game. You weren't invited.
You're really going to kick me out? That's rude.
Snipe_4_Lyfe: We don't know you.
You can *get* to know me.

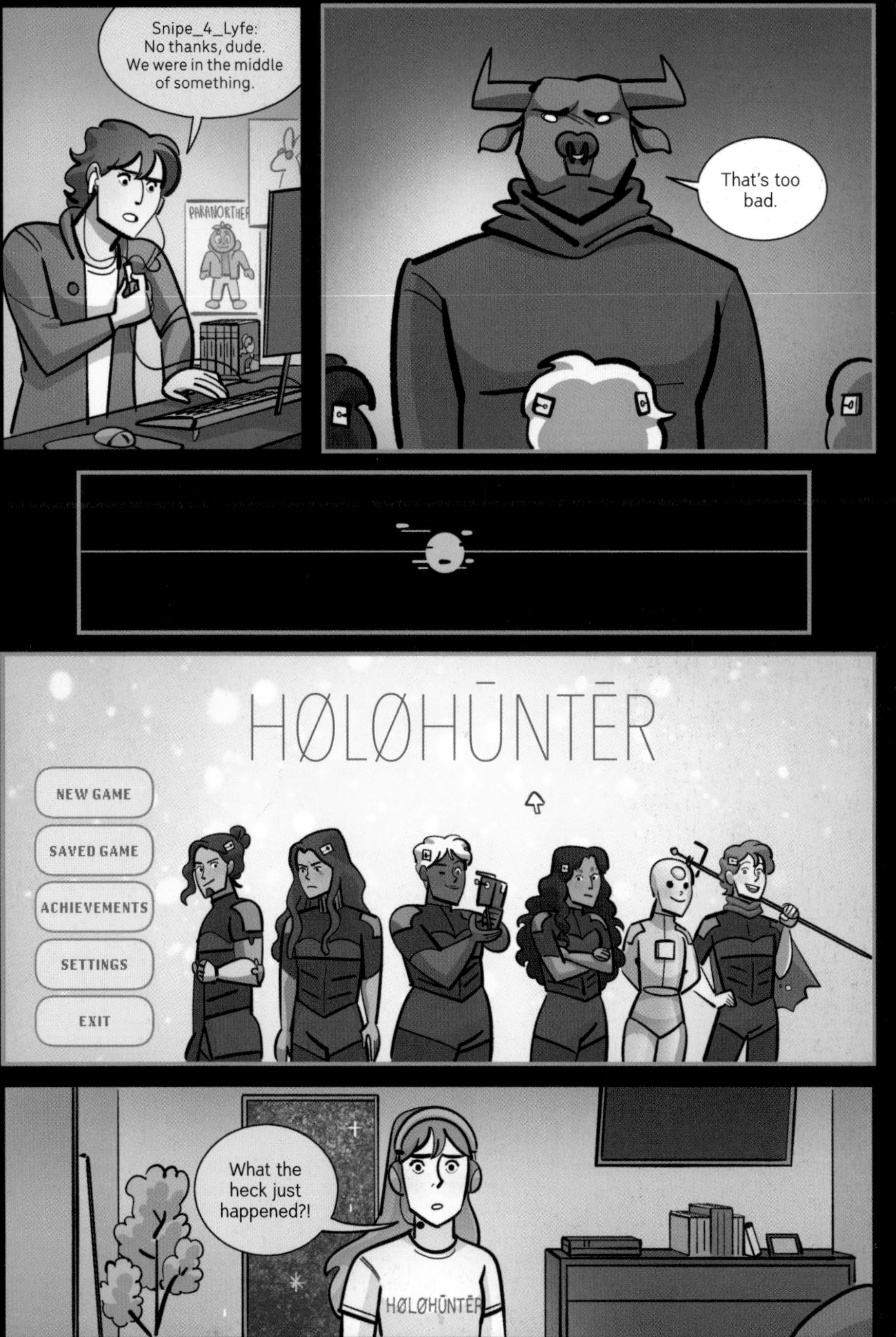

Snipe_4_Lyfe: No thanks, dude. We were in the middle of something.
PARANORTHER
That's too bad.
HØLØHŪNTĒR
NEW GAME
SAVED GAME
ACHIEVEMENTS
SETTINGS
EXIT
What the heck just happened?!
HØLØHŪNTĒR

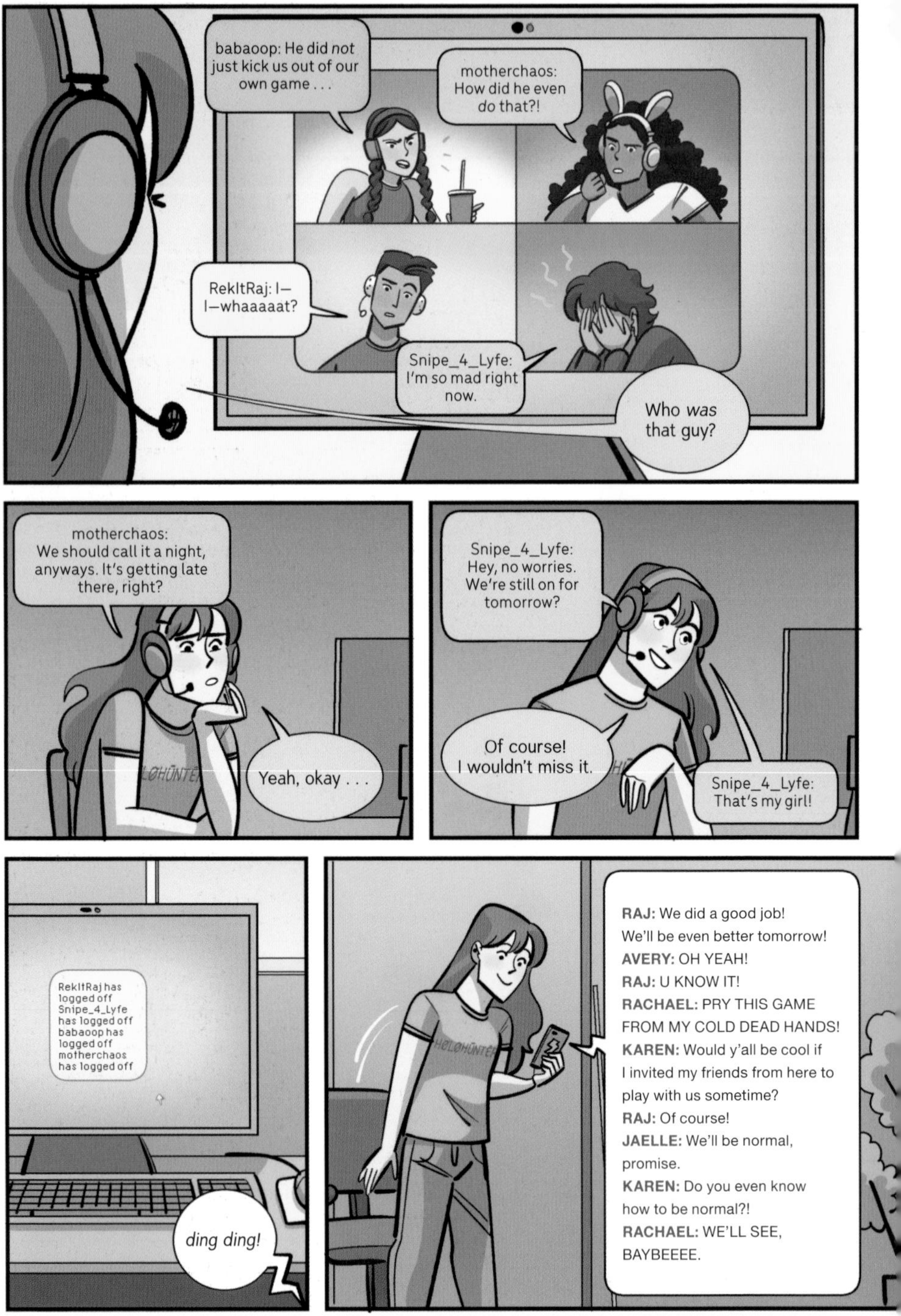
babaoop: He did *not* just kick us out of our own game . . .
motherchaos: How did he even *do* that?!
RekItRaj: I—I—whaaaaat?
Snipe_4_Lyfe: I'm so mad right now.
Who *was* that guy?
motherchaos: We should call it a night, anyways. It's getting late there, right?
Yeah, okay . . .
Snipe_4_Lyfe: Hey, no worries. We're still on for tomorrow?
Of course! I wouldn't miss it.
Snipe_4_Lyfe: That's my girl!
RekItRaj has logged off
Snipe_4_Lyfe has logged off
babaoop has logged off
motherchaos has logged off
ding ding!
RAJ: We did a good job! We'll be even better tomorrow!
AVERY: OH YEAH!
RAJ: U KNOW IT!
RACHAEL: PRY THIS GAME FROM MY COLD DEAD HANDS!
KAREN: Would y'all be cool if I invited my friends from here to play with us sometime?
RAJ: Of course!
JAELLE: We'll be normal, promise.
KAREN: Do you even know how to be normal?!
RACHAEL: WE'LL SEE, BAYBEEEE.

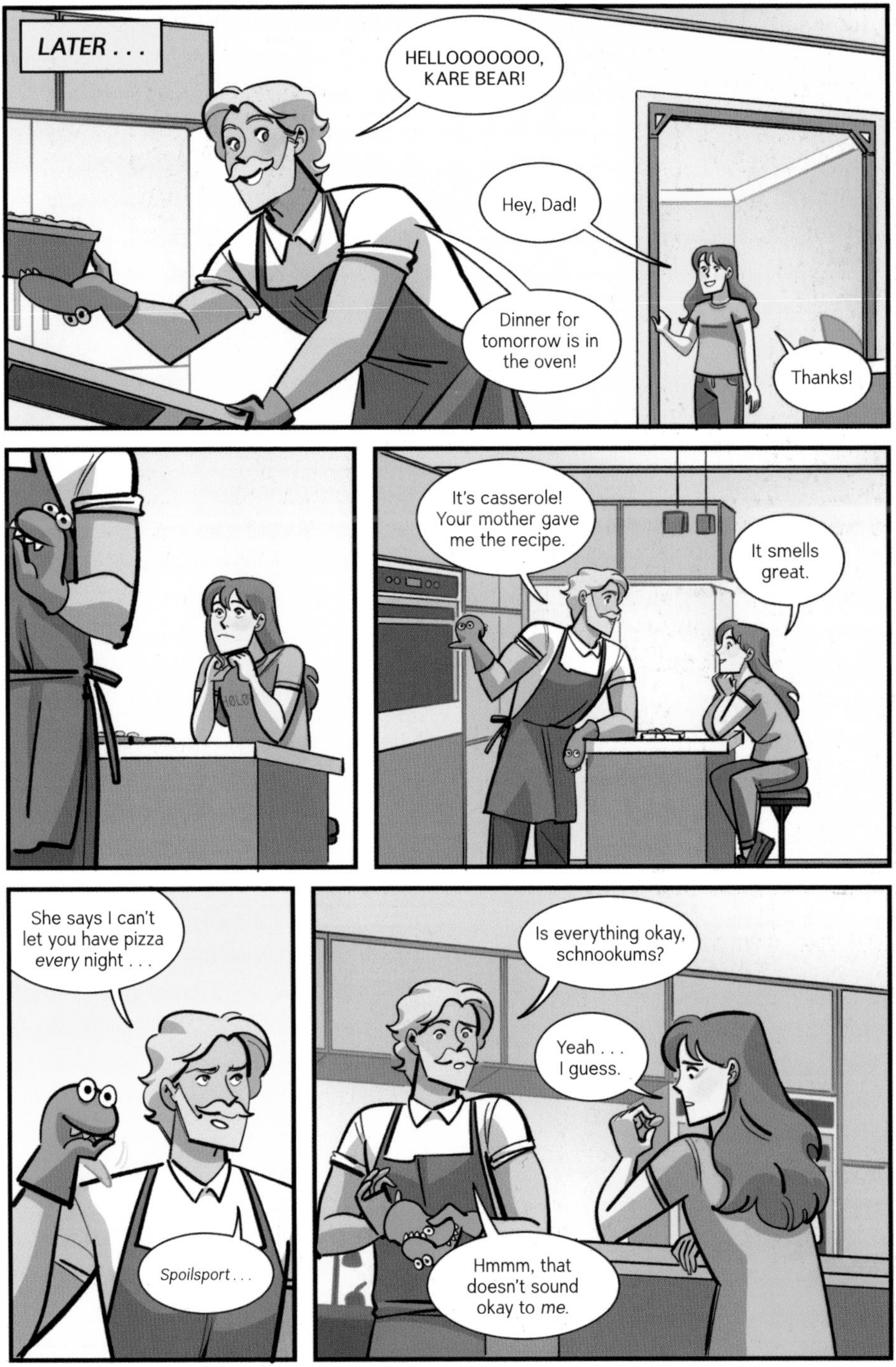
LATER . . .
HELLOOOOOOO, KARE BEAR!
Hey, Dad!
Dinner for tomorrow is in the oven!
Thanks!
It's casserole! Your mother gave me the recipe.
It smells great.
She says I can't let you have pizza *every* night . . .
Spoilsport . . .
Is everything okay, schnookums?
Yeah . . . I guess.
Hmmm, that doesn't sound okay to *me*.

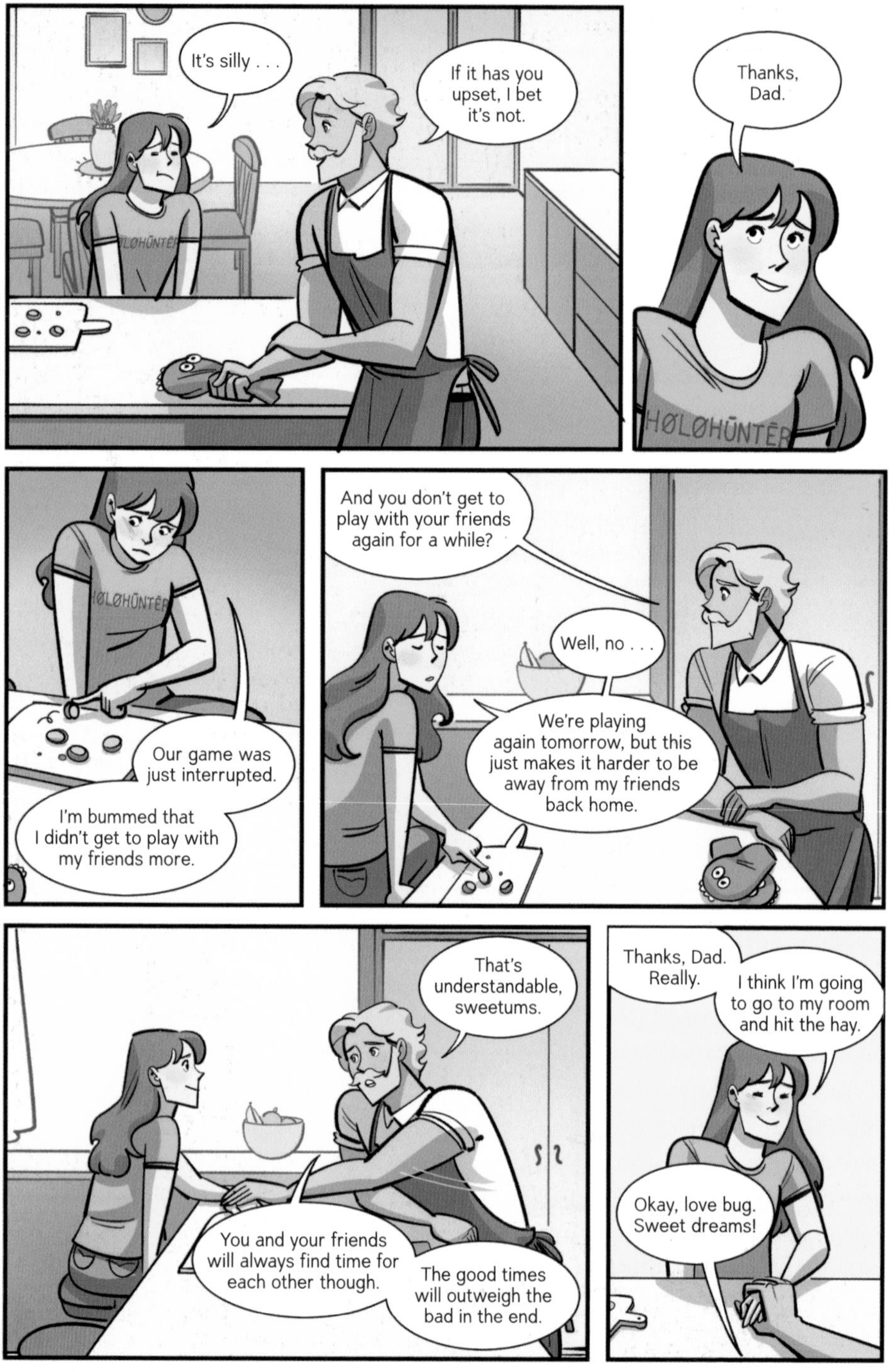
It's silly . . .
If it has you upset, I bet it's not.
Thanks, Dad.
HØLØHŪNTĒR
Our game was just interrupted.
I'm bummed that I didn't get to play with my friends more.
And you don't get to play with your friends again for a while?
Well, no . . .
We're playing again tomorrow, but this just makes it harder to be away from my friends back home.
That's understandable, sweetums.
You and your friends will always find time for each other though.
The good times will outweigh the bad in the end.
Thanks, Dad. Really.
I think I'm going to go to my room and hit the hay.
Okay, love bug. Sweet dreams!

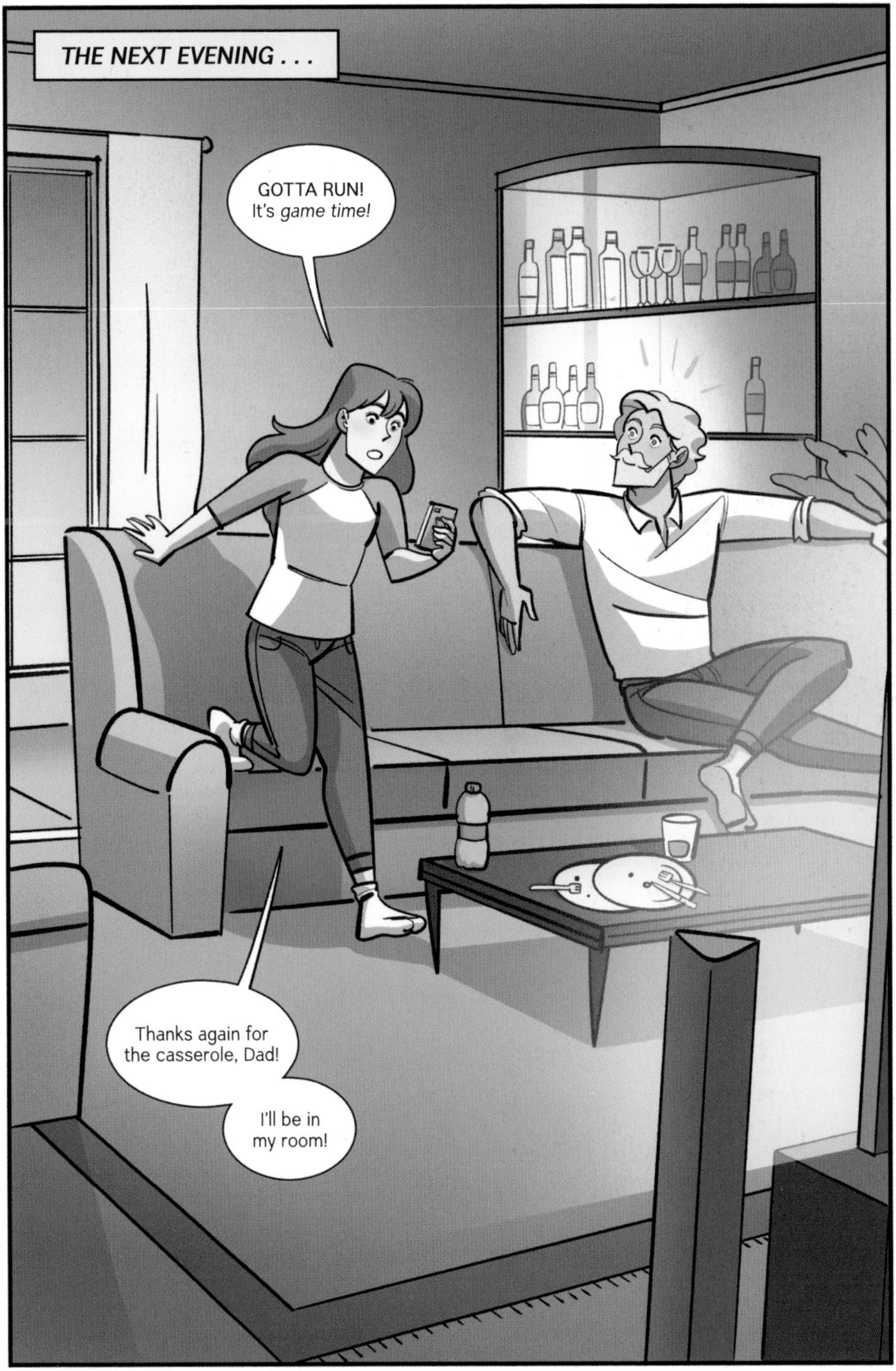
THE NEXT EVENING . . .
GOTTA RUN! It's *game time!*
Thanks again for the casserole, Dad!
I'll be in my room!

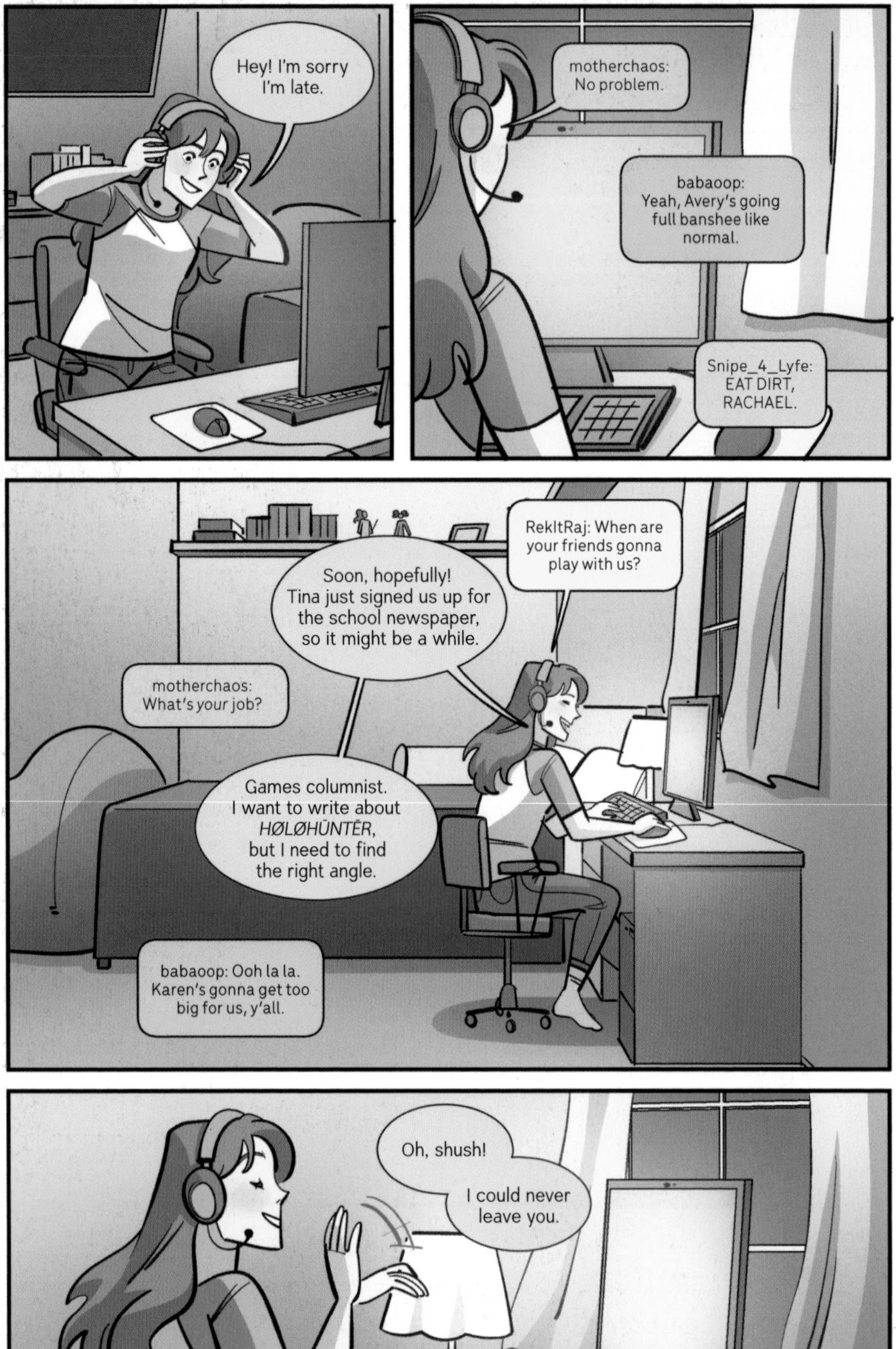
Hey! I'm sorry I'm late.
motherchaos: No problem.
babaoop: Yeah, Avery's going full banshee like normal.
Snipe_4_Lyfe: EAT DIRT, RACHAEL.
RekItRaj: When are your friends gonna play with us?
Soon, hopefully! Tina just signed us up for the school newspaper, so it might be a while.
motherchaos: What's *your* job?
Games columnist. I want to write about *HØLØHŪNTĒR*, but I need to find the right angle.
babaoop: Ooh la la. Karen's gonna get too big for us, y'all.
Oh, shush!
I could never leave you.

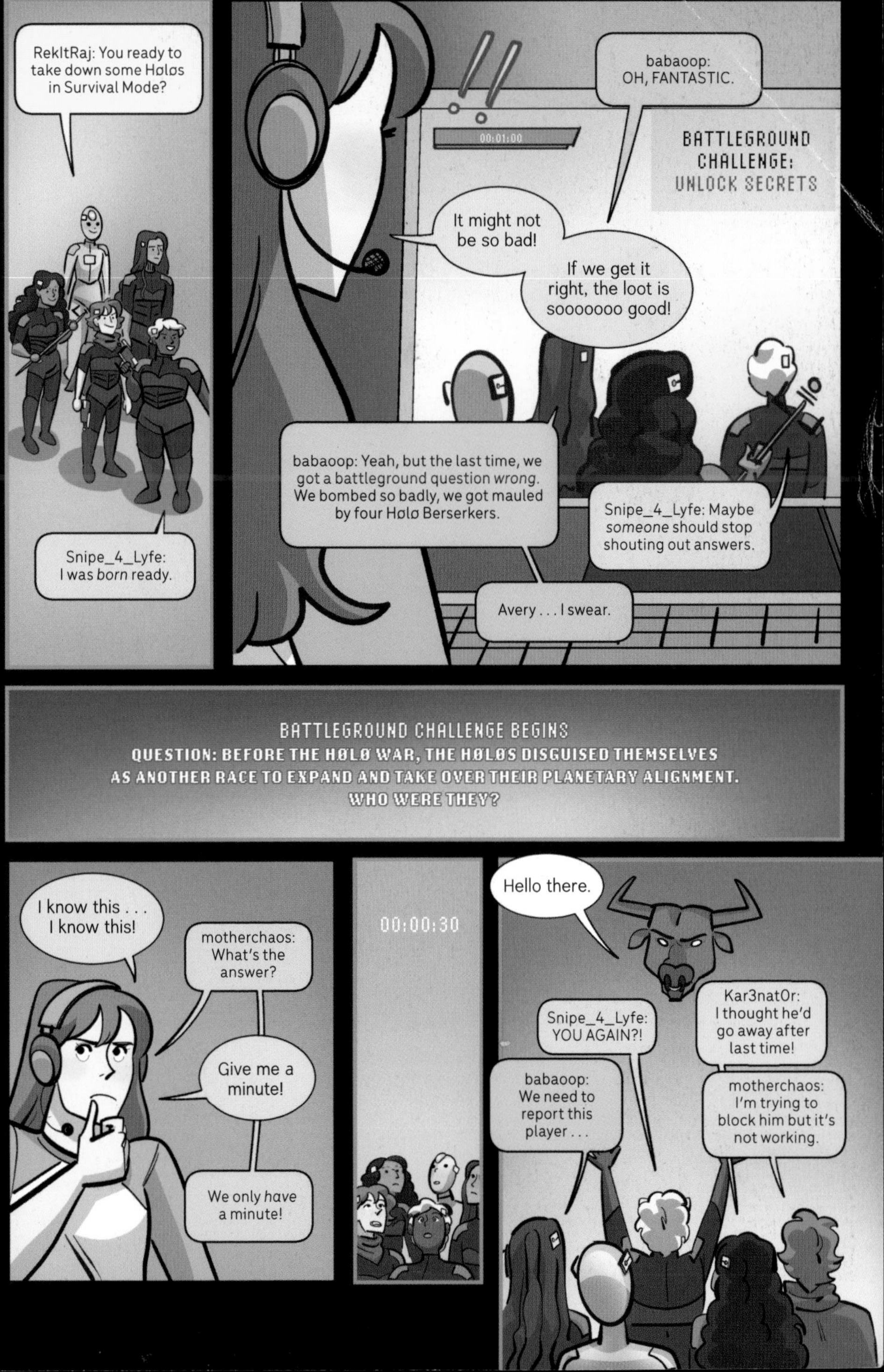
RekItRaj: You ready to take down some Høløs in Survival Mode?
Snipe_4_Lyfe: I was *born* ready.
babaoop: OH, FANTASTIC.
00:01:00
BATTLEGROUND CHALLENGE: UNLOCK SECRETS
It might not be so bad!
If we get it right, the loot is soooooo good!
babaoop: Yeah, but the last time, we got a battleground question *wrong*. We bombed so badly, we got mauled by four Hølø Berserkers.
Snipe_4_Lyfe: Maybe *someone* should stop shouting out answers.
Avery . . . I swear.
BATTLEGROUND CHALLENGE BEGINS
QUESTION: BEFORE THE HØLØ WAR, THE HØLØS DISGUISED THEMSELVES AS ANOTHER RACE TO EXPAND AND TAKE OVER THEIR PLANETARY ALIGNMENT. WHO WERE THEY?
I know this . . . I know this!
motherchaos: What's the answer?
Give me a minute!
We only *have* a minute!
00:00:30
Hello there.
Snipe_4_Lyfe: YOU AGAIN?!
Kar3natOr: I thought he'd go away after last time!
babaoop: We need to report this player . . .
motherchaos: I'm trying to block him but it's not working.

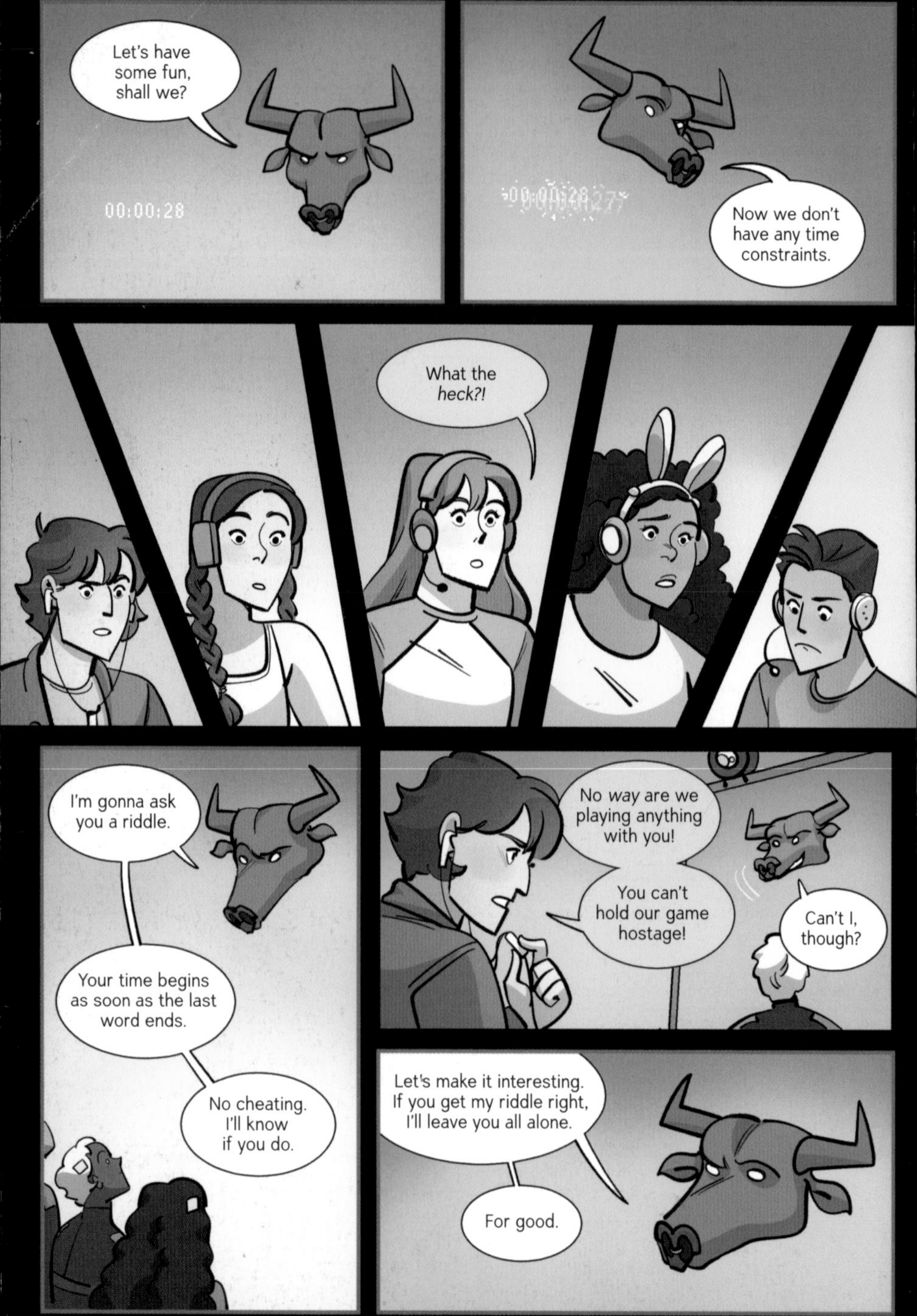
Let's have some fun, shall we?
00:00:28
Now we don't have any time constraints.
What the *heck?!*
I'm gonna ask you a riddle.
Your time begins as soon as the last word ends.
No cheating. I'll know if you do.
No *way* are we playing anything with you!
You can't hold our game hostage!
Can't I, though?
Let's make it interesting. If you get my riddle right, I'll leave you all alone.
For good.

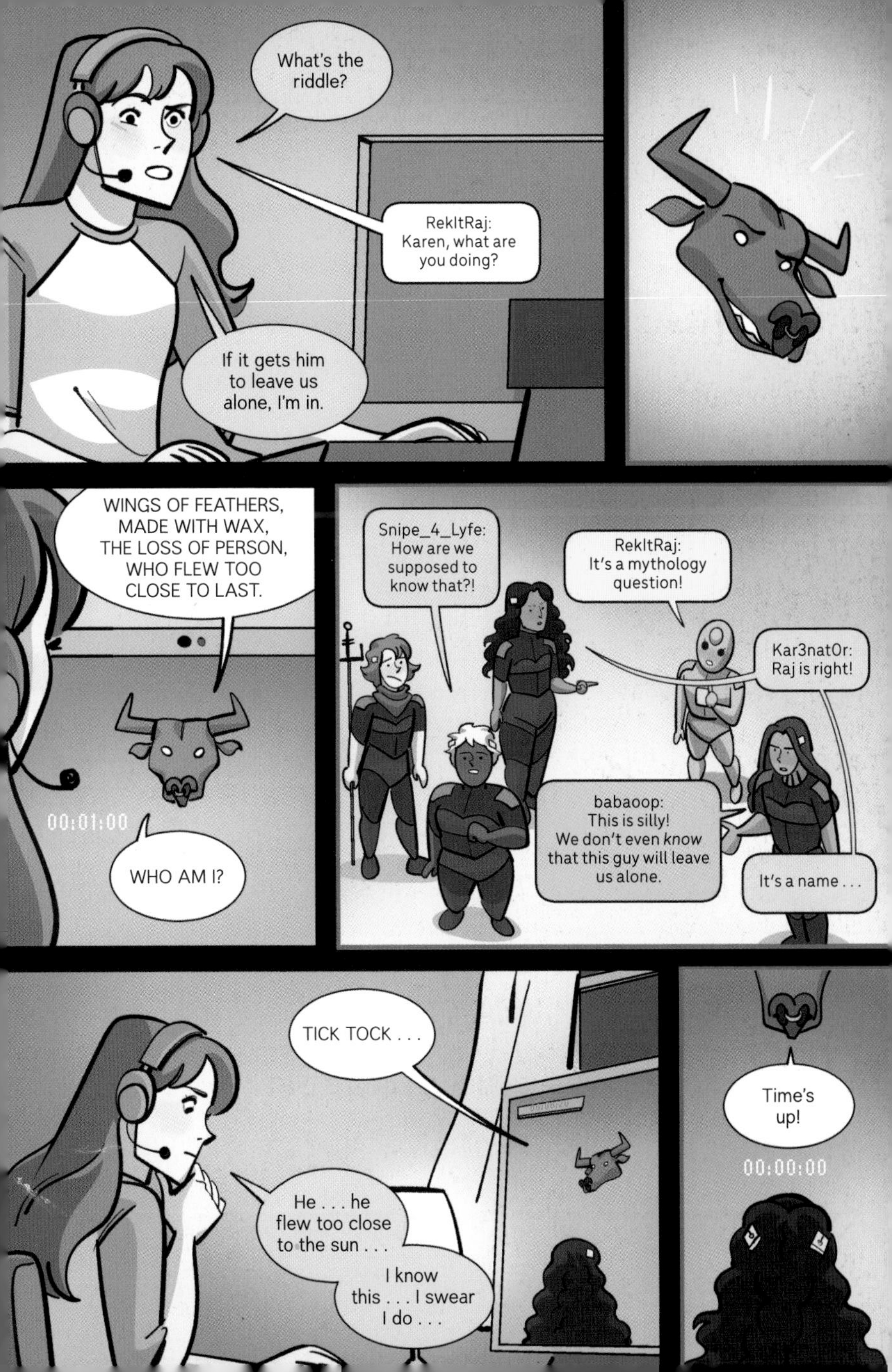
What's the riddle?
RekItRaj: Karen, what are you doing?
If it gets him to leave us alone, I'm in.
WINGS OF FEATHERS, MADE WITH WAX, THE LOSS OF PERSON, WHO FLEW TOO CLOSE TO LAST.
00:01:00
WHO AM I?
Snipe_4_Lyfe: How are we supposed to know that?!
RekItRaj: It's a mythology question!
Kar3natOr: Raj is right!
babaoop: This is silly! We don't even *know* that this guy will leave us alone.
It's a name . . .
TICK TOCK . . .
He . . . he flew too close to the sun . . .
I know this . . . I swear I do . . .
Time's up!
00:00:00

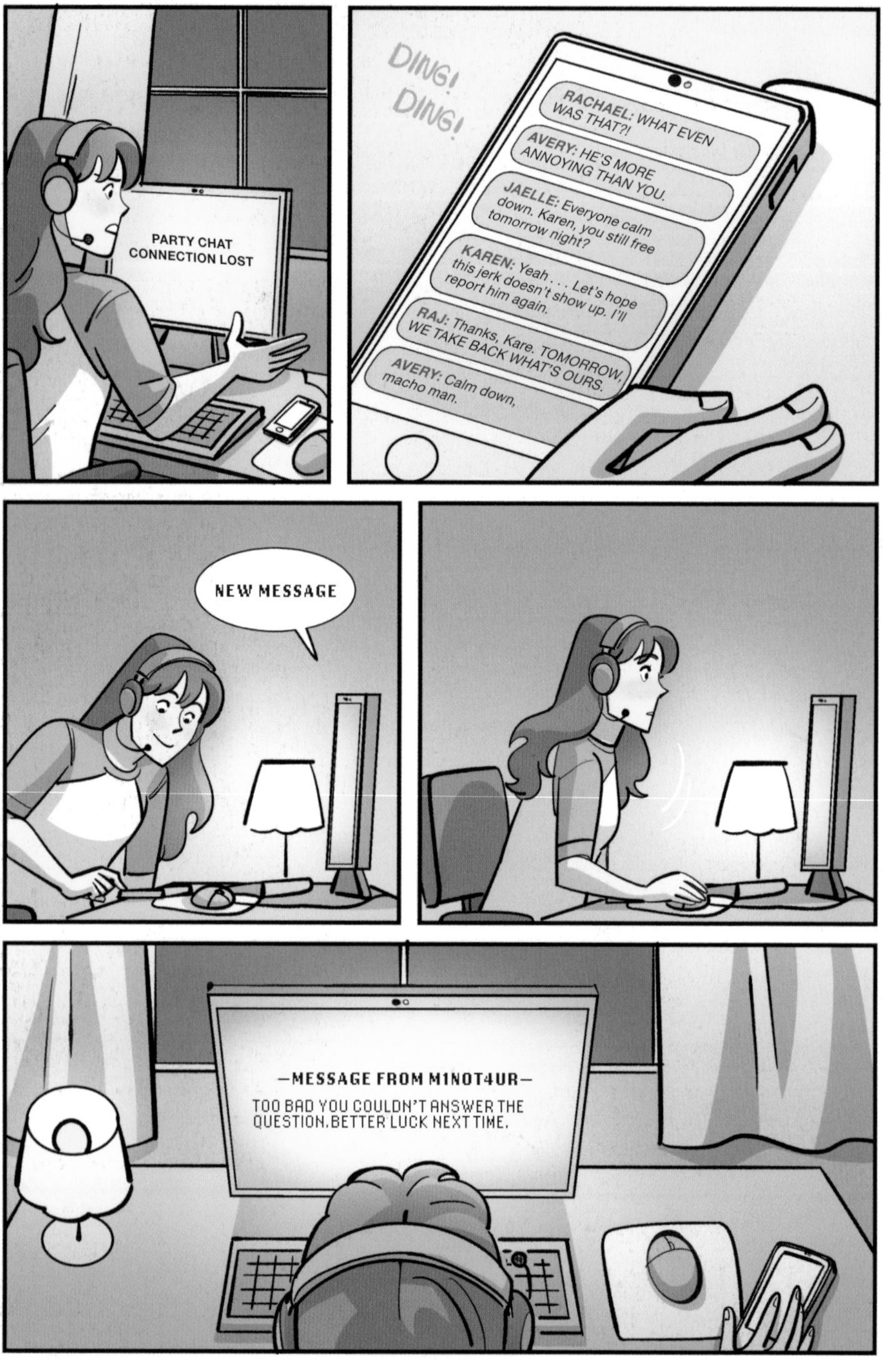
PARTY CHAT CONNECTION LOST
DING! DING!
RACHAEL: WHAT EVEN WAS THAT?!
AVERY: HE'S MORE ANNOYING THAN YOU.
JAELLE: Everyone calm down. Karen, you still free tomorrow night?
KAREN: Yeah . . . Let's hope this jerk doesn't show up. I'll report him again.
RAJ: Thanks, Kare. TOMORROW, WE TAKE BACK WHAT'S OURS.
AVERY: Calm down, macho man.
NEW MESSAGE
—MESSAGE FROM M1NOT4UR—
TOO BAD YOU COULDN'T ANSWER THE QUESTION. BETTER LUCK NEXT TIME.

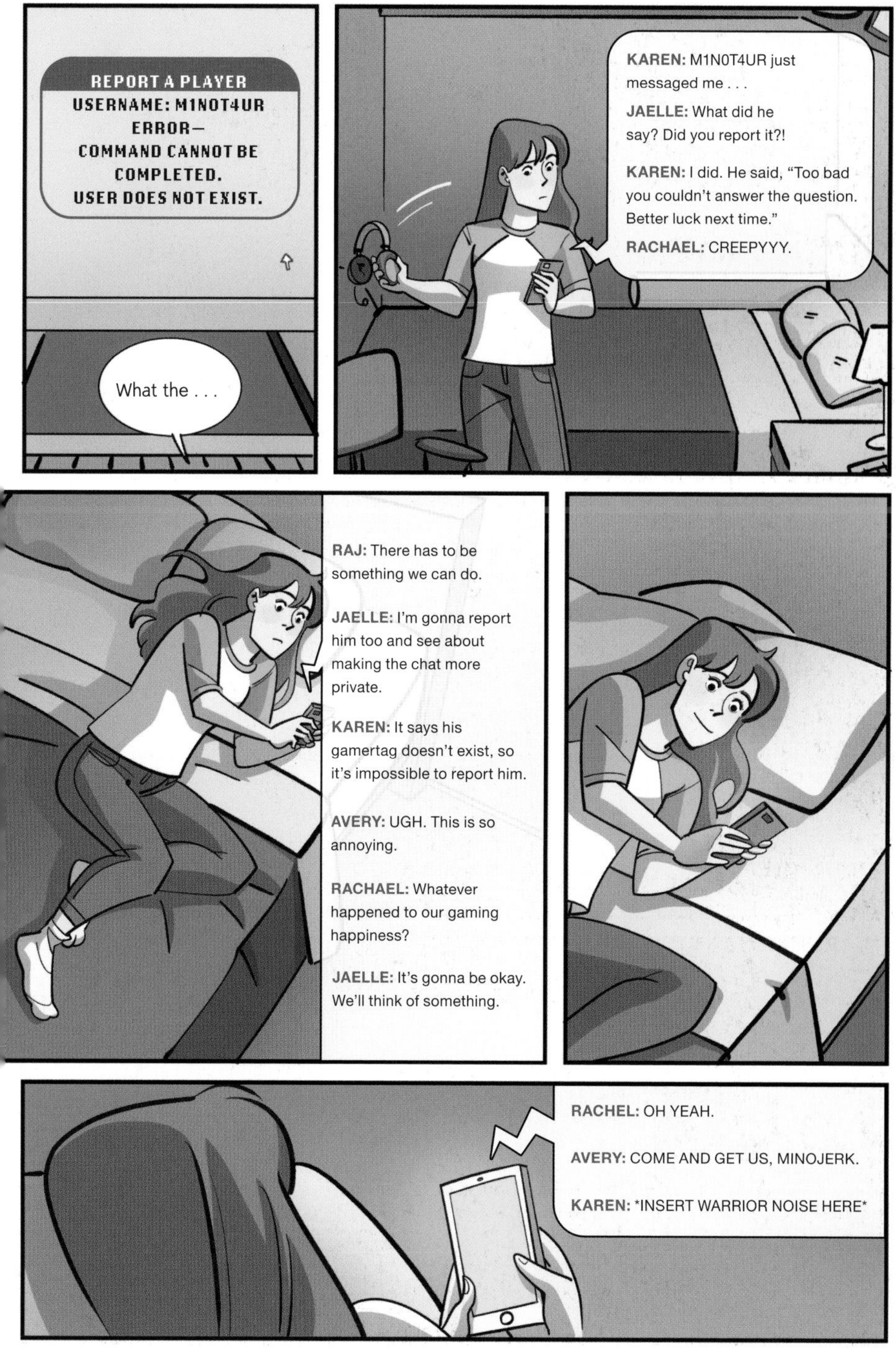
REPORT A PLAYER
USERNAME: M1NOT4UR
ERROR—
COMMAND CANNOT BE COMPLETED.
USER DOES NOT EXIST.
What the . . .
KAREN: M1N0T4UR just messaged me . . .
JAELLE: What did he say? Did you report it?!
KAREN: I did. He said, "Too bad you couldn't answer the question. Better luck next time."
RACHAEL: CREEPYYY.
RAJ: There has to be something we can do.
JAELLE: I'm gonna report him too and see about making the chat more private.
KAREN: It says his gamertag doesn't exist, so it's impossible to report him.
AVERY: UGH. This is so annoying.
RACHAEL: Whatever happened to our gaming happiness?
JAELLE: It's gonna be okay. We'll think of something.
RACHEL: OH YEAH.
AVERY: COME AND GET US, MINOJERK.
KAREN: *INSERT WARRIOR NOISE HERE*

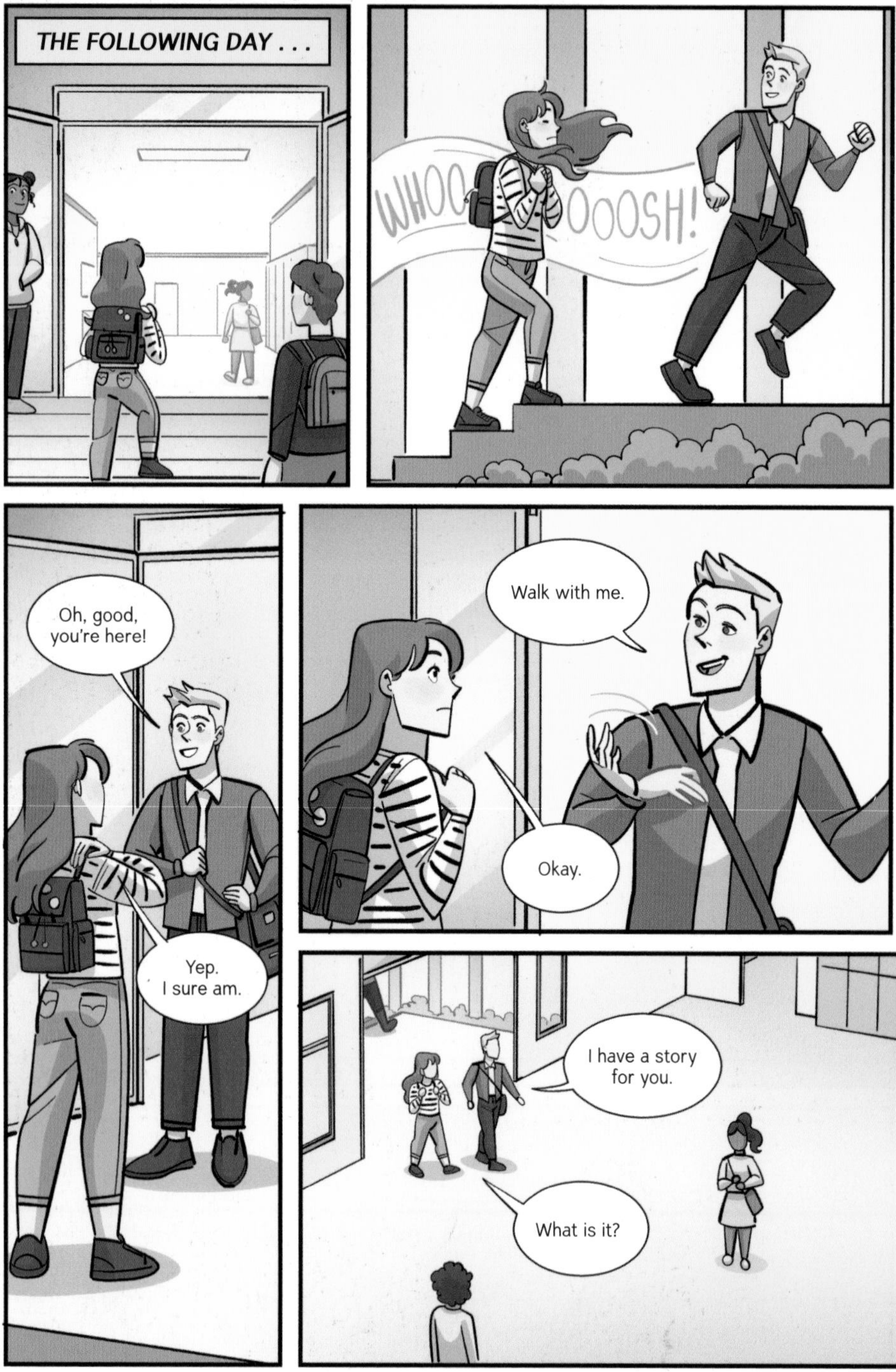
THE FOLLOWING DAY . . .
WHOOOOOOSH!
Oh, good, you're here!
Yep. I sure am.
Walk with me.
Okay.
I have a story for you.
What is it?

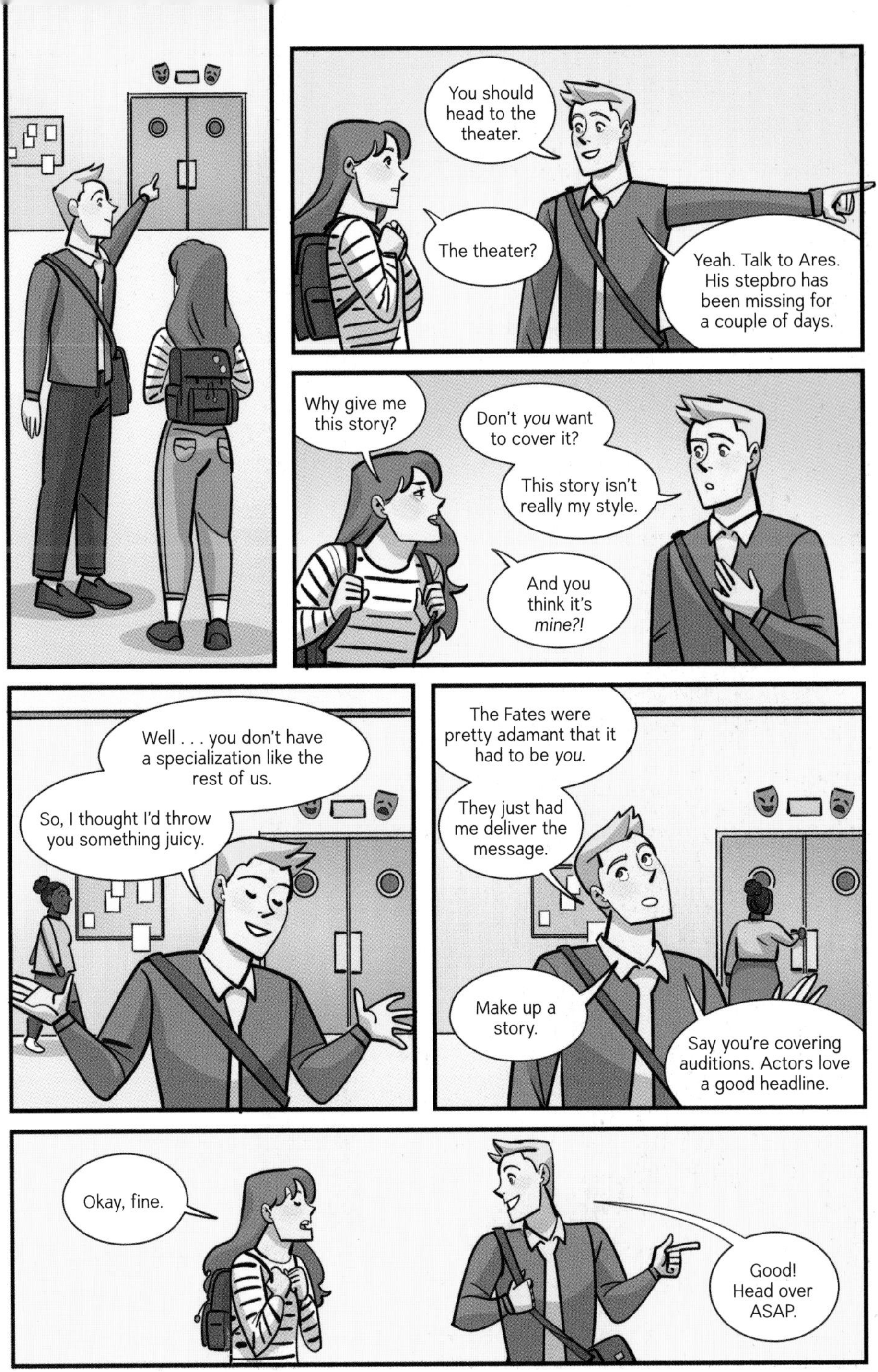
You should head to the theater.
The theater?
Yeah. Talk to Ares. His stepbro has been missing for a couple of days.
Why give me this story?
Don't *you* want to cover it?
This story isn't really my style.
And you think it's *mine?!*
Well . . . you don't have a specialization like the rest of us.
So, I thought I'd throw you something juicy.
The Fates were pretty adamant that it had to be *you.*
They just had me deliver the message.
Make up a story.
Say you're covering auditions. Actors love a good headline.
Okay, fine.
Good! Head over ASAP.

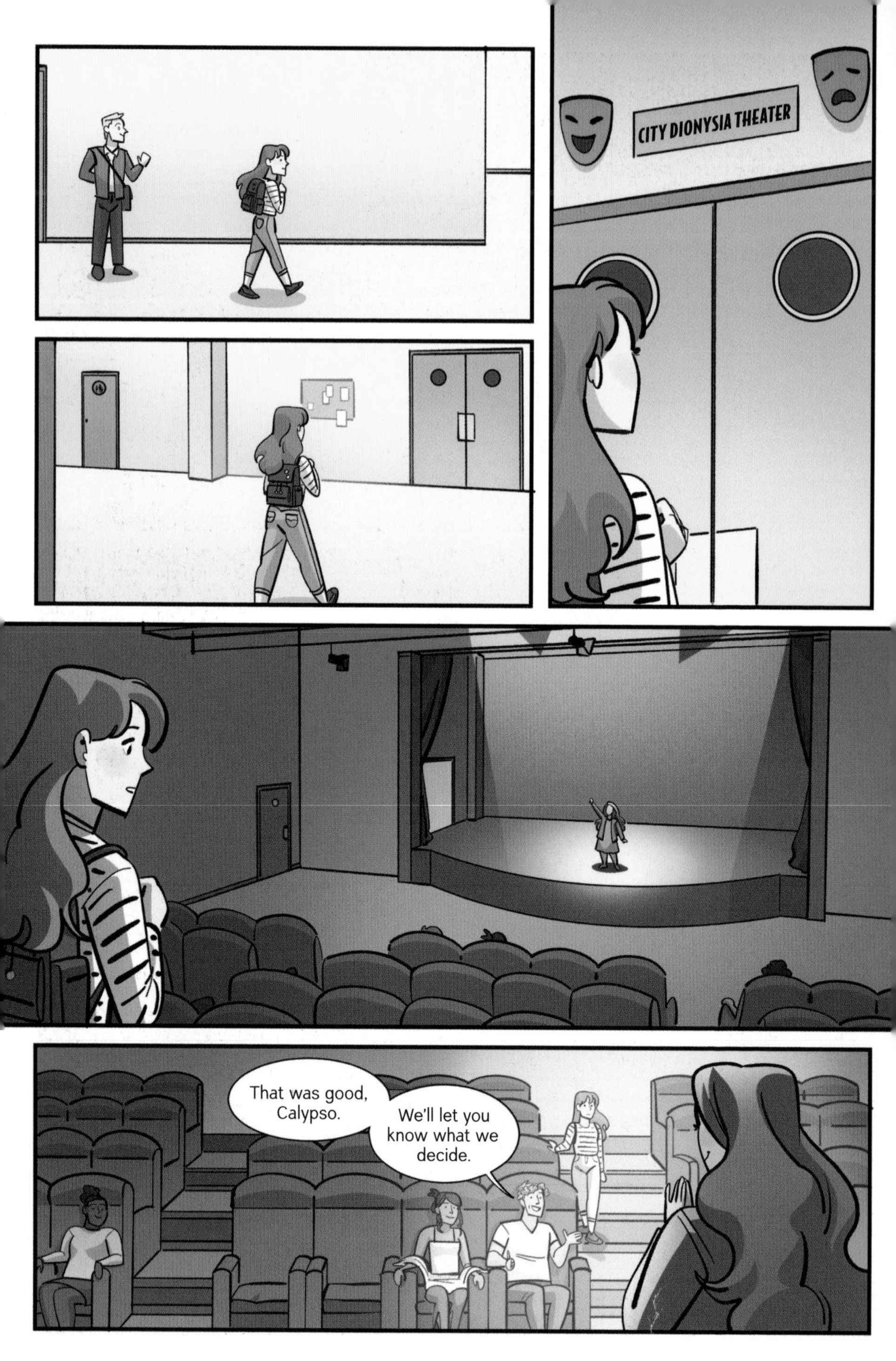
CITY DIONYSIA THEATER
That was good, Calypso.
We'll let you know what we decide.

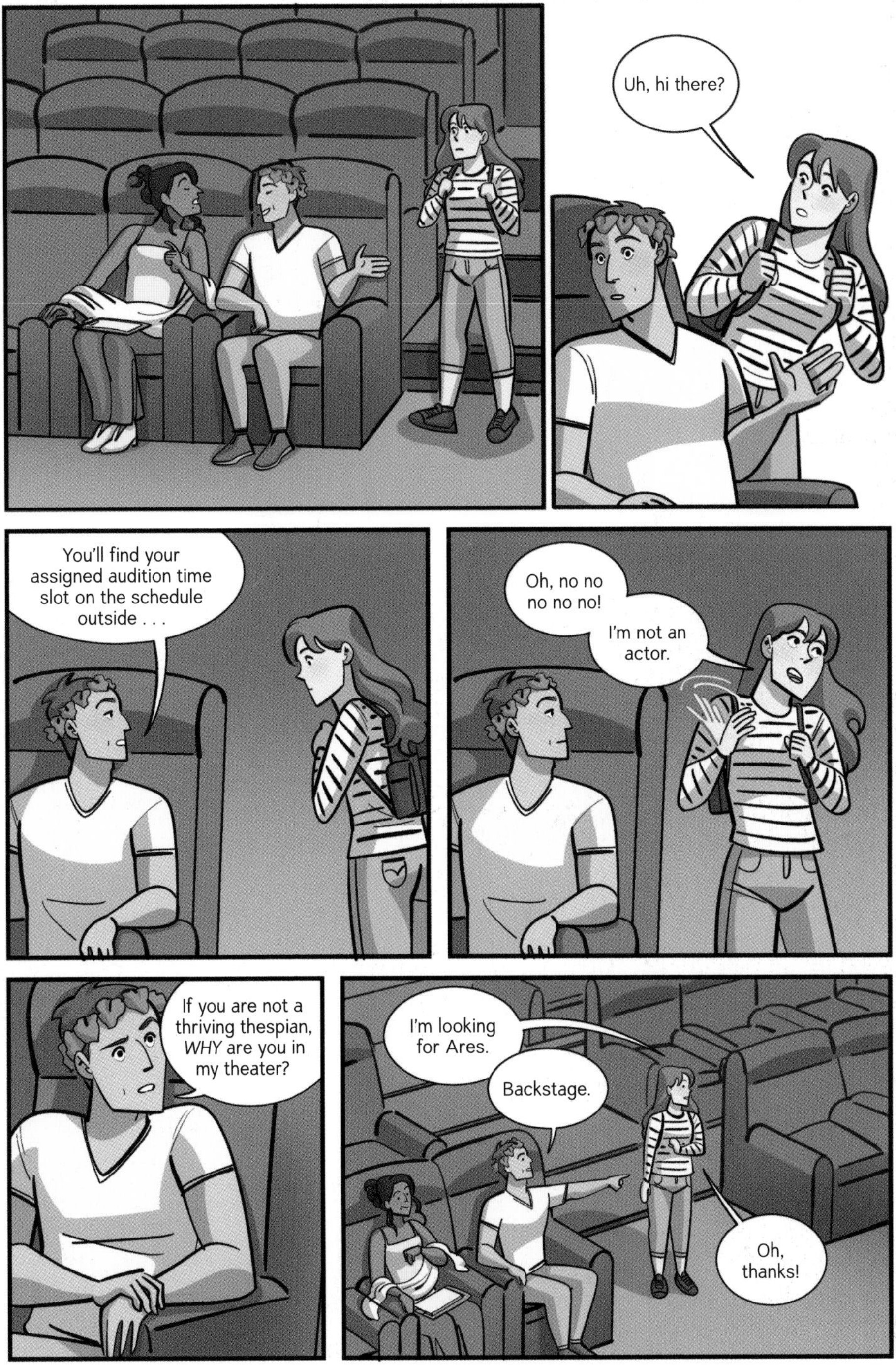
Uh, hi there?
You'll find your assigned audition time slot on the schedule outside . . .
Oh, no no no no no!
I'm not an actor.
If you are not a thriving thespian, *WHY* are you in my theater?
I'm looking for Ares.
Backstage.
Oh, thanks!

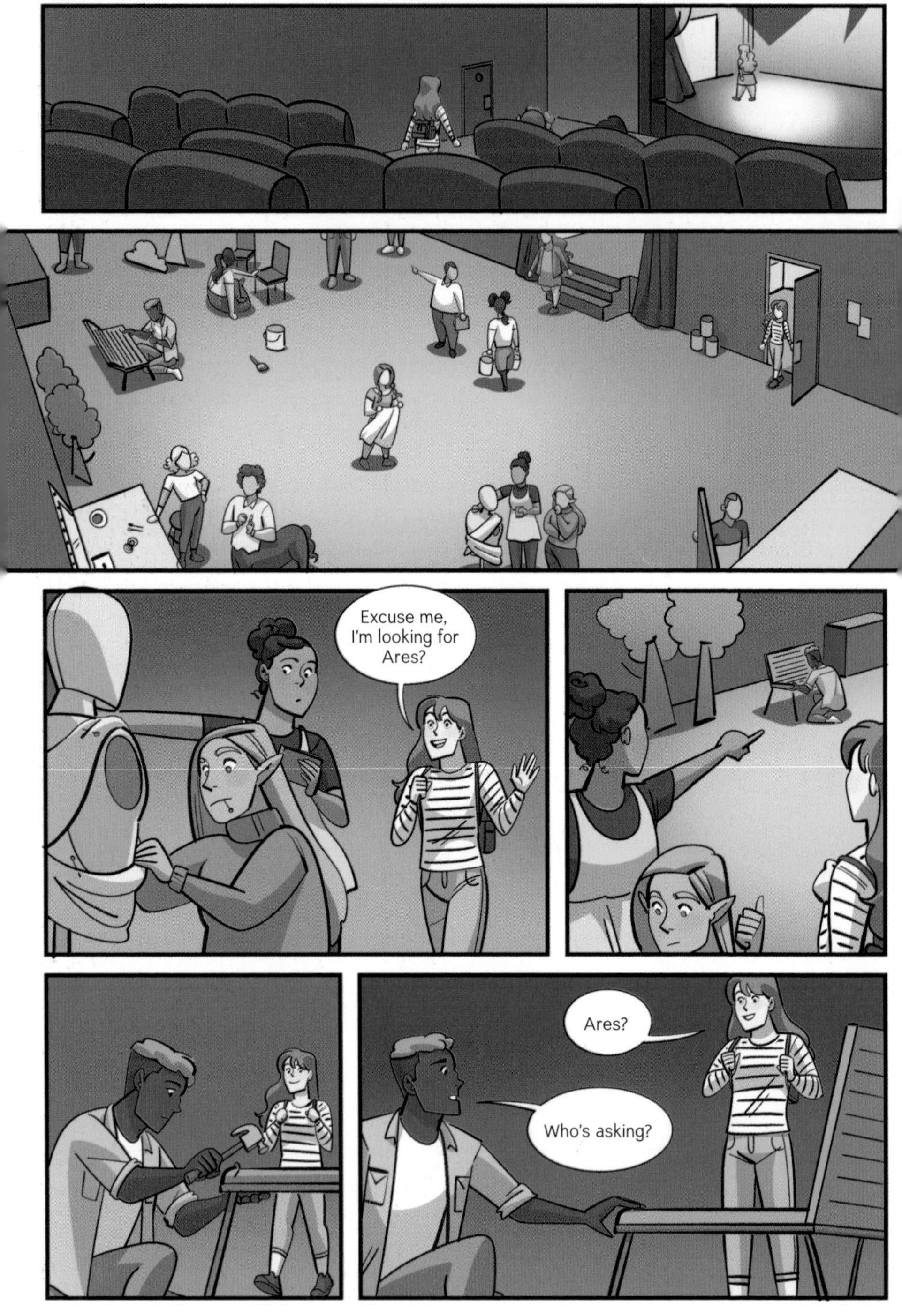
Excuse me, I'm looking for Ares?
Ares?
Who's asking?

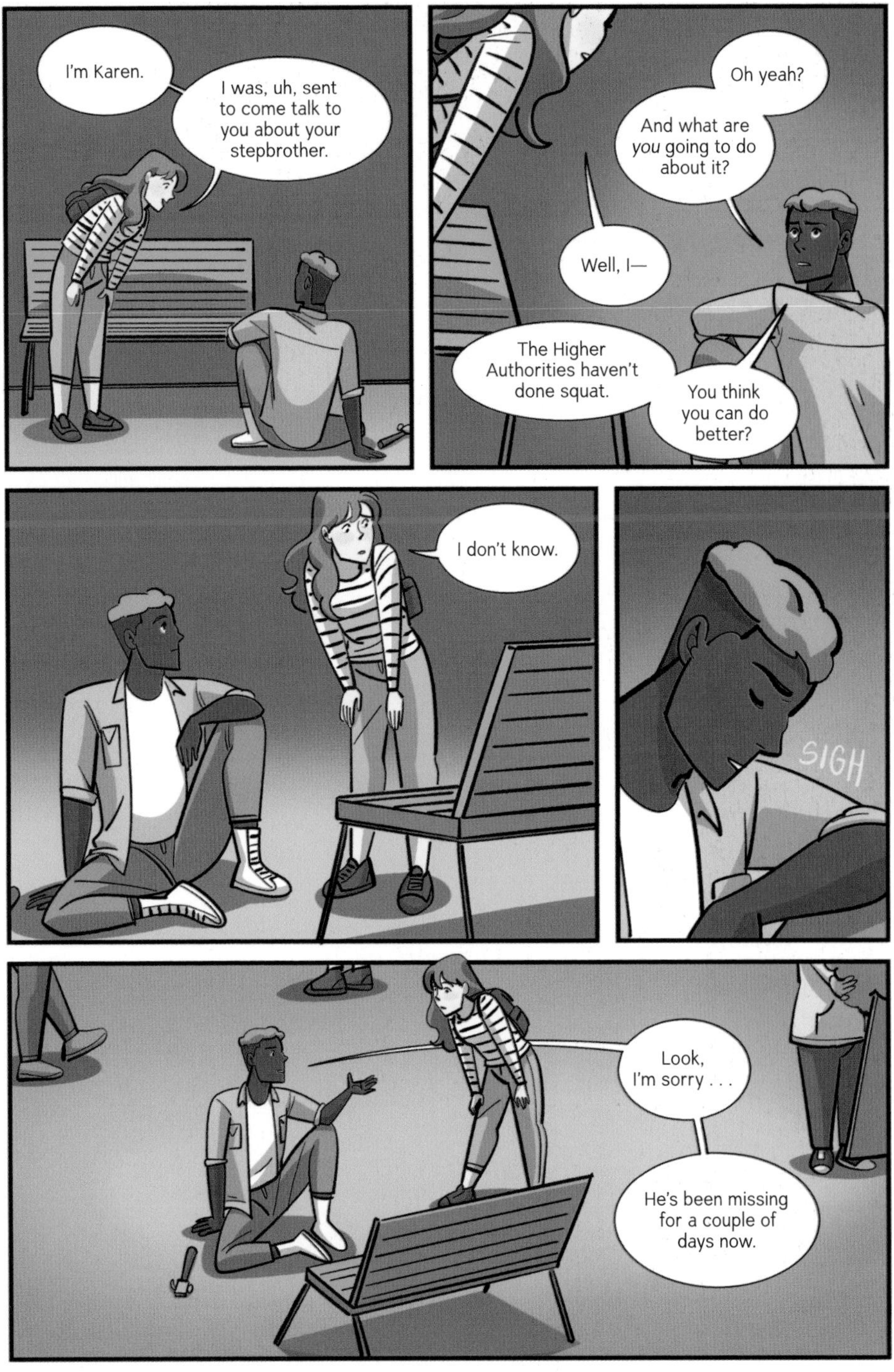
I'm Karen.
I was, uh, sent to come talk to you about your stepbrother.
Oh yeah?
And what are *you* going to do about it?
Well, I—
The Higher Authorities haven't done squat.
You think you can do better?
I don't know.
SIGH
Look, I'm sorry . . .
He's been missing for a couple of days now.

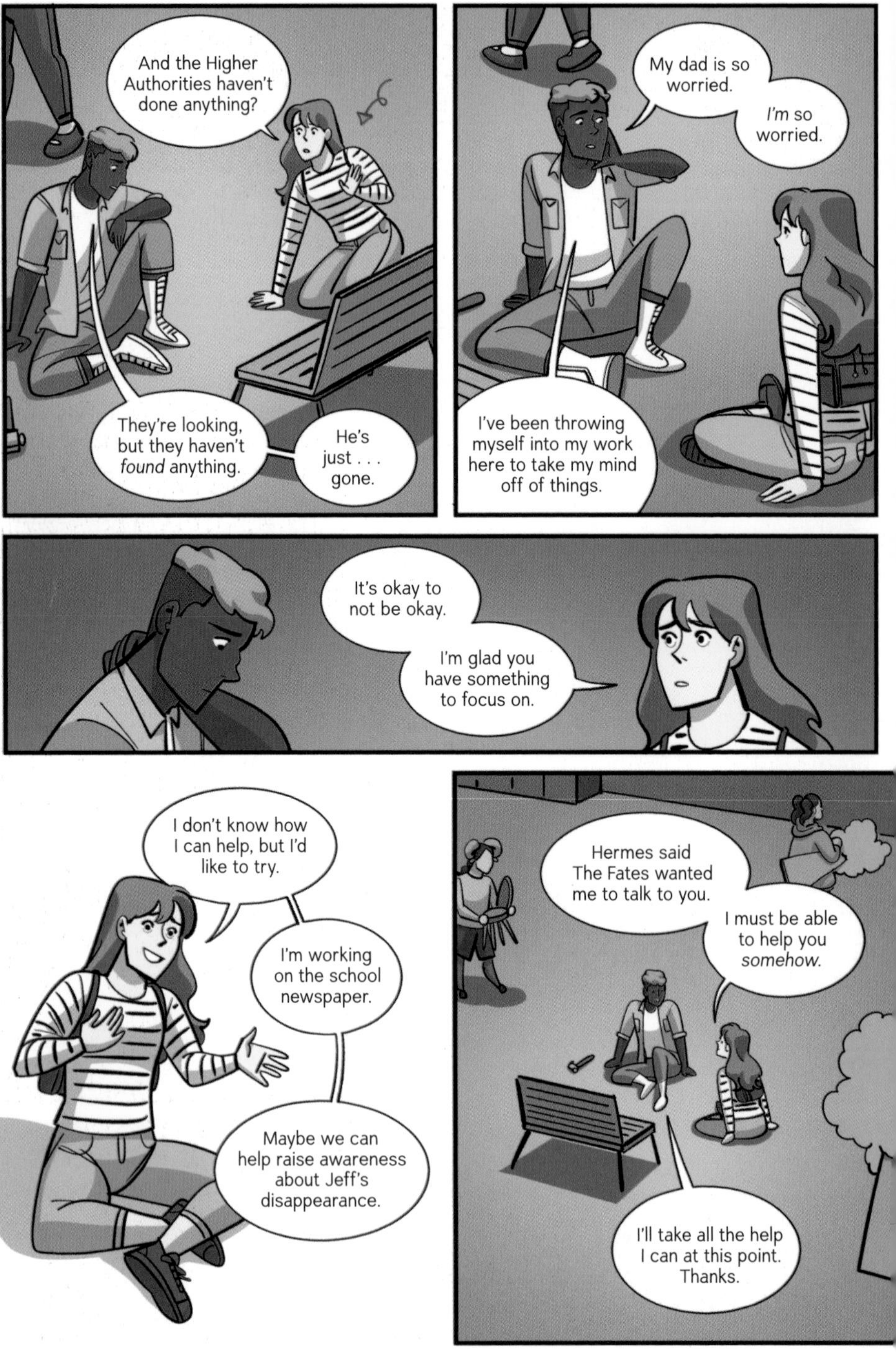
And the Higher Authorities haven't done anything?
They're looking, but they haven't *found* anything.
He's just . . . gone.
My dad is so worried.
I'm so worried.
I've been throwing myself into my work here to take my mind off of things.
It's okay to not be okay.
I'm glad you have something to focus on.
I don't know how I can help, but I'd like to try.
I'm working on the school newspaper.
Maybe we can help raise awareness about Jeff's disappearance.
Hermes said The Fates wanted me to talk to you.
I must be able to help you *somehow.*
I'll take all the help I can at this point. Thanks.

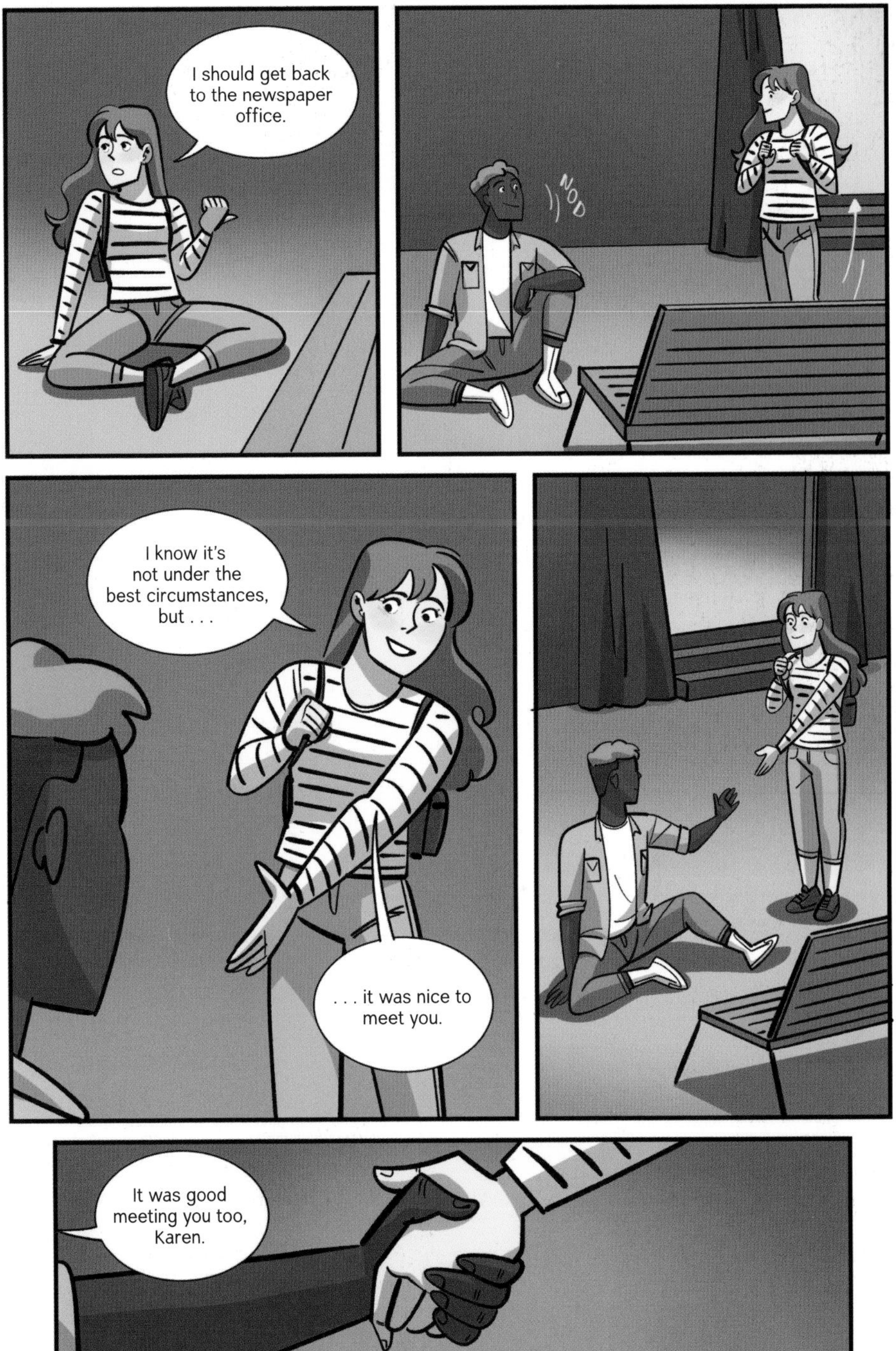
I should get back to the newspaper office.
NOD
I know it's not under the best circumstances, but . . .
. . . it was nice to meet you.
It was good meeting you too, Karen.

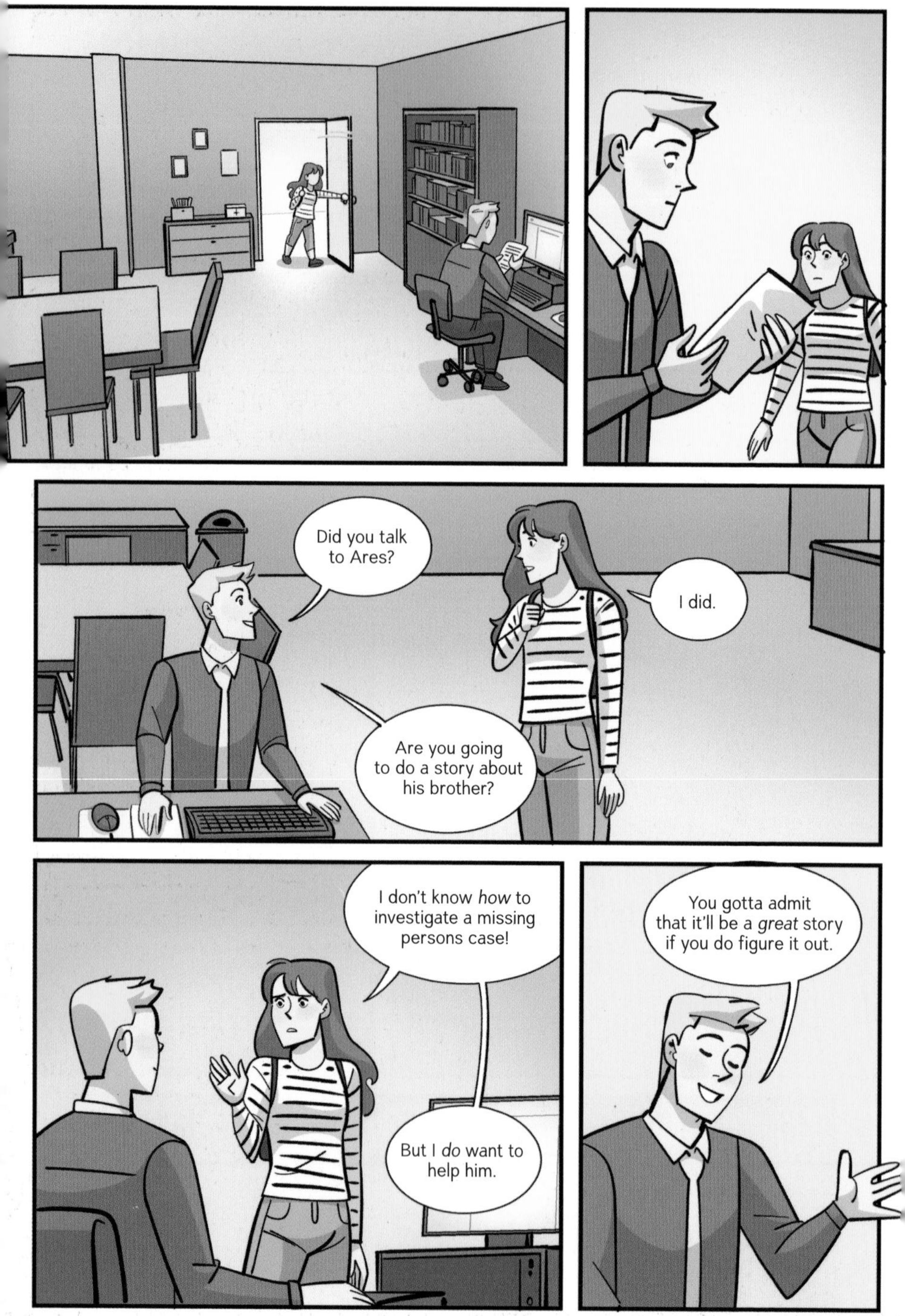
Did you talk to Ares?
I did.
Are you going to do a story about his brother?
I don't know *how* to investigate a missing persons case!
But I *do* want to help him.
You gotta admit that it'll be a *great* story if you do figure it out.

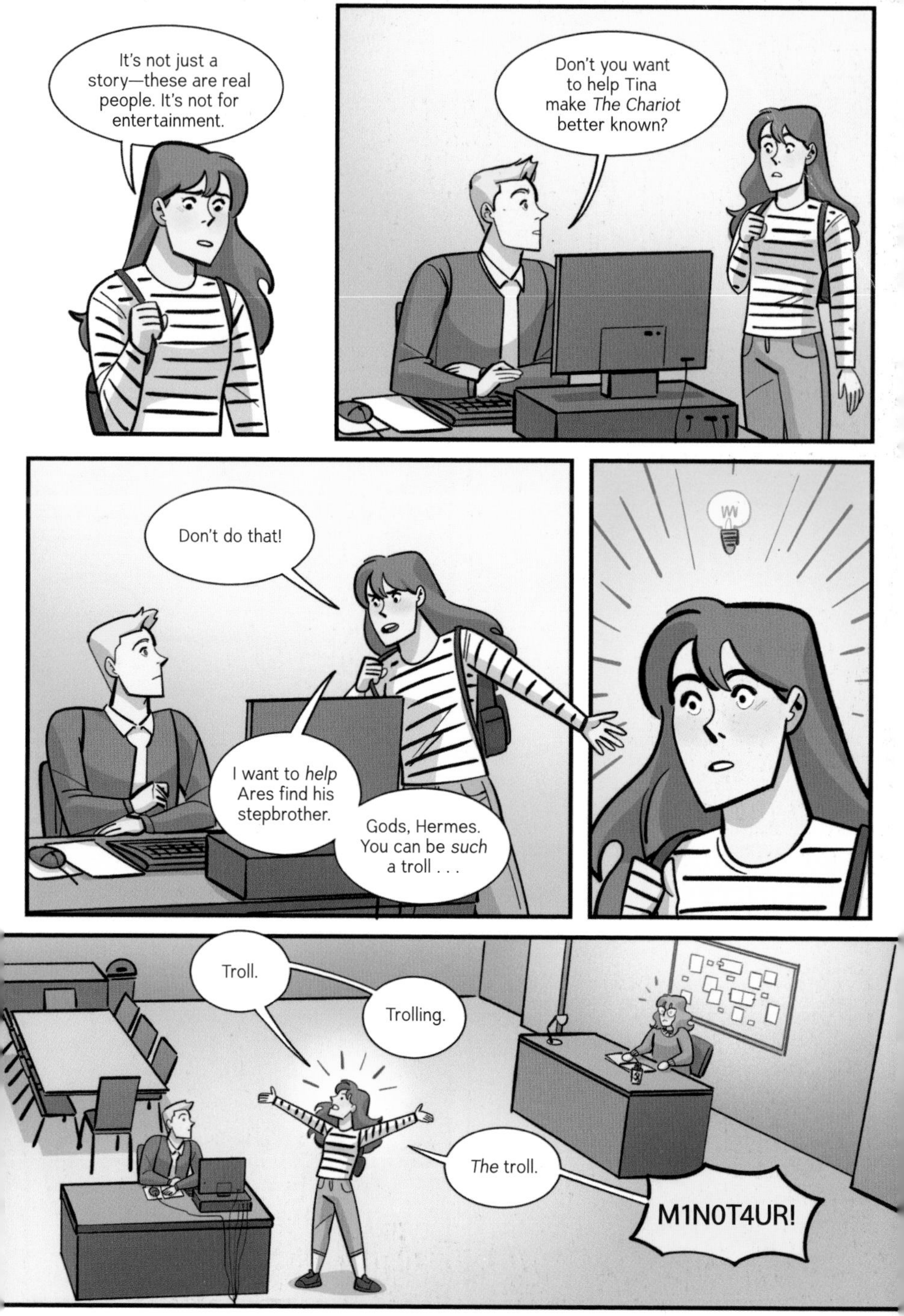
It's not just a story—these are real people. It's not for entertainment.
Don't you want to help Tina make *The Chariot* better known?
Don't do that!
I want to *help* Ares find his stepbrother.
Gods, Hermes. You can be *such* a troll . . .
Troll.
Trolling.
The troll.
M1N0T4UR!

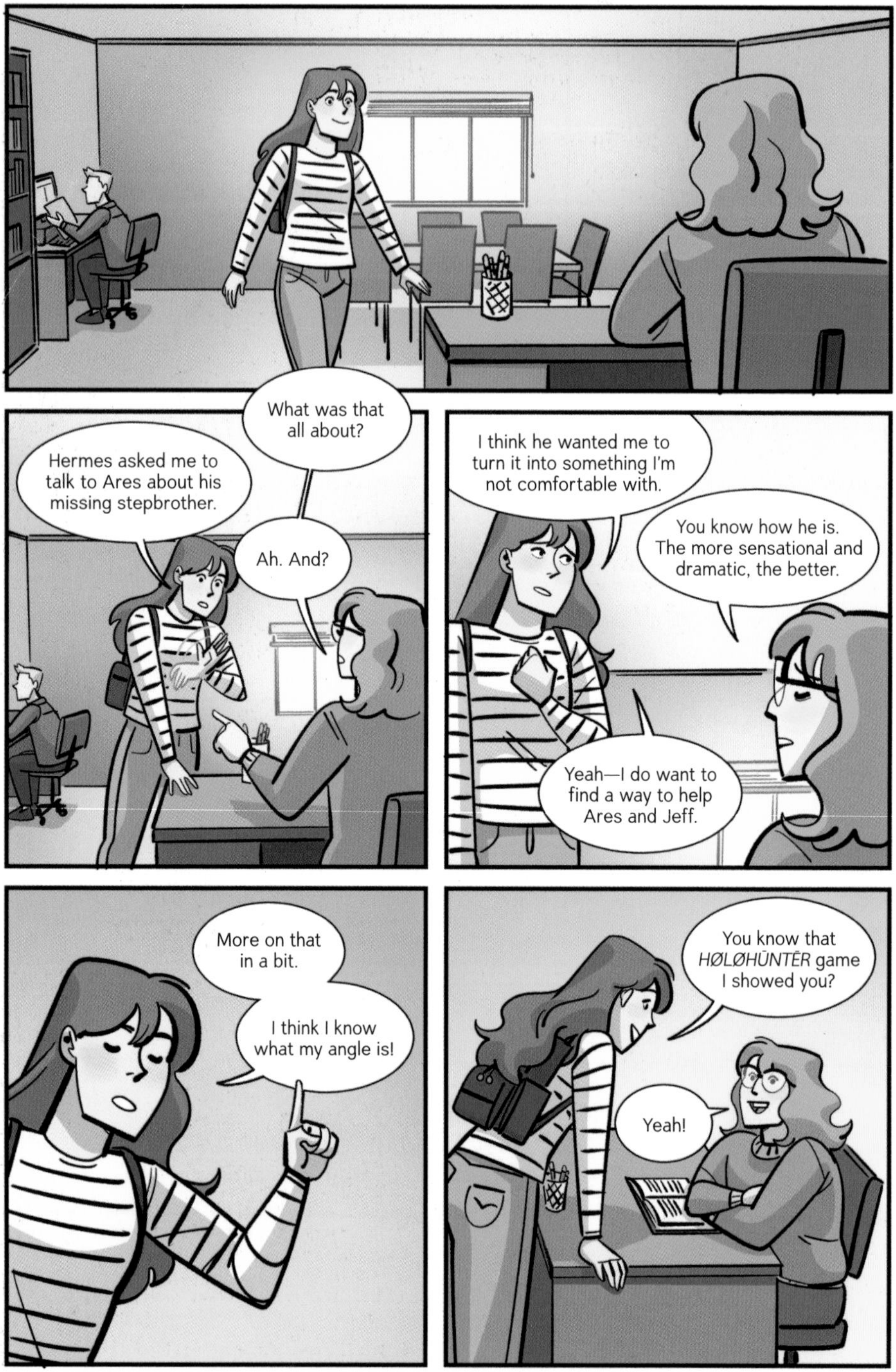
What was that all about?
Hermes asked me to talk to Ares about his missing stepbrother.
Ah. And?
I think he wanted me to turn it into something I'm not comfortable with.
You know how he is. The more sensational and dramatic, the better.
Yeah—I do want to find a way to help Ares and Jeff.
More on that in a bit.
I think I know what my angle is!
You know that *HØLØHŪNTĒR* game I showed you?
Yeah!

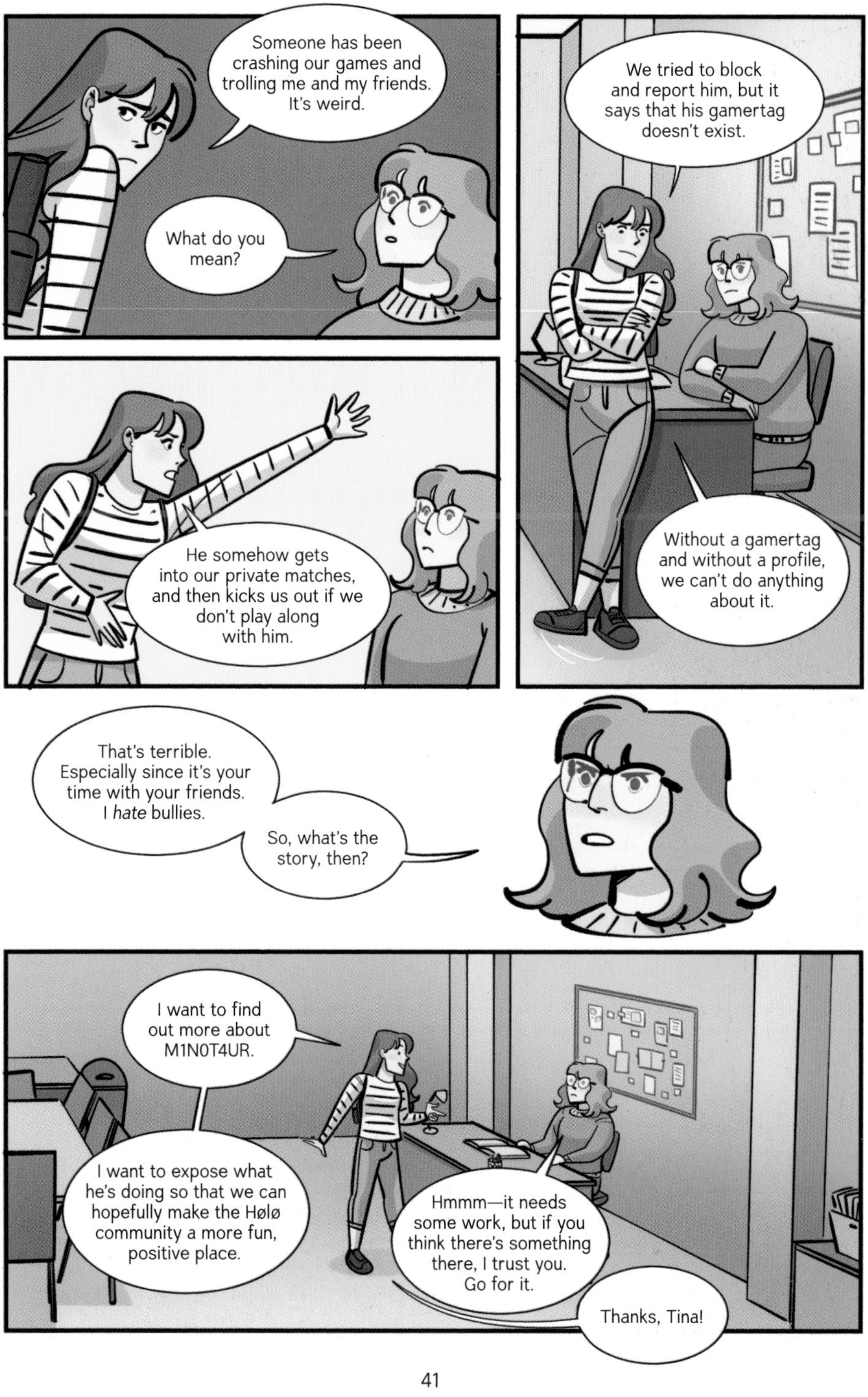
Someone has been crashing our games and trolling me and my friends. It's weird.
What do you mean?
We tried to block and report him, but it says that his gamertag doesn't exist.
He somehow gets into our private matches, and then kicks us out if we don't play along with him.
Without a gamertag and without a profile, we can't do anything about it.
That's terrible. Especially since it's your time with your friends. I *hate* bullies.
So, what's the story, then?
I want to find out more about M1N0T4UR.
I want to expose what he's doing so that we can hopefully make the Hølø community a more fun, positive place.
Hmmm—it needs some work, but if you think there's something there, I trust you. Go for it.
Thanks, Tina!

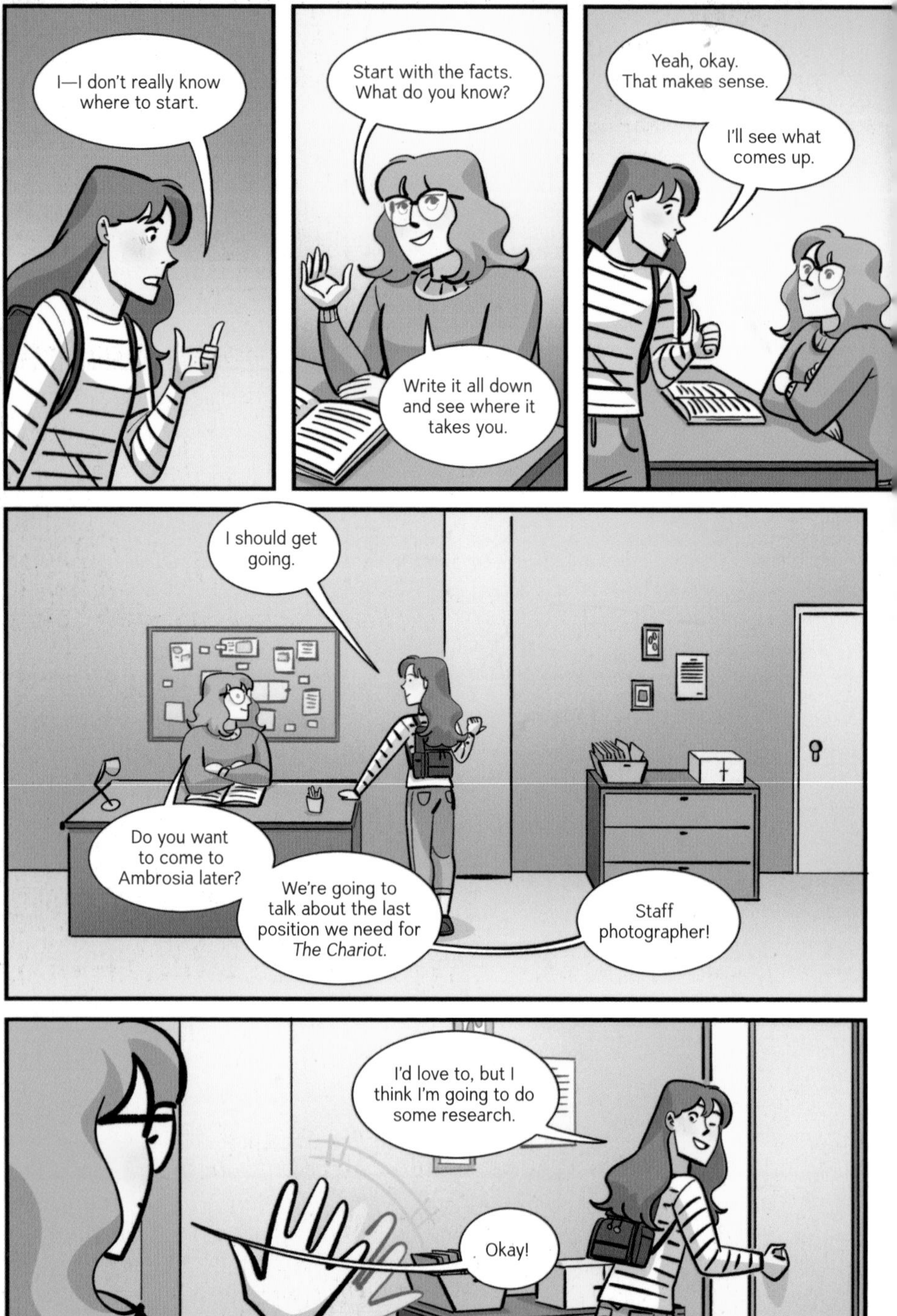
I—I don't really know where to start.
Start with the facts. What do you know?
Write it all down and see where it takes you.
Yeah, okay. That makes sense.
I'll see what comes up.
I should get going.
Do you want to come to Ambrosia later?
We're going to talk about the last position we need for *The Chariot*.
Staff photographer!
I'd love to, but I think I'm going to do some research.
Okay!

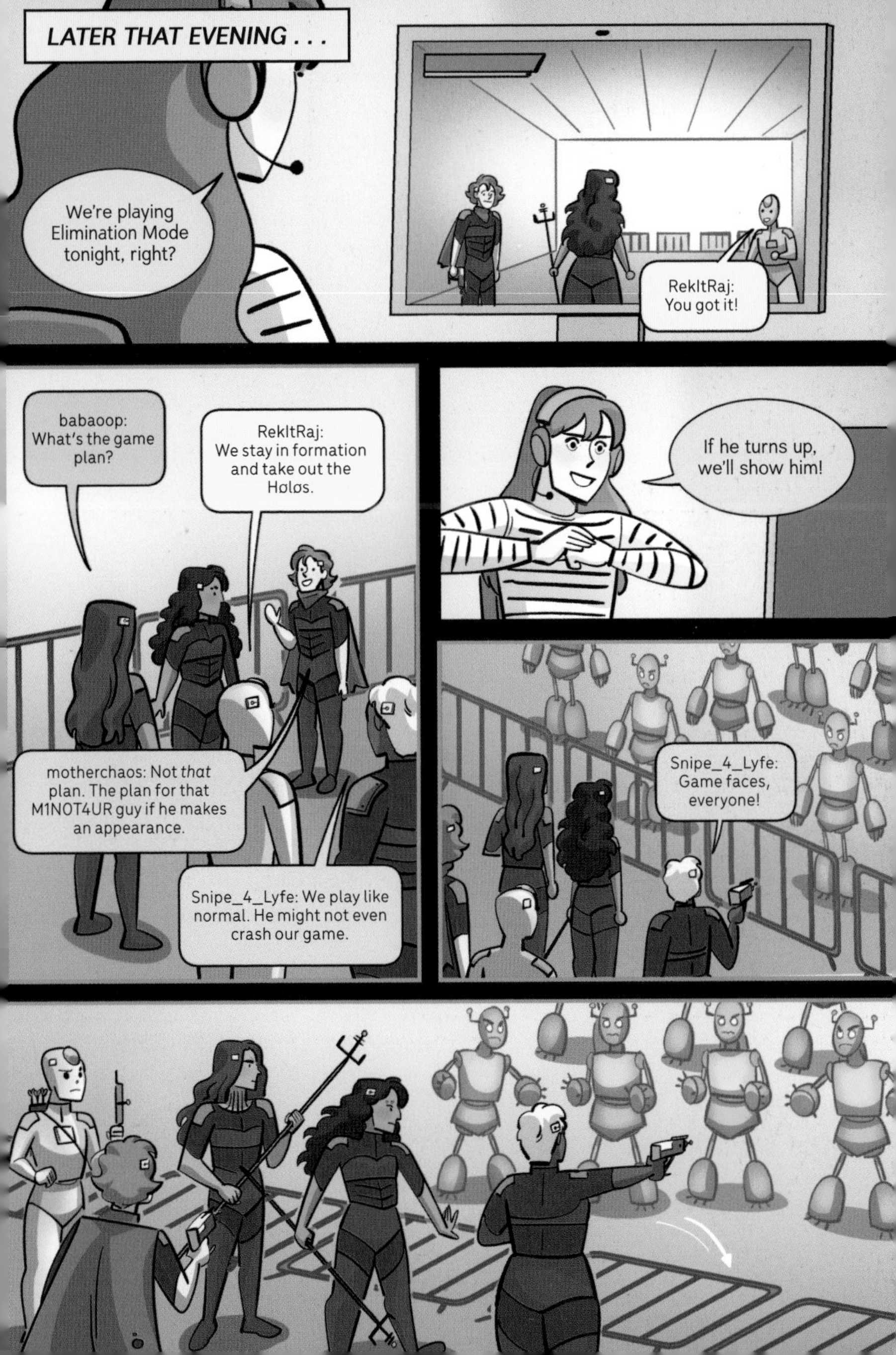
LATER THAT EVENING . . .
We're playing Elimination Mode tonight, right?
RekItRaj: You got it!
babaoop: What's the game plan?
RekItRaj: We stay in formation and take out the Høløs.
motherchaos: Not *that* plan. The plan for that M1NOT4UR guy if he makes an appearance.
Snipe_4_Lyfe: We play like normal. He might not even crash our game.
If he turns up, we'll show him!
Snipe_4_Lyfe: Game faces, everyone!

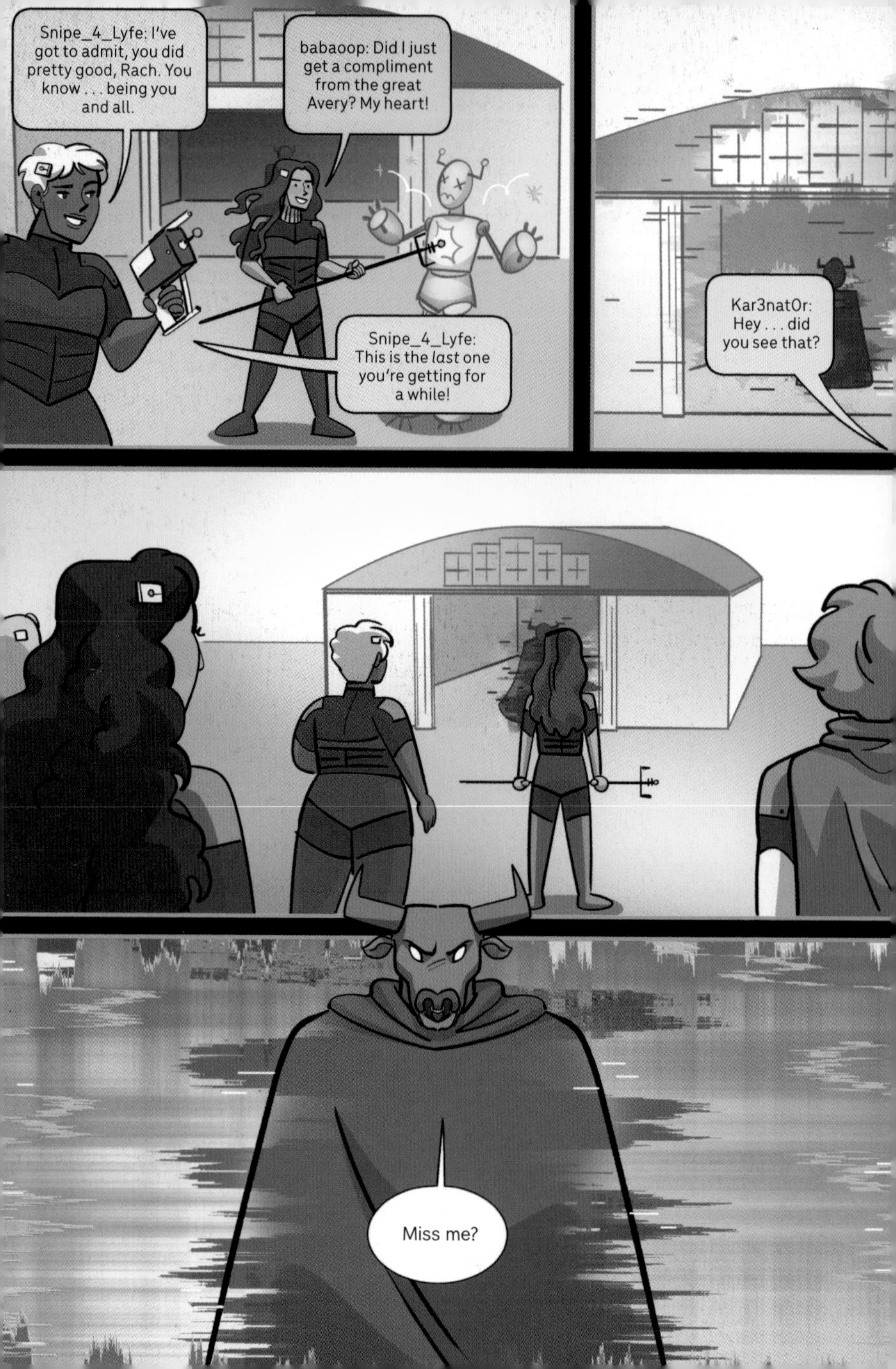
Snipe_4_Lyfe: I've got to admit, you did pretty good, Rach. You know . . . being you and all.
babaoop: Did I just get a compliment from the great Avery? My heart!
Snipe_4_Lyfe: This is the *last* one you're getting for a while!
Kar3nat0r: Hey . . . did you see that?
Miss me?

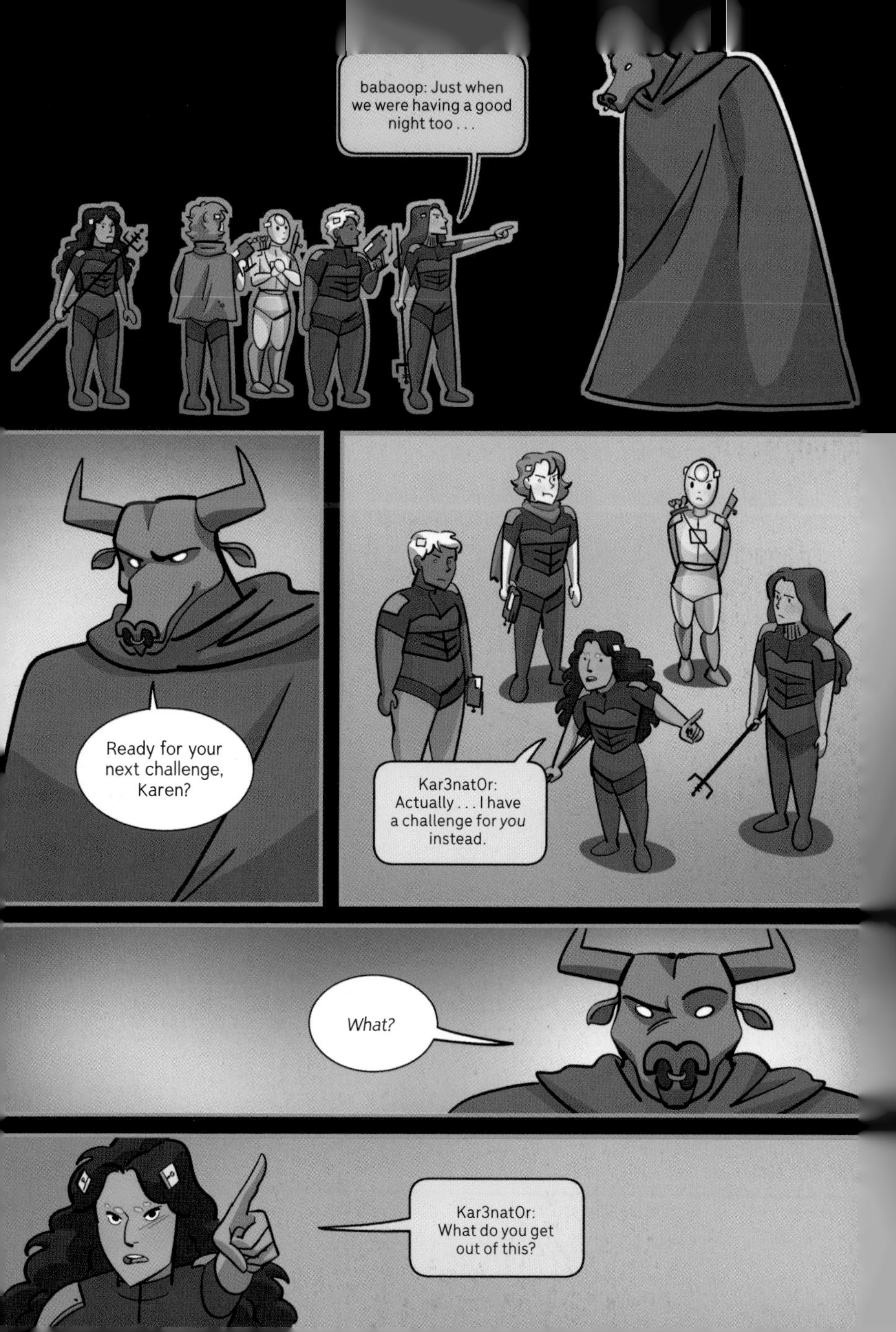
babaoop: Just when we were having a good night too . . .
Ready for your next challenge, Karen?
Kar3nat0r: Actually . . . I have a challenge for *you* instead.
What?
Kar3nat0r: What do you get out of this?

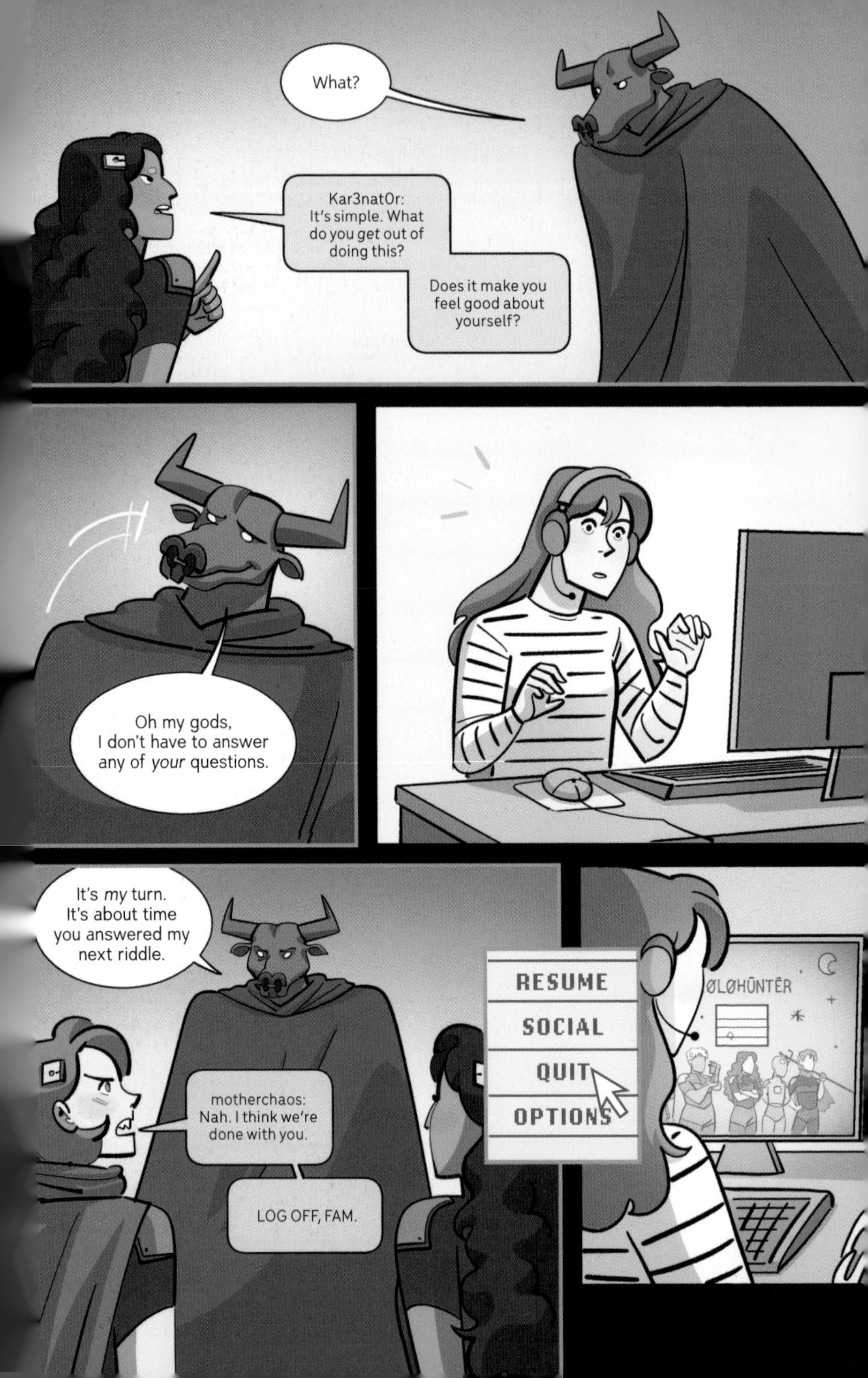
What?
Kar3nat0r:
It's simple. What do you *get* out of doing this?
Does it make you feel good about yourself?
Oh my gods, I don't have to answer any of *your* questions.
It's *my* turn. It's about time you answered my next riddle.
RESUME
SOCIAL
QUIT
OPTIONS
ØLØHŪNTĒR
motherchaos:
Nah. I think we're done with you.
LOG OFF, FAM.

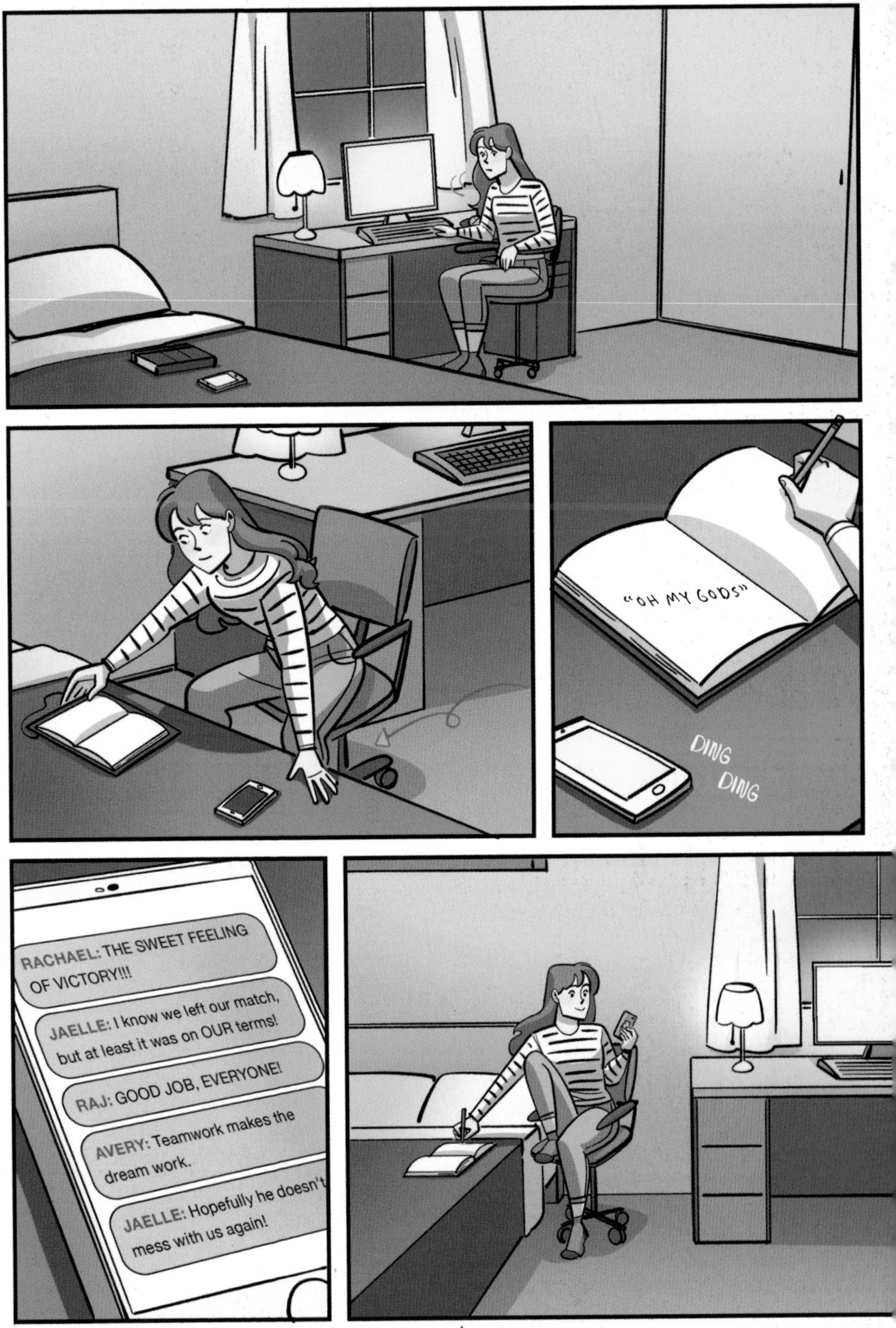
"OH MY GODS"
DING
DING
RACHAEL: THE SWEET FEELING OF VICTORY!!!
JAELLE: I know we left our match, but at least it was on OUR terms!
RAJ: GOOD JOB, EVERYONE!
AVERY: Teamwork makes the dream work.
JAELLE: Hopefully he doesn't mess with us again!

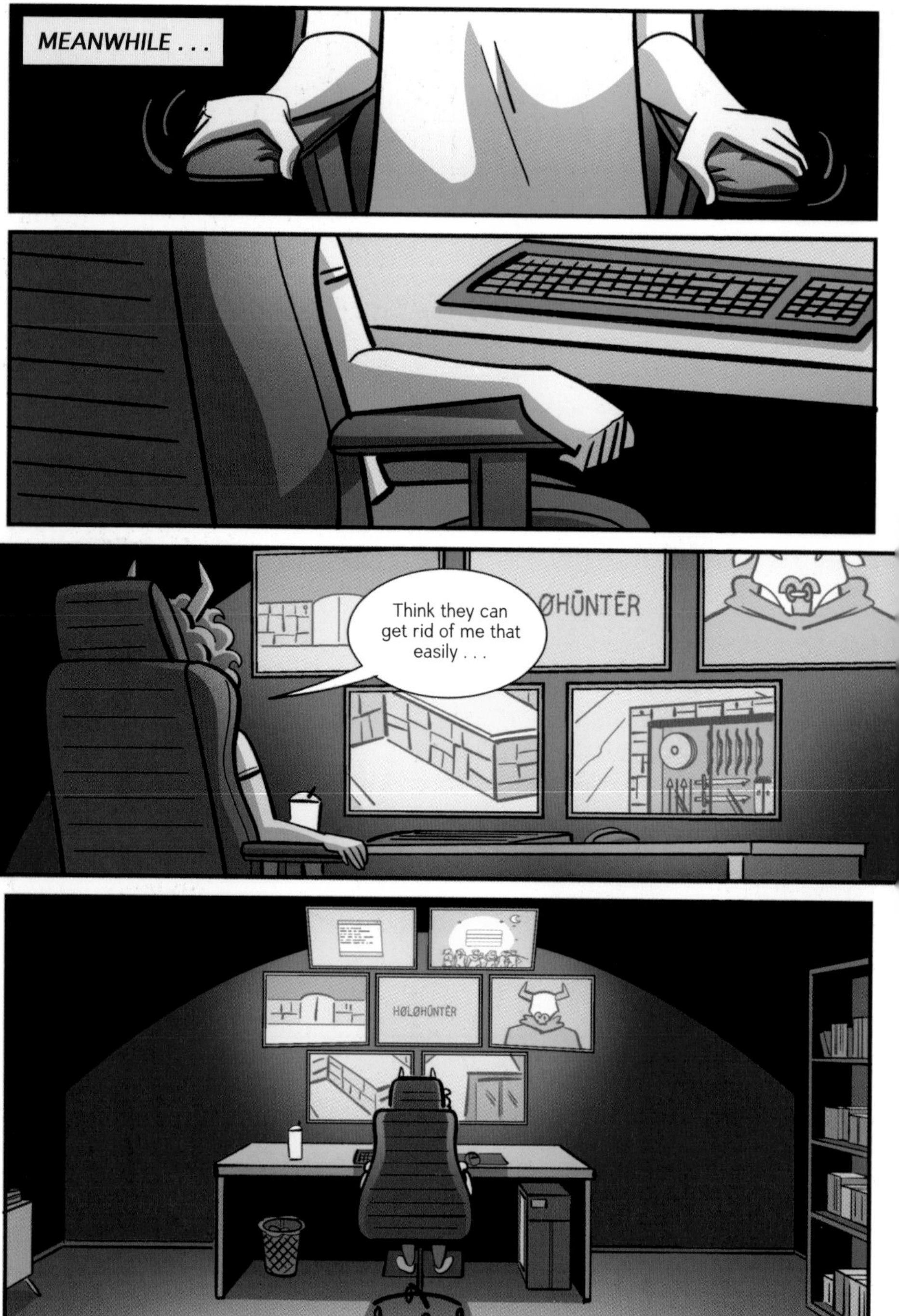
MEANWHILE . . .
Think they can get rid of me that easily . . .
HØLØHŪNTĒR

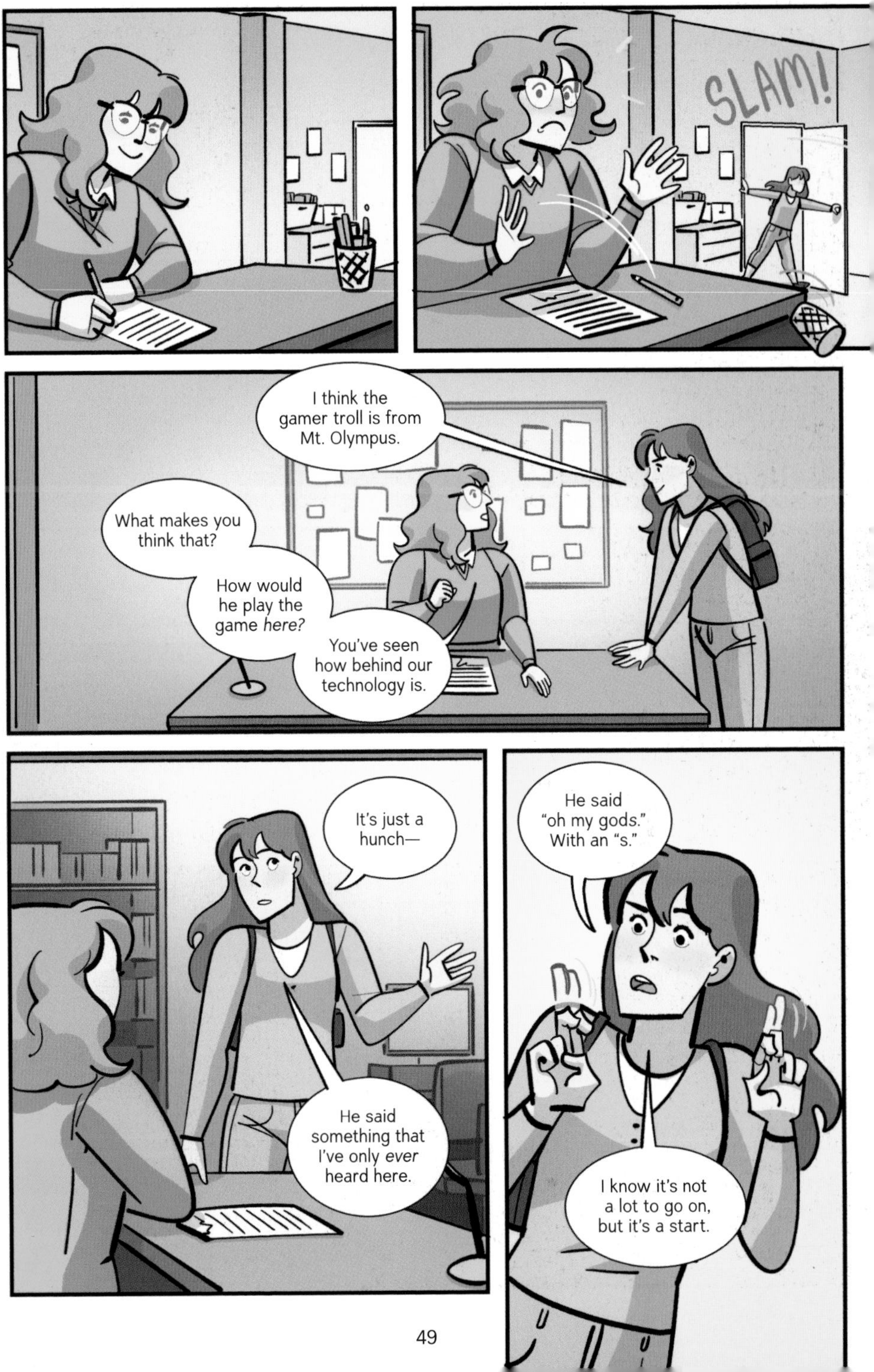
SLAM!
I think the gamer troll is from Mt. Olympus.
What makes you think that?
How would he play the game *here?*
You've seen how behind our technology is.
It's just a hunch—
He said something that I've only *ever* heard here.
He said "oh my gods." With an "s."
I know it's not a lot to go on, but it's a start.

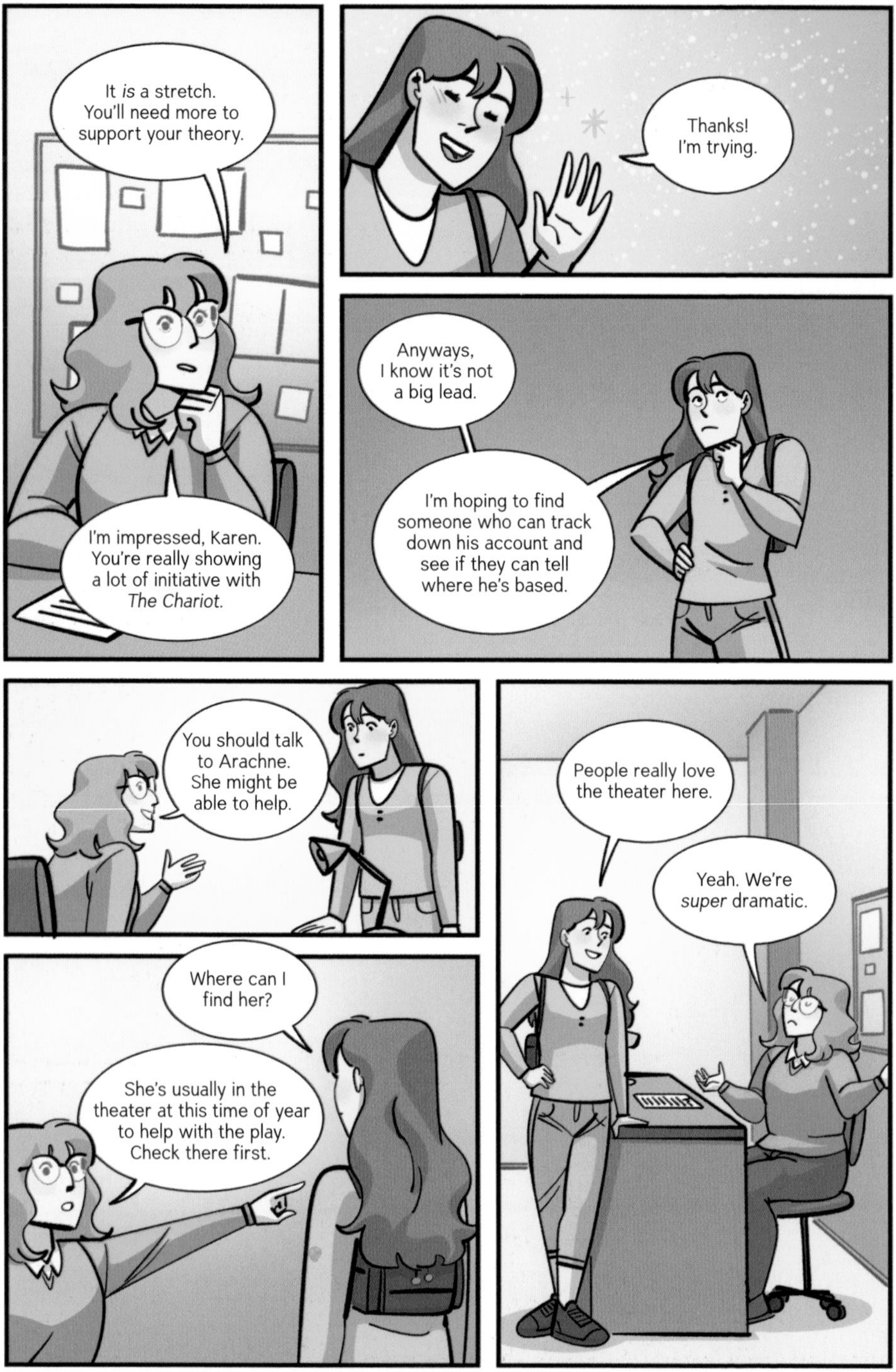
It *is* a stretch.
You'll need more to support your theory.
I'm impressed, Karen. You're really showing a lot of initiative with *The Chariot*.
Thanks! I'm trying.
Anyways, I know it's not a big lead.
I'm hoping to find someone who can track down his account and see if they can tell where he's based.
You should talk to Arachne. She might be able to help.
Where can I find her?
She's usually in the theater at this time of year to help with the play. Check there first.
People really love the theater here.
Yeah. We're *super* dramatic.

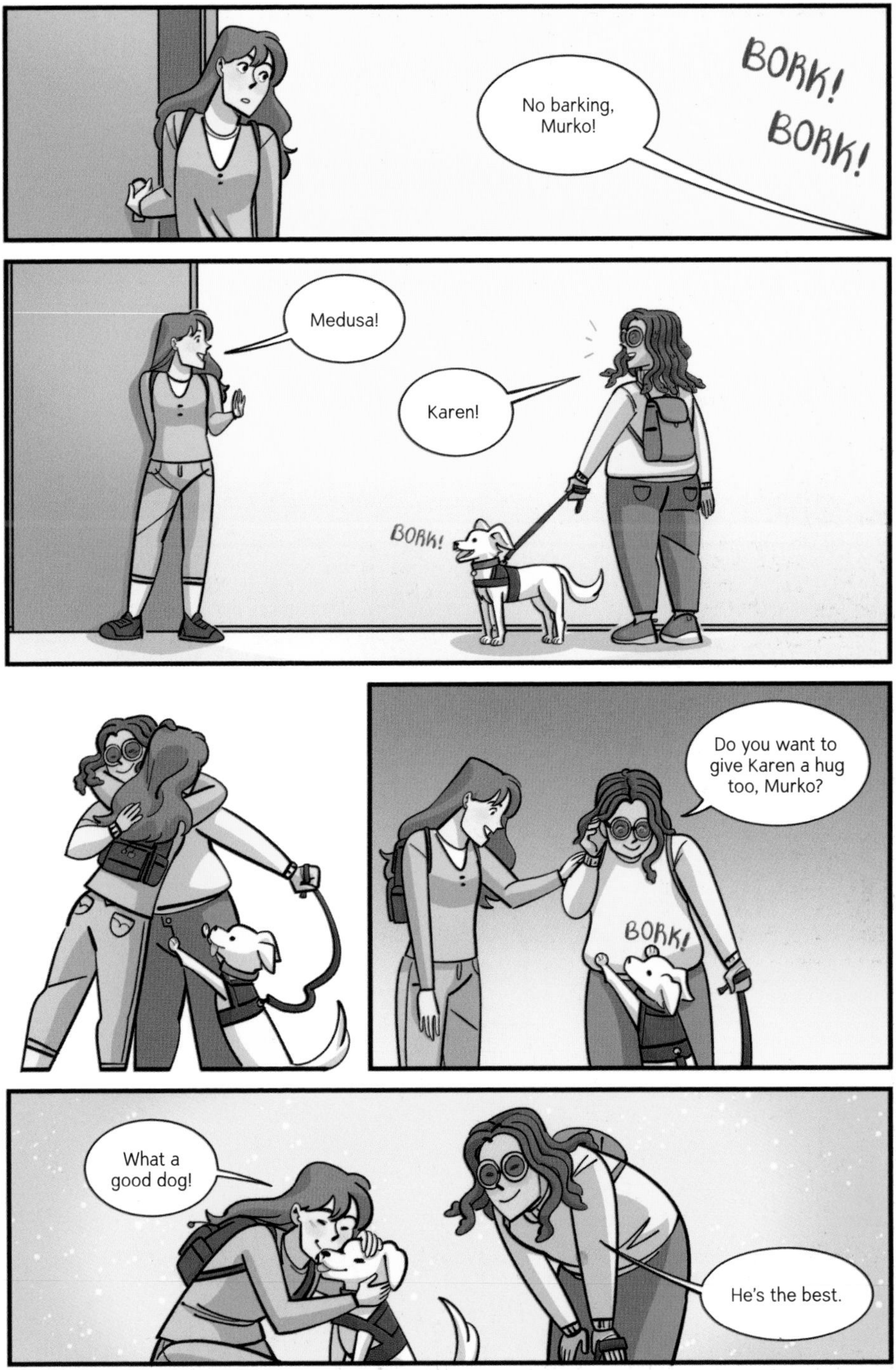
BORK! BORK!
No barking, Murko!
Medusa!
Karen!
BORK!
BORK!
Do you want to give Karen a hug too, Murko?
What a good dog!
He's the best.

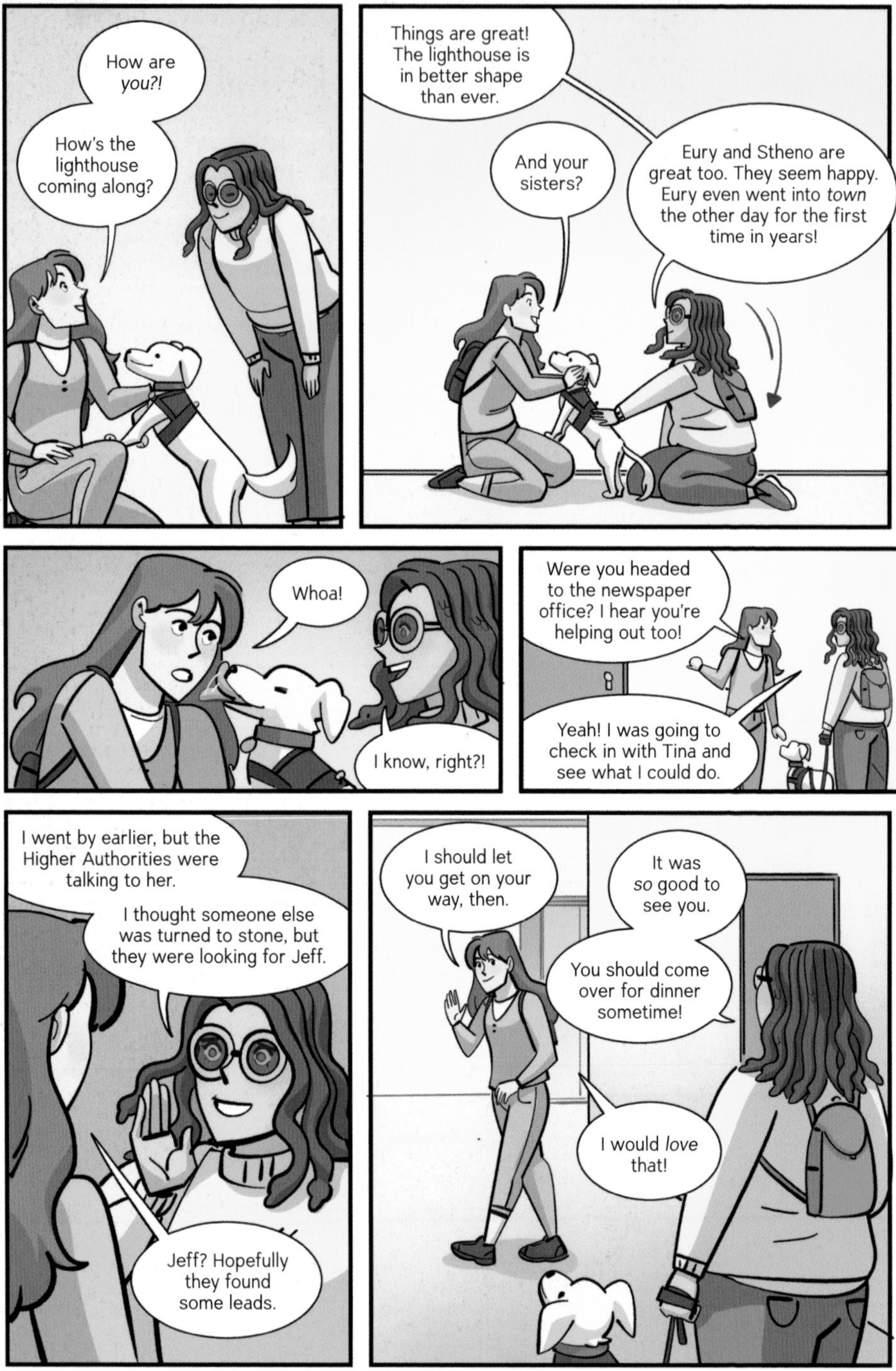
How are *you?!*
How's the lighthouse coming along?
Things are great! The lighthouse is in better shape than ever.
And your sisters?
Eury and Stheno are great too. They seem happy. Eury even went into *town* the other day for the first time in years!
Whoa!
I know, right?!
Were you headed to the newspaper office? I hear you're helping out too!
Yeah! I was going to check in with Tina and see what I could do.
I went by earlier, but the Higher Authorities were talking to her.
I thought someone else was turned to stone, but they were looking for Jeff.
Jeff? Hopefully they found some leads.
I should let you get on your way, then.
It was *so* good to see you.
You should come over for dinner sometime!
I would *love* that!

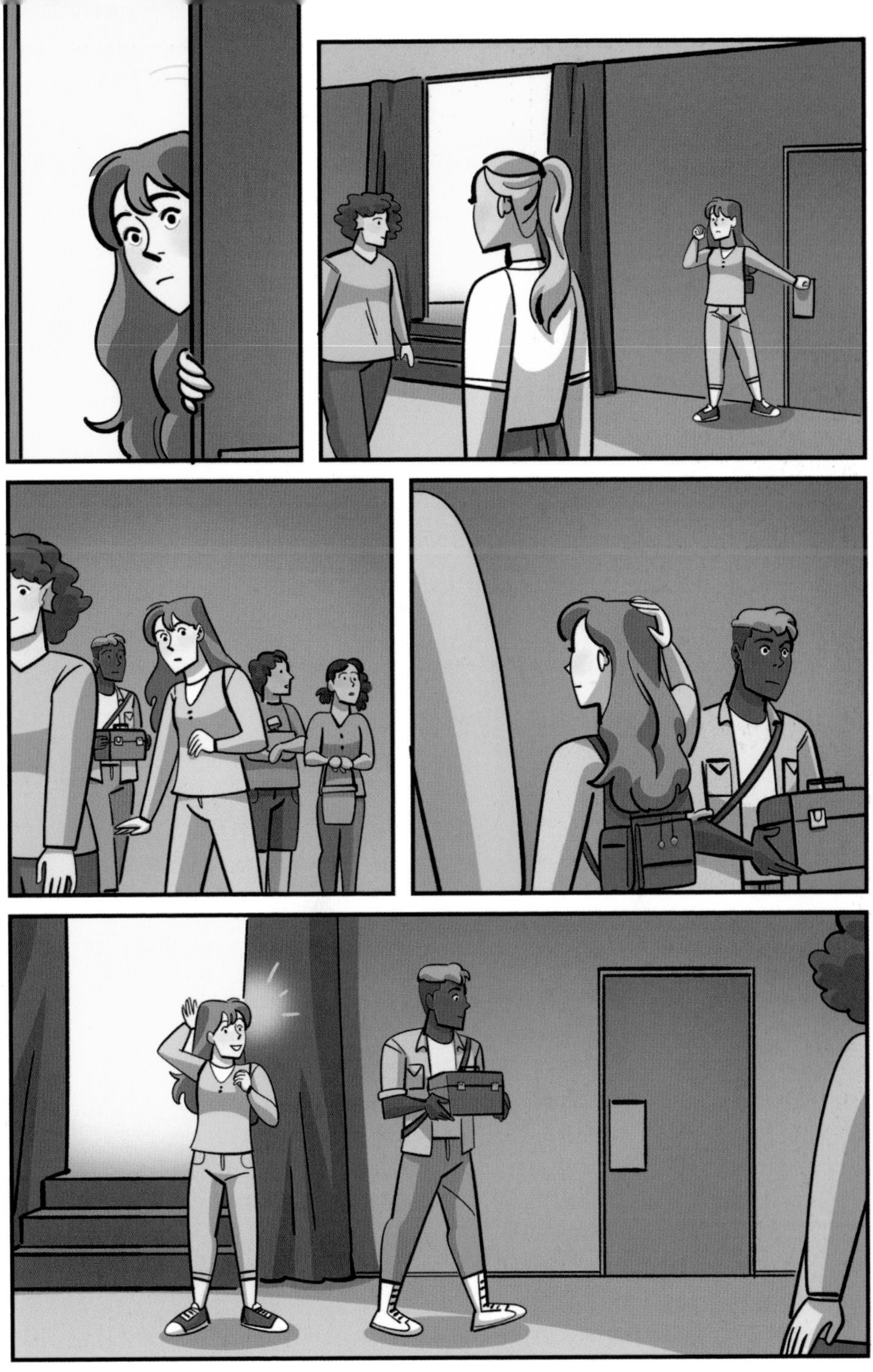

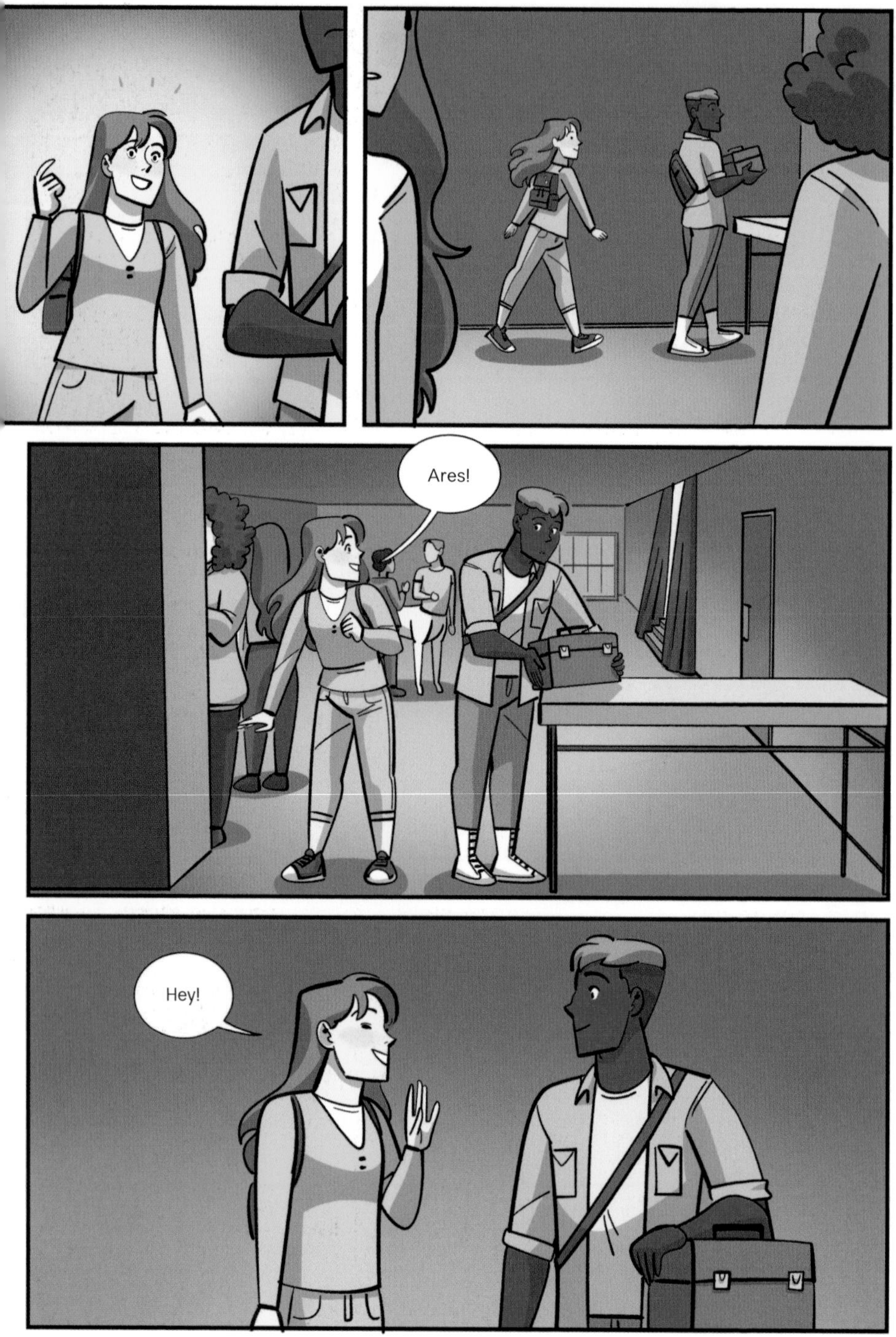
Ares!
Hey!

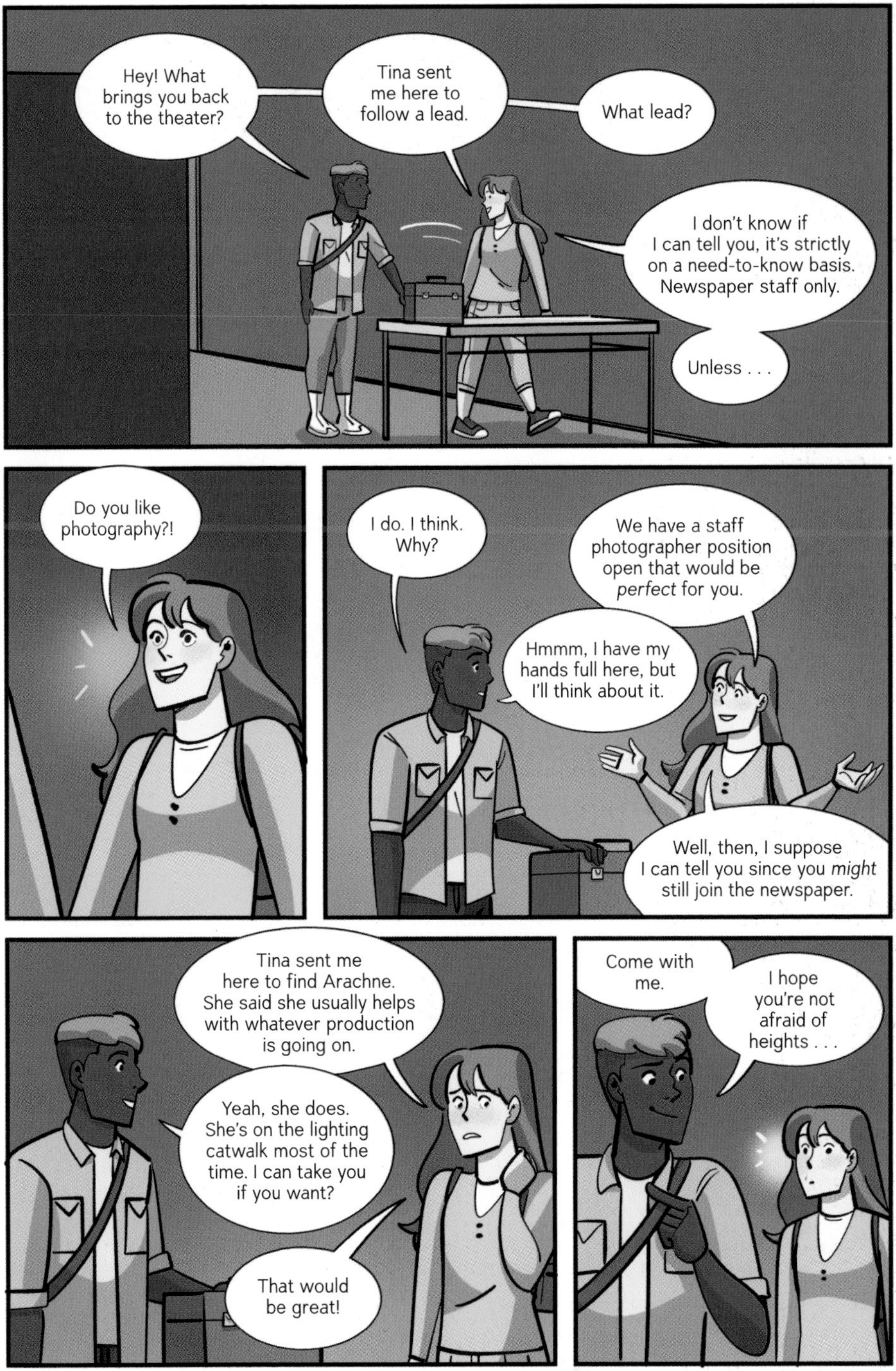
Hey! What brings you back to the theater?
Tina sent me here to follow a lead.
What lead?
I don't know if I can tell you, it's strictly on a need-to-know basis. Newspaper staff only.
Unless . . .
Do you like photography?!
I do. I think. Why?
We have a staff photographer position open that would be *perfect* for you.
Hmmm, I have my hands full here, but I'll think about it.
Well, then, I suppose I can tell you since you *might* still join the newspaper.
Tina sent me here to find Arachne. She said she usually helps with whatever production is going on.
Yeah, she does. She's on the lighting catwalk most of the time. I can take you if you want?
That would be great!
Come with me.
I hope you're not afraid of heights . . .

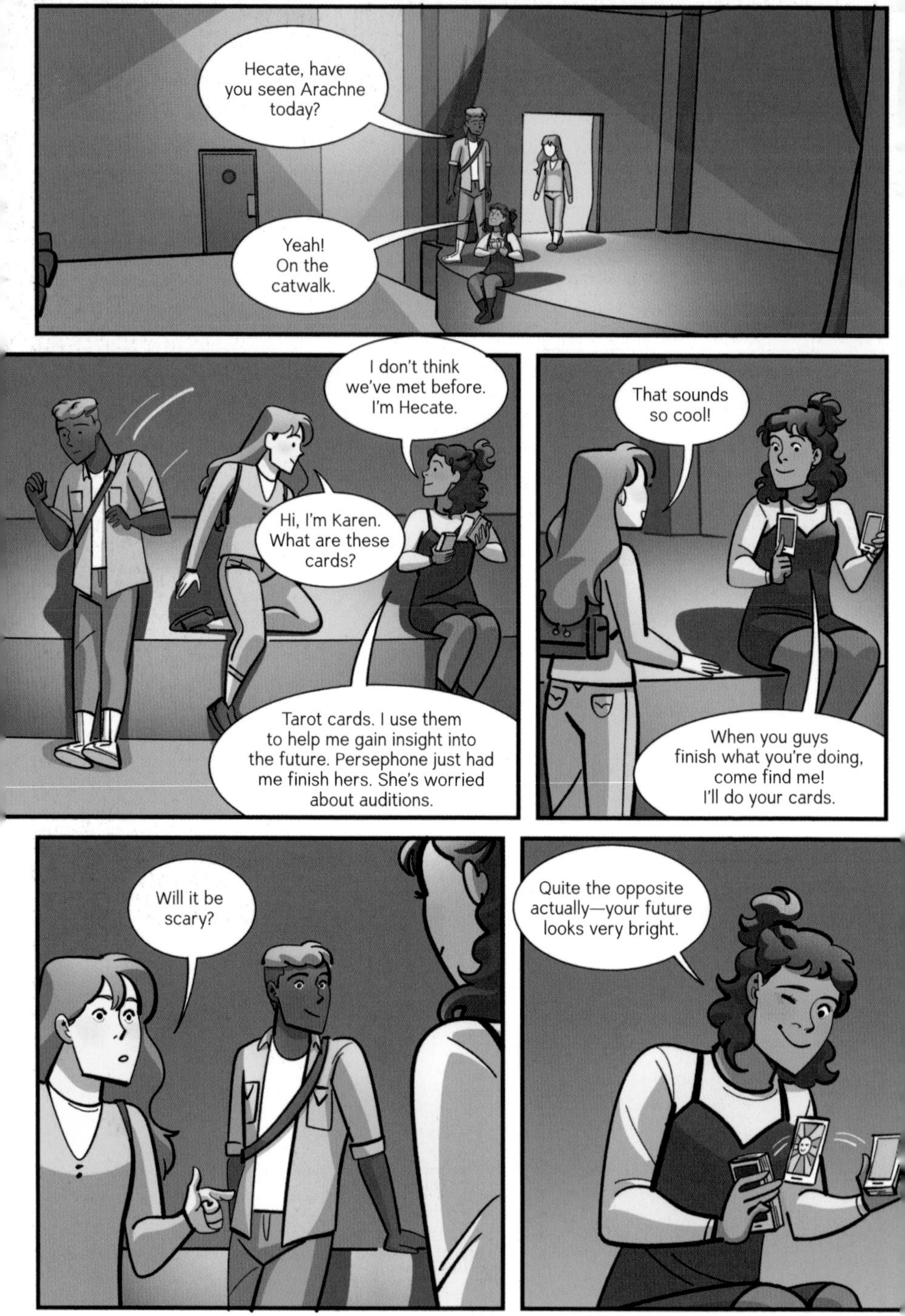
Hecate, have you seen Arachne today?
Yeah! On the catwalk.
I don't think we've met before. I'm Hecate.
Hi, I'm Karen. What are these cards?
Tarot cards. I use them to help me gain insight into the future. Persephone just had me finish hers. She's worried about auditions.
That sounds so cool!
When you guys finish what you're doing, come find me! I'll do your cards.
Will it be scary?
Quite the opposite actually—your future looks very bright.

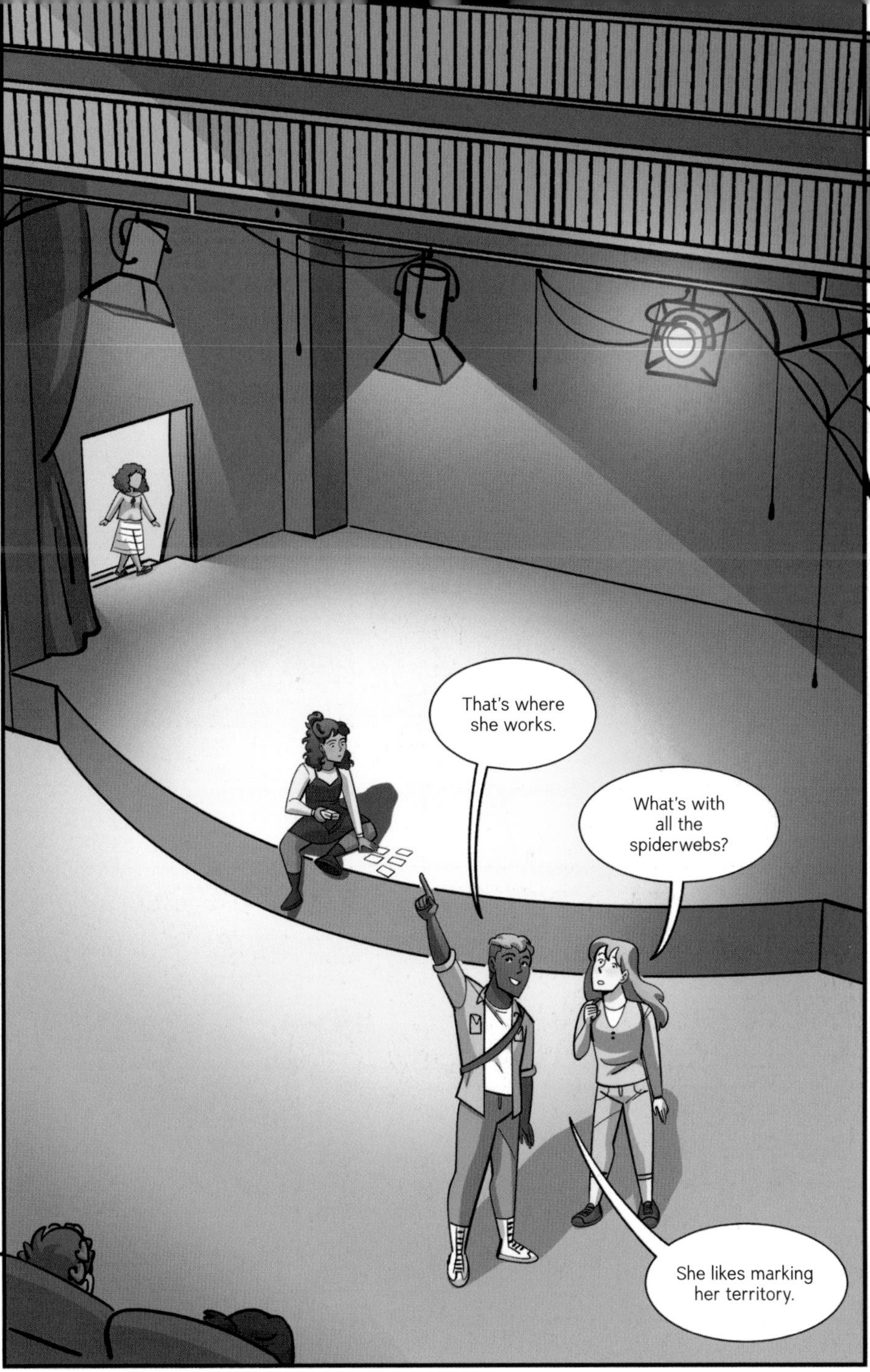
That's where she works.
What's with all the spiderwebs?
She likes marking her territory.

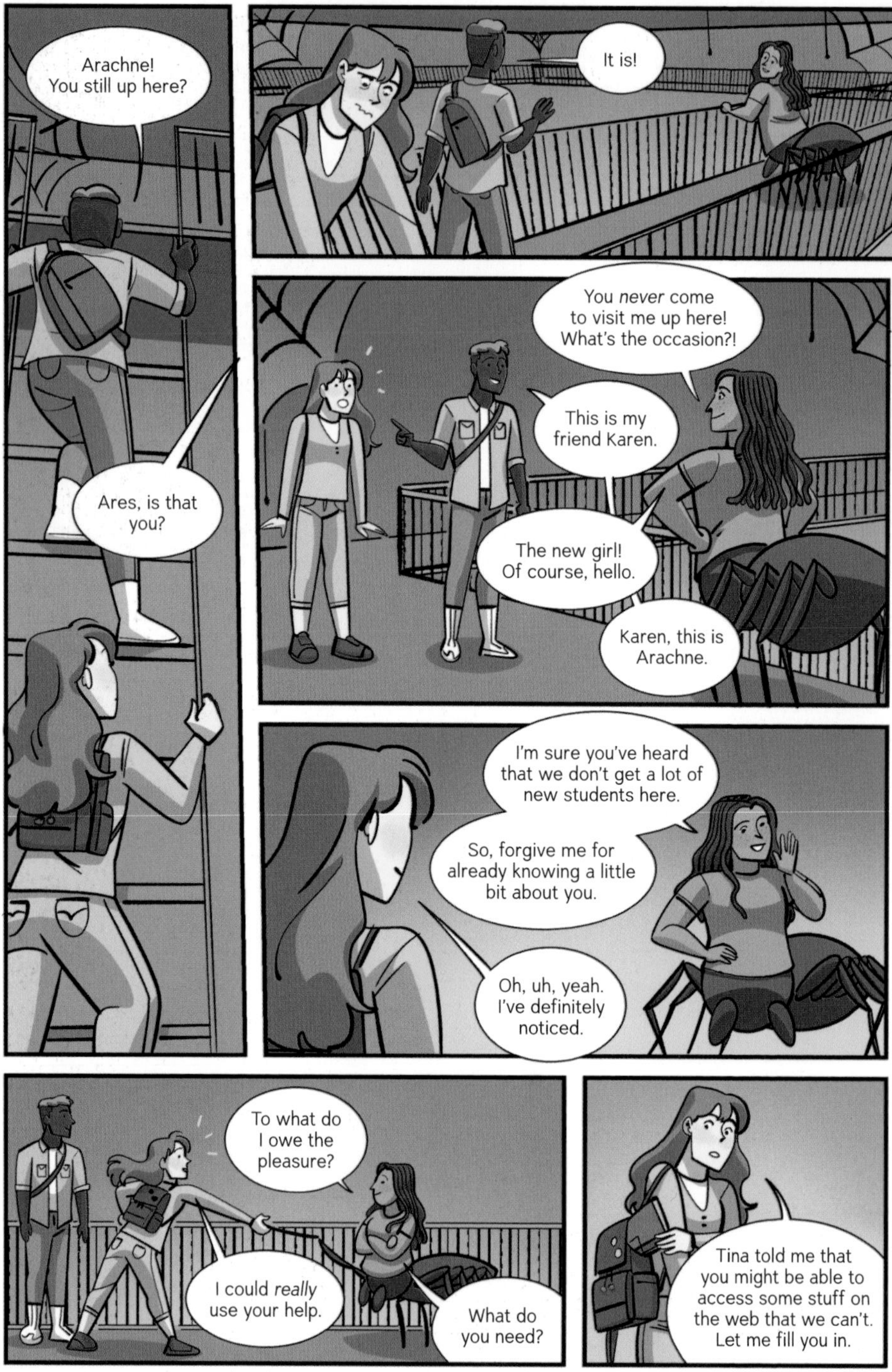

Arachne! You still up here?
It is!
Ares, is that you?
You *never* come to visit me up here! What's the occasion?!
This is my friend Karen.
The new girl! Of course, hello.
Karen, this is Arachne.
I'm sure you've heard that we don't get a lot of new students here.
So, forgive me for already knowing a little bit about you.
Oh, uh, yeah. I've definitely noticed.
To what do I owe the pleasure?
I could *really* use your help.
What do you need?
Tina told me that you might be able to access some stuff on the web that we can't. Let me fill you in.

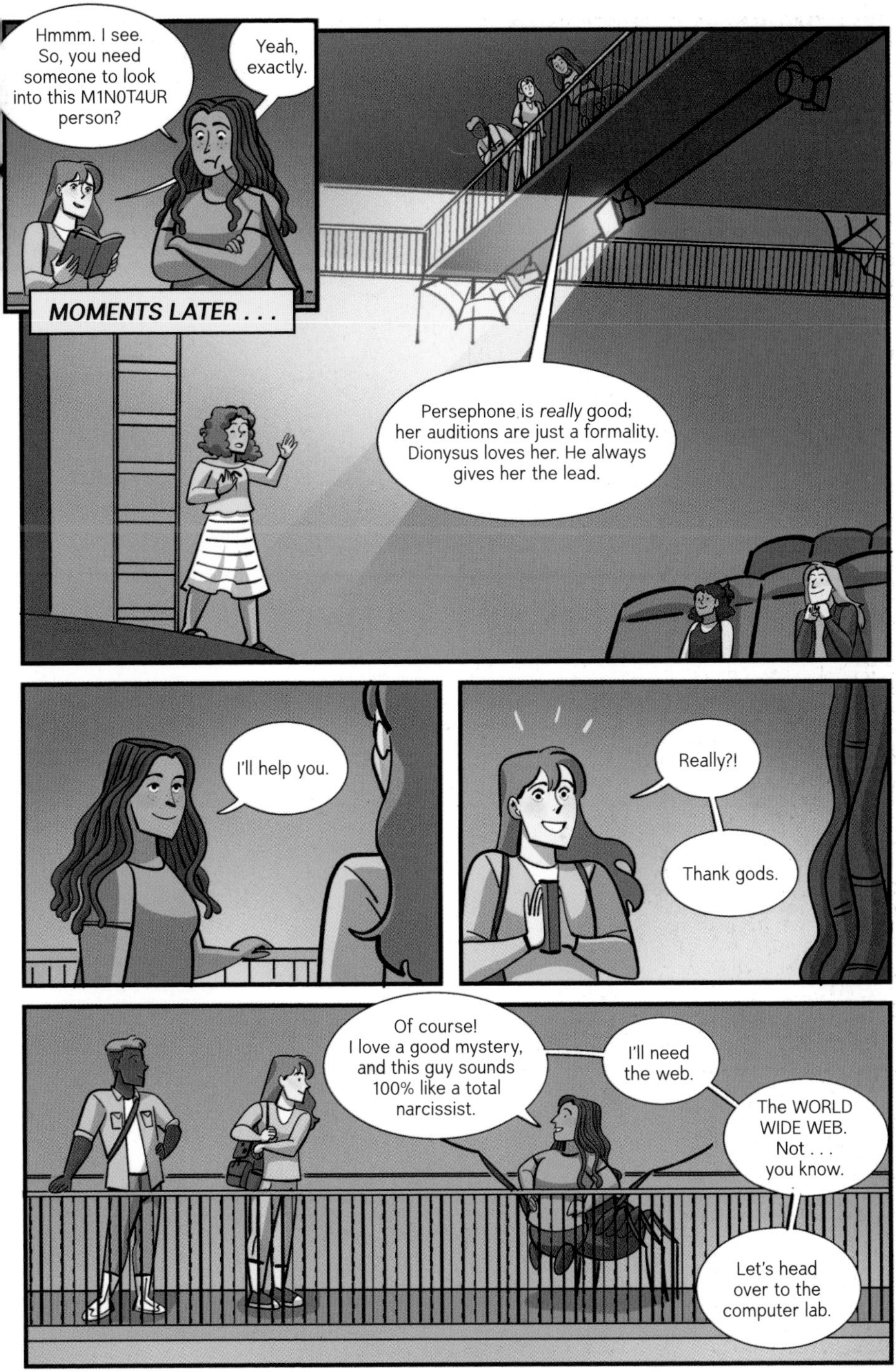
Hmmm. I see. So, you need someone to look into this M1N0T4UR person?
Yeah, exactly.
MOMENTS LATER . . .
Persephone is *really* good; her auditions are just a formality. Dionysus loves her. He always gives her the lead.
I'll help you.
Really?!
Thank gods.
Of course! I love a good mystery, and this guy sounds 100% like a total narcissist.
I'll need the web.
The WORLD WIDE WEB. Not . . . you know.
Let's head over to the computer lab.

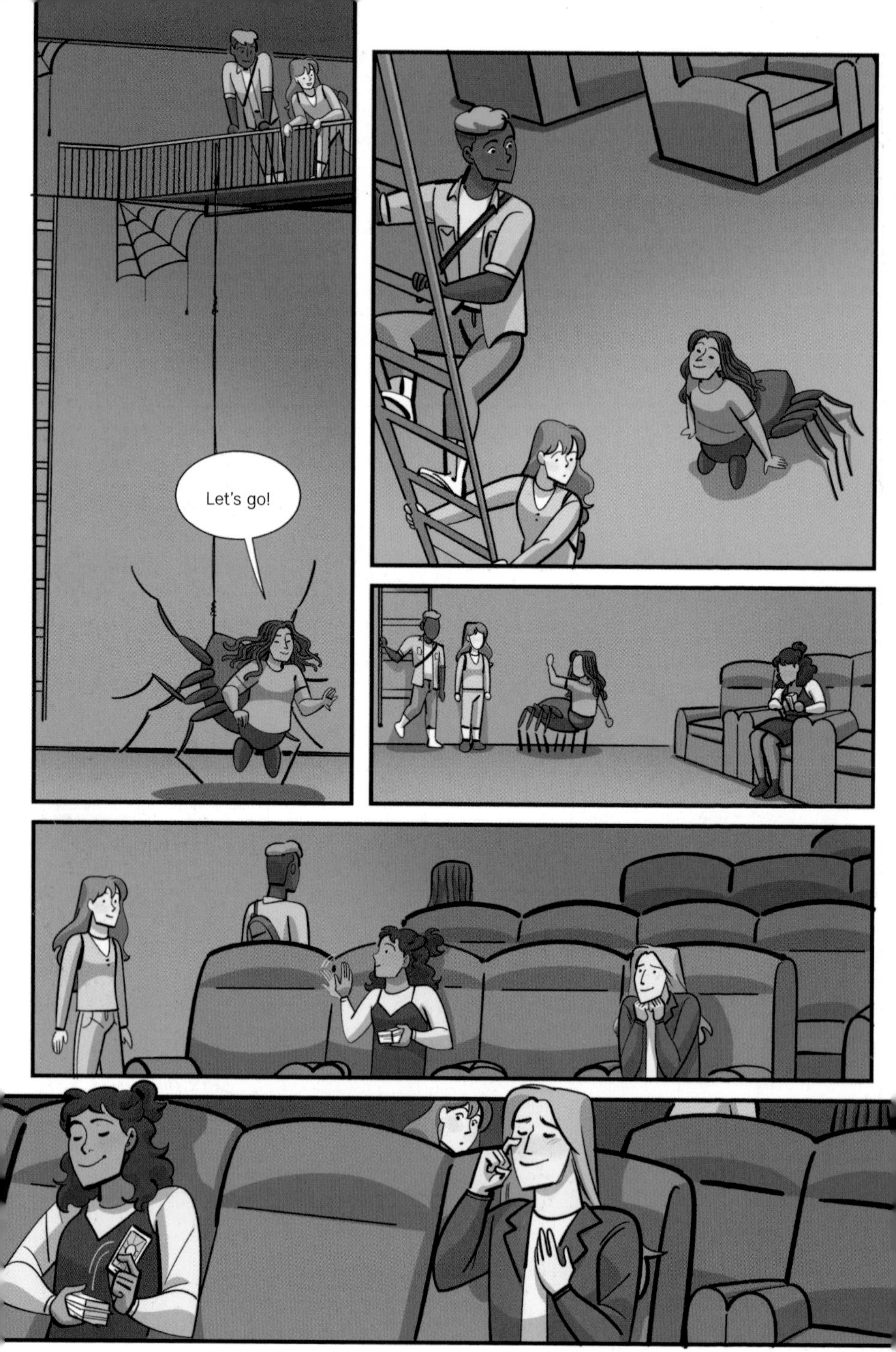
Let's go!

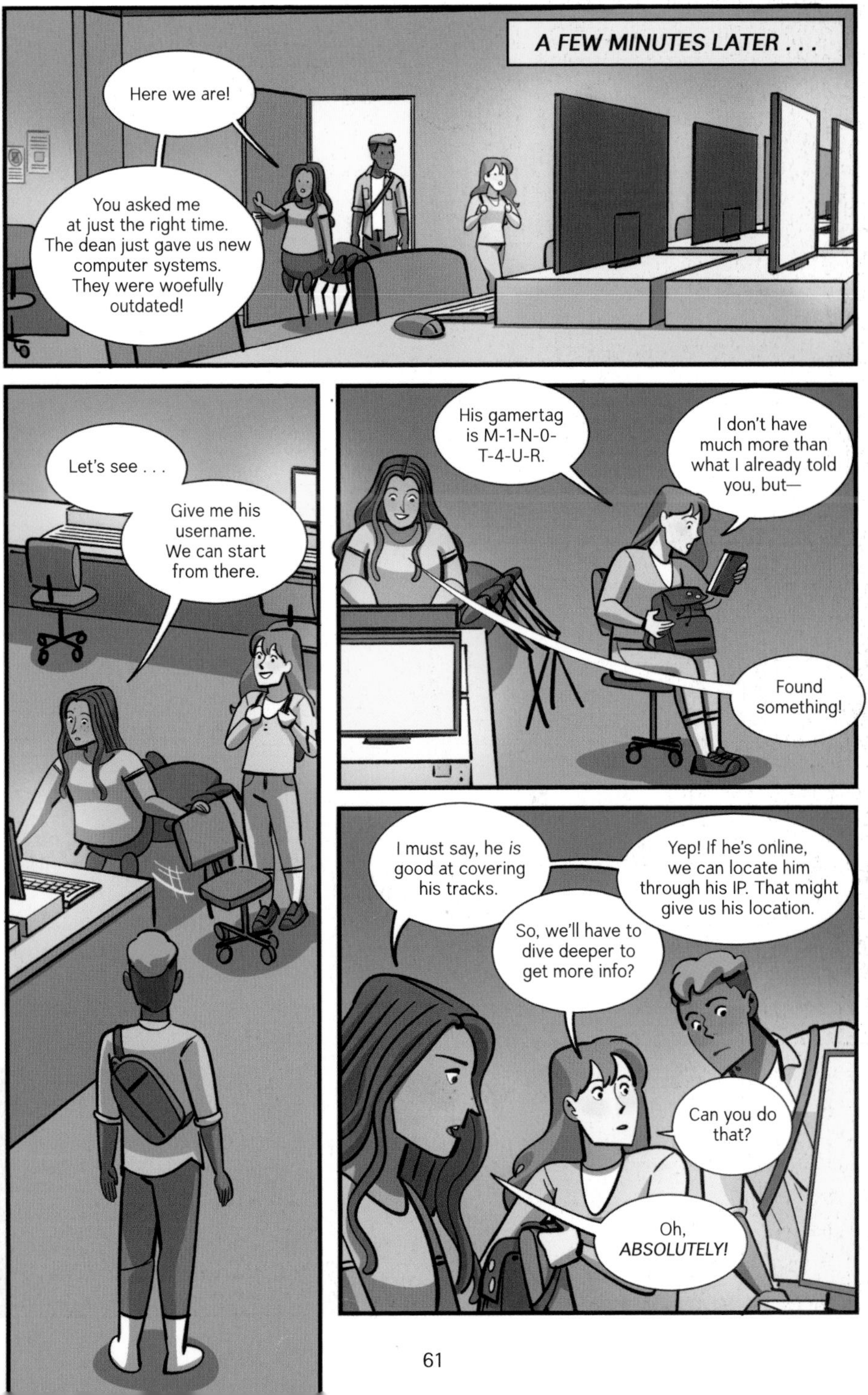
A FEW MINUTES LATER . . .
Here we are!
You asked me at just the right time. The dean just gave us new computer systems. They were woefully outdated!
Let's see . . .
Give me his username. We can start from there.
His gamertag is M-1-N-0-T-4-U-R.
I don't have much more than what I already told you, but—
Found something!
I must say, he *is* good at covering his tracks.
Yep! If he's online, we can locate him through his IP. That might give us his location.
So, we'll have to dive deeper to get more info?
Can you do that?
Oh, *ABSOLUTELY!*

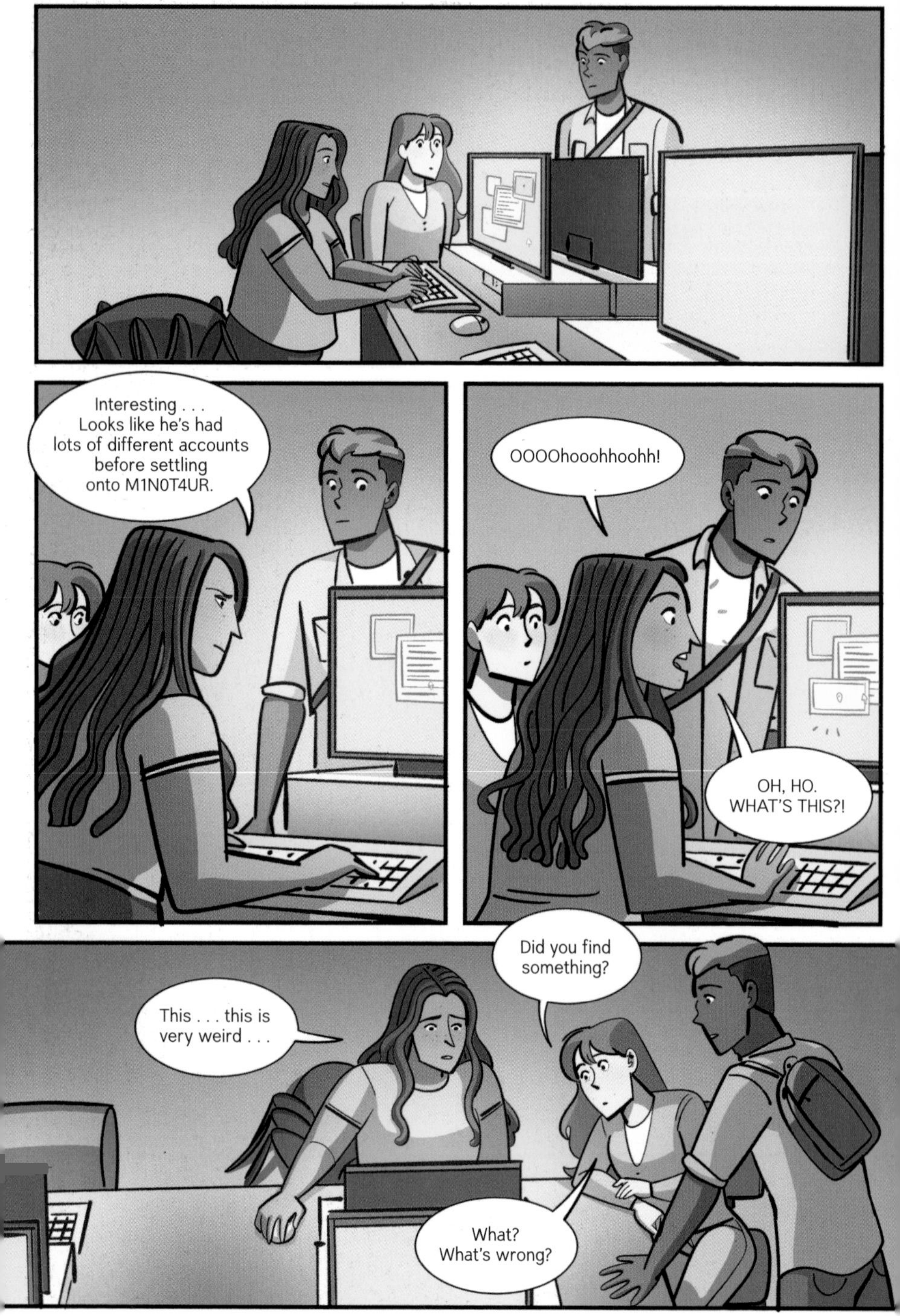
Interesting . . . Looks like he's had lots of different accounts before settling onto M1N0T4UR.
OOOOhooohhoohh!
OH, HO. WHAT'S THIS?!
This . . . this is very weird . . .
Did you find something?
What? What's wrong?

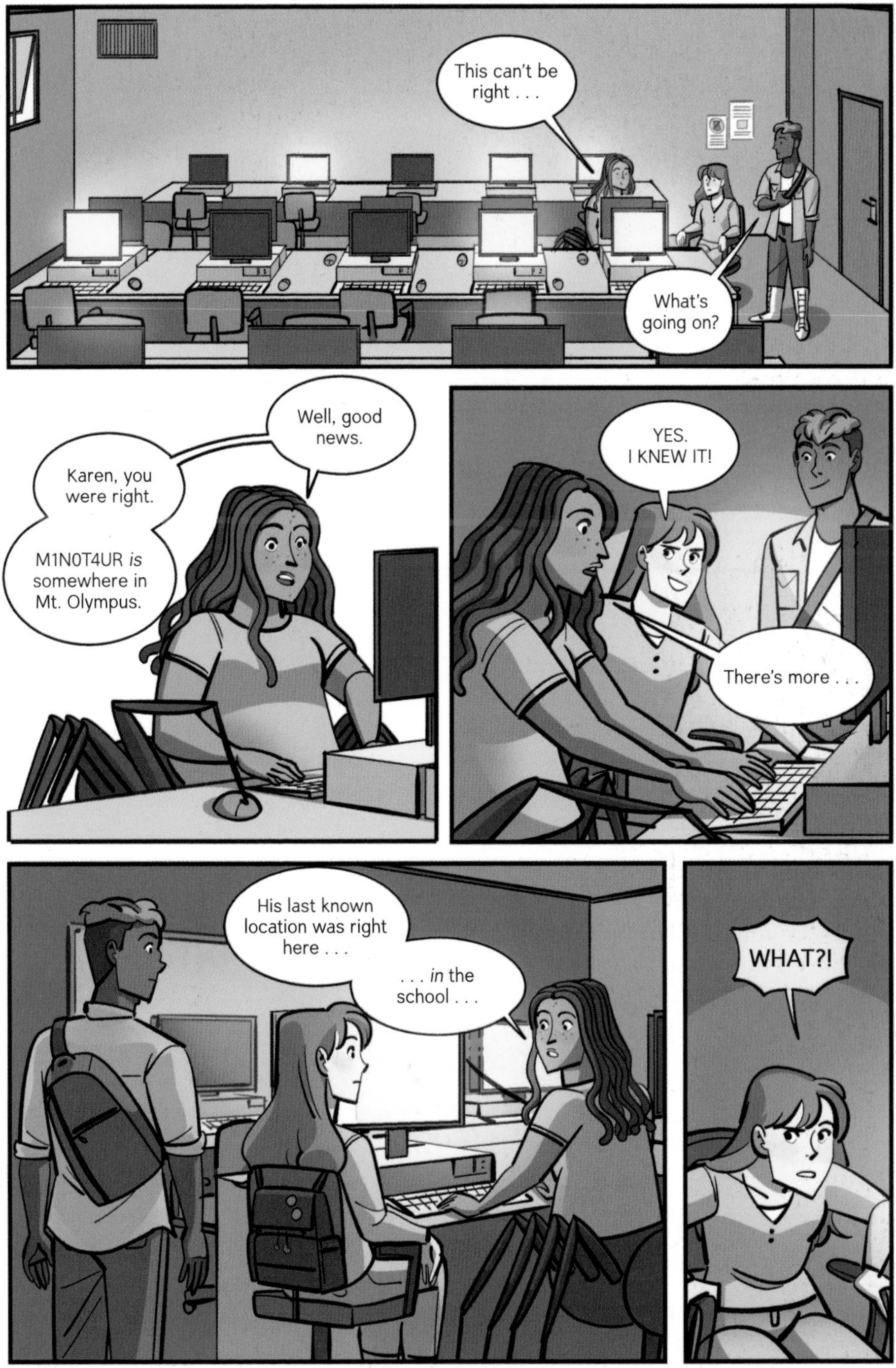
This can't be right . . .
What's going on?
Well, good news.
Karen, you were right.
M1N0T4UR *is* somewhere in Mt. Olympus.
YES. I KNEW IT!
There's more . . .
His last known location was right here . . .
. . . *in* the school . . .
WHAT?!

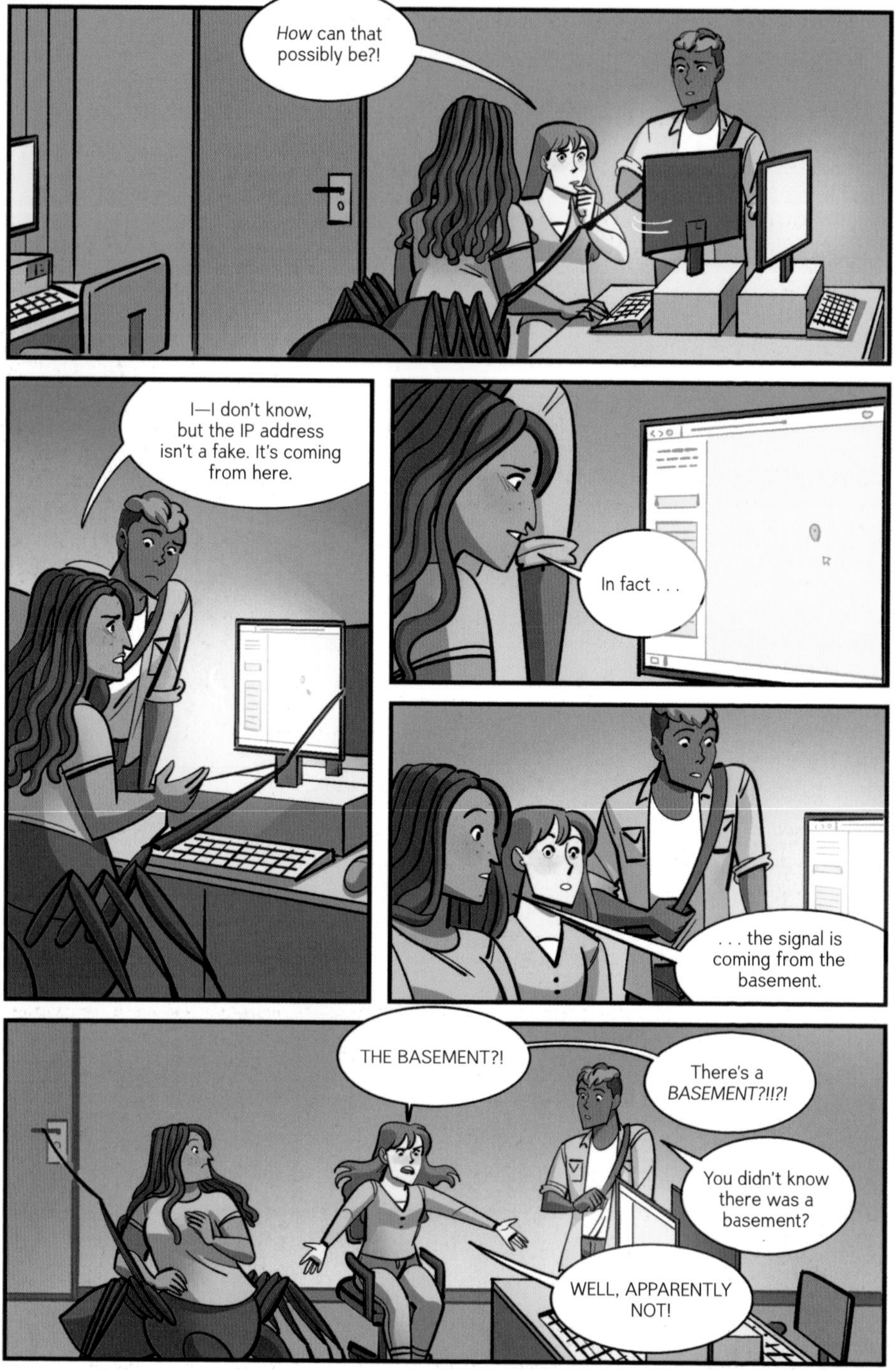

How can that possibly be?!
I—I don't know, but the IP address isn't a fake. It's coming from here.
In fact . . .
. . . the signal is coming from the basement.
THE BASEMENT?!
There's a *BASEMENT?!!?!*
You didn't know there was a basement?
WELL, APPARENTLY NOT!

Well, to be fair, no one talks about it much these days.

There *used* to be this survivalist course in the basement.

It was meant to train students on track for the Hero Academy.

Hero Academy?

As they modernized the school, and the outside world changed, there wasn't really a need for it anymore.

So the course was shut down, and people stopped going down to the basement except to put stuff into storage.

But a *course*? In the *basement?!*

The new school was built over top of it, but it's still there.

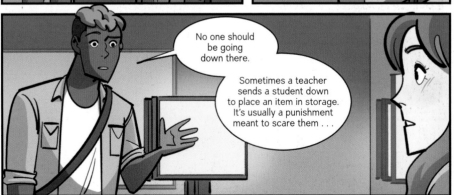

No one should be going down there.

Sometimes a teacher sends a student down to place an item in storage. It's usually a punishment meant to scare them . . .

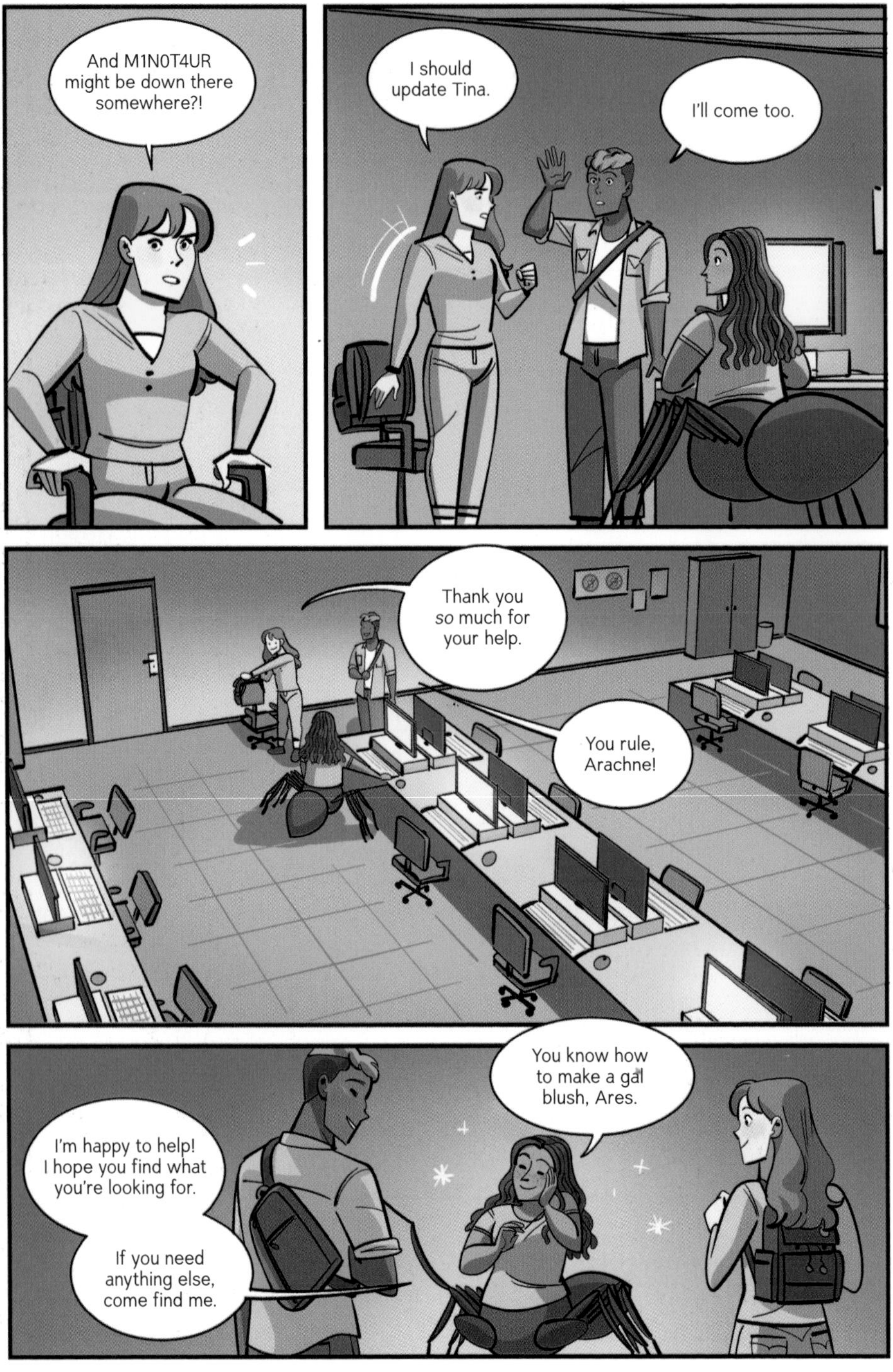
And M1N0T4UR might be down there somewhere?!
I should update Tina.
I'll come too.
Thank you *so* much for your help.
You rule, Arachne!
I'm happy to help! I hope you find what you're looking for.
If you need anything else, come find me.
You know how to make a gal blush, Ares.

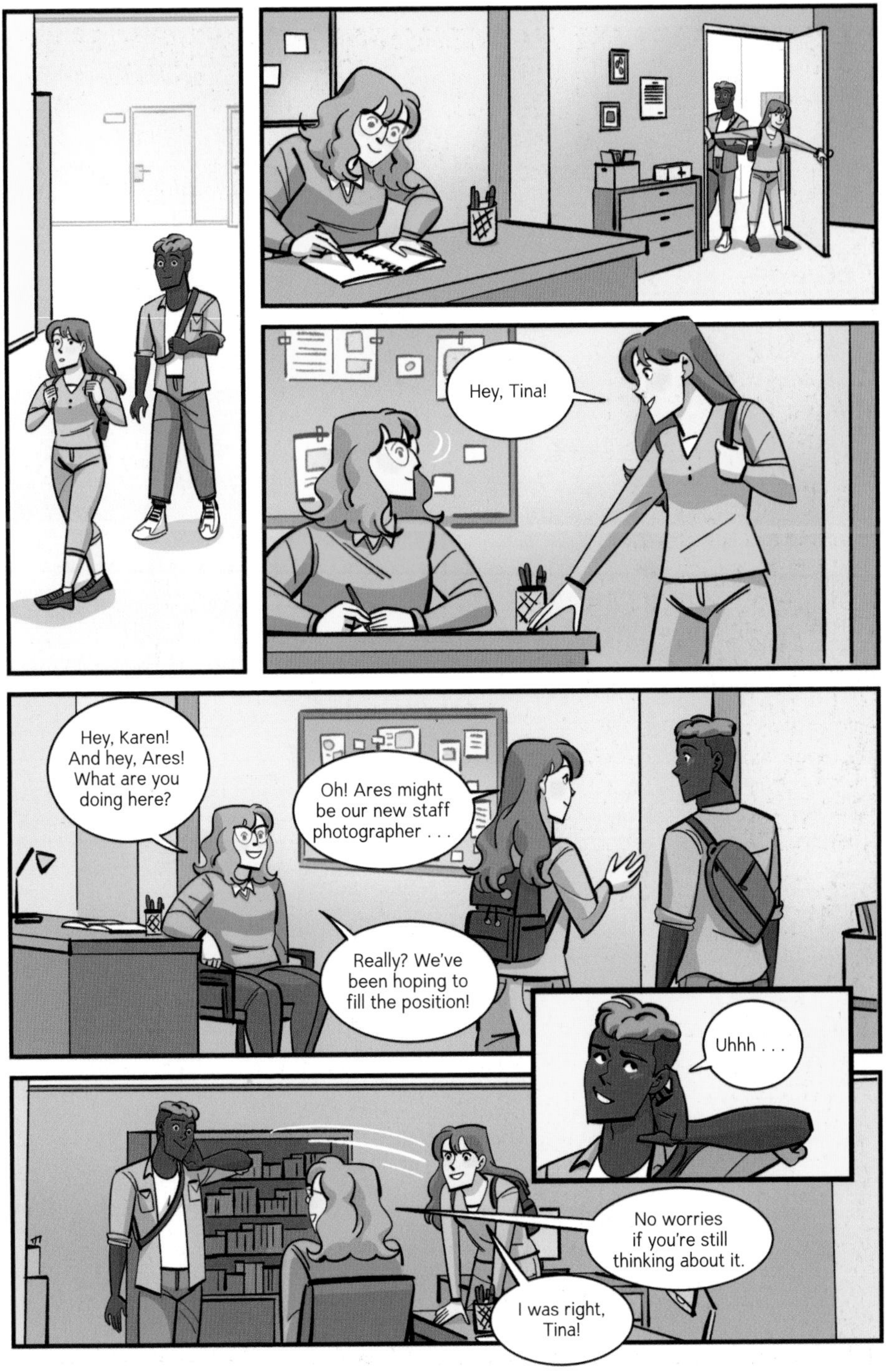
Hey, Tina!
Hey, Karen! And hey, Ares! What are you doing here?
Oh! Ares might be our new staff photographer . . .
Really? We've been hoping to fill the position!
Uhhh . . .
No worries if you're still thinking about it.
I was right, Tina!

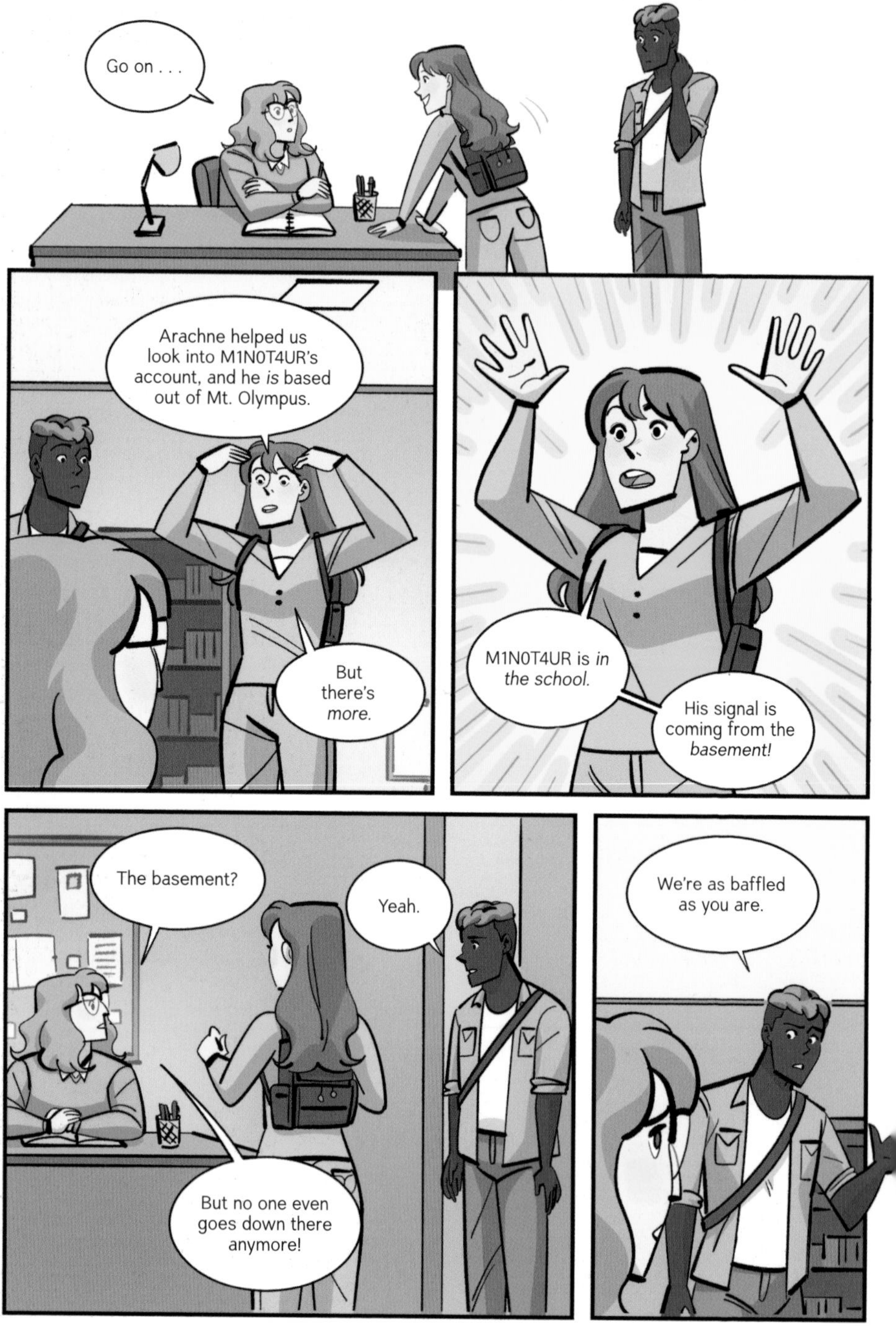
Go on . . .
Arachne helped us look into M1N0T4UR's account, and he *is* based out of Mt. Olympus.
But there's *more.*
M1N0T4UR is *in the school.*
His signal is coming from the *basement!*
The basement?
Yeah.
But no one even goes down there anymore!
We're as baffled as you are.

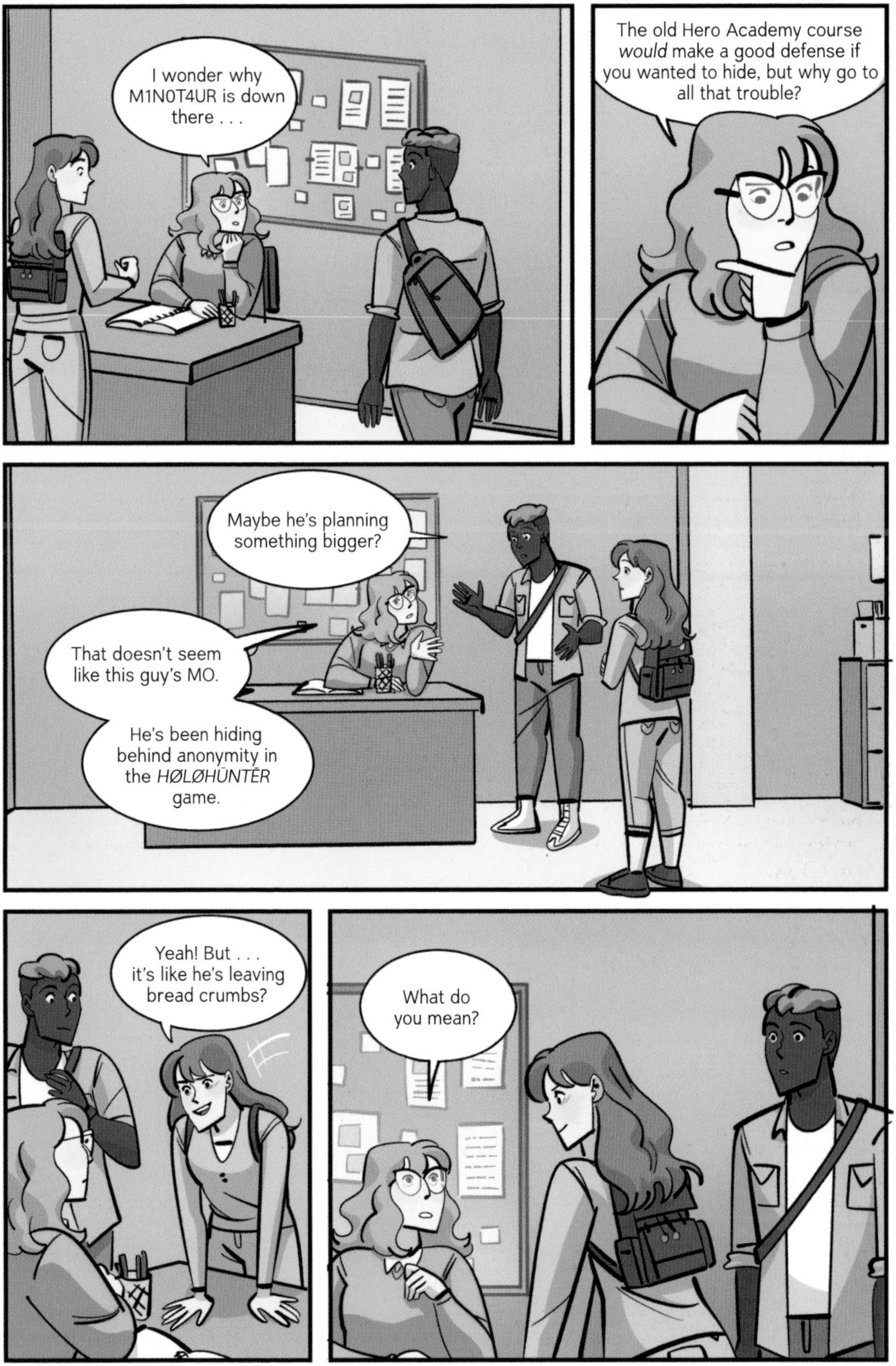
I wonder why M1N0T4UR is down there . . .
The old Hero Academy course *would* make a good defense if you wanted to hide, but why go to all that trouble?
Maybe he's planning something bigger?
That doesn't seem like this guy's MO.
He's been hiding behind anonymity in the *HØLØHŪNTĒR* game.
Yeah! But . . . it's like he's leaving bread crumbs?
What do you mean?

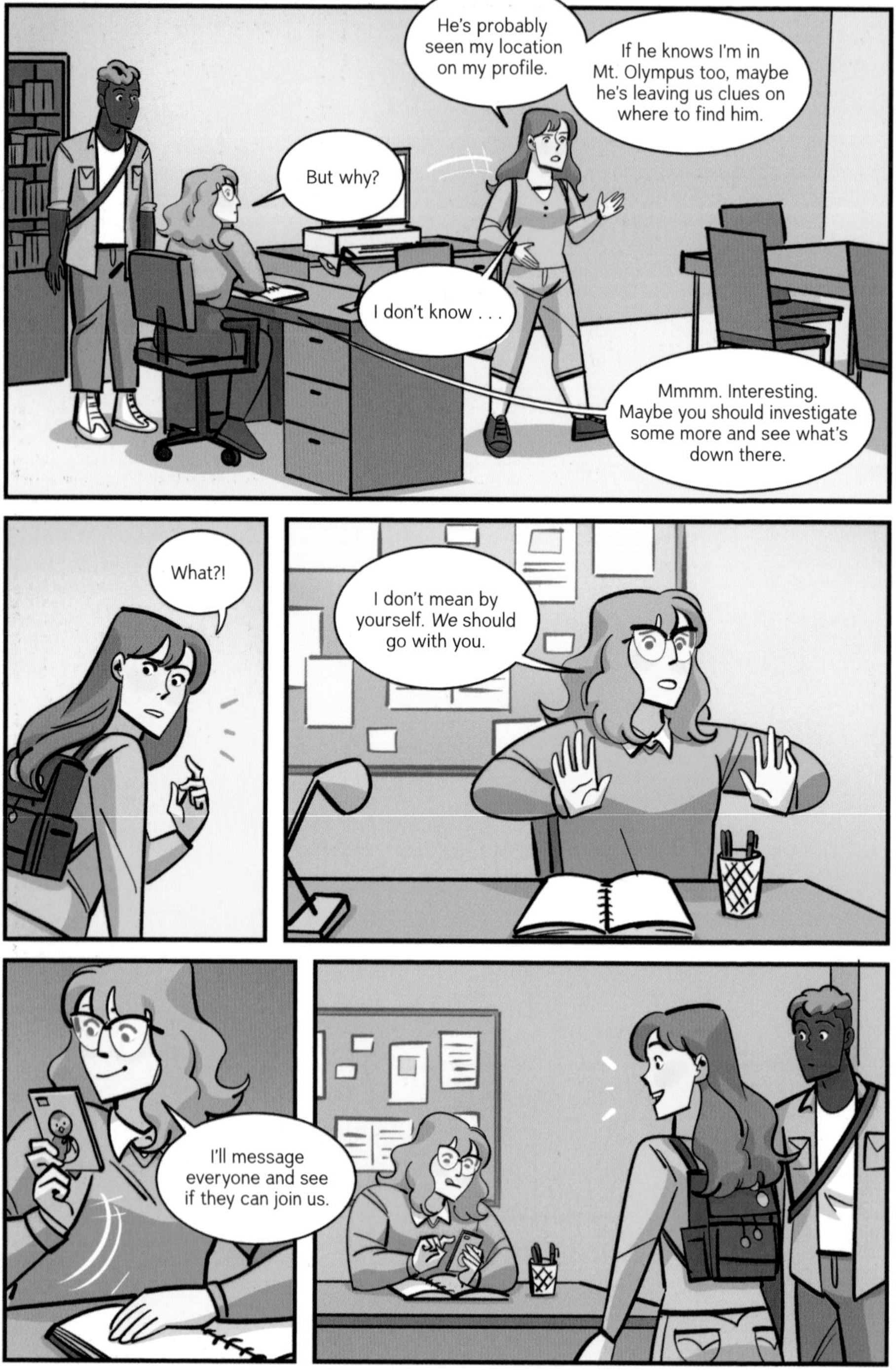
He's probably seen my location on my profile.
If he knows I'm in Mt. Olympus too, maybe he's leaving us clues on where to find him.
But why?
I don't know . . .
Mmmm. Interesting. Maybe you should investigate some more and see what's down there.
What?!
I don't mean by yourself. *We* should go with you.
I'll message everyone and see if they can join us.

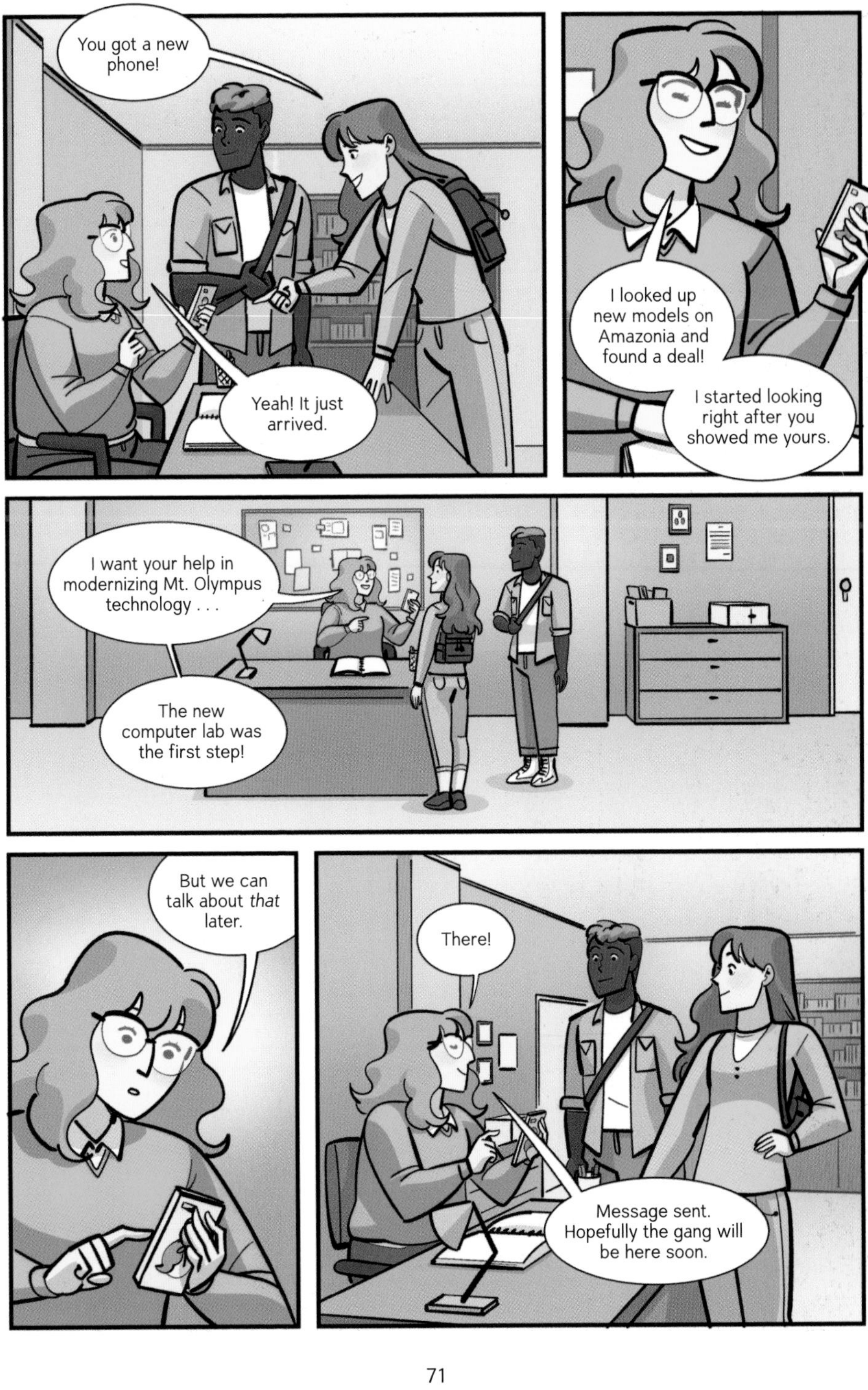
You got a new phone!
Yeah! It just arrived.
I looked up new models on Amazonia and found a deal!
I started looking right after you showed me yours.
I want your help in modernizing Mt. Olympus technology . . .
The new computer lab was the first step!
But we can talk about *that* later.
There!
Message sent. Hopefully the gang will be here soon.

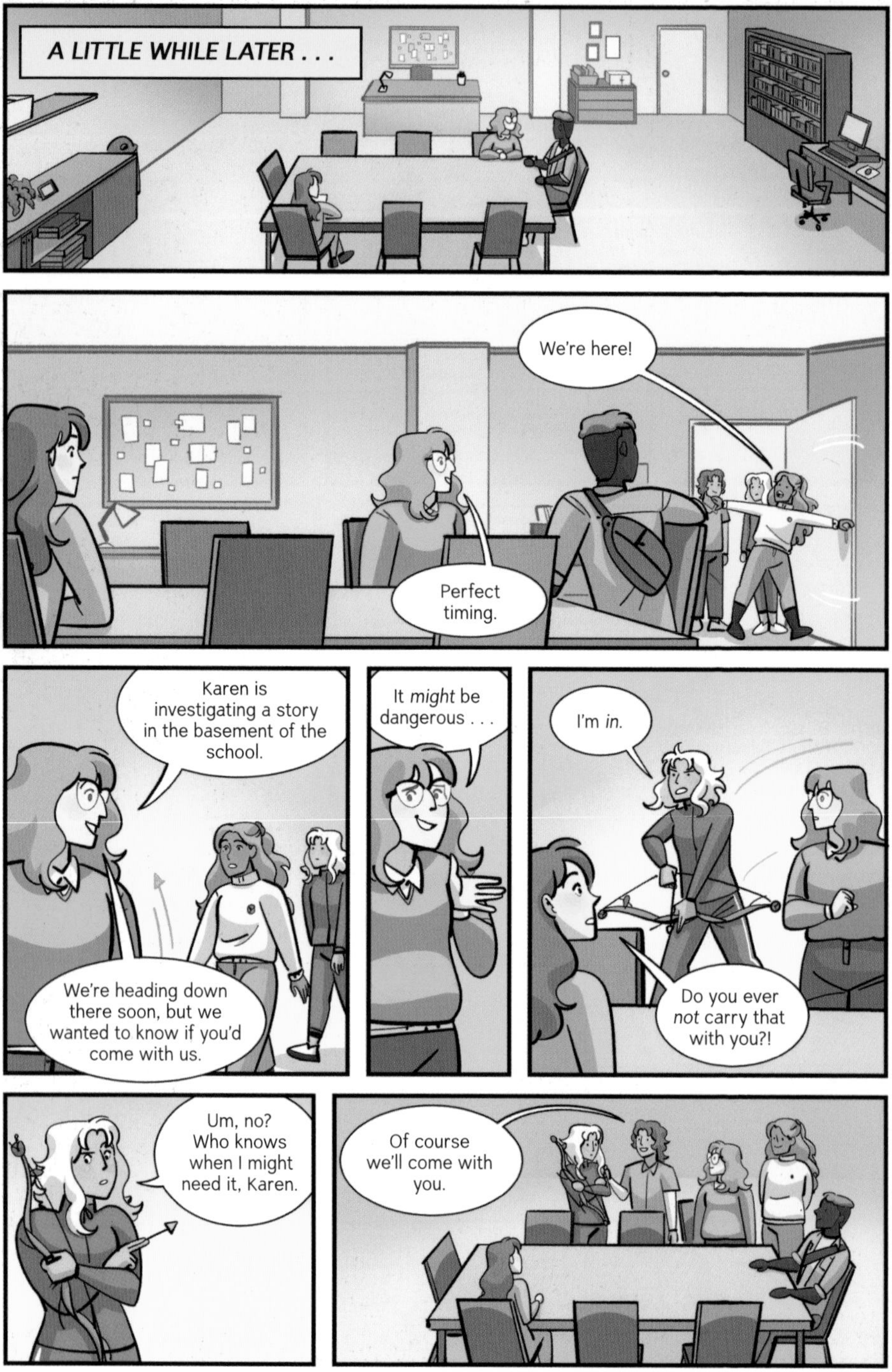
A LITTLE WHILE LATER . . .
We're here!
Perfect timing.
Karen is investigating a story in the basement of the school.
We're heading down there soon, but we wanted to know if you'd come with us.
It *might* be dangerous . . .
I'm *in*.
Do you ever *not* carry that with you?!
Um, no? Who knows when I might need it, Karen.
Of course we'll come with you.

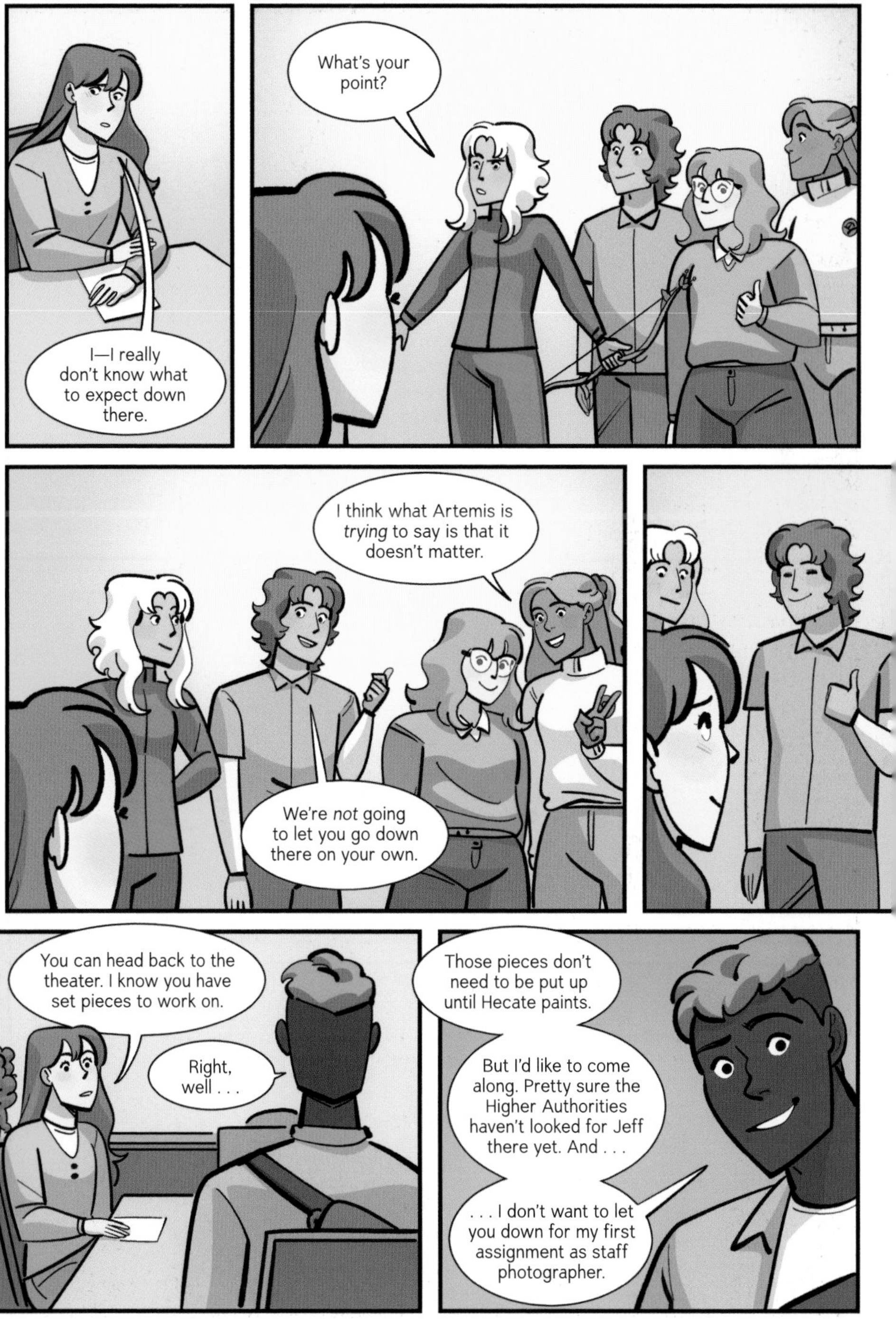
I—I really don't know what to expect down there.
What's your point?
I think what Artemis is *trying* to say is that it doesn't matter.
We're *not* going to let you go down there on your own.
You can head back to the theater. I know you have set pieces to work on.
Right, well . . .
Those pieces don't need to be put up until Hecate paints.
But I'd like to come along. Pretty sure the Higher Authorities haven't looked for Jeff there yet. And . . .
. . . I don't want to let you down for my first assignment as staff photographer.

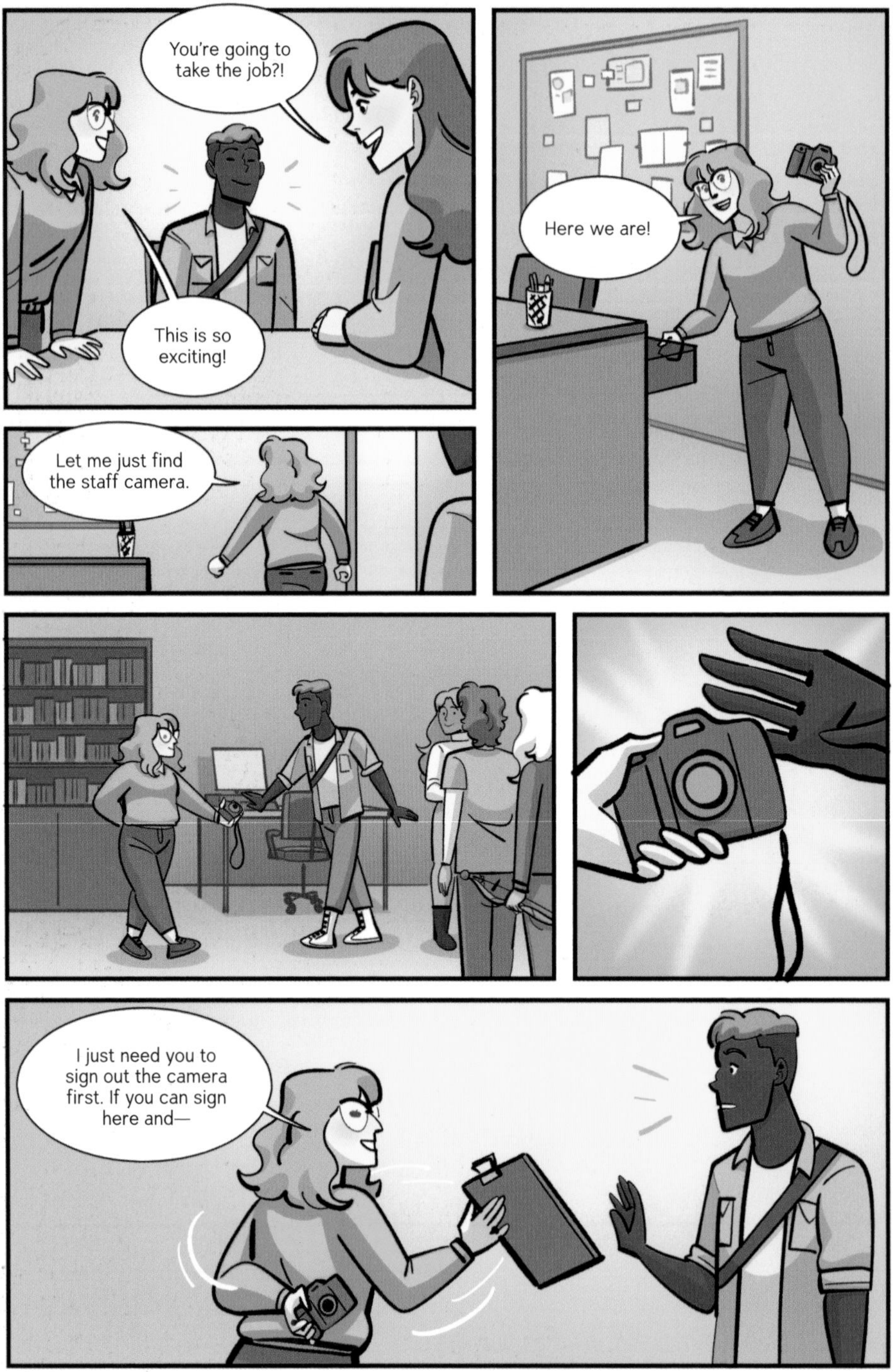
You're going to take the job?!
This is so exciting!
Let me just find the staff camera.
Here we are!
I just need you to sign out the camera first. If you can sign here and—

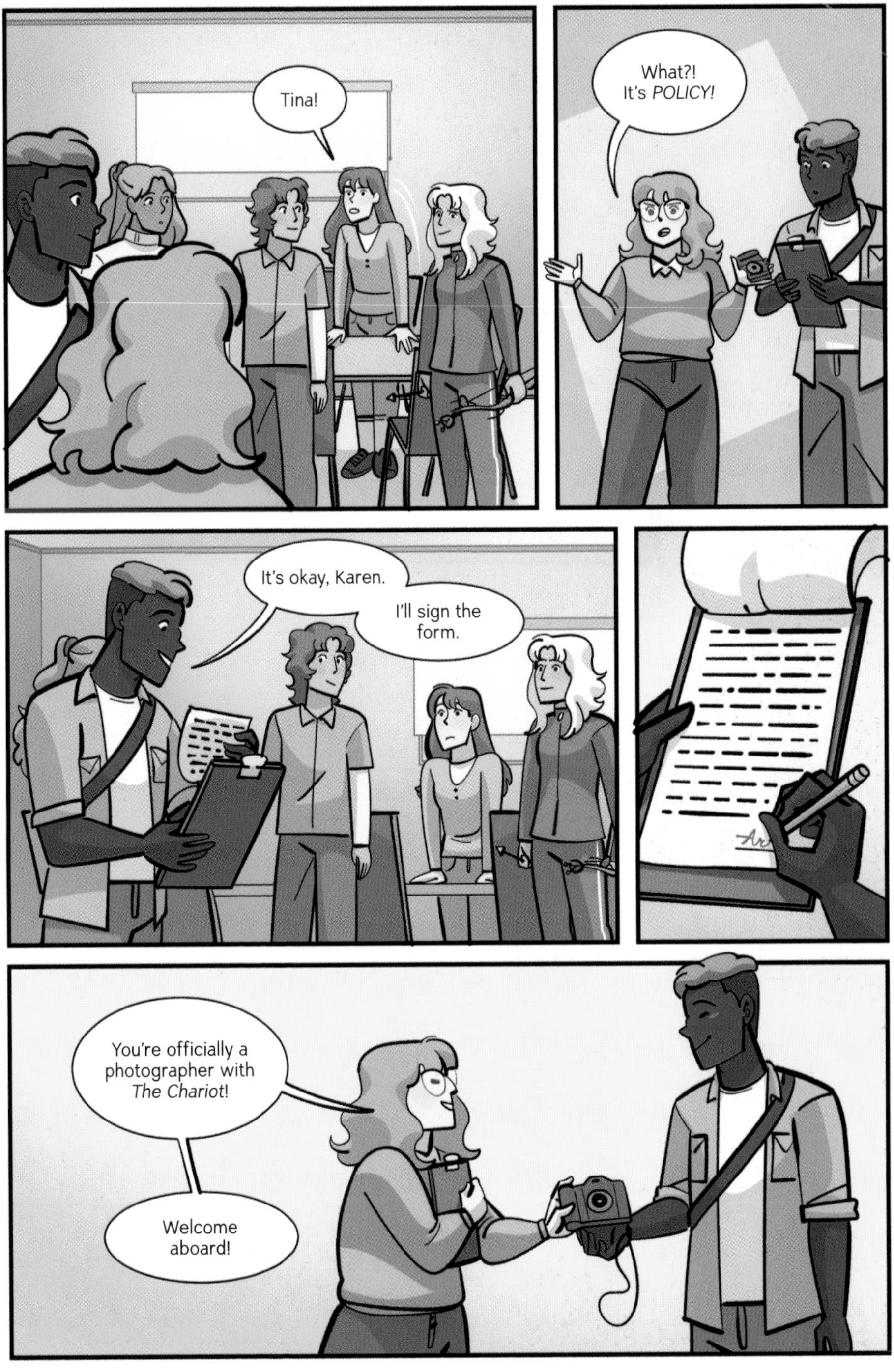
Tina!
What?! It's *POLICY!*
It's okay, Karen.
I'll sign the form.
You're officially a photographer with *The Chariot*!
Welcome aboard!

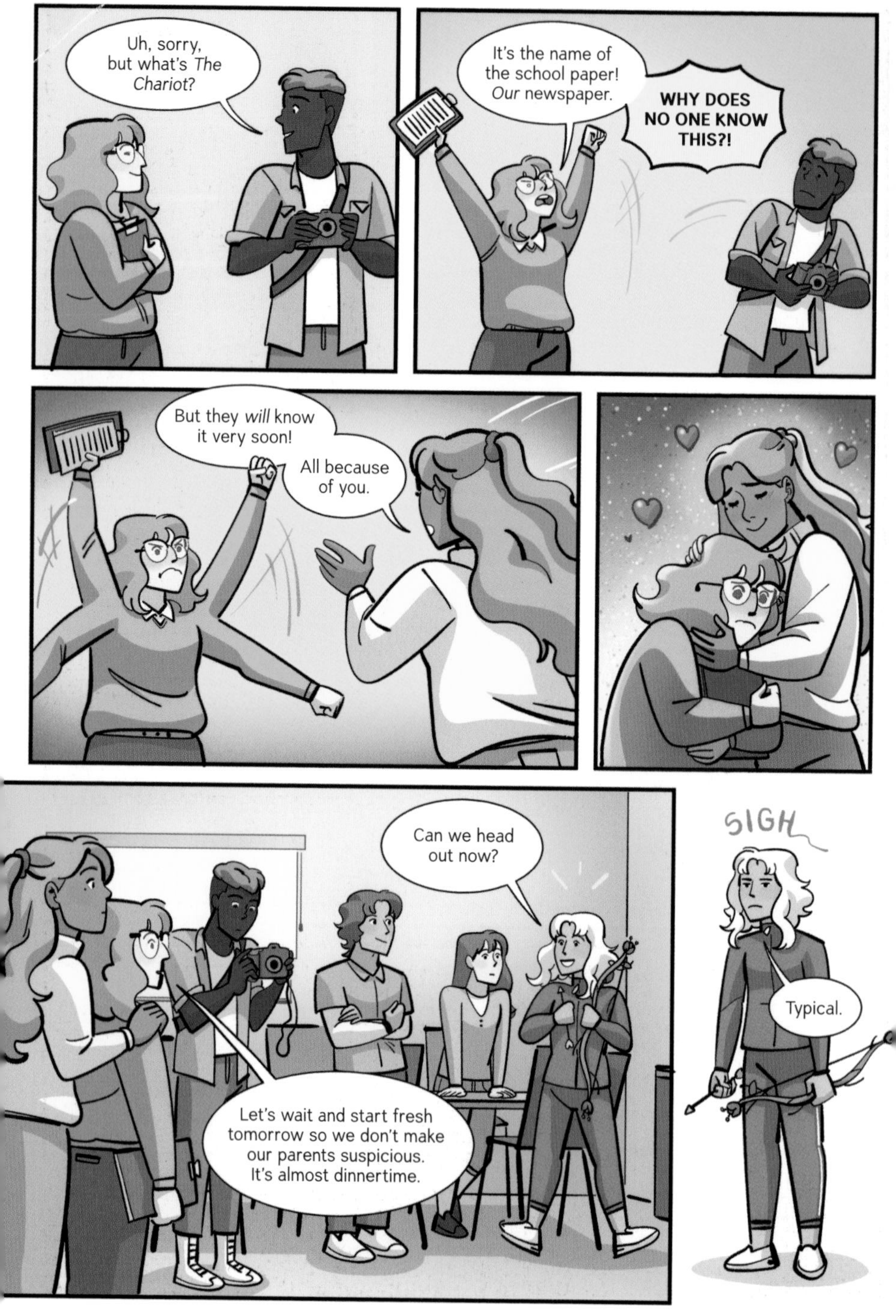

Uh, sorry, but what's *The Chariot*?
It's the name of the school paper! *Our* newspaper.
WHY DOES NO ONE KNOW THIS?!
But they *will* know it very soon!
All because of you.
Can we head out now?
Let's wait and start fresh tomorrow so we don't make our parents suspicious. It's almost dinnertime.
SIGH
Typical.

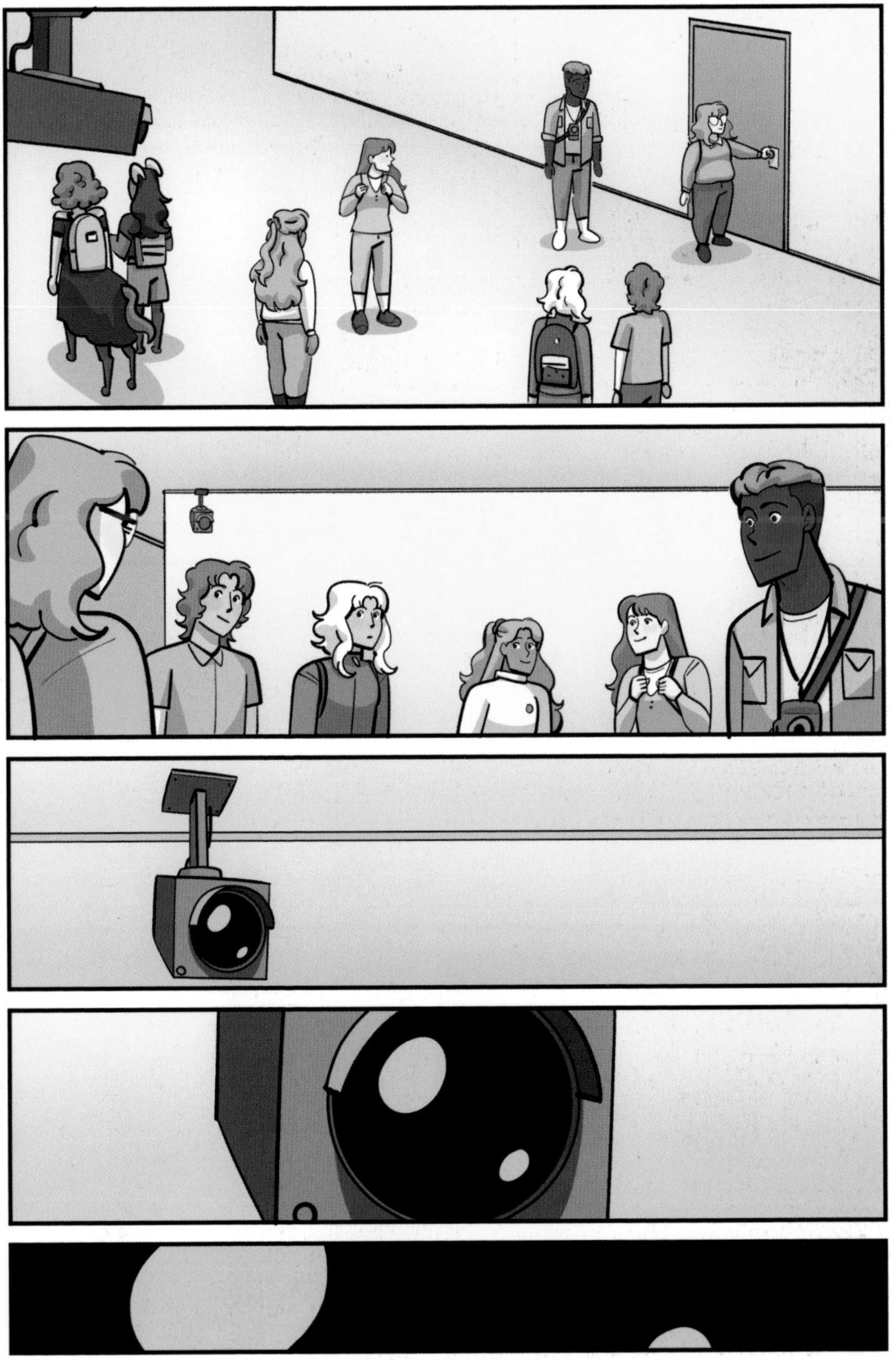

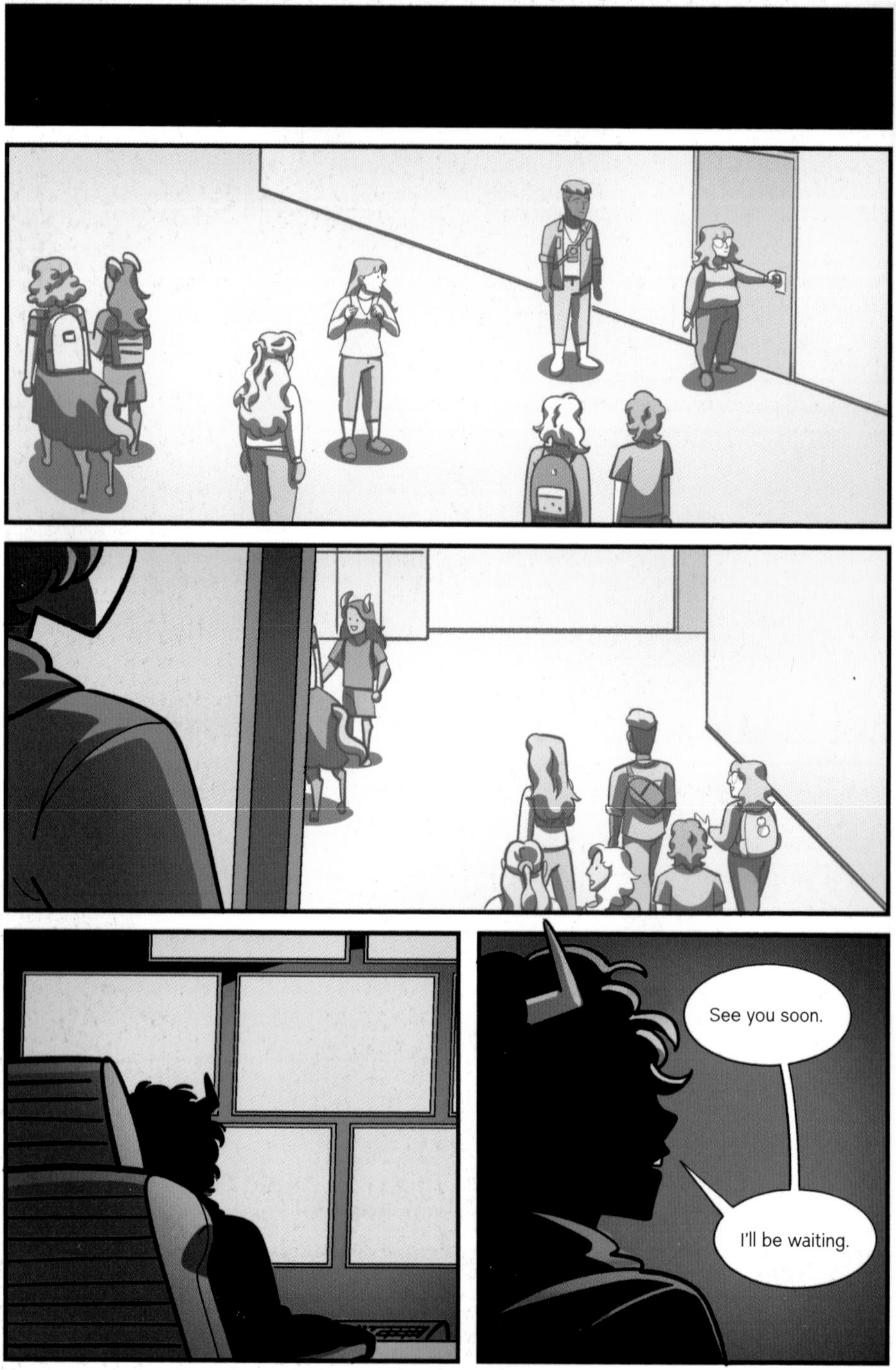
See you soon.
I'll be waiting.

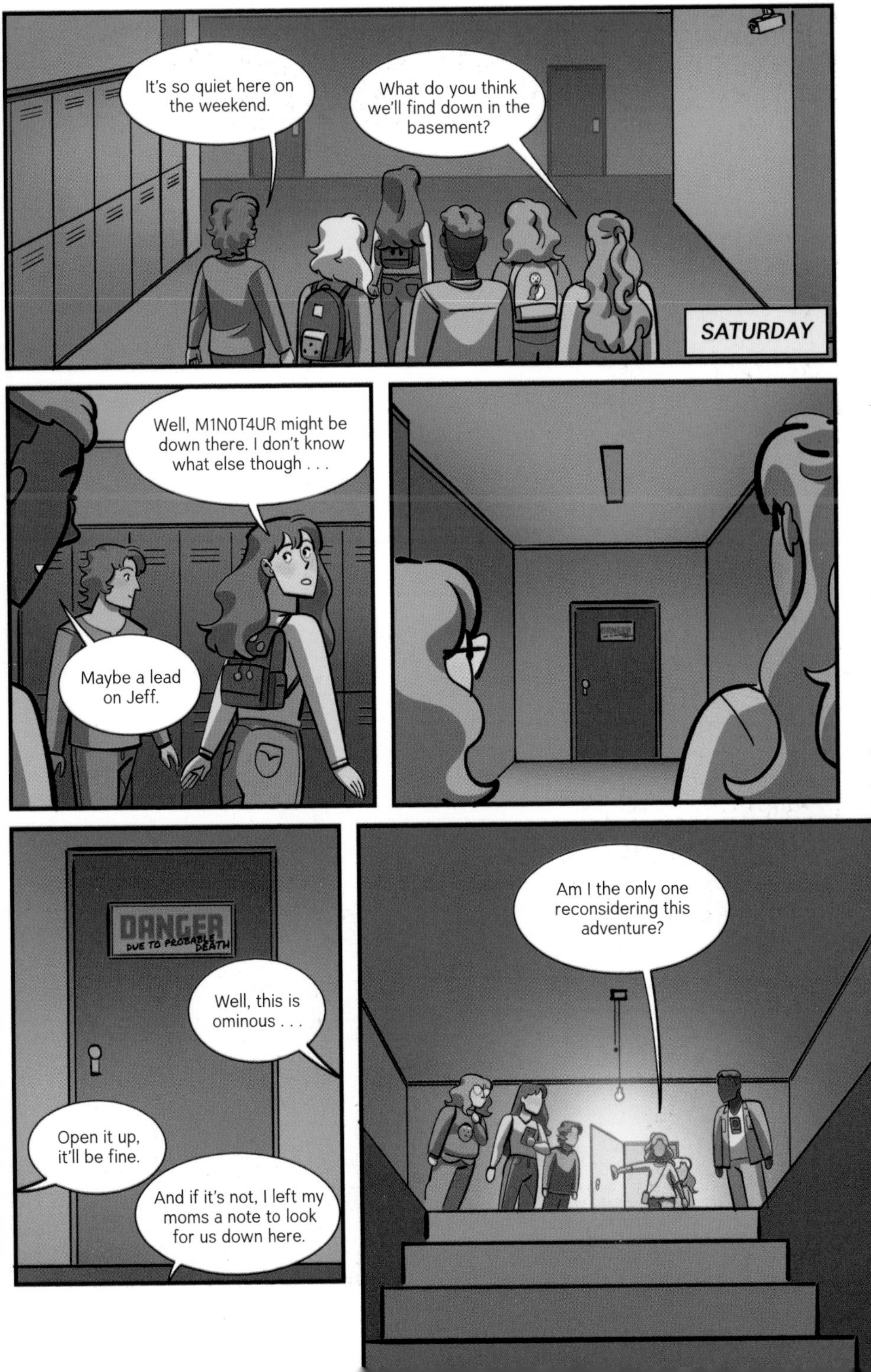
It's so quiet here on the weekend.
What do you think we'll find down in the basement?
SATURDAY
Well, M1N0T4UR might be down there. I don't know what else though . . .
Maybe a lead on Jeff.
DANGER DUE TO PROBABLE DEATH
Well, this is ominous . . .
Open it up, it'll be fine.
And if it's not, I left my moms a note to look for us down here.
Am I the only one reconsidering this adventure?

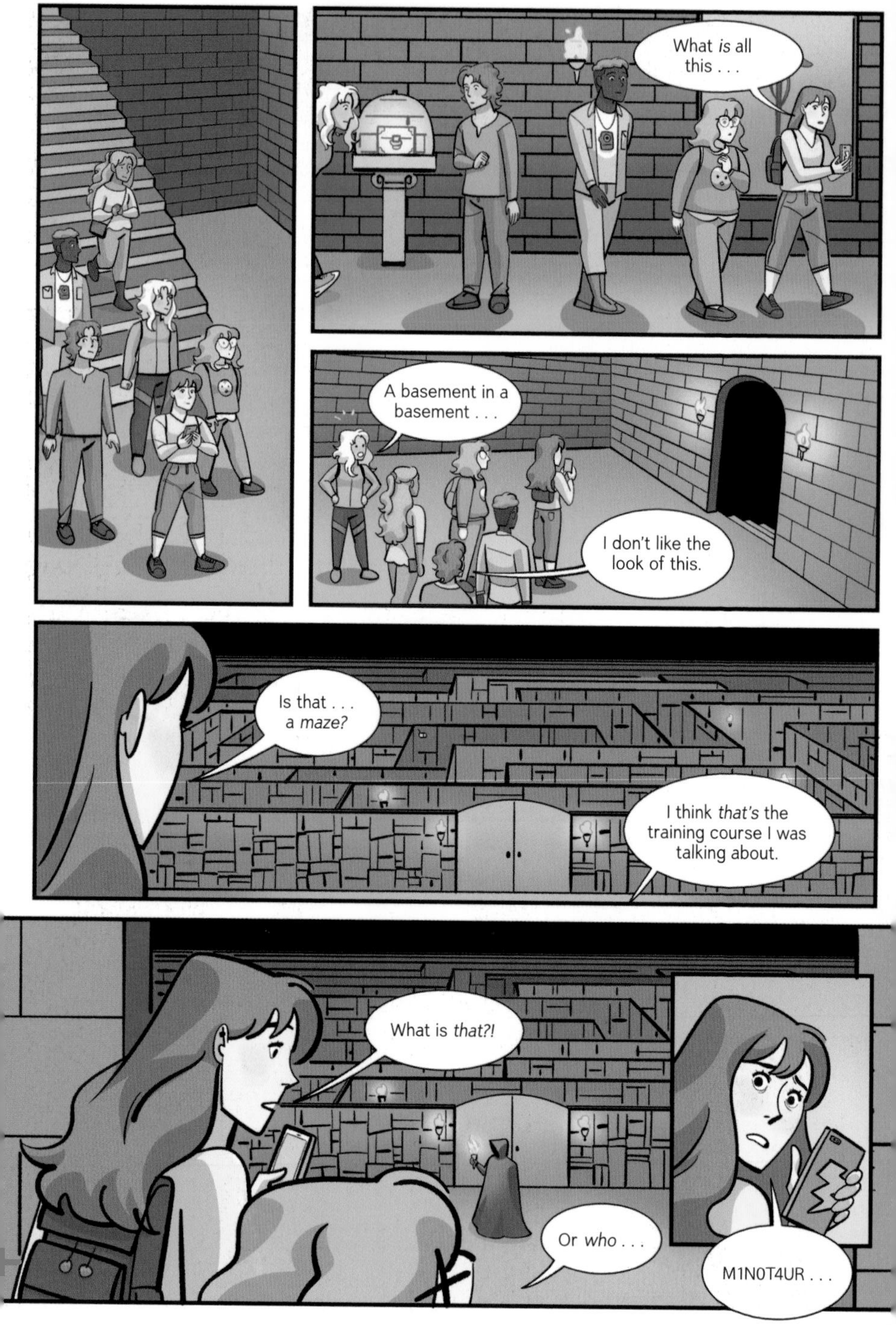
What *is* all this . . .
A basement in a basement . . .
I don't like the look of this.
Is that . . . a *maze?*
I think *that's* the training course I was talking about.
What is *that?!*
Or *who* . . .
M1N0T4UR . . .

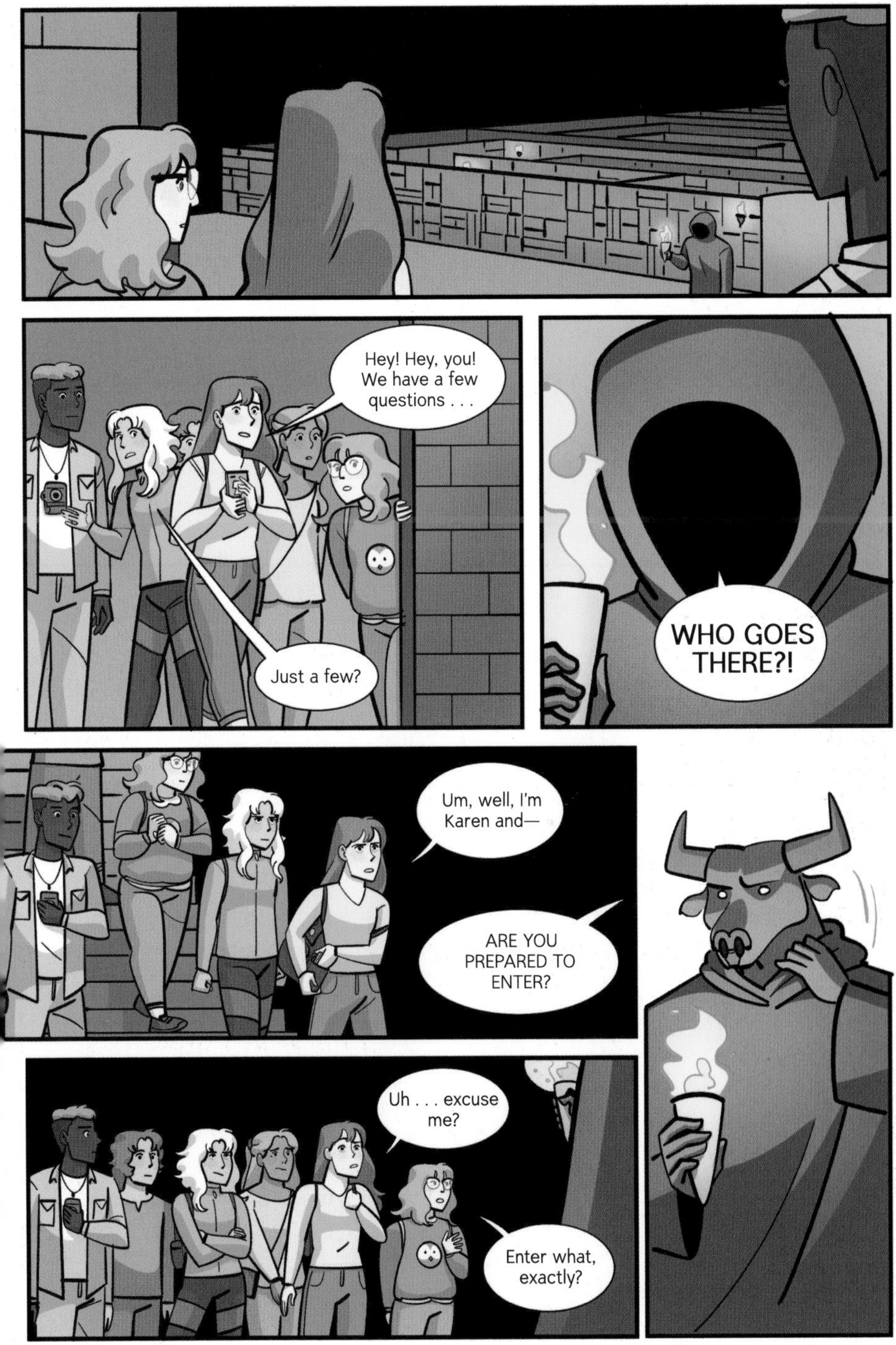
Hey! Hey, you! We have a few questions . . .
Just a few?
WHO GOES THERE?!
Um, well, I'm Karen and—
ARE YOU PREPARED TO ENTER?
Uh . . . excuse me?
Enter what, exactly?

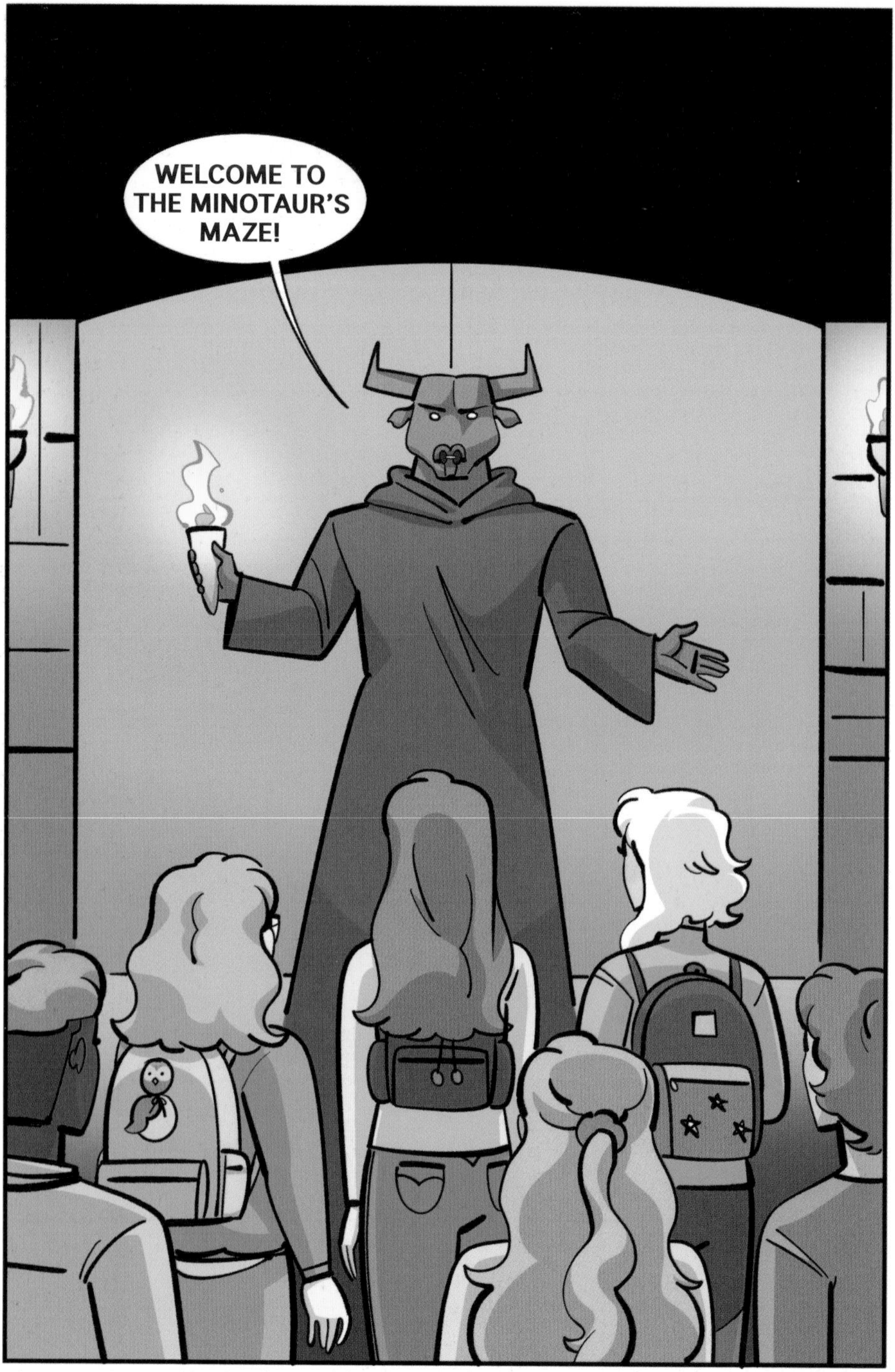
WELCOME TO THE MINOTAUR'S MAZE!

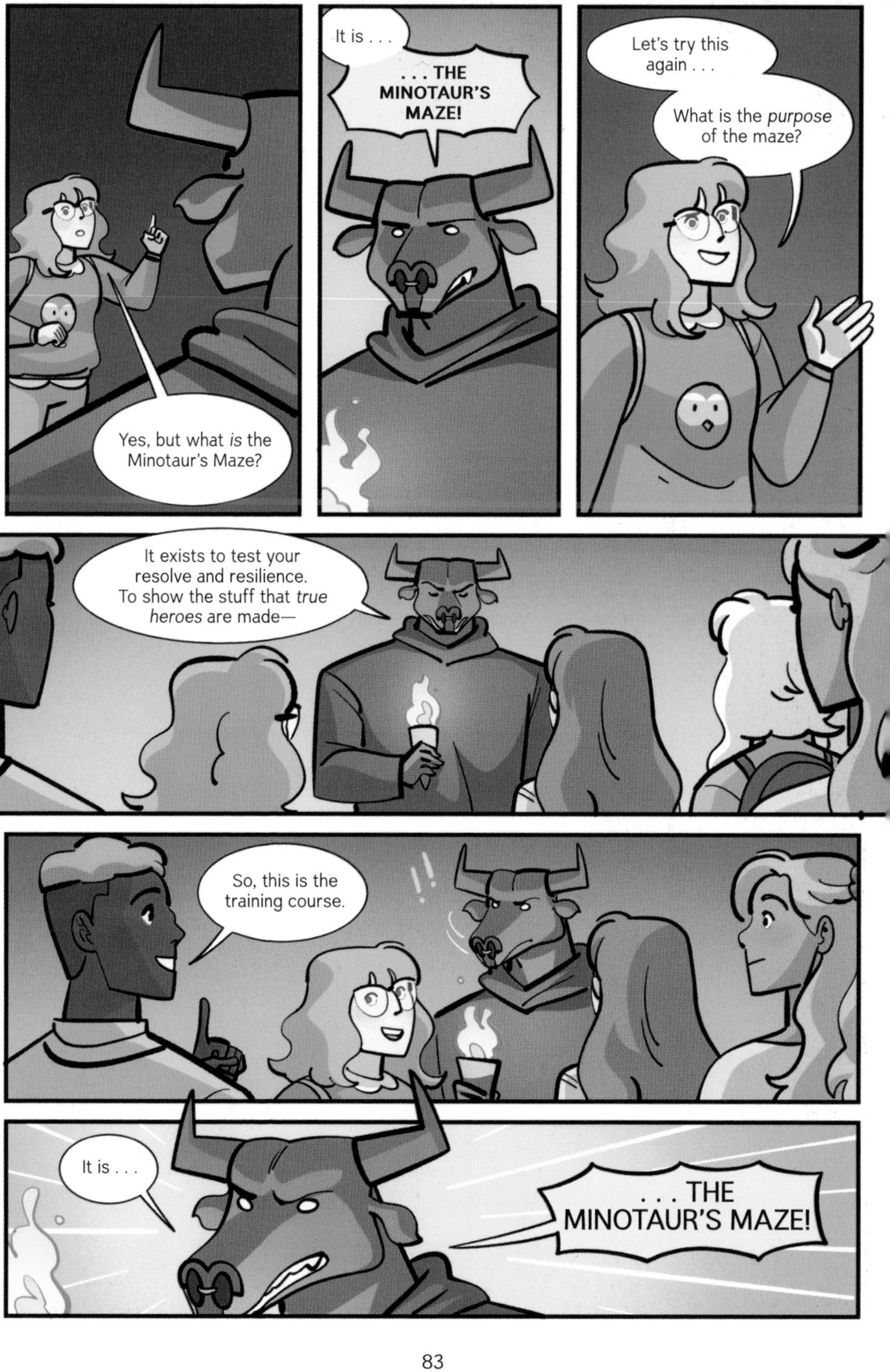
Yes, but what *is* the Minotaur's Maze?
It is . . .
. . . THE MINOTAUR'S MAZE!
Let's try this again . . .
What is the *purpose* of the maze?
It exists to test your resolve and resilience. To show the stuff that *true heroes* are made—
So, this is the training course.
!!
It is . . .
. . . THE MINOTAUR'S MAZE!

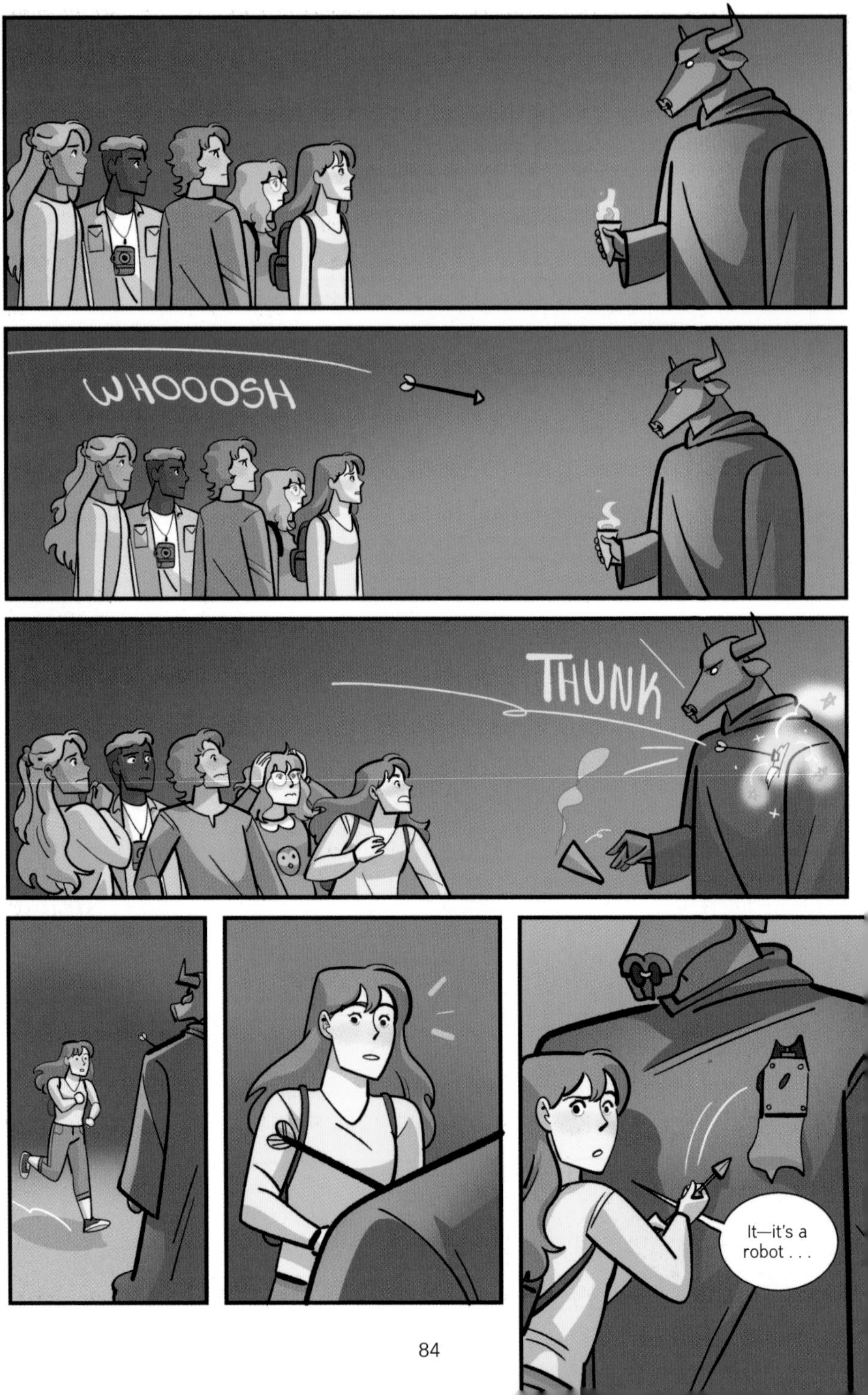
WHOOOSH
THUNK
It—it's a robot . . .

WELCOME TO THE MINOTAUR'S MAZE!

Fascinating. It appears to be programmed . . .

I wonder if the *whole* maze is programmed?

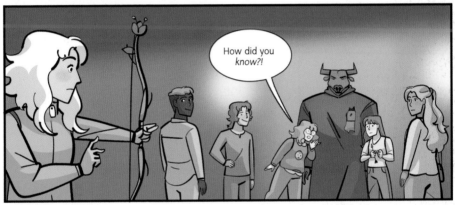

How did you *know?!*

I didn't.

SHRUG

WHAT?!

What if it was real and then it *attacked us?!*

I had a hunch! And I was right.

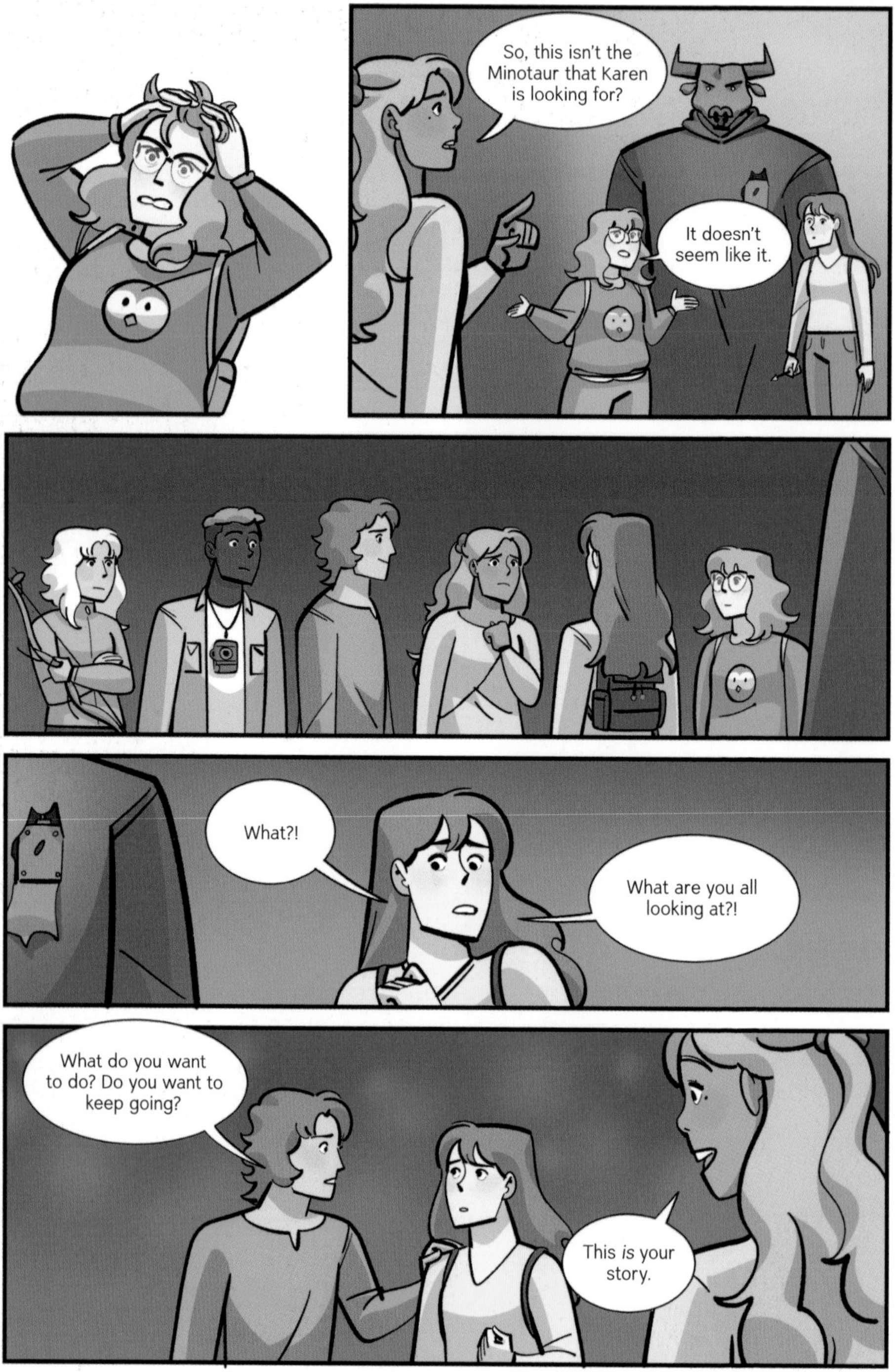
So, this isn't the Minotaur that Karen is looking for?
It doesn't seem like it.
What?!
What are you all looking at?!
What do you want to do? Do you want to keep going?
This *is* your story.

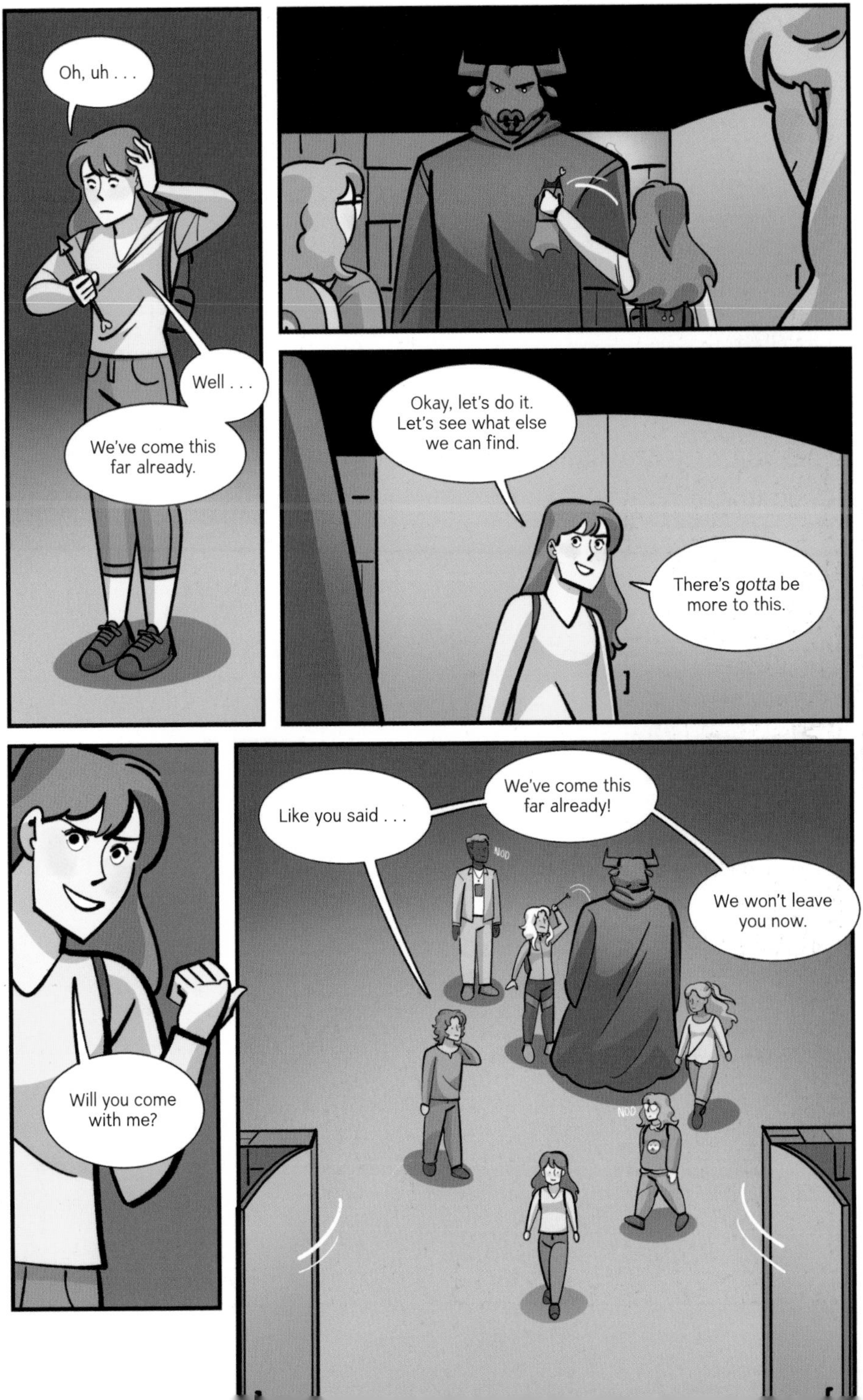
Oh, uh . . .
Well . . .
We've come this far already.
Okay, let's do it. Let's see what else we can find.
There's *gotta* be more to this.
Will you come with me?
Like you said . . .
We've come this far already!
NOD
We won't leave you now.
NOD

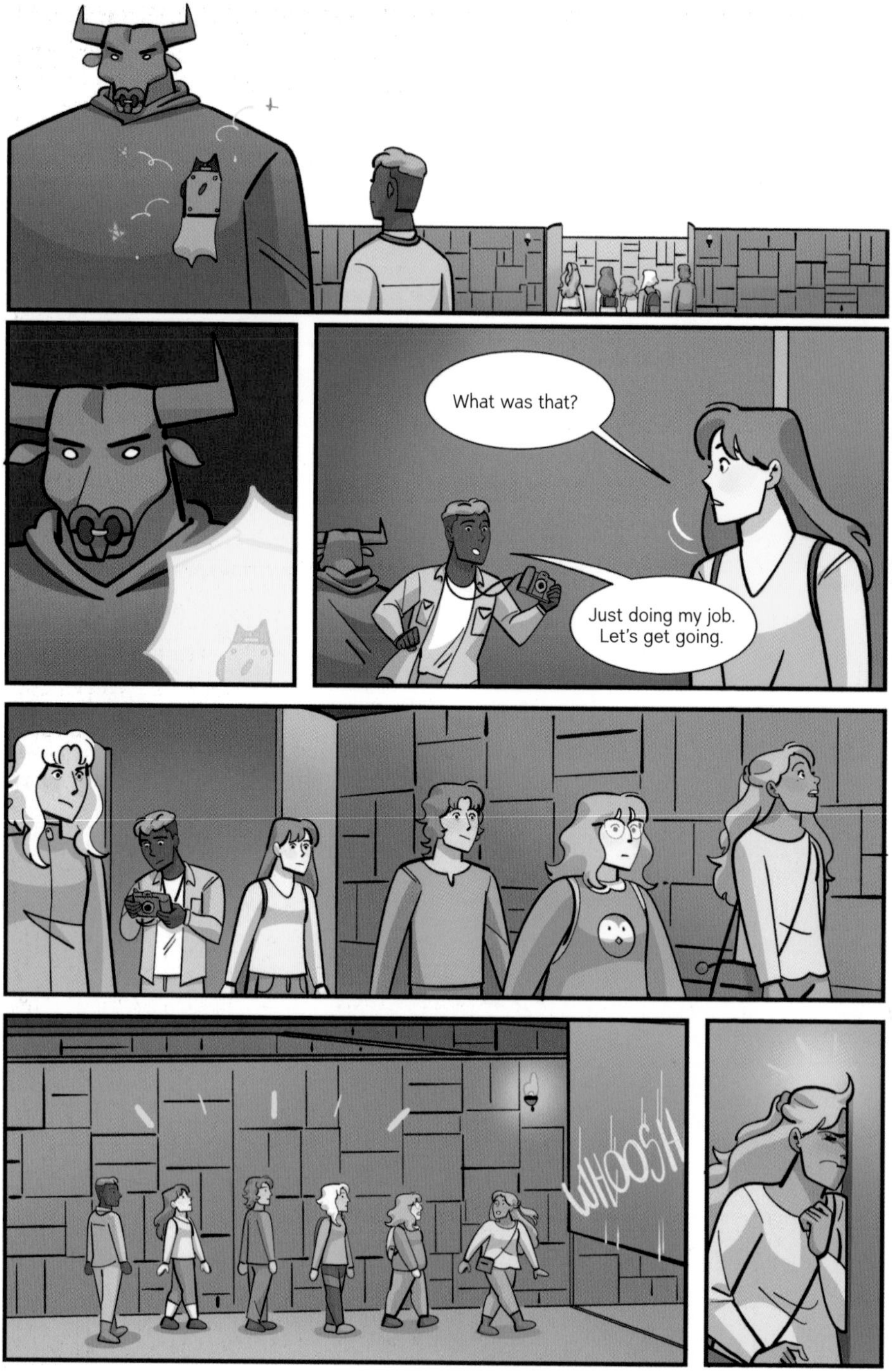
What was that?
Just doing my job. Let's get going.
WHOOSH

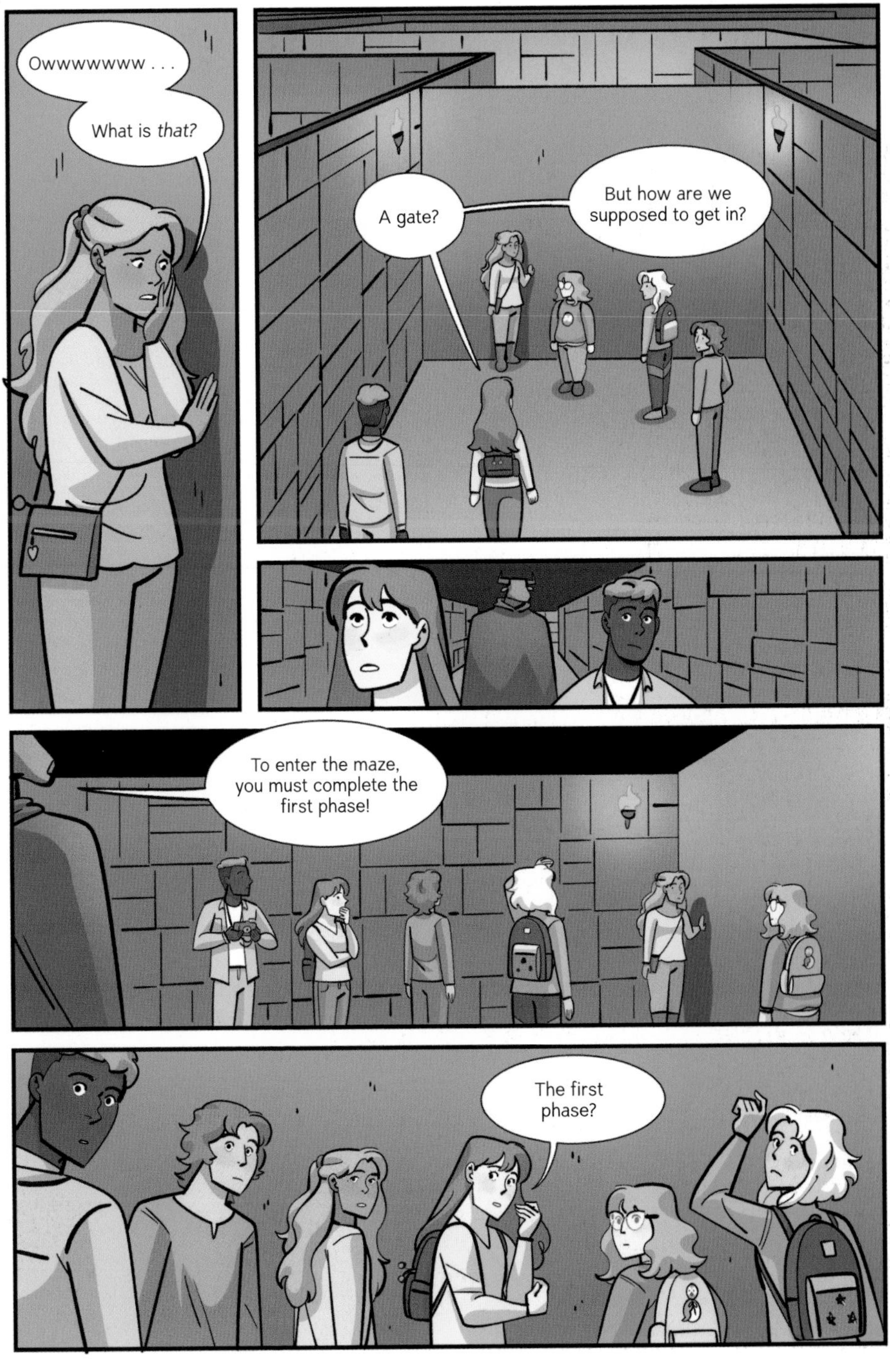
Owwwwwww . . .
What is *that?*
A gate?
But how are we supposed to get in?
To enter the maze, you must complete the first phase!
The first phase?

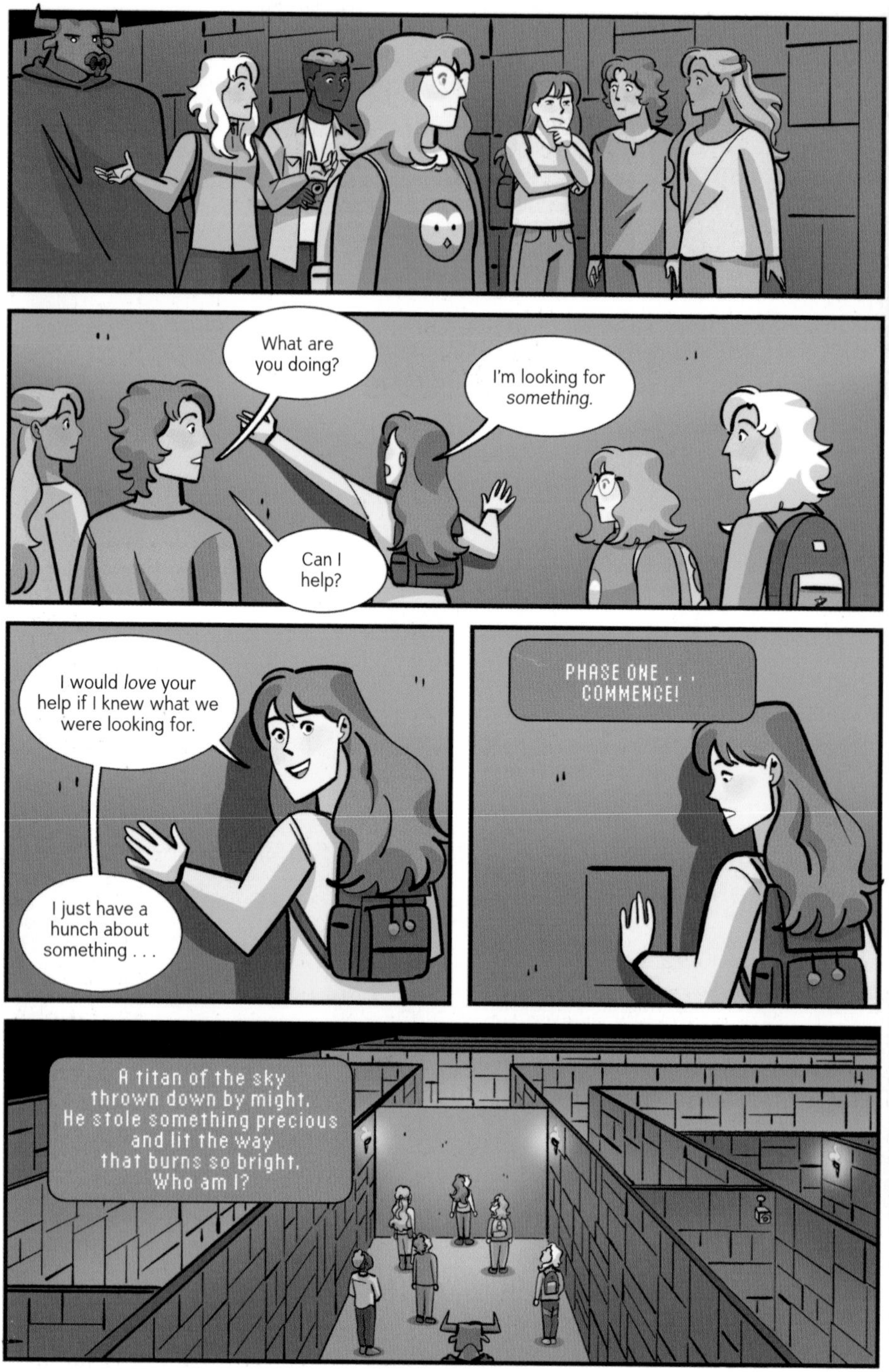
What are you doing?
I'm looking for *something.*
Can I help?
I would *love* your help if I knew what we were looking for.
I just have a hunch about something . . .
PHASE ONE . . . COMMENCE!
A titan of the sky thrown down by might. He stole something precious and lit the way that burns so bright. Who am I?

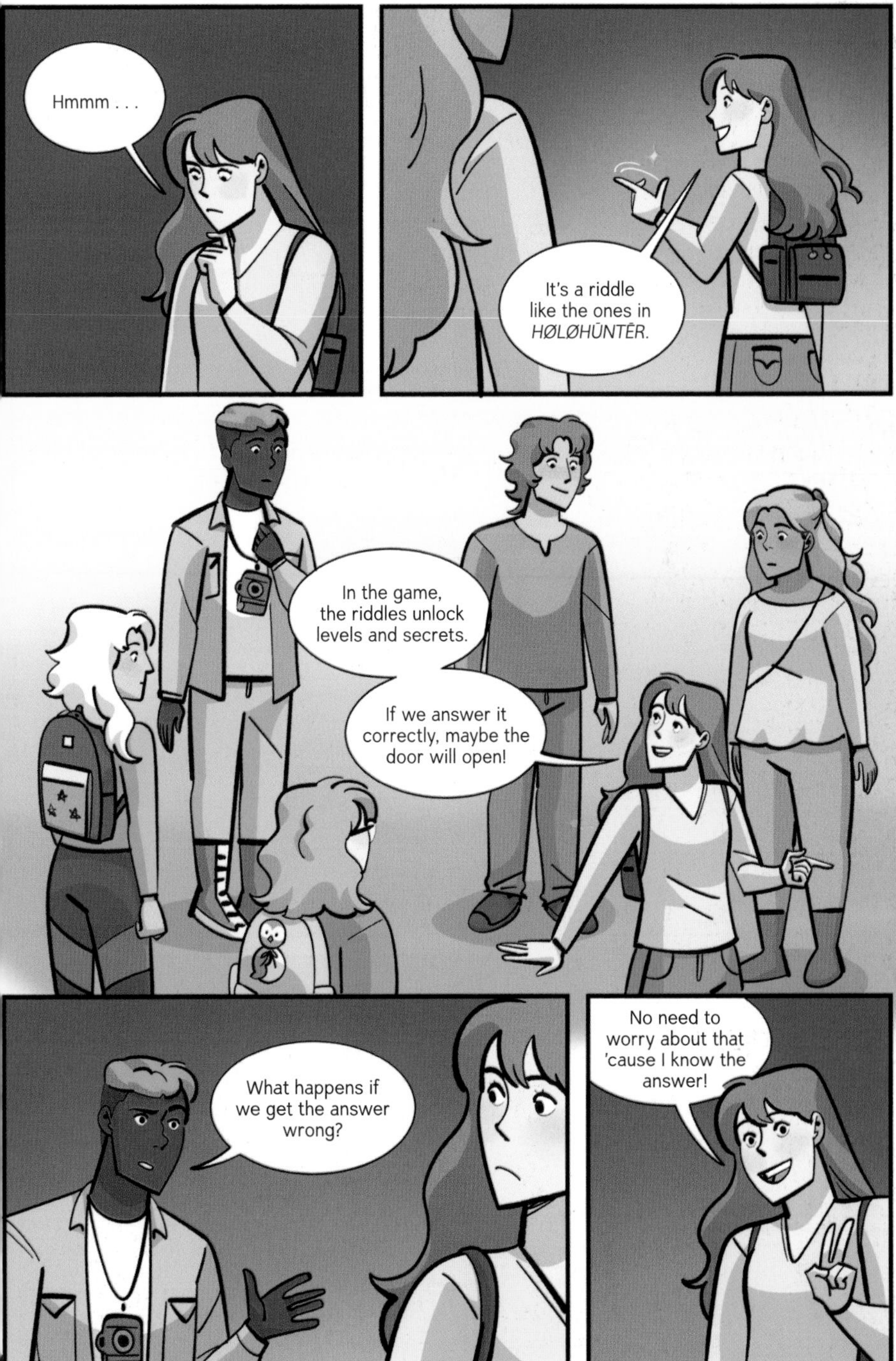
Hmmm . . .
It's a riddle like the ones in *HØLØHŪNTĒR*.
In the game, the riddles unlock levels and secrets.
If we answer it correctly, maybe the door will open!
What happens if we get the answer wrong?
No need to worry about that 'cause I know the answer!

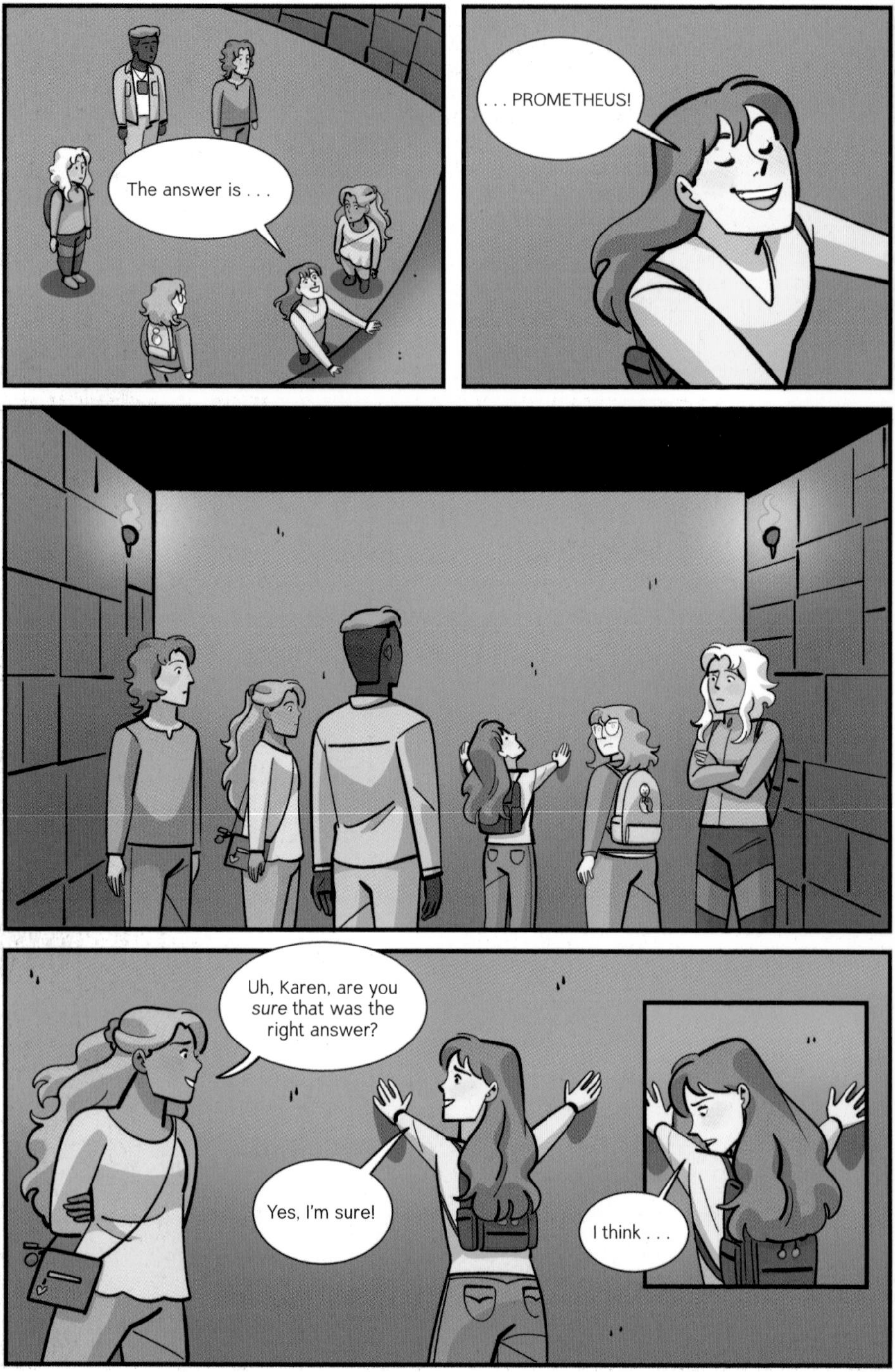
The answer is . . .
. . . PROMETHEUS!
Uh, Karen, are you *sure* that was the right answer?
Yes, I'm sure!
I think . . .

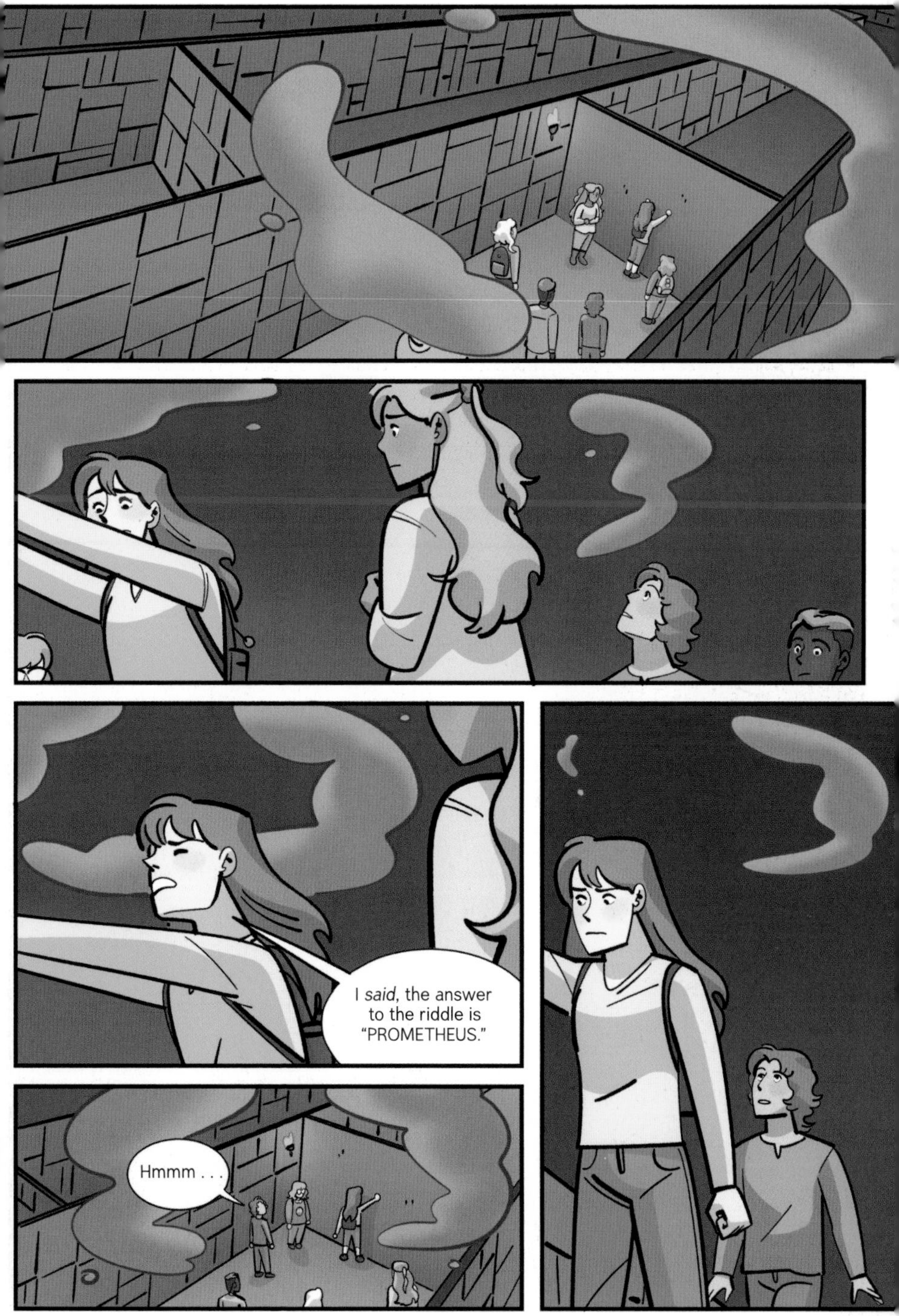
I *said*, the answer to the riddle is "PROMETHEUS."
Hmmm . . .

Earthquake?!

No, look! It's the door!

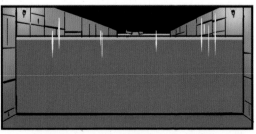

Congrats on completing the first phase. The *other* phases will not be so easy . . .

Ha ha ha ha ha ha . . .

That voice . . .

. . . M1N0T4UR.

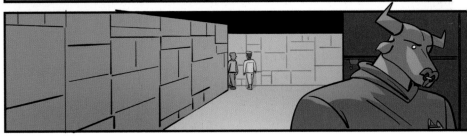

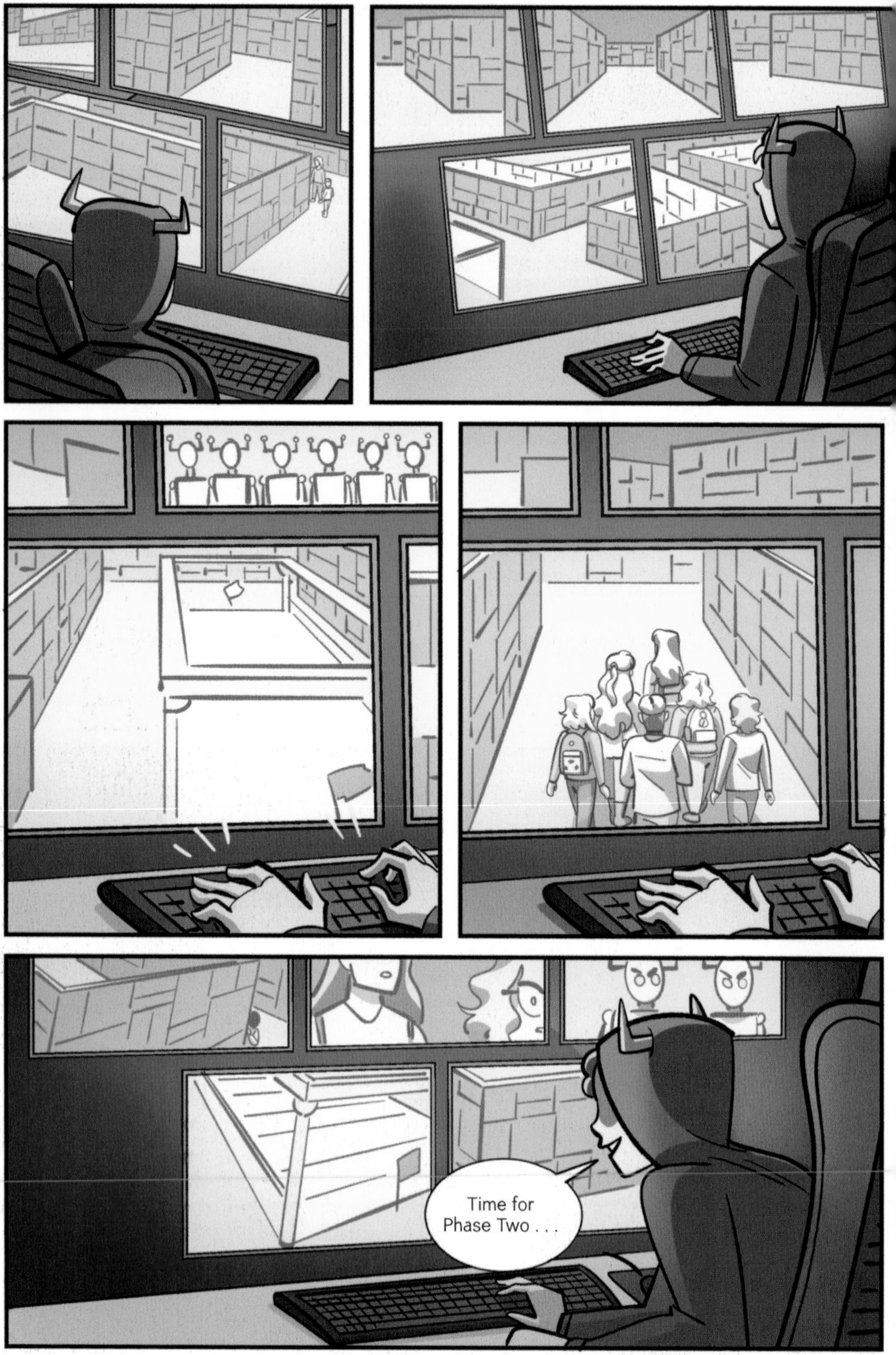
Time for
Phase Two . . .

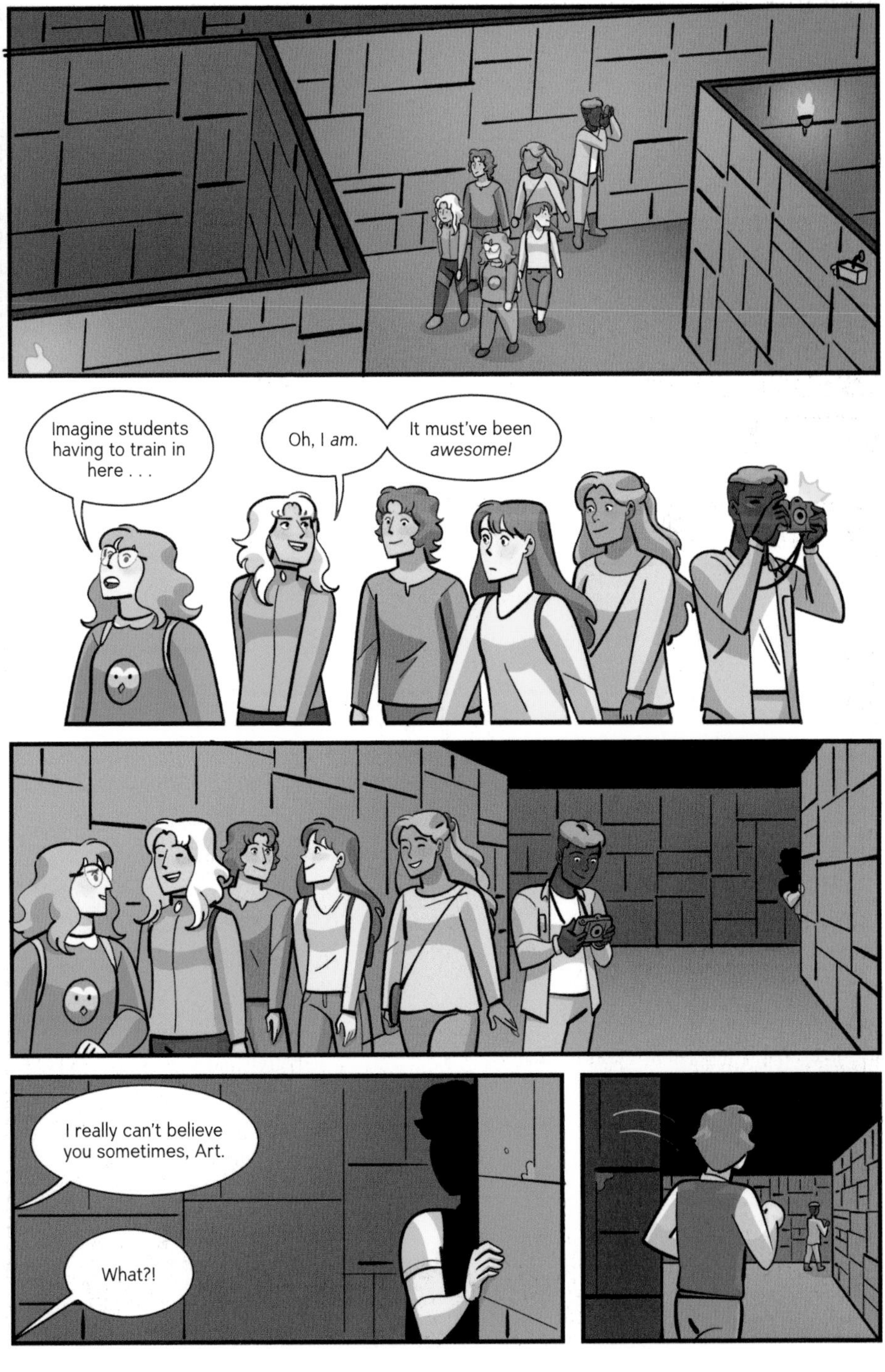
Imagine students having to train in here . . .
Oh, I *am*.
It must've been *awesome!*
I really can't believe you sometimes, Art.
What?!

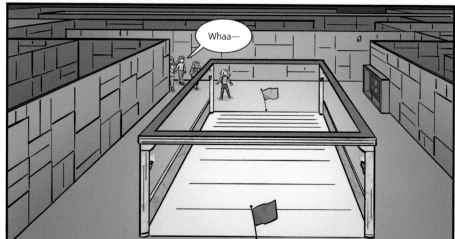

Whaa—

I'm glad you could make it.

I hope you like what I've done with the place.

Hmmm . . .

What is it, Karen?

This must be the next phase of the maze.

I think he's replicating Capture the Flag from *HØLØHÜNTÉR.*

98

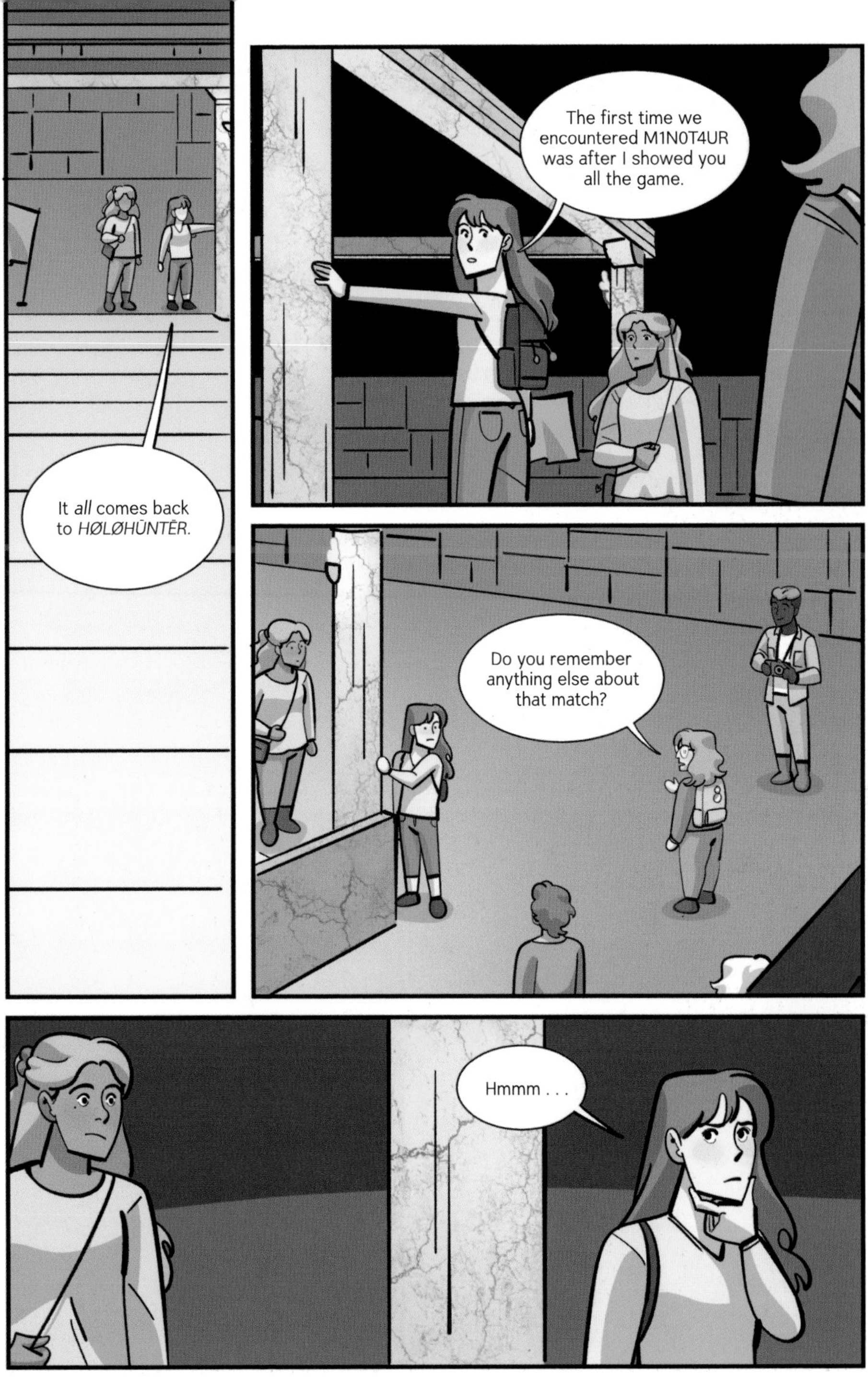
It *all* comes back to *HØLØHŪNTĒR.*
The first time we encountered M1N0T4UR was after I showed you all the game.
Do you remember anything else about that match?
Hmmm . . .

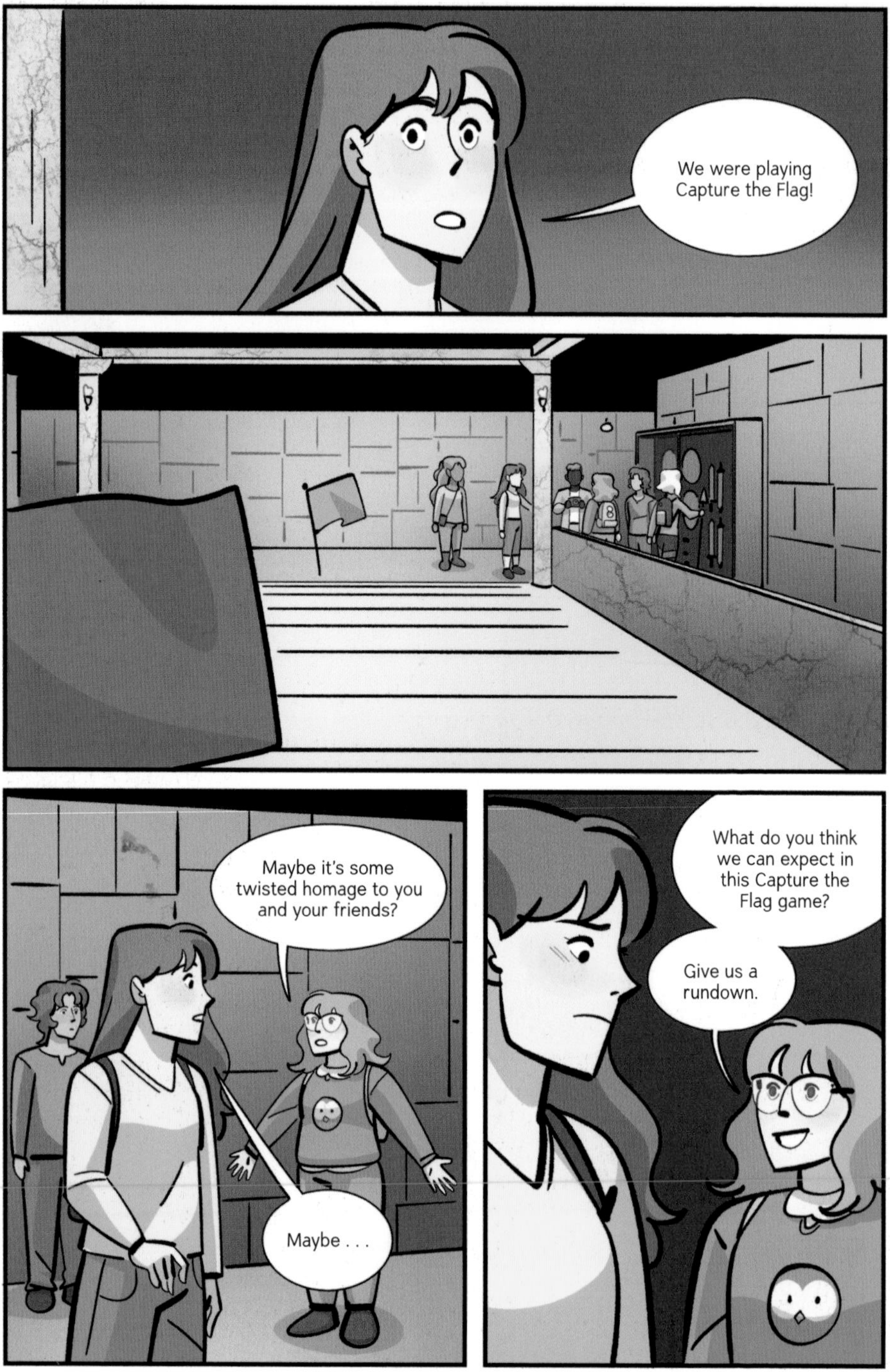
We were playing Capture the Flag!
Maybe it's some twisted homage to you and your friends?
Maybe . . .
What do you think we can expect in this Capture the Flag game?
Give us a rundown.

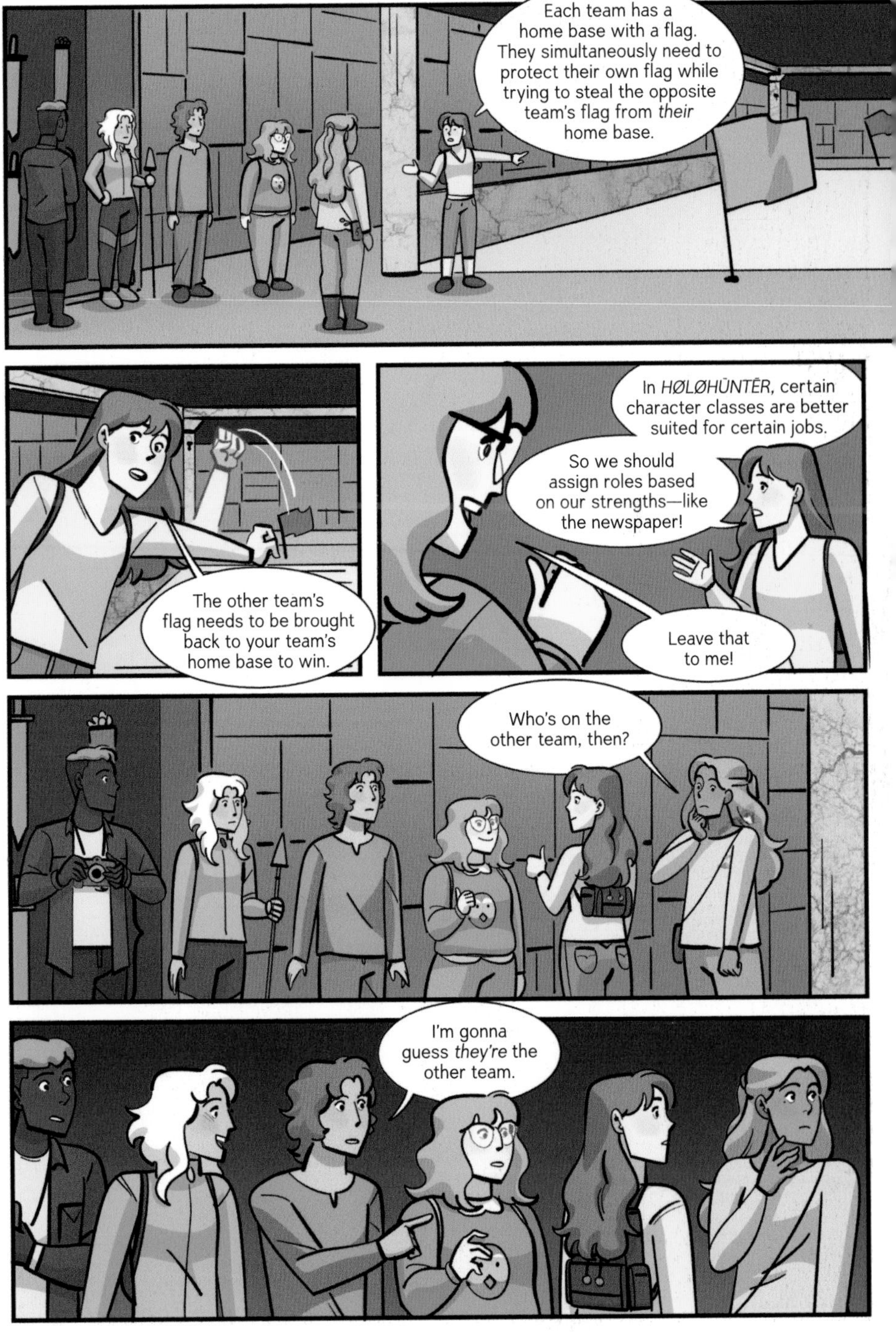
Each team has a home base with a flag. They simultaneously need to protect their own flag while trying to steal the opposite team's flag from *their* home base.
The other team's flag needs to be brought back to your team's home base to win.
In *HØLØHÜNTĒR*, certain character classes are better suited for certain jobs.
So we should assign roles based on our strengths—like the newspaper!
Leave that to me!
Who's on the other team, then?
I'm gonna guess *they're* the other team.

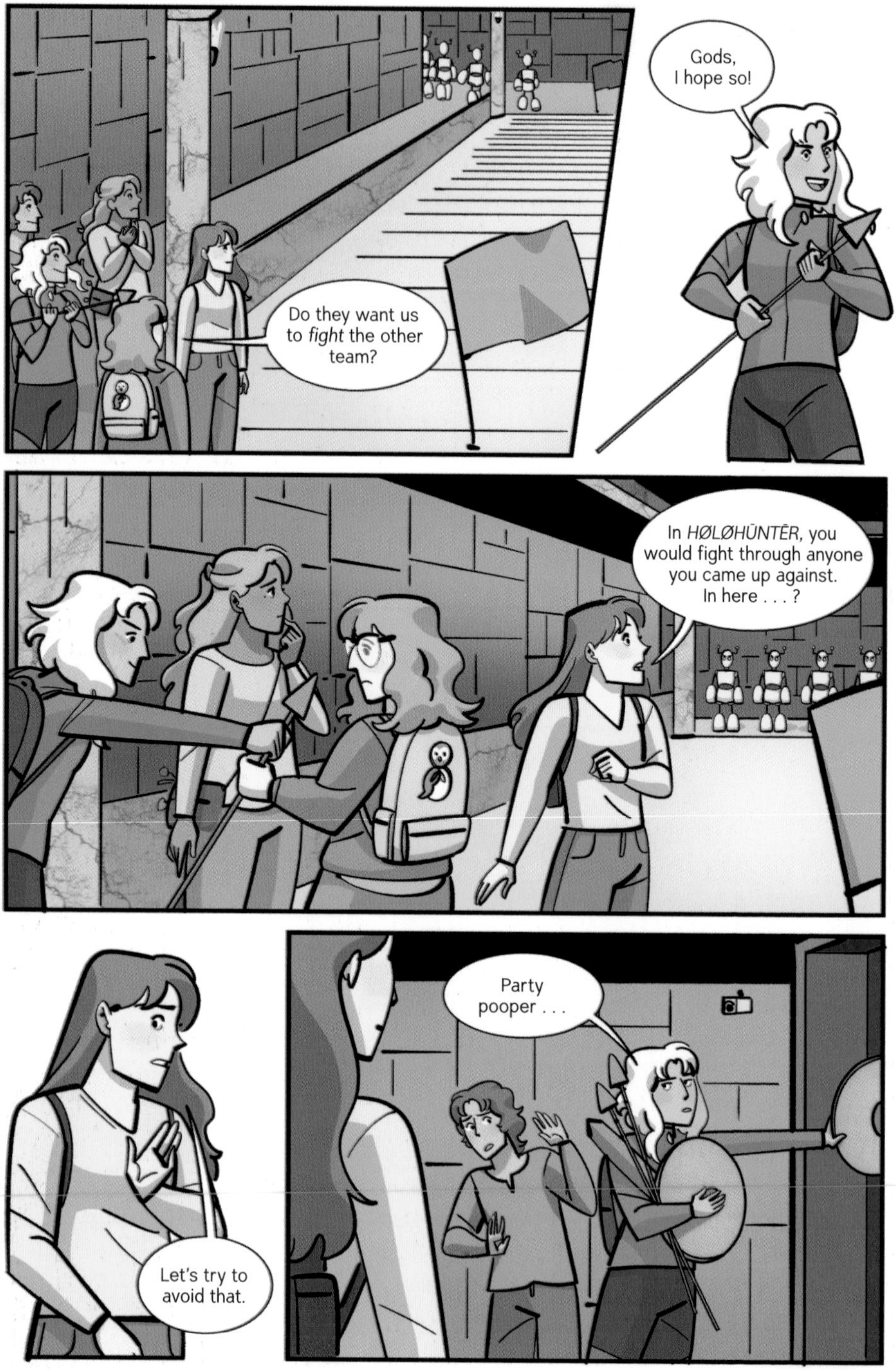
Do they want us to *fight* the other team?
Gods, I hope so!
In *HØLØHŪNTĒR*, you would fight through anyone you came up against. In here . . . ?
Let's try to avoid that.
Party pooper . . .

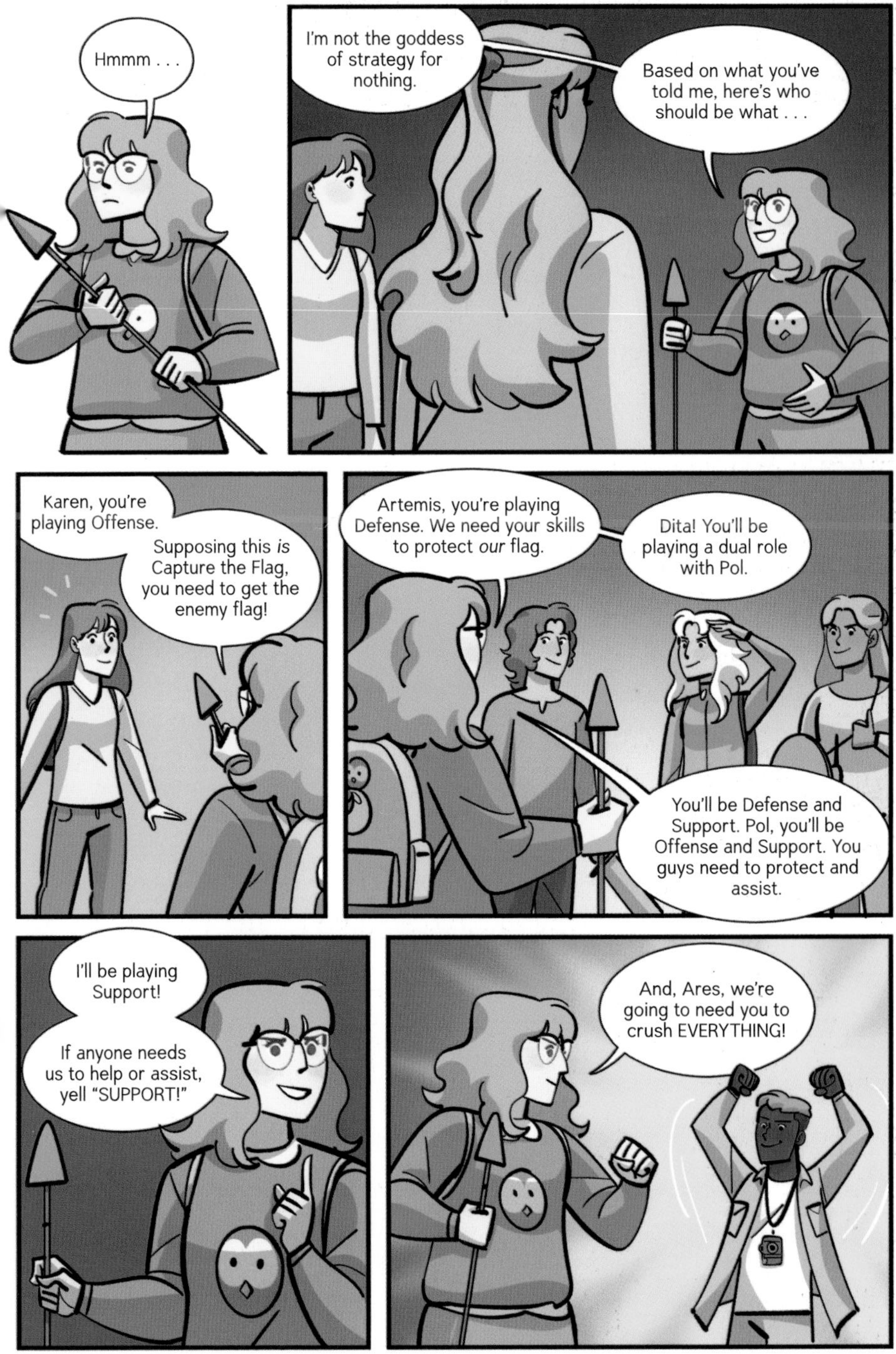
Hmmm . . .
I'm not the goddess of strategy for nothing.
Based on what you've told me, here's who should be what . . .
Karen, you're playing Offense.
Supposing this *is* Capture the Flag, you need to get the enemy flag!
Artemis, you're playing Defense. We need your skills to protect *our* flag.
Dita! You'll be playing a dual role with Pol.
You'll be Defense and Support. Pol, you'll be Offense and Support. You guys need to protect and assist.
I'll be playing Support!
If anyone needs us to help or assist, yell "SUPPORT!"
And, Ares, we're going to need you to crush EVERYTHING!

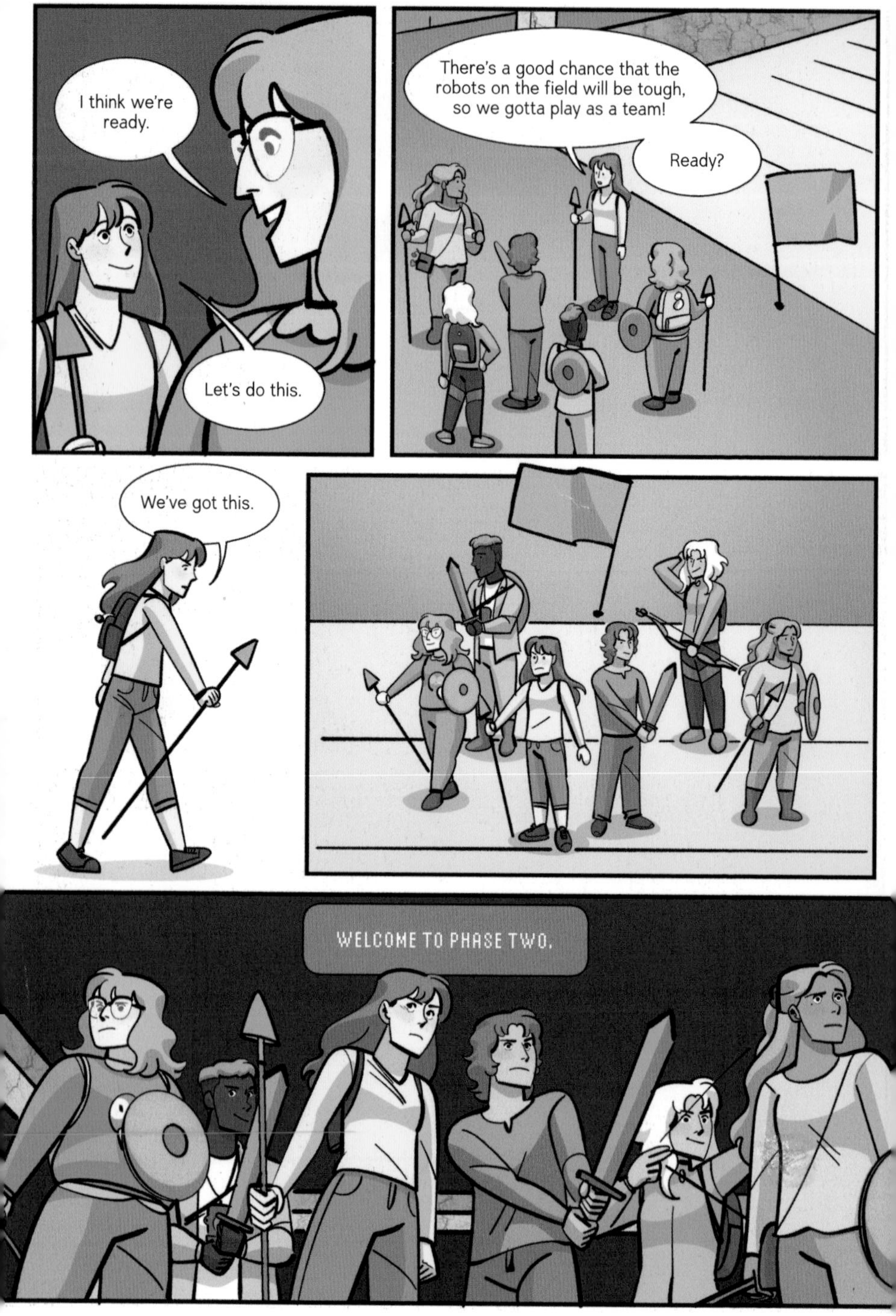
I think we're ready.
Let's do this.
There's a good chance that the robots on the field will be tough, so we gotta play as a team!
Ready?
We've got this.
WELCOME TO PHASE TWO.

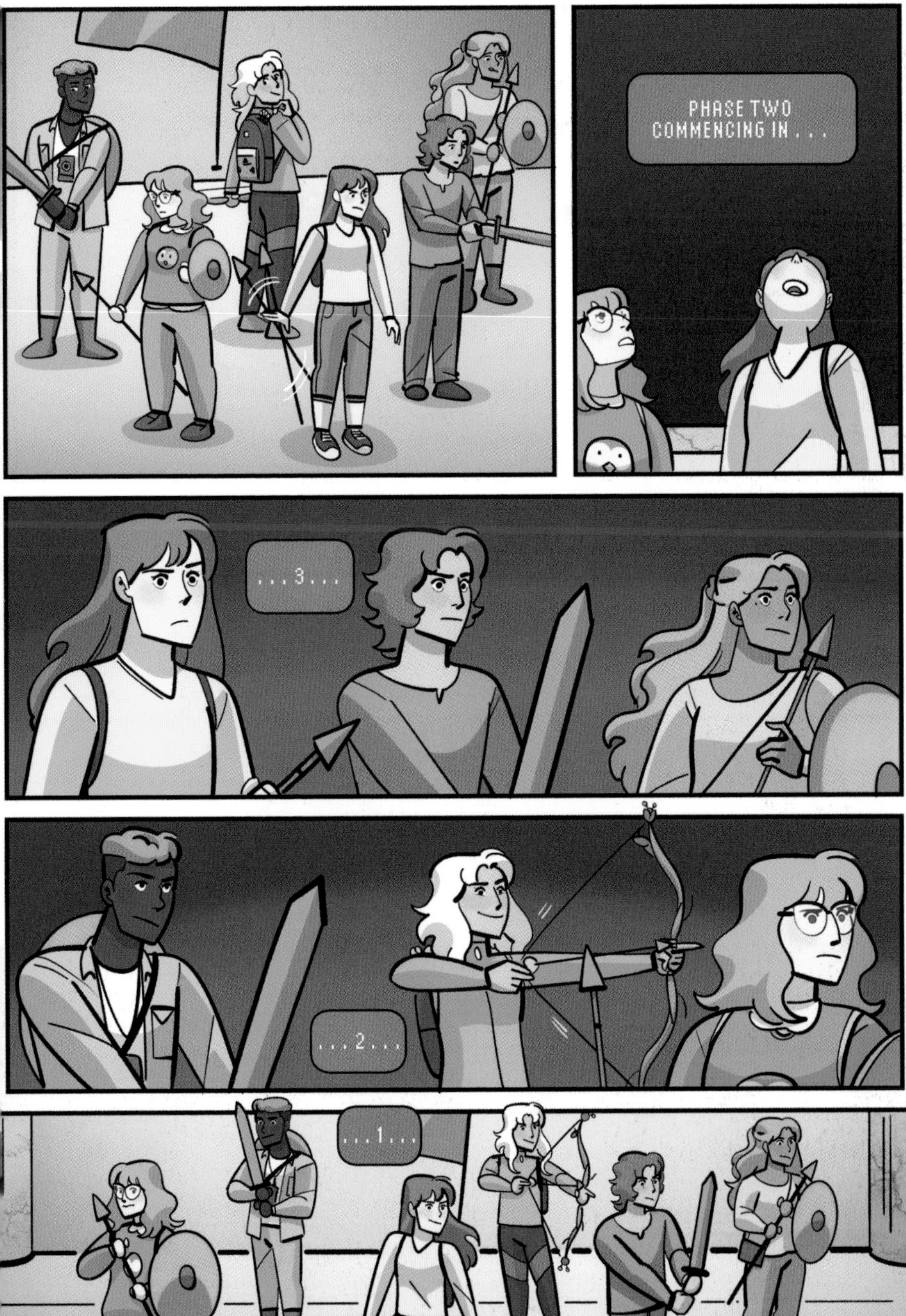
PHASE TWO COMMENCING IN . . .
. . . 3 . . .
. . . 2 . . .
. . . 1 . . .

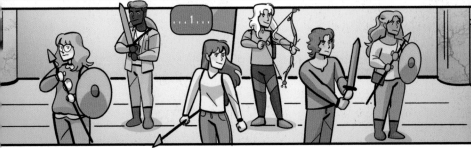

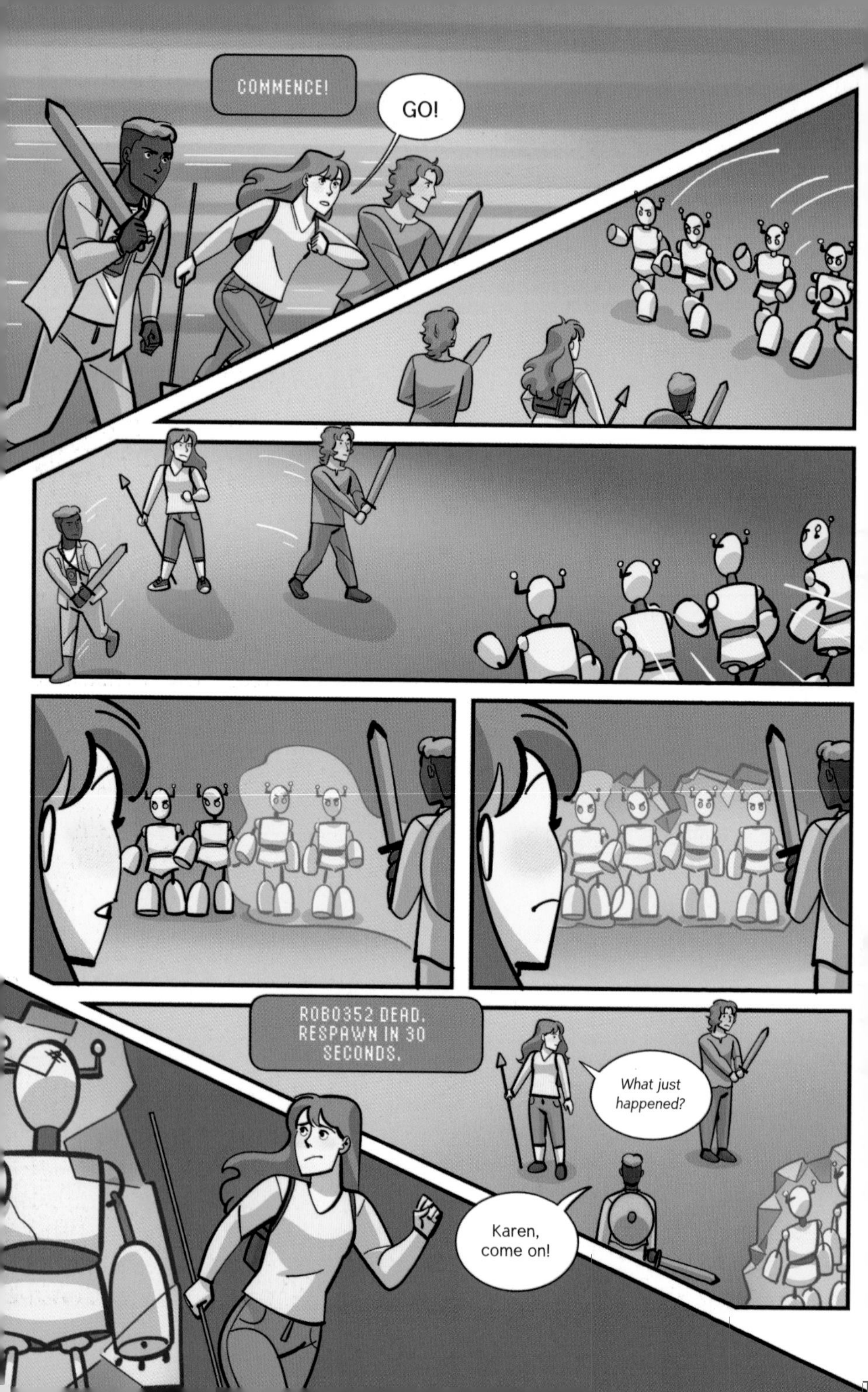
COMMENCE!
GO!
ROBO352 DEAD. RESPAWN IN 30 SECONDS.
What just happened?
Karen, come on!

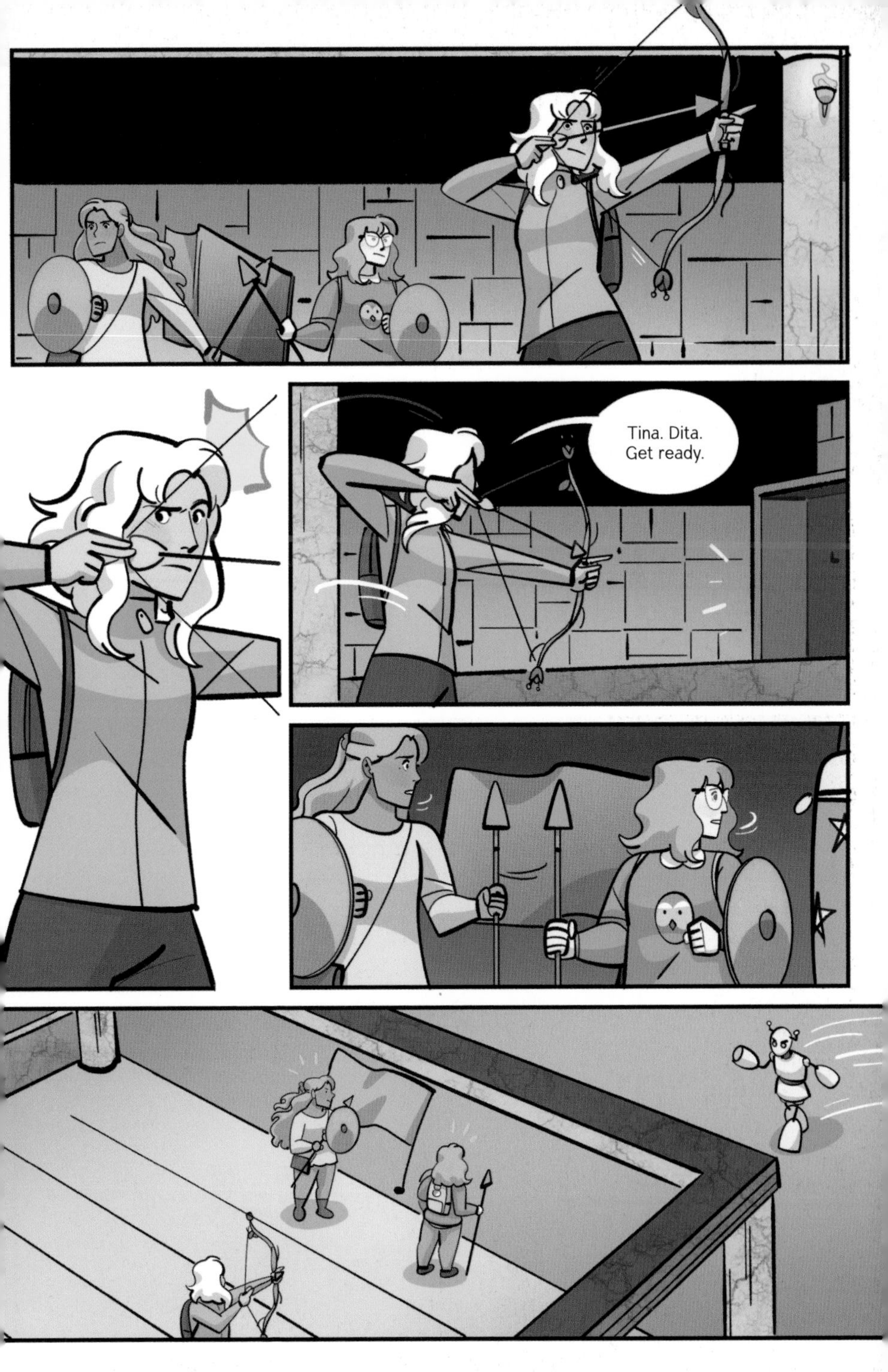
Tina. Dita.
Get ready.

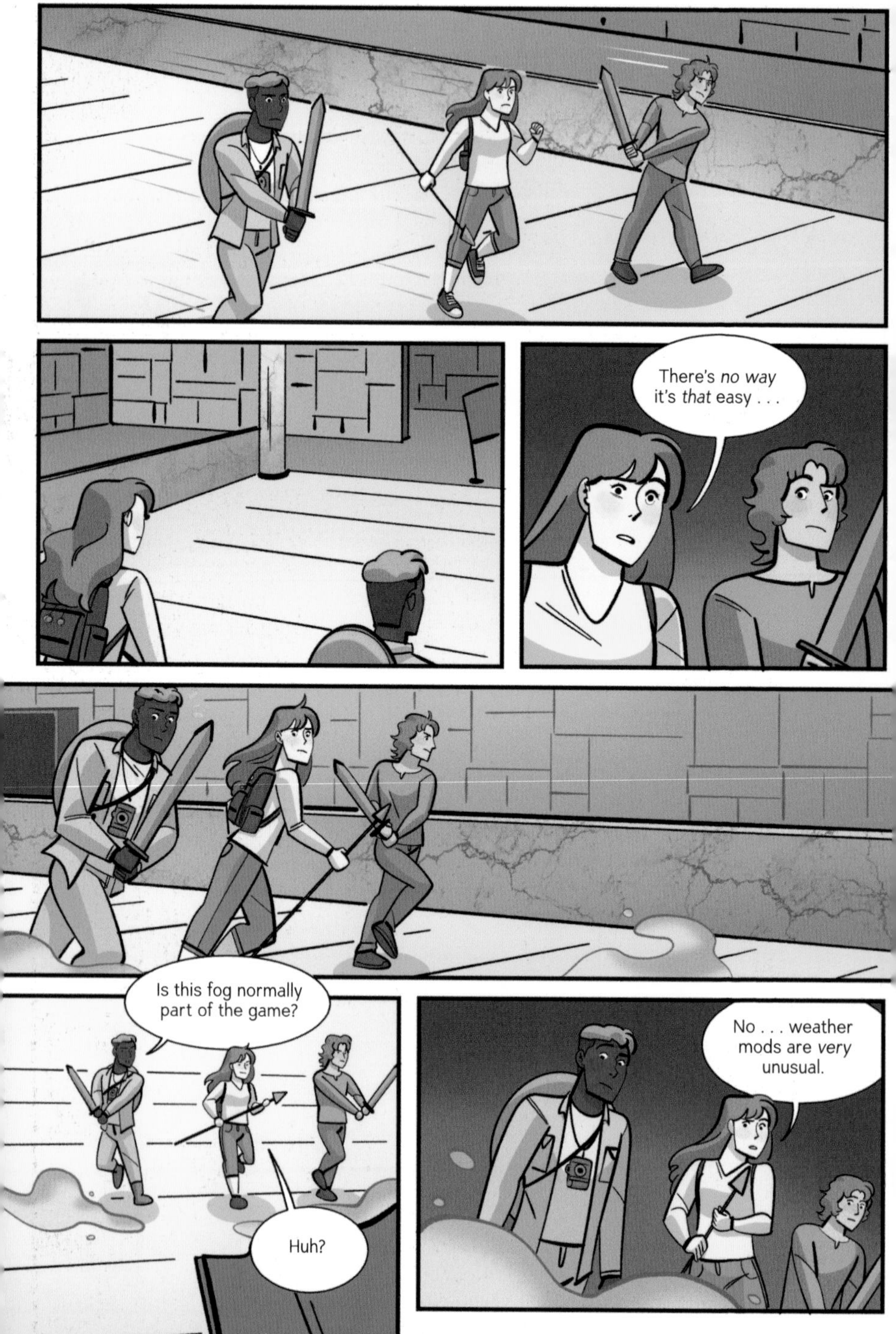
There's *no way* it's *that* easy . . .
Is this fog normally part of the game?
Huh?
No . . . weather mods are *very* unusual.

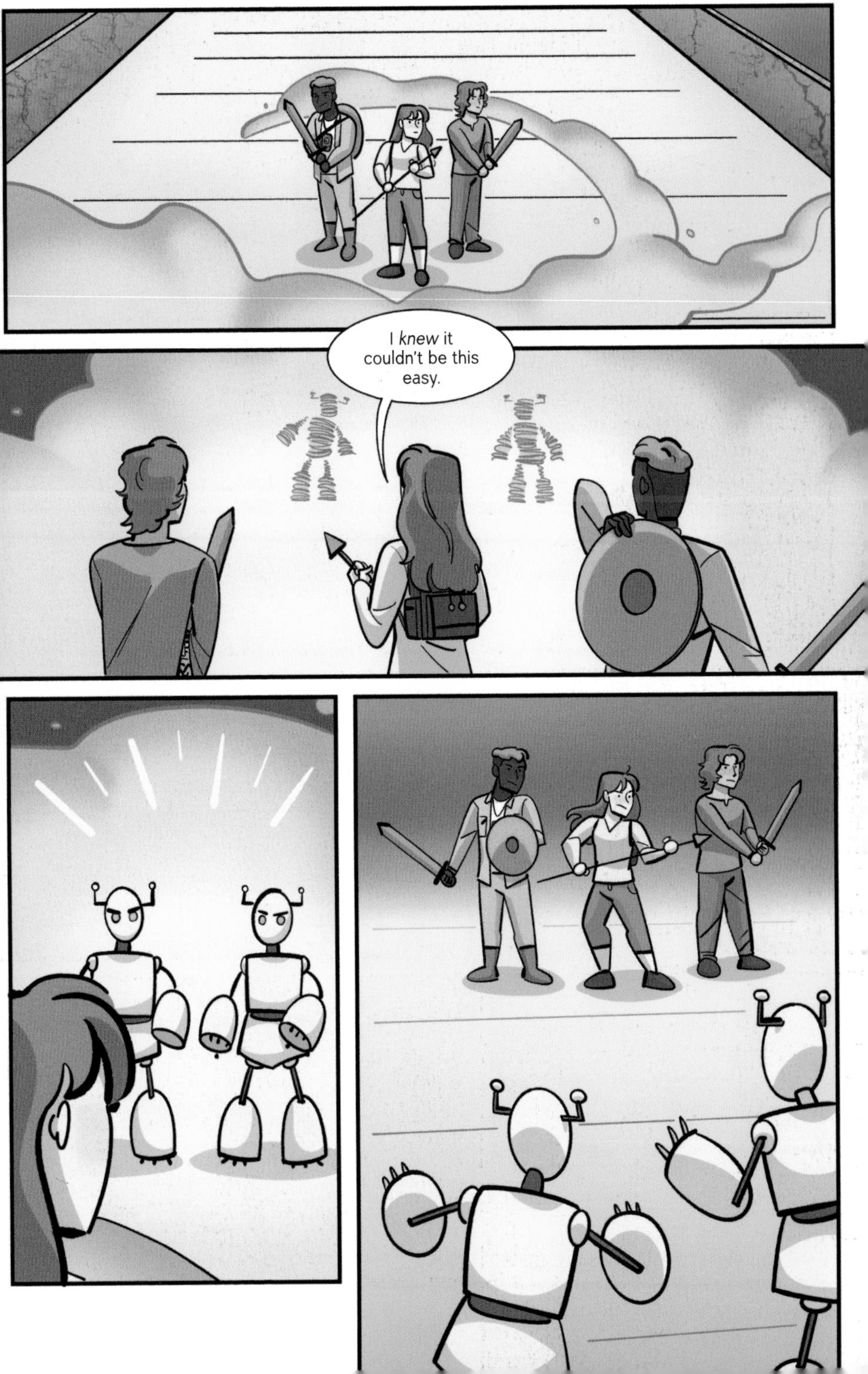
I *knew* it couldn't be this easy.

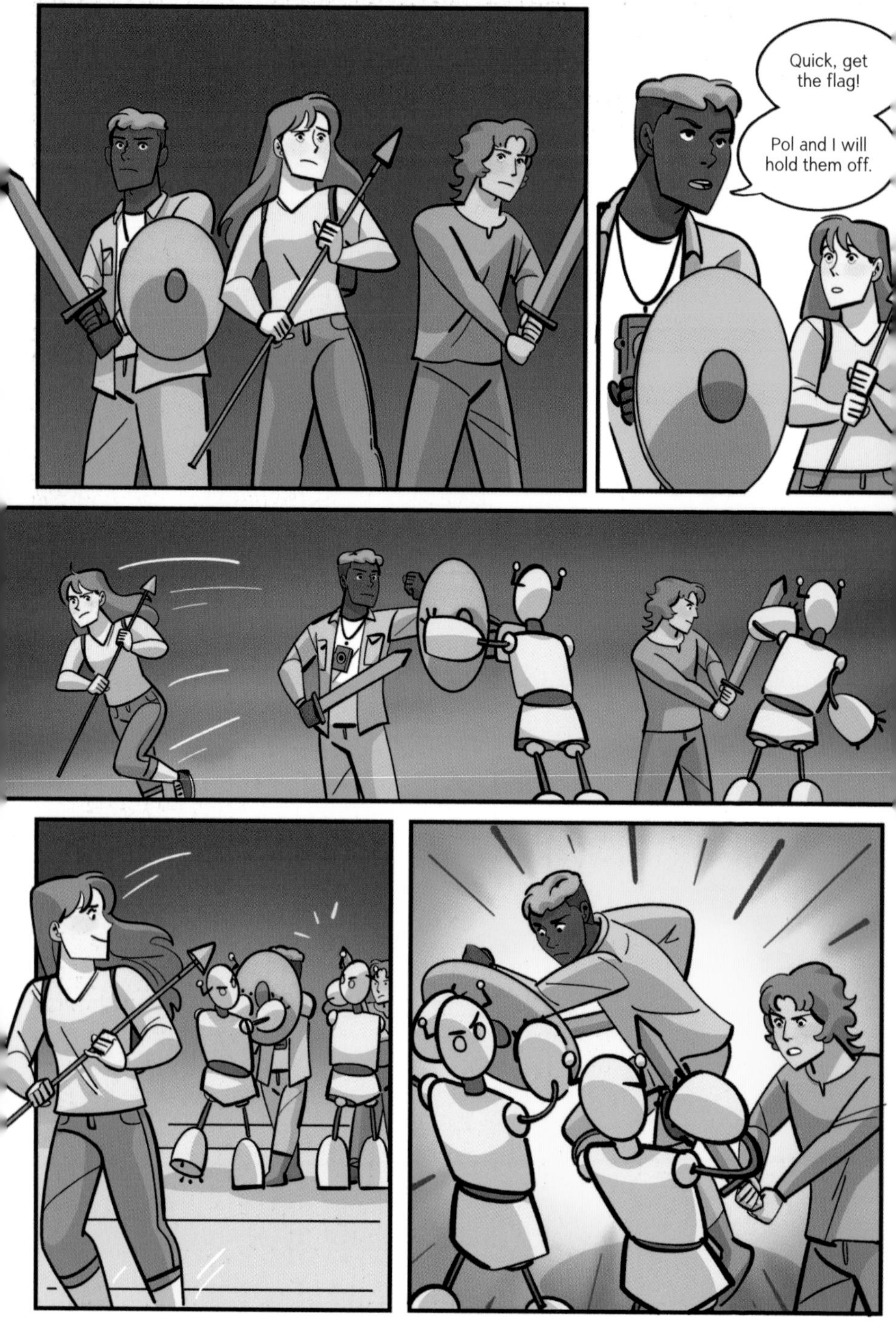
Quick, get the flag!
Pol and I will hold them off.

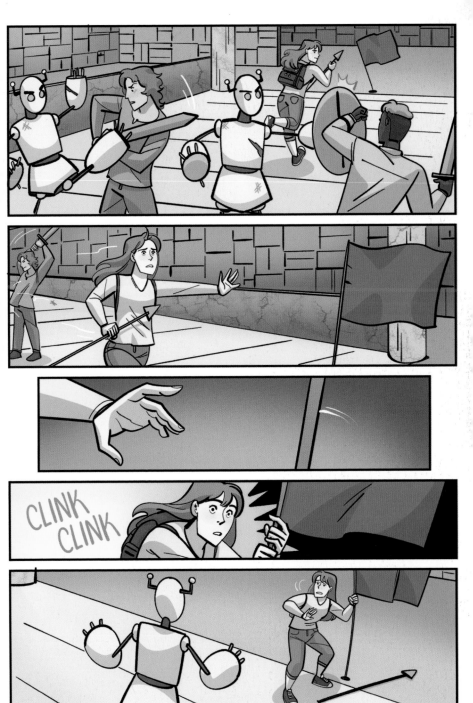

CLINK
CLINK

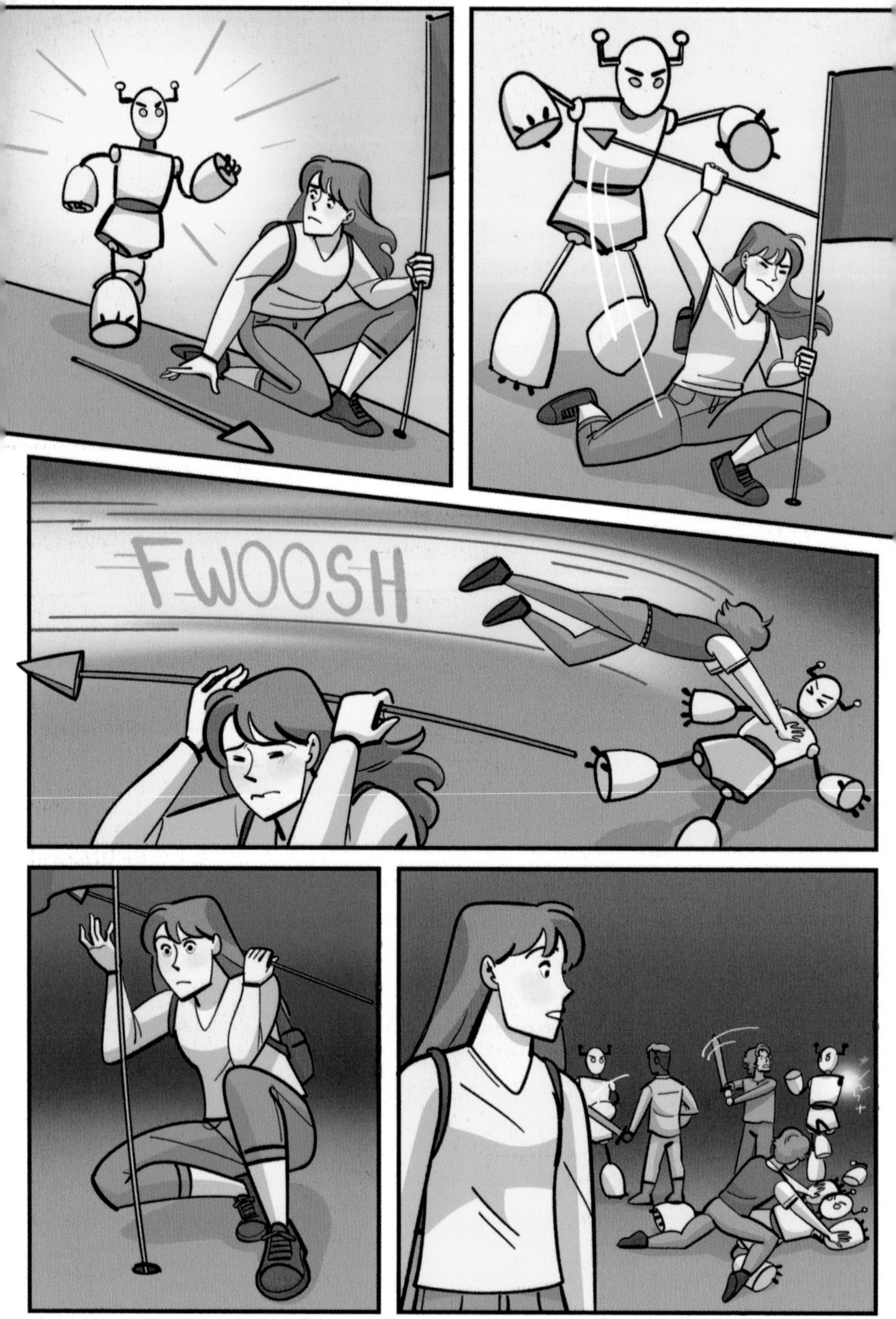
FWOOSH

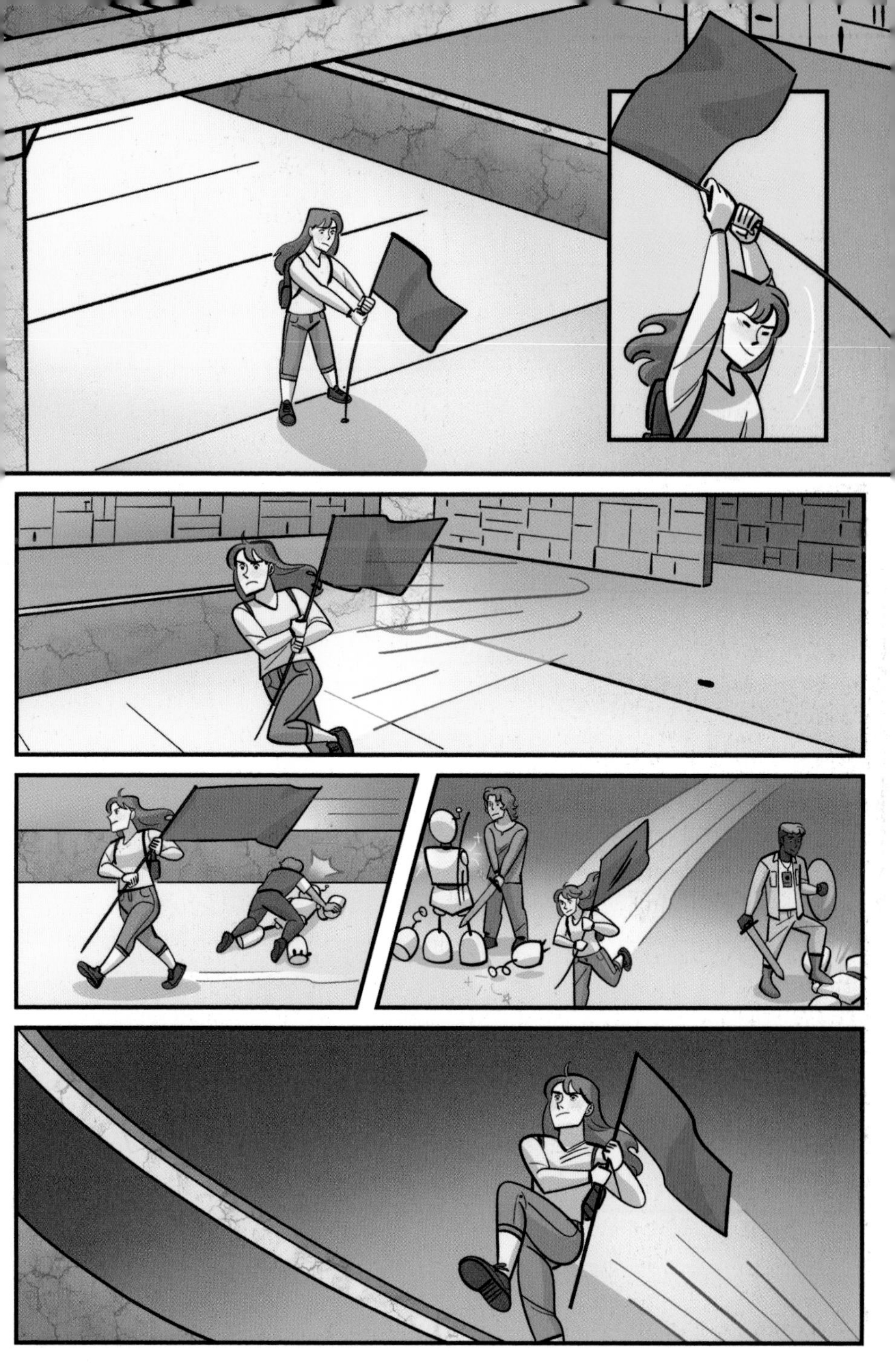

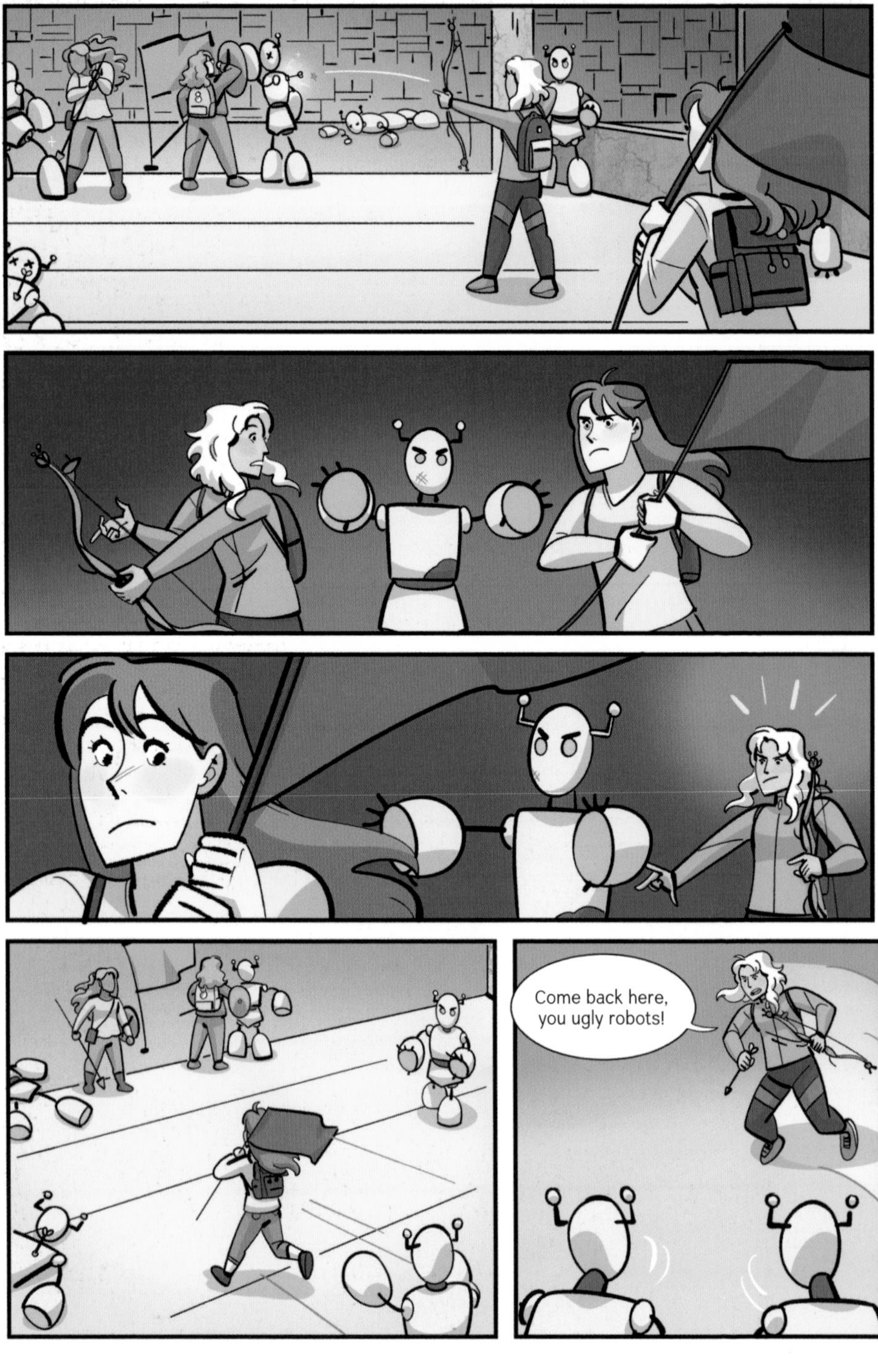
Come back here, you ugly robots!

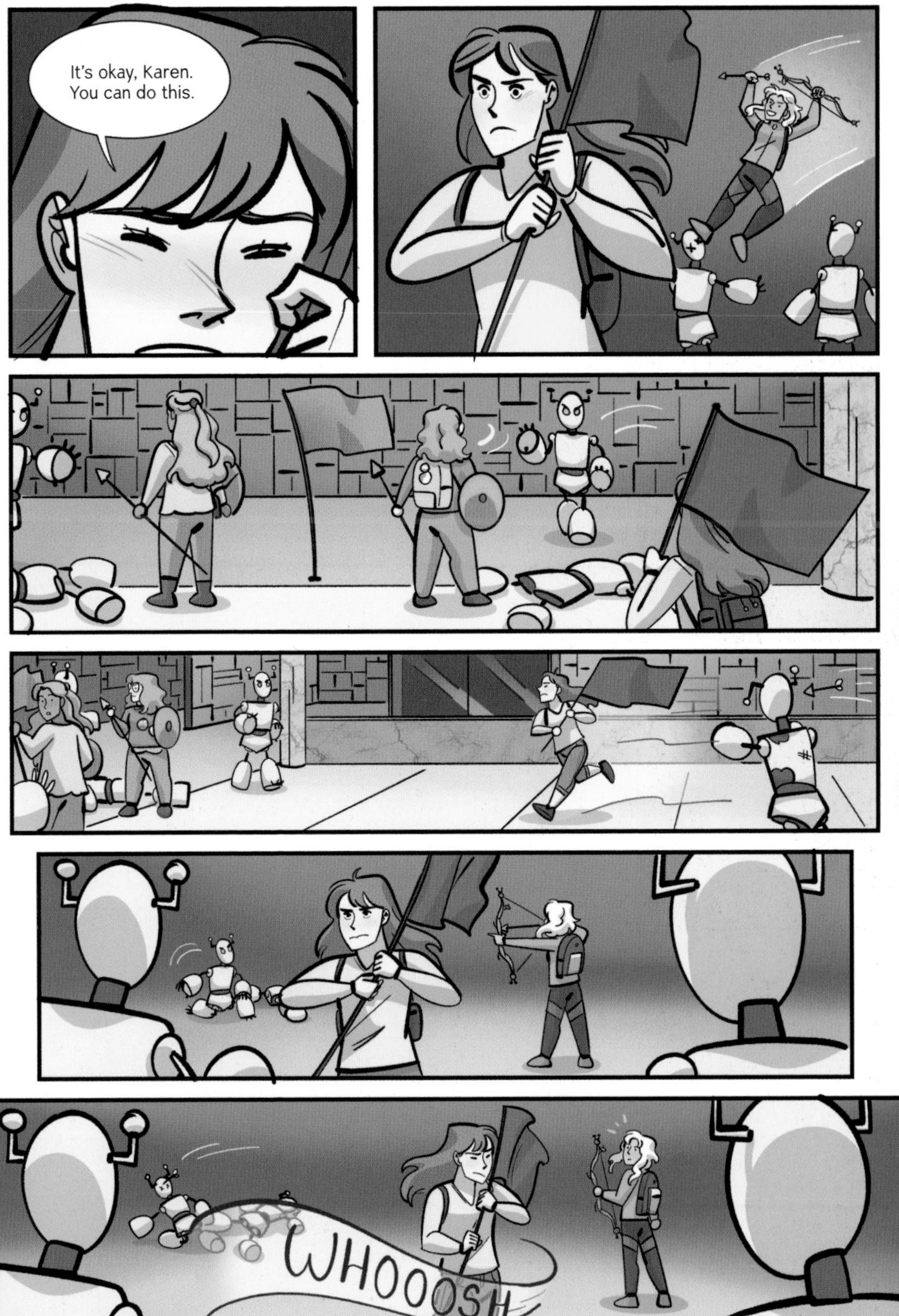
It's okay, Karen.
You can do this.
WHOOOOSH

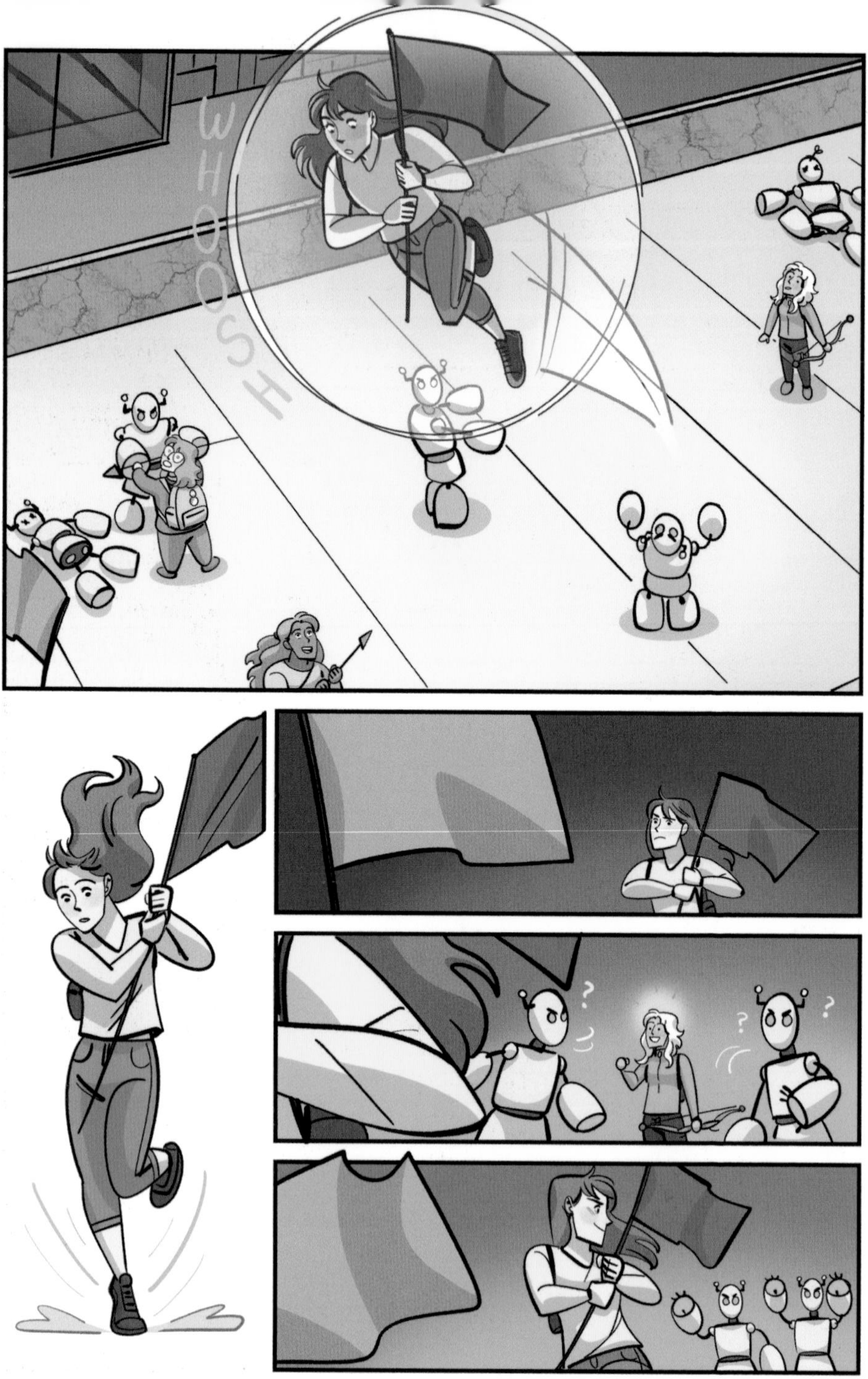
WHOOSH
?
? ?

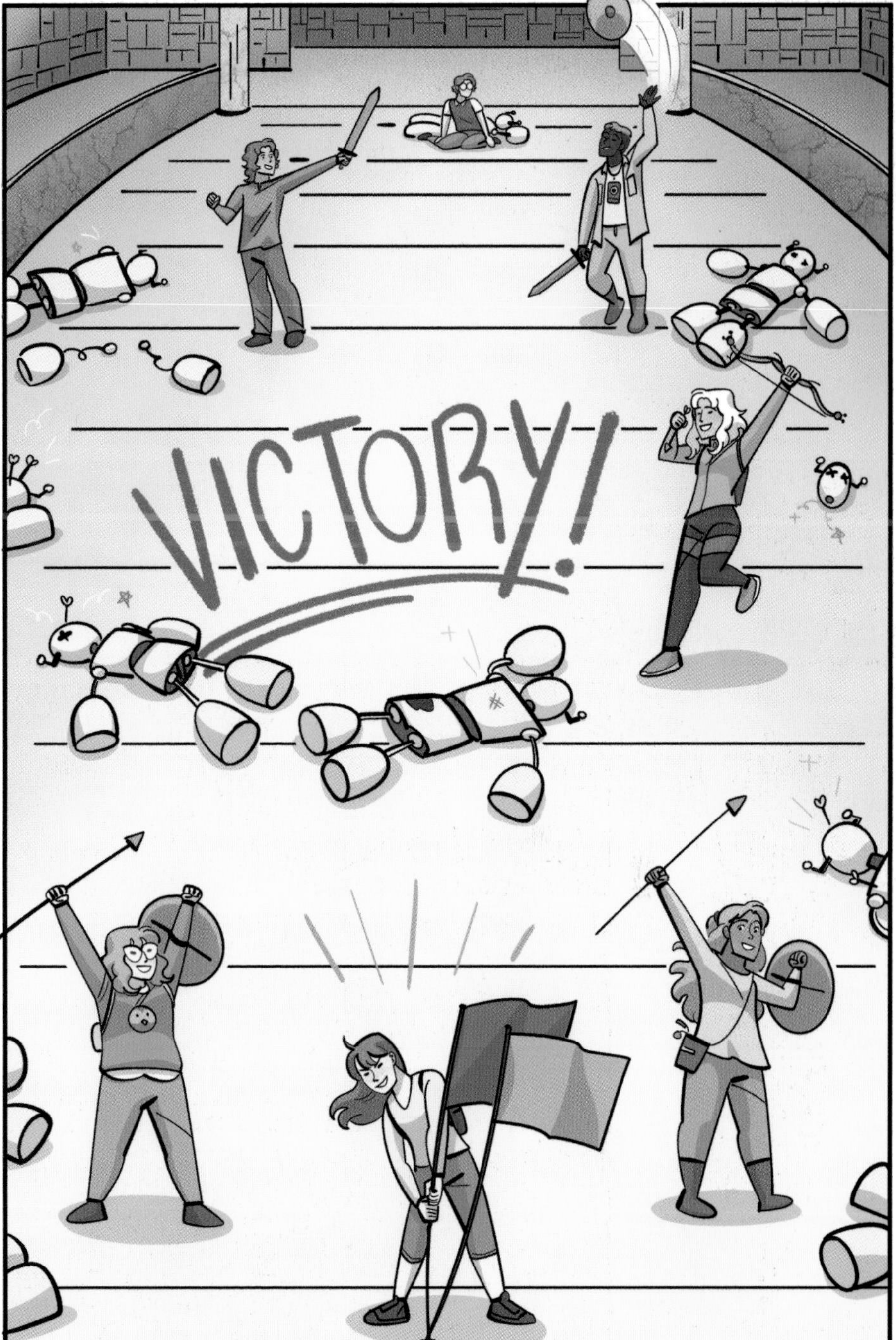
VICTORY!

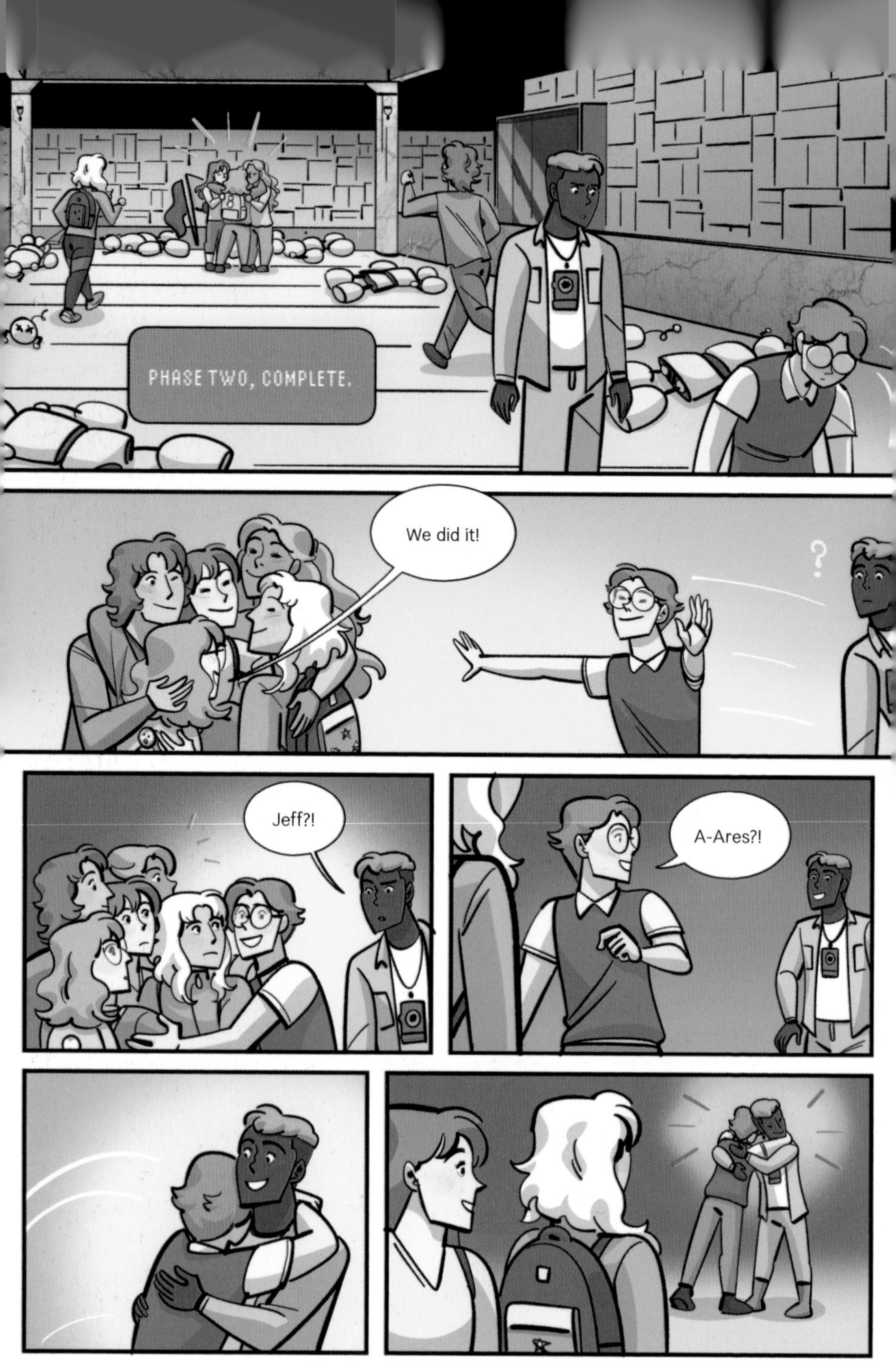
PHASE TWO, COMPLETE.
We did it!
?
Jeff?!
A-Ares?!

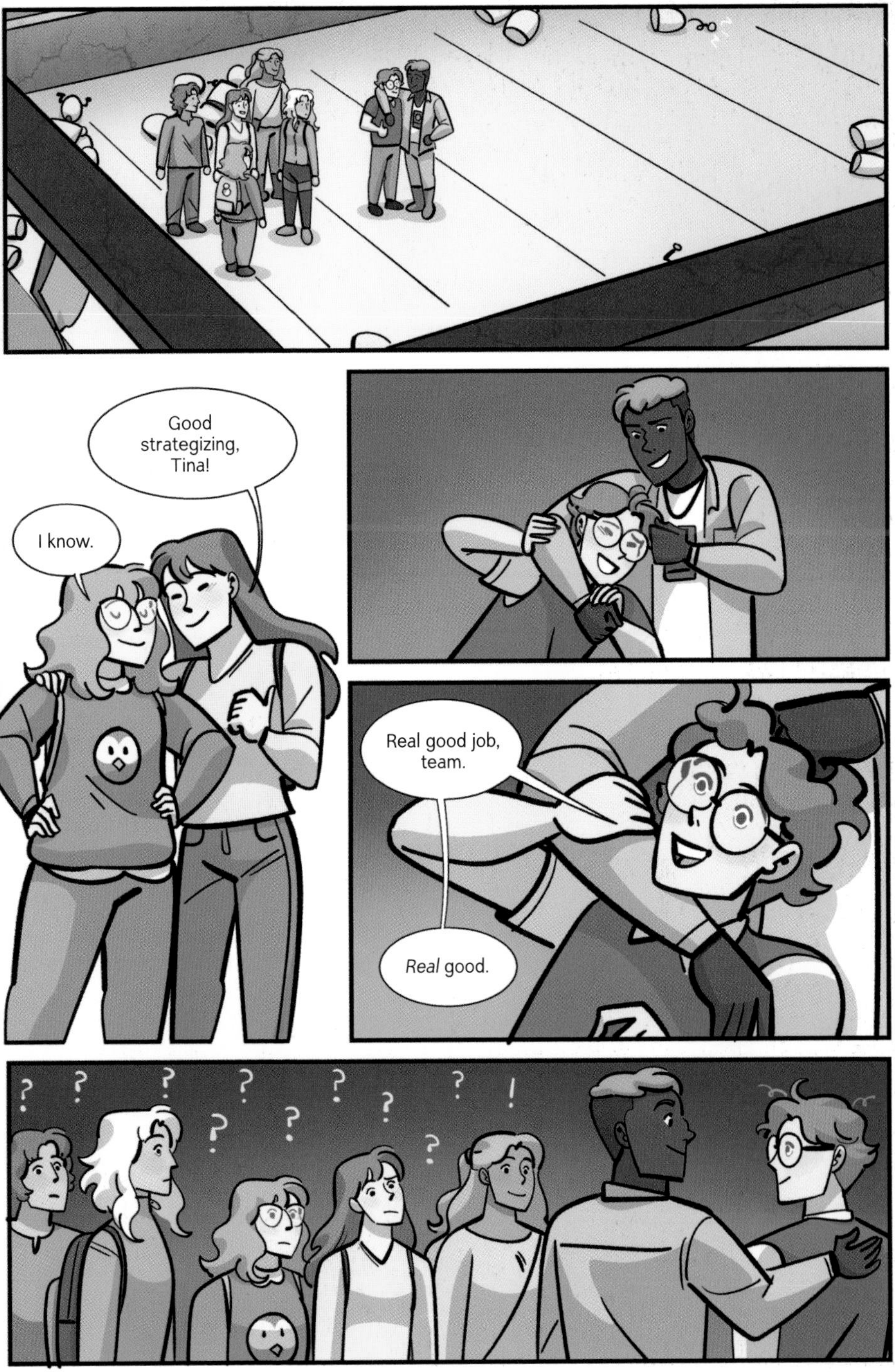
Good strategizing, Tina!
I know.
Real good job, team.
Real good.

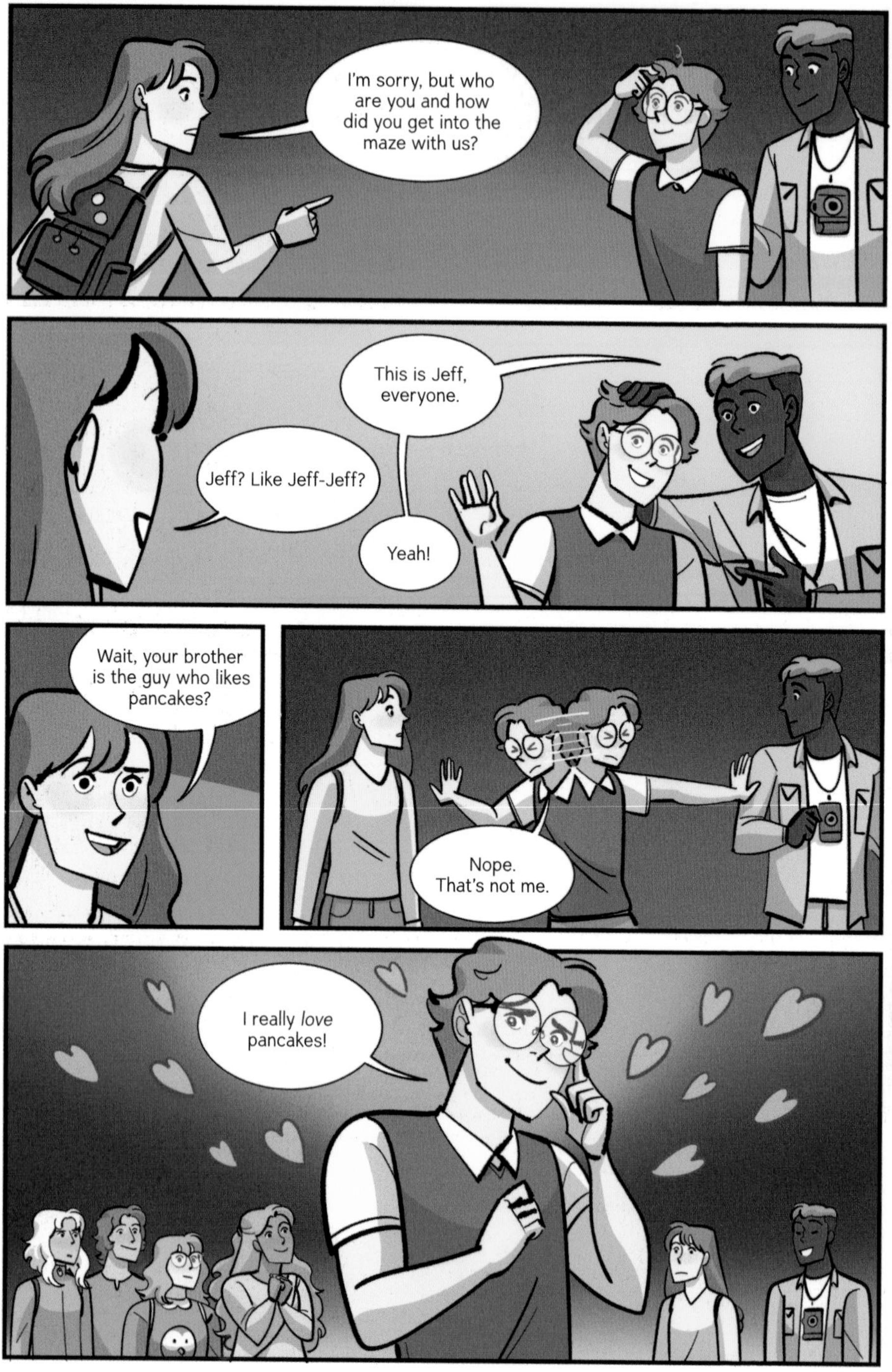
I'm sorry, but who are you and how did you get into the maze with us?
This is Jeff, everyone.
Jeff? Like Jeff-Jeff?
Yeah!
Wait, your brother is the guy who likes pancakes?
Nope. That's not me.
I really *love* pancakes!

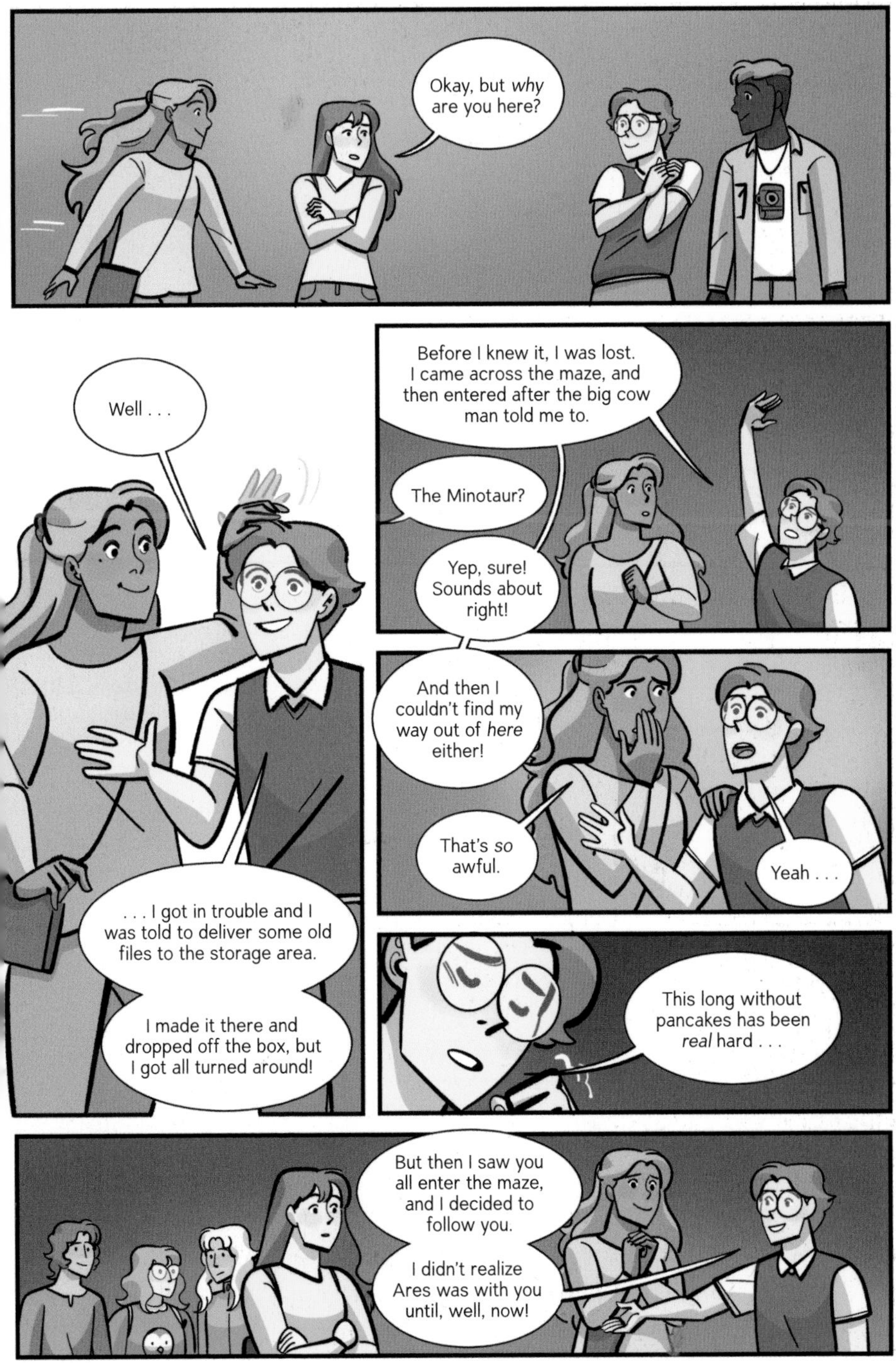

Okay, but *why* are you here?
Well . . .
. . . I got in trouble and I was told to deliver some old files to the storage area.
I made it there and dropped off the box, but I got all turned around!
Before I knew it, I was lost. I came across the maze, and then entered after the big cow man told me to.
The Minotaur?
Yep, sure! Sounds about right!
And then I couldn't find my way out of *here* either!
That's *so* awful.
Yeah . . .
This long without pancakes has been *real* hard . . .
But then I saw you all enter the maze, and I decided to follow you.
I didn't realize Ares was with you until, well, now!

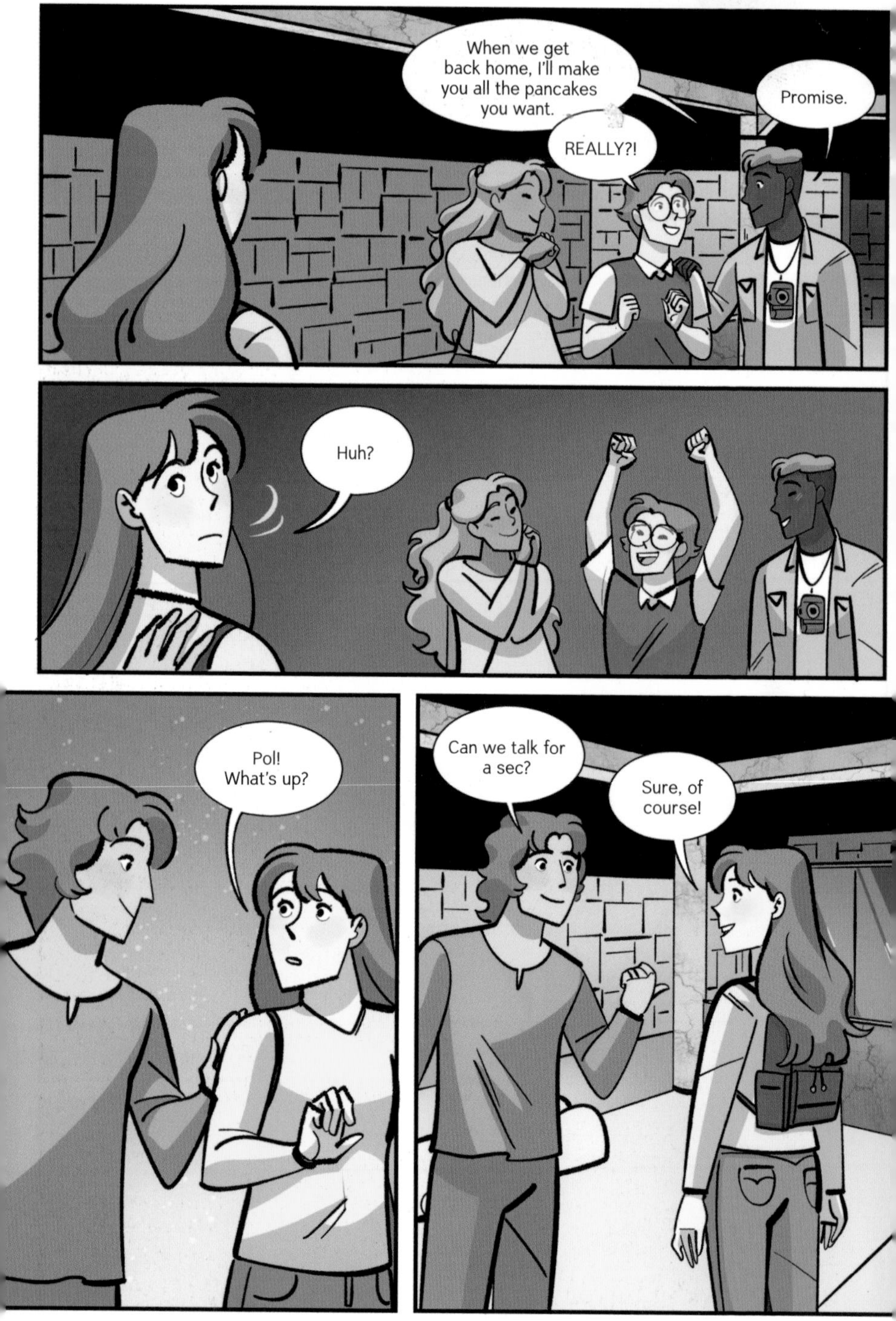
When we get back home, I'll make you all the pancakes you want.
REALLY?!
Promise.
Huh?
Pol! What's up?
Can we talk for a sec?
Sure, of course!

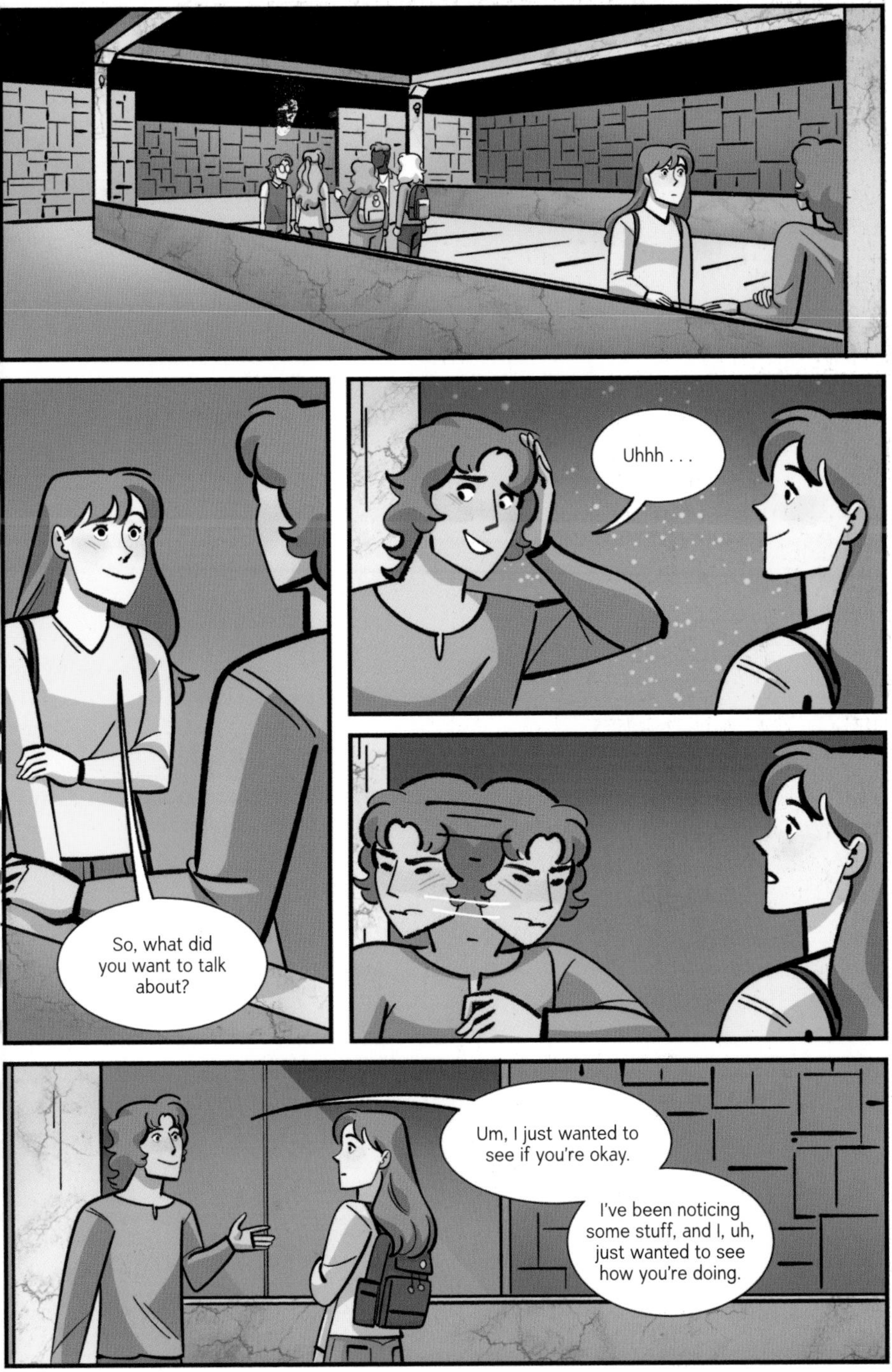
So, what did you want to talk about?
Uhhh . . .
Um, I just wanted to see if you're okay.
I've been noticing some stuff, and I, uh, just wanted to see how you're doing.

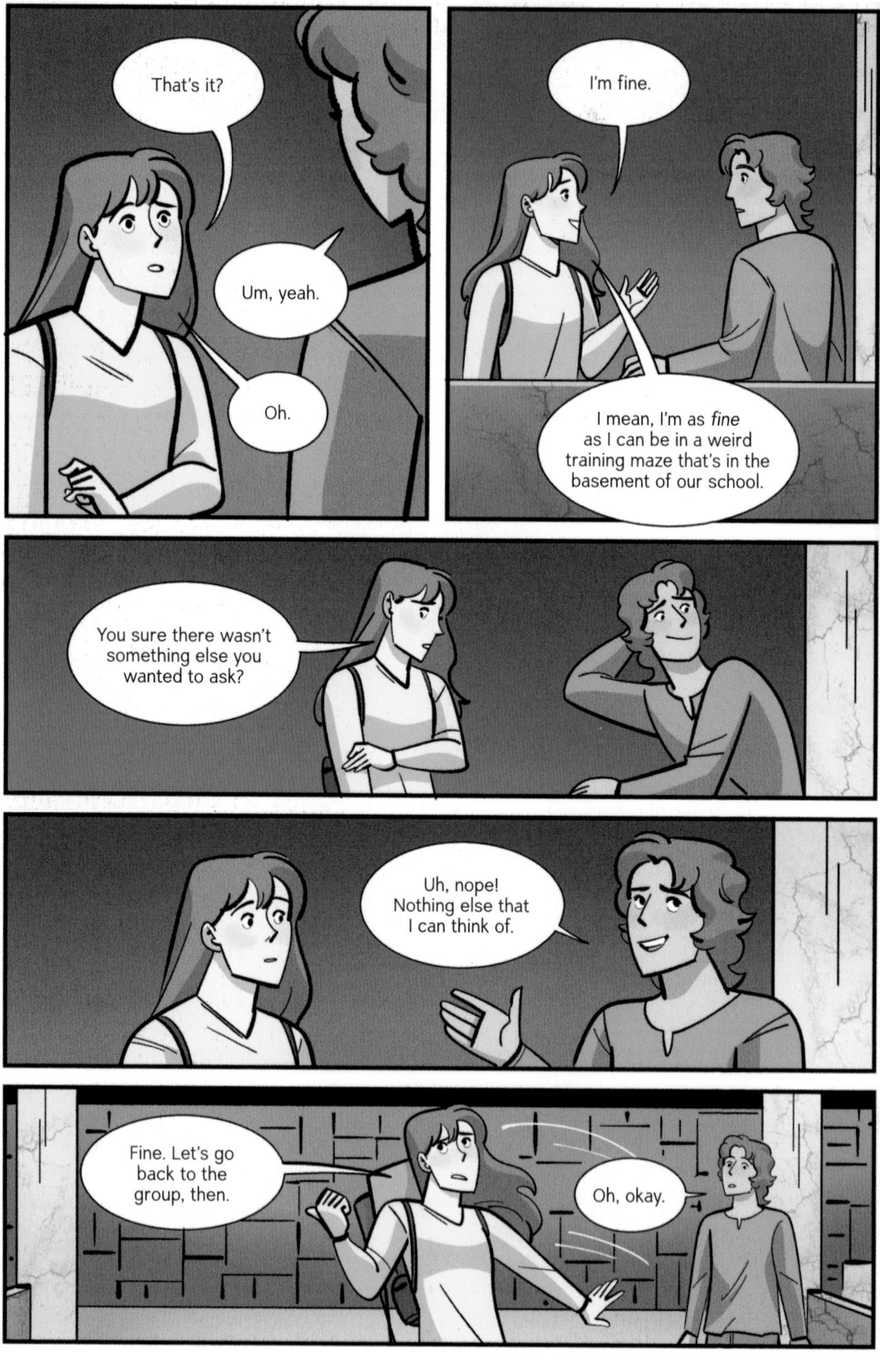
That's it?
Um, yeah.
Oh.
I'm fine.
I mean, I'm as *fine* as I can be in a weird training maze that's in the basement of our school.
You sure there wasn't something else you wanted to ask?
Uh, nope! Nothing else that I can think of.
Fine. Let's go back to the group, then.
Oh, okay.

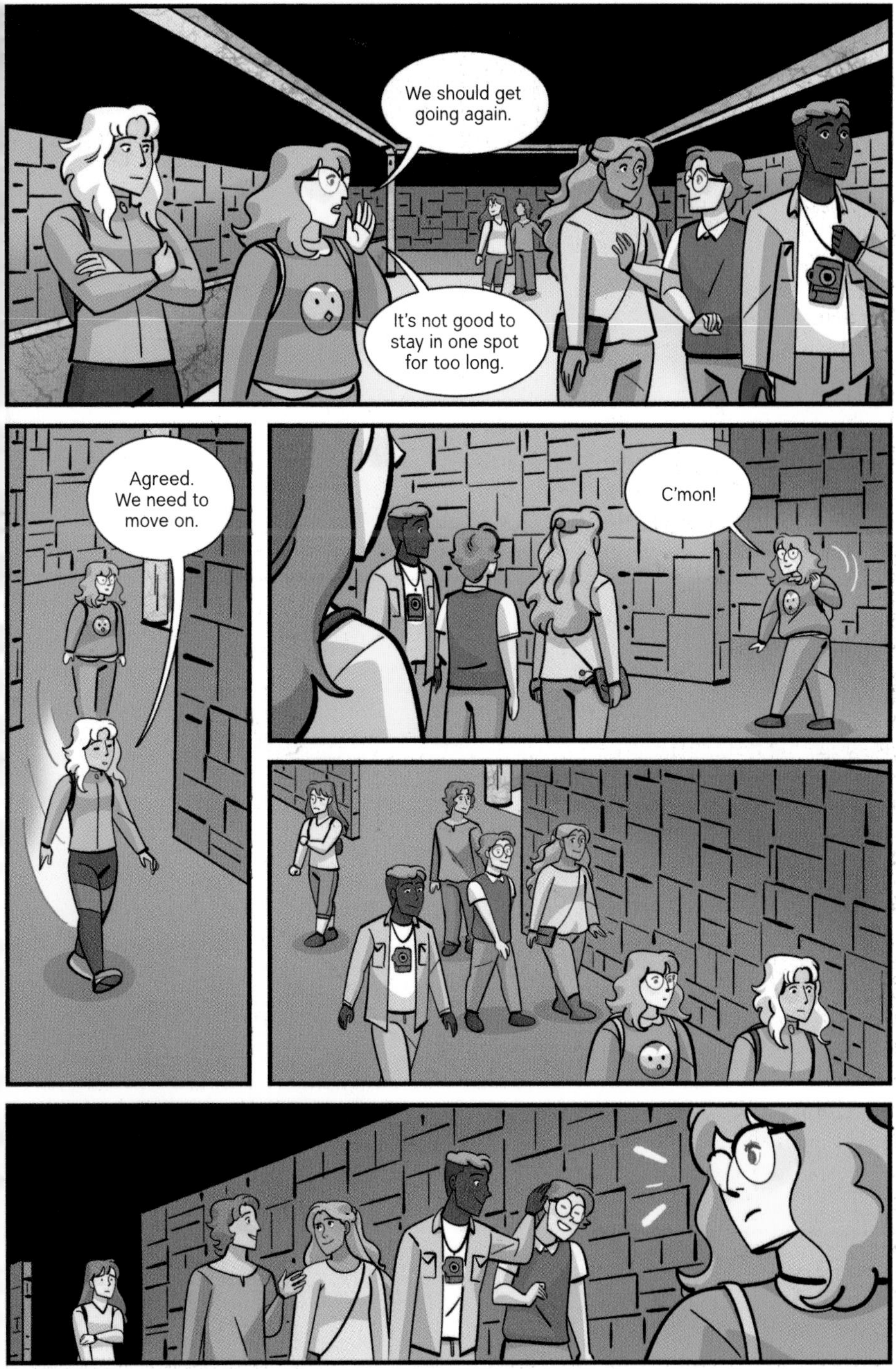
We should get going again.
It's not good to stay in one spot for too long.
Agreed. We need to move on.
C'mon!

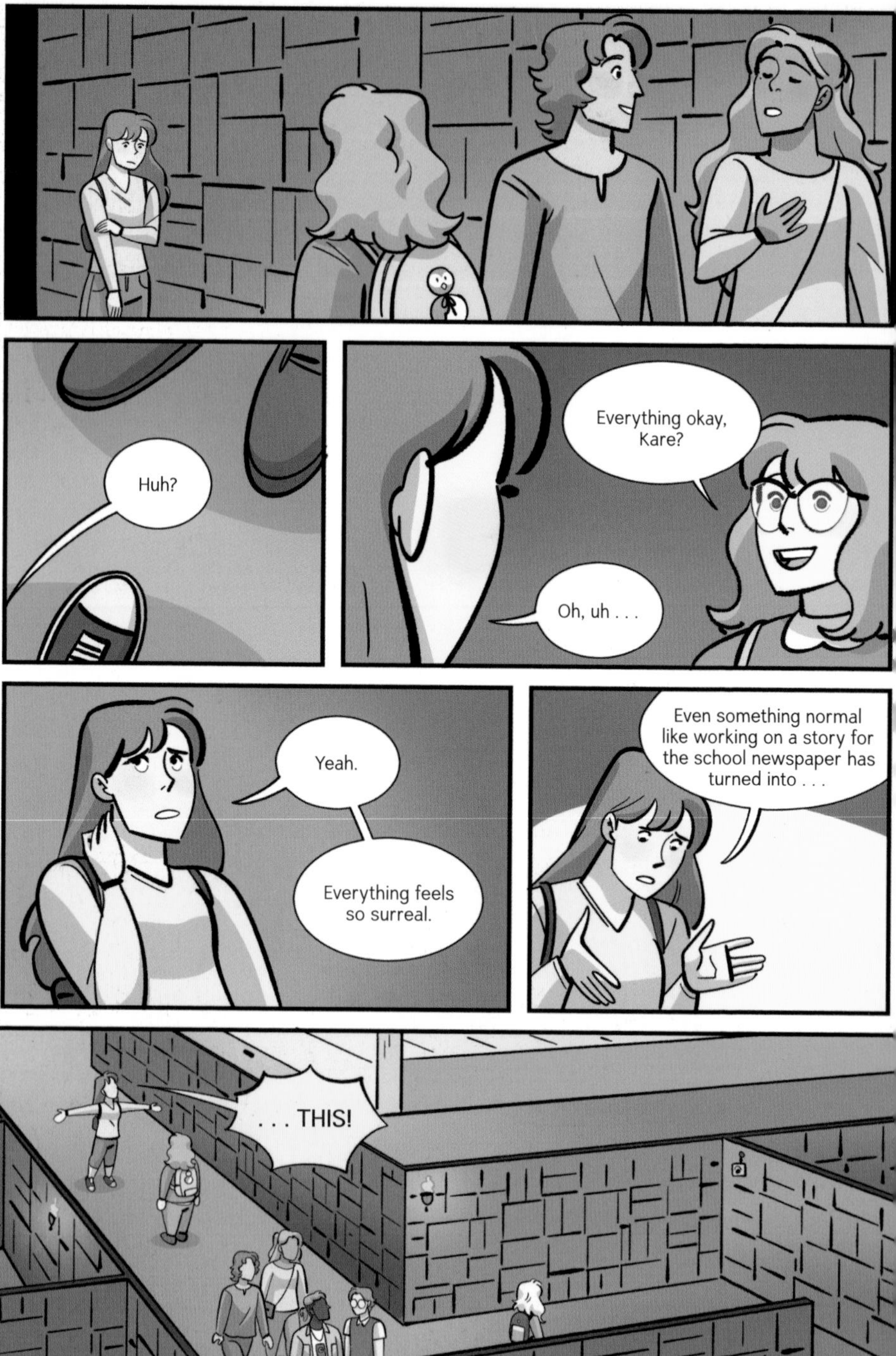
Huh?
Everything okay, Kare?
Oh, uh . . .
Yeah.
Everything feels so surreal.
Even something normal like working on a story for the school newspaper has turned into . . .
. . . THIS!

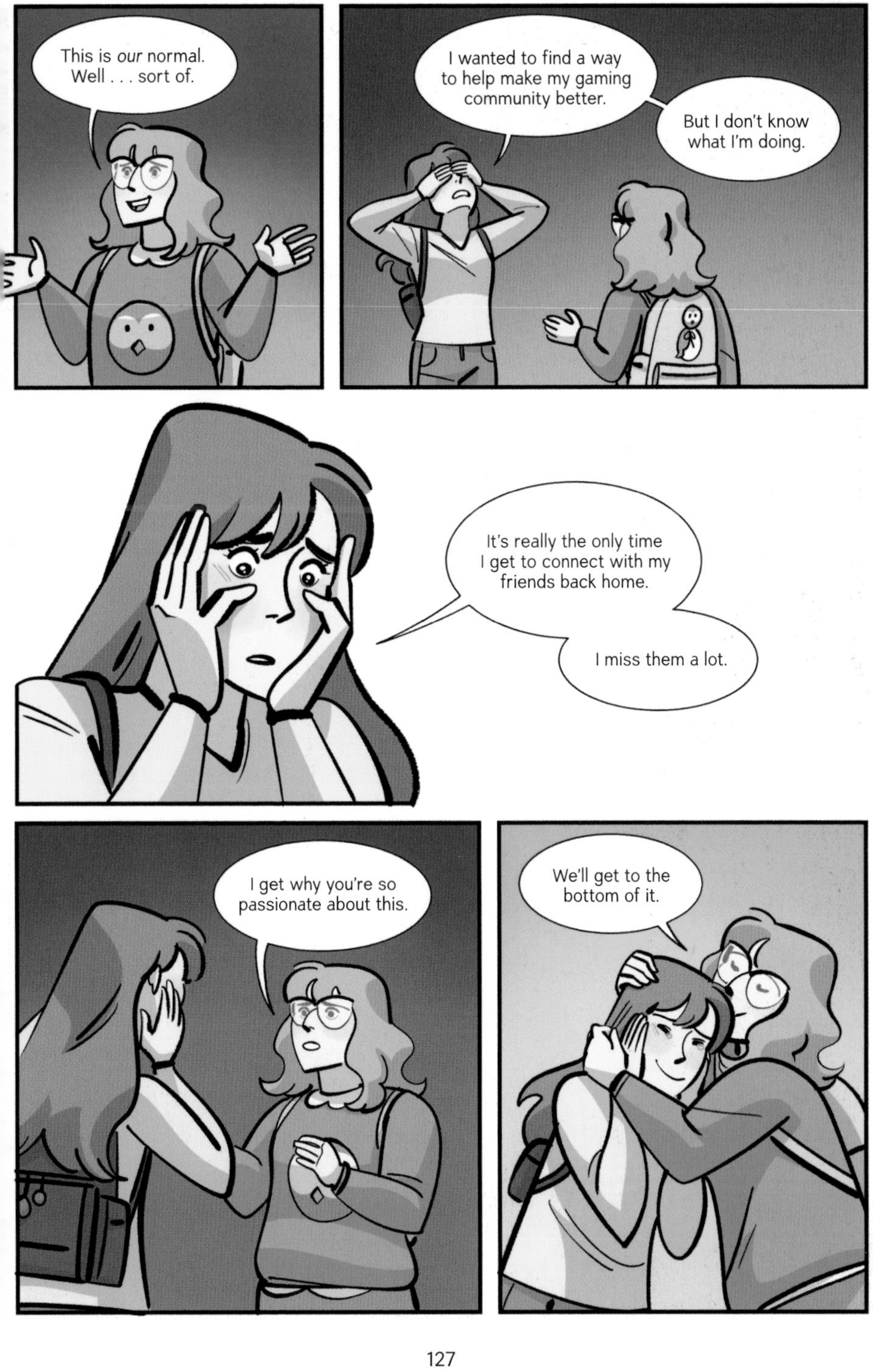
This is *our* normal.
Well . . . sort of.
I wanted to find a way to help make my gaming community better.
But I don't know what I'm doing.
It's really the only time I get to connect with my friends back home.
I miss them a lot.
I get why you're so passionate about this.
We'll get to the bottom of it.

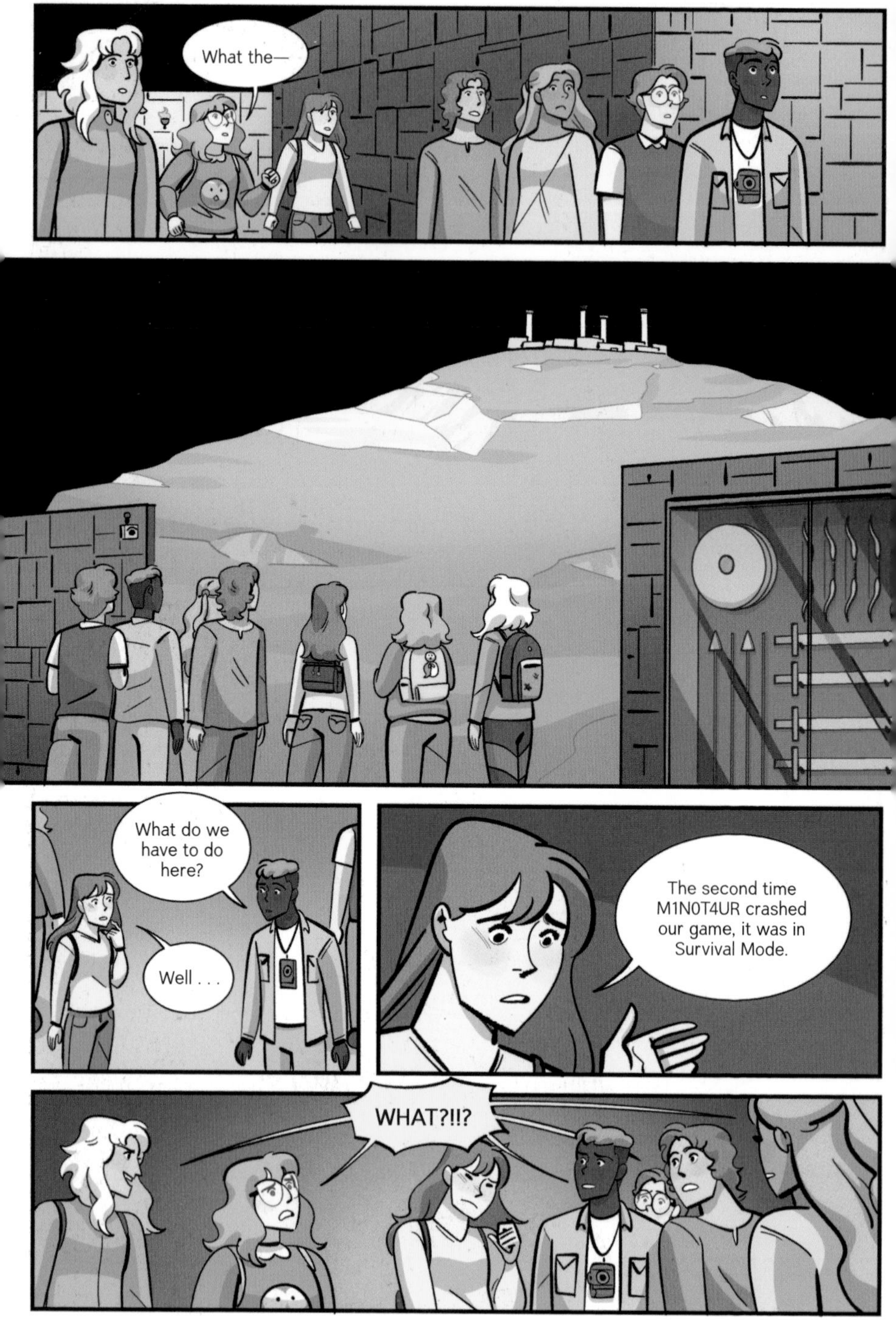
What the—
What do we have to do here?
Well . . .
The second time M1N0T4UR crashed our game, it was in Survival Mode.
WHAT?!!?

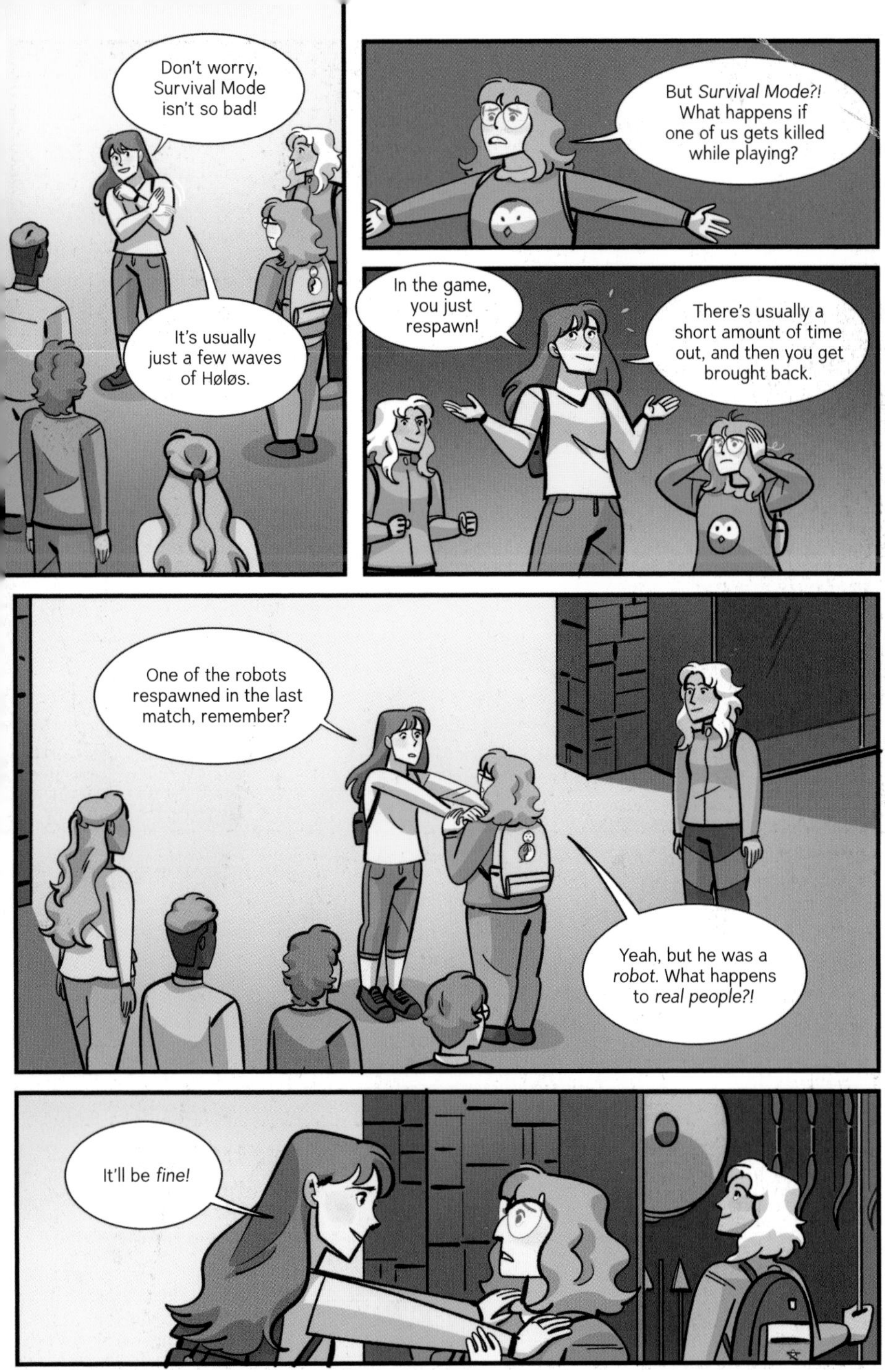
Don't worry, Survival Mode isn't so bad!
It's usually just a few waves of Høløs.
But *Survival Mode?!* What happens if one of us gets killed while playing?
In the game, you just respawn!
There's usually a short amount of time out, and then you get brought back.
One of the robots respawned in the last match, remember?
Yeah, but he was a *robot*. What happens to *real people?!*
It'll be *fine!*

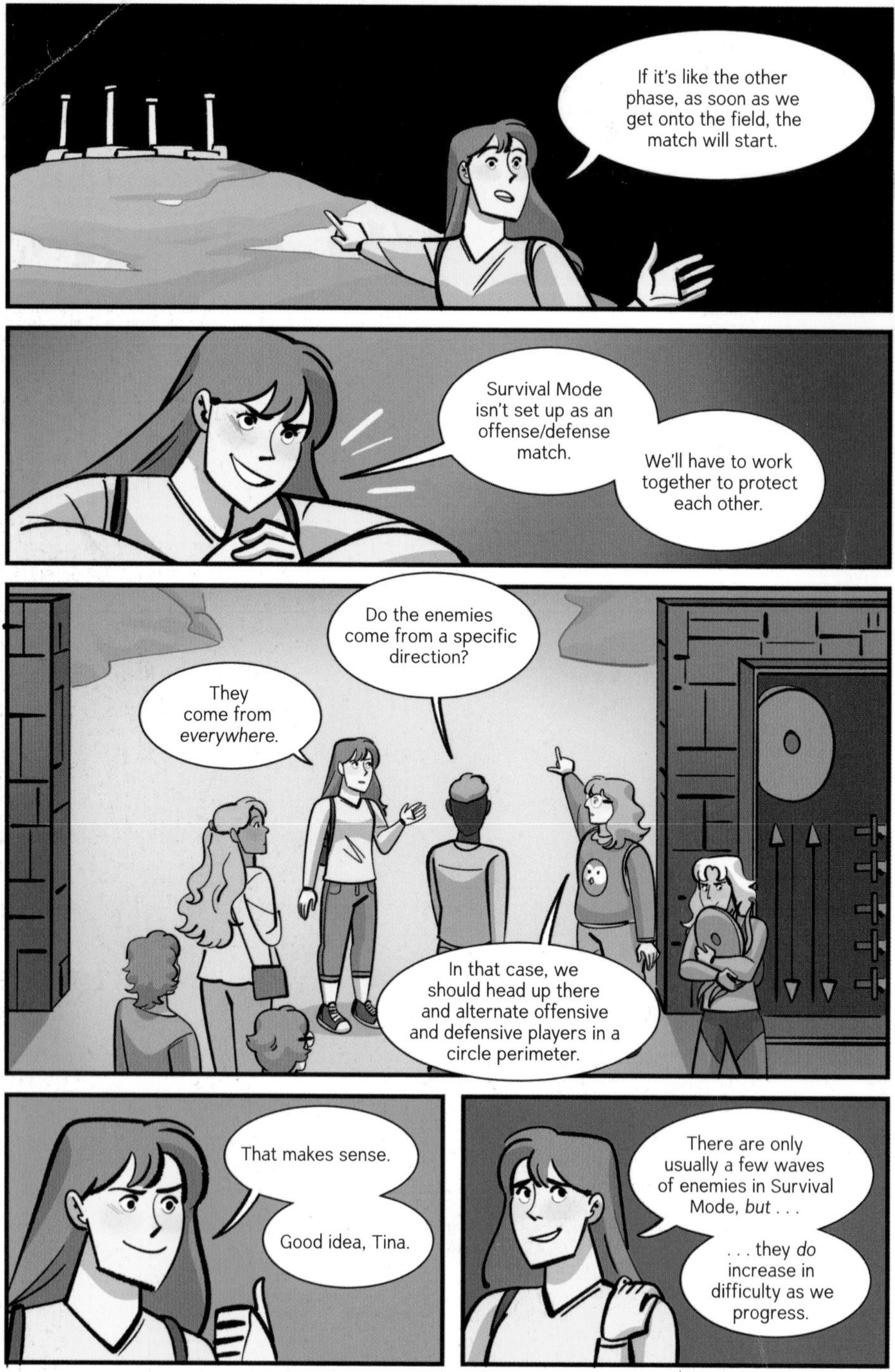
If it's like the other phase, as soon as we get onto the field, the match will start.
Survival Mode isn't set up as an offense/defense match.
We'll have to work together to protect each other.
Do the enemies come from a specific direction?
They come from *everywhere.*
In that case, we should head up there and alternate offensive and defensive players in a circle perimeter.
That makes sense.
Good idea, Tina.
There are only usually a few waves of enemies in Survival Mode, *but* . . .
. . . they *do* increase in difficulty as we progress.

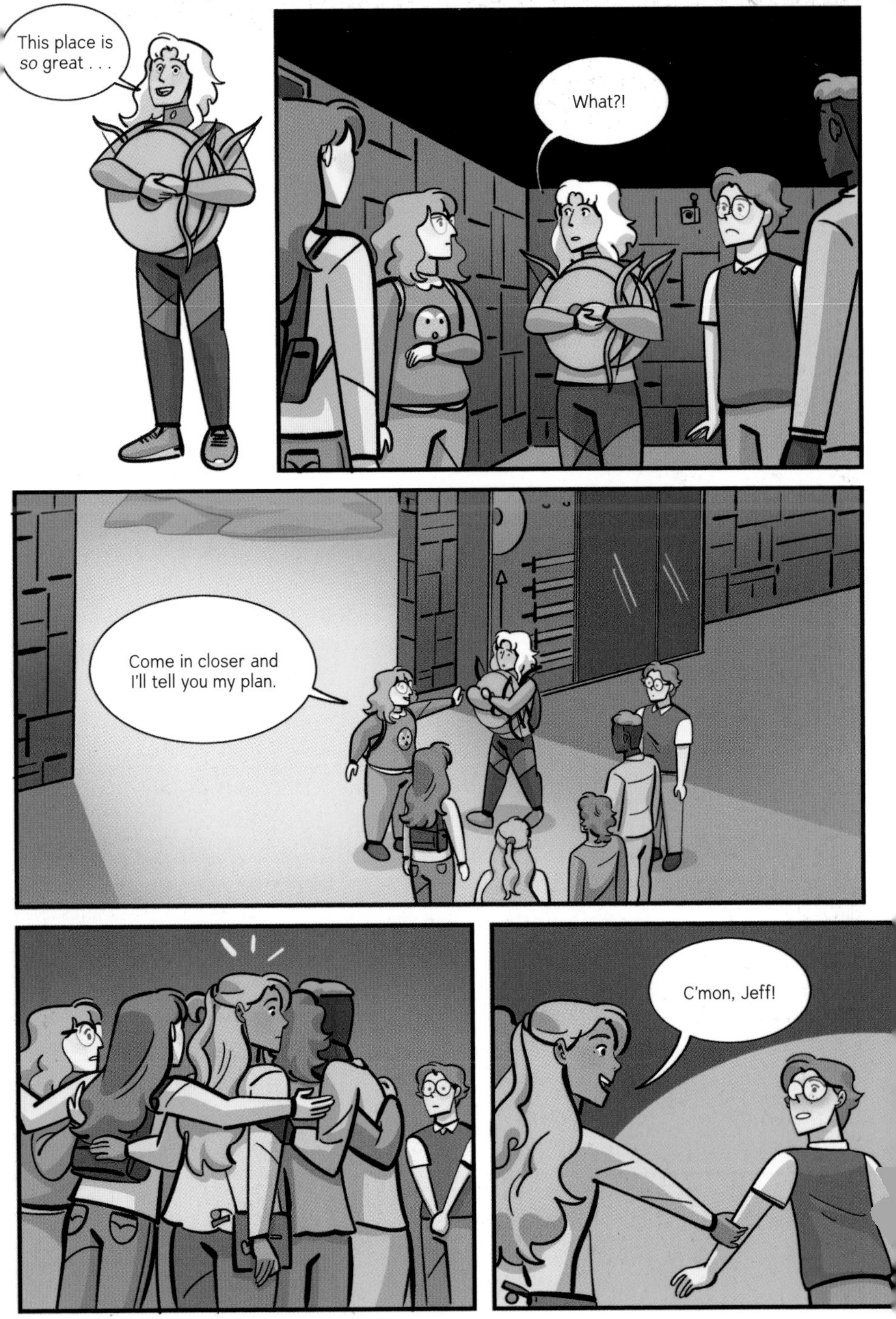
This place is *so* great . . .
What?!
Come in closer and I'll tell you my plan.
C'mon, Jeff!

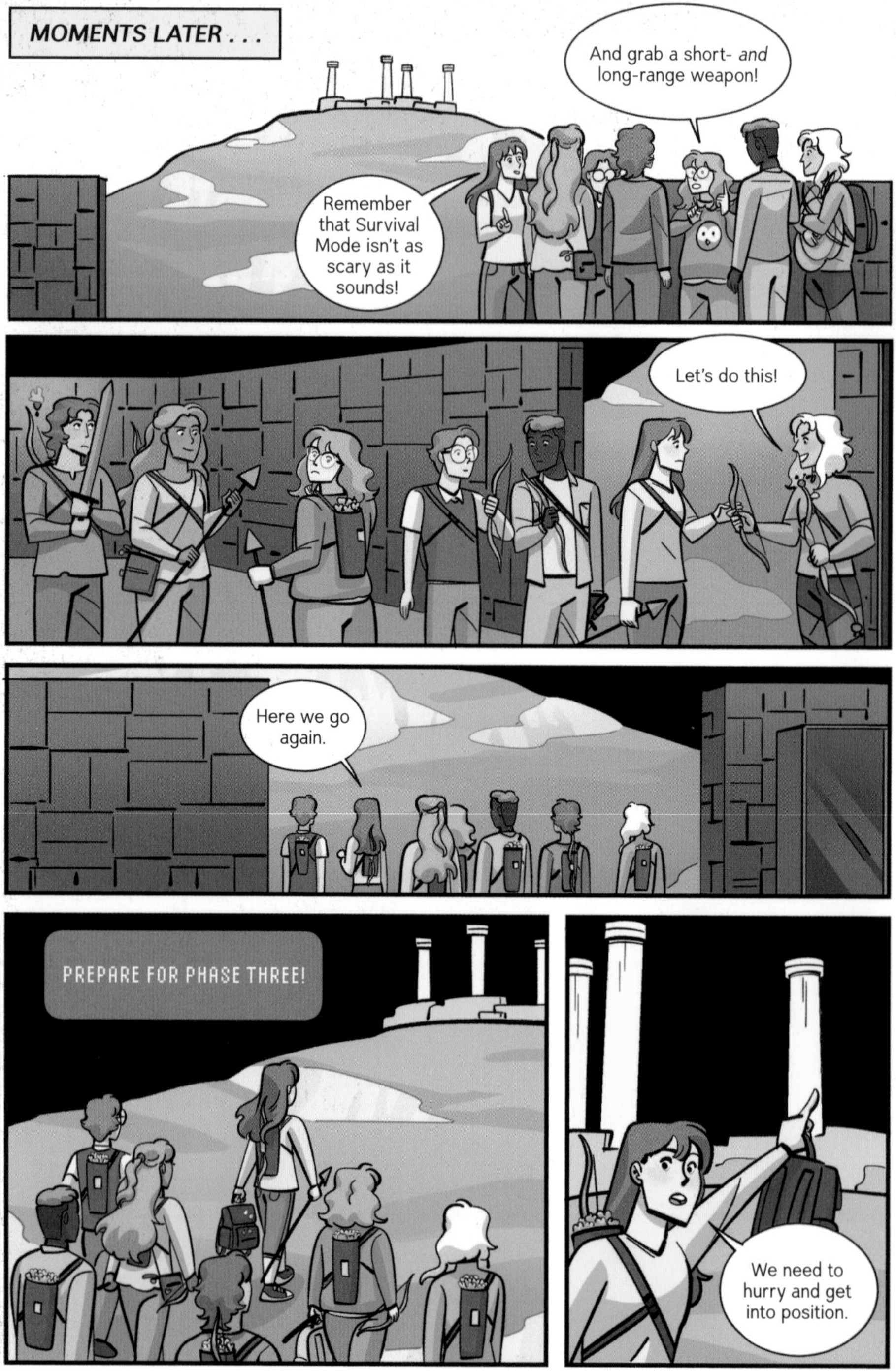
MOMENTS LATER . . .
Remember that Survival Mode isn't as scary as it sounds!
And grab a short- *and* long-range weapon!
Let's do this!
Here we go again.
PREPARE FOR PHASE THREE!
We need to hurry and get into position.

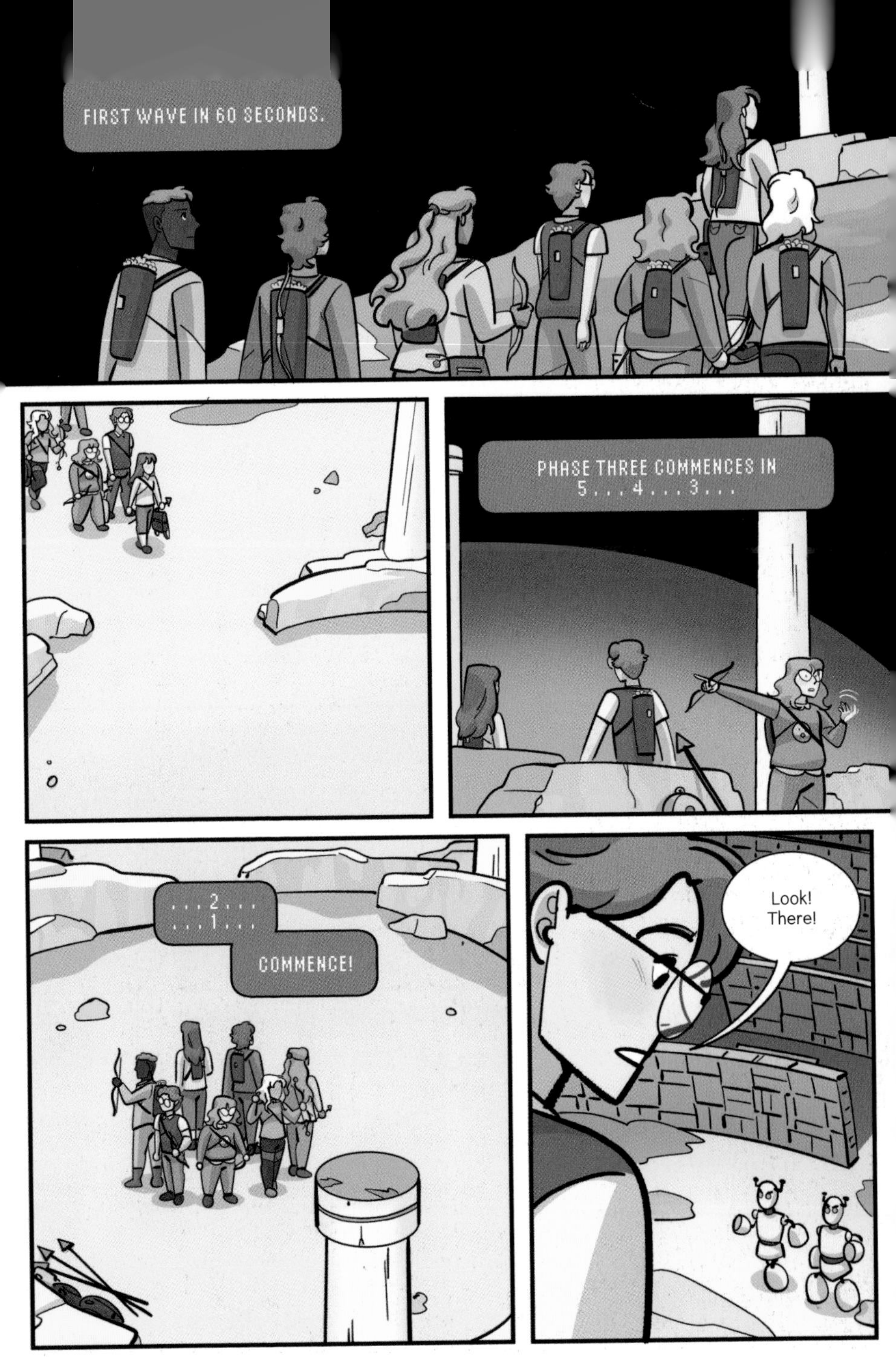
FIRST WAVE IN 60 SECONDS.
PHASE THREE COMMENCES IN 5 . . . 4 . . . 3 . . .
. . . 2 . . .
. . . 1 . . .
COMMENCE!
Look! There!

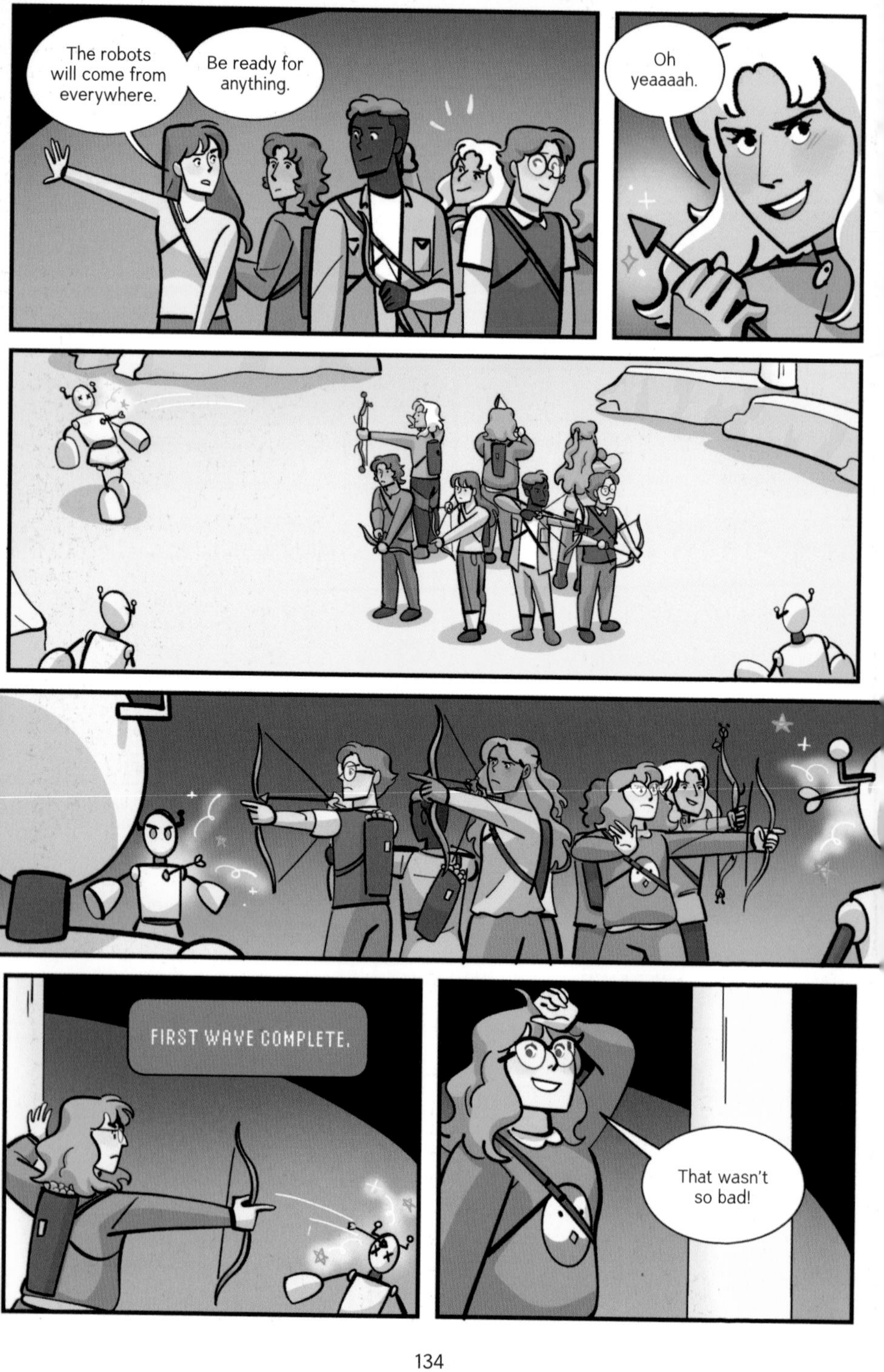

The robots will come from everywhere.
Be ready for anything.
Oh yeaaaah.
FIRST WAVE COMPLETE.
That wasn't so bad!

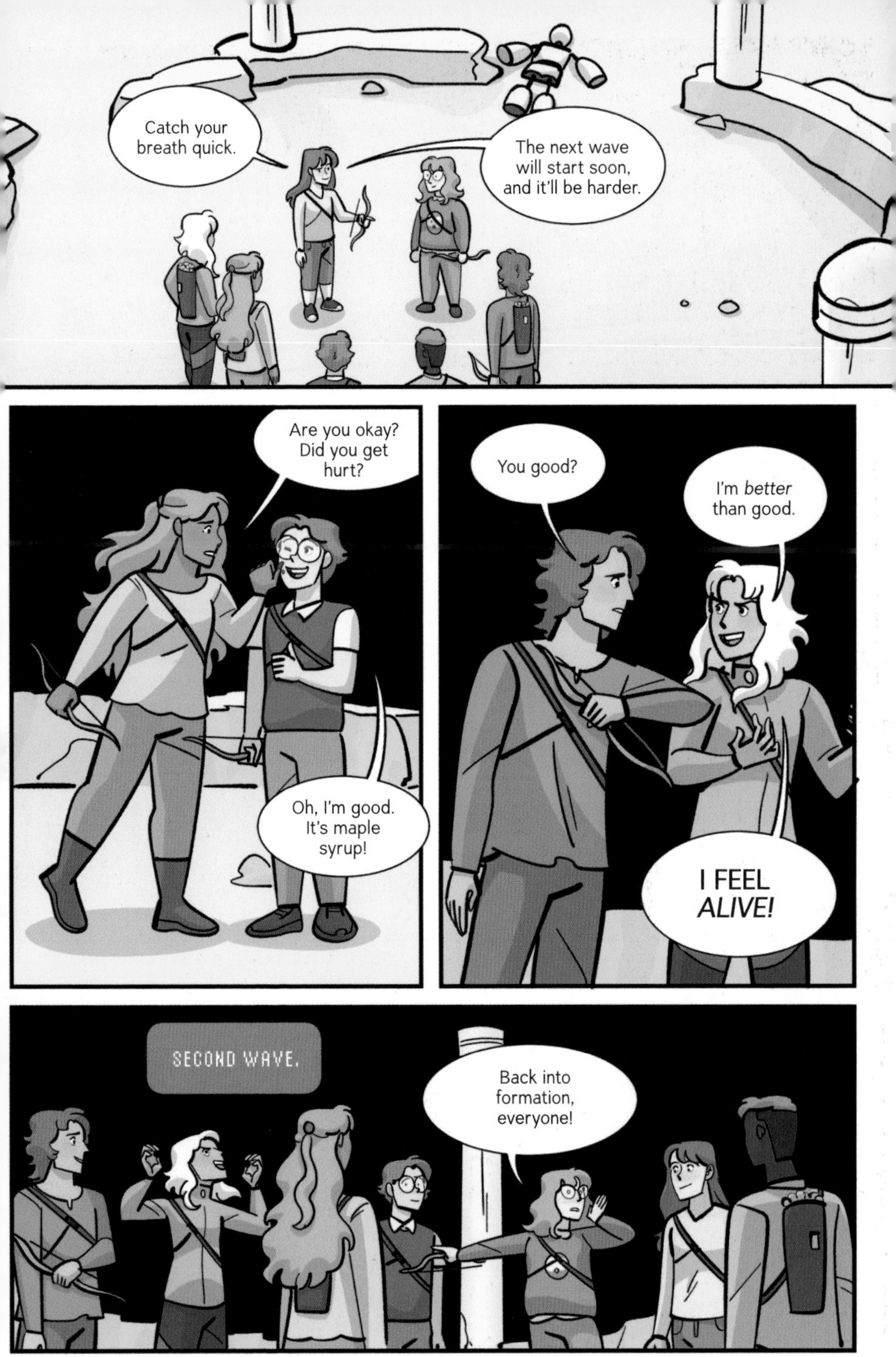
Catch your breath quick.
The next wave will start soon, and it'll be harder.
Are you okay? Did you get hurt?
Oh, I'm good. It's maple syrup!
You good?
I'm *better* than good.
I FEEL *ALIVE!*
SECOND WAVE.
Back into formation, everyone!

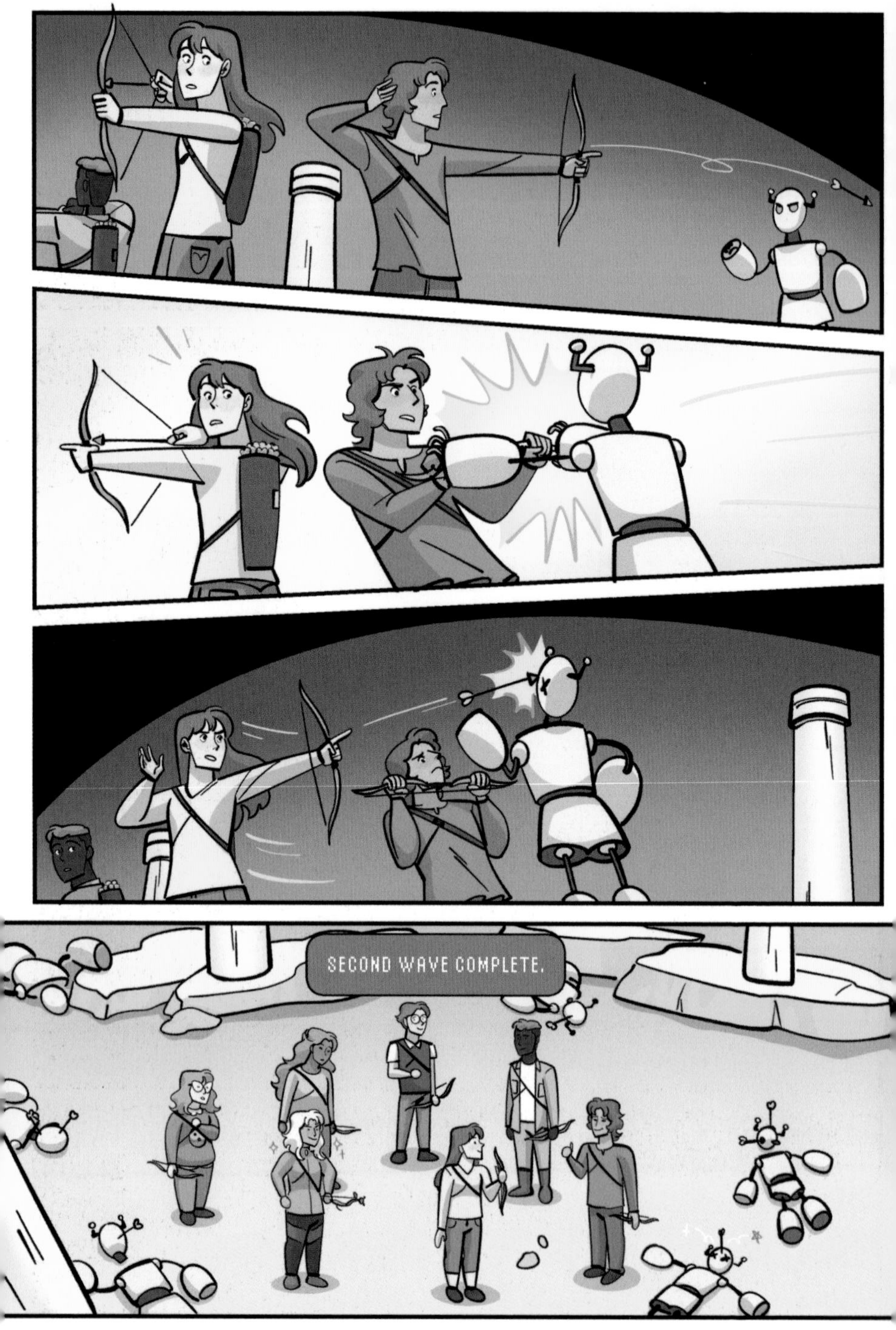
SECOND WAVE COMPLETE.

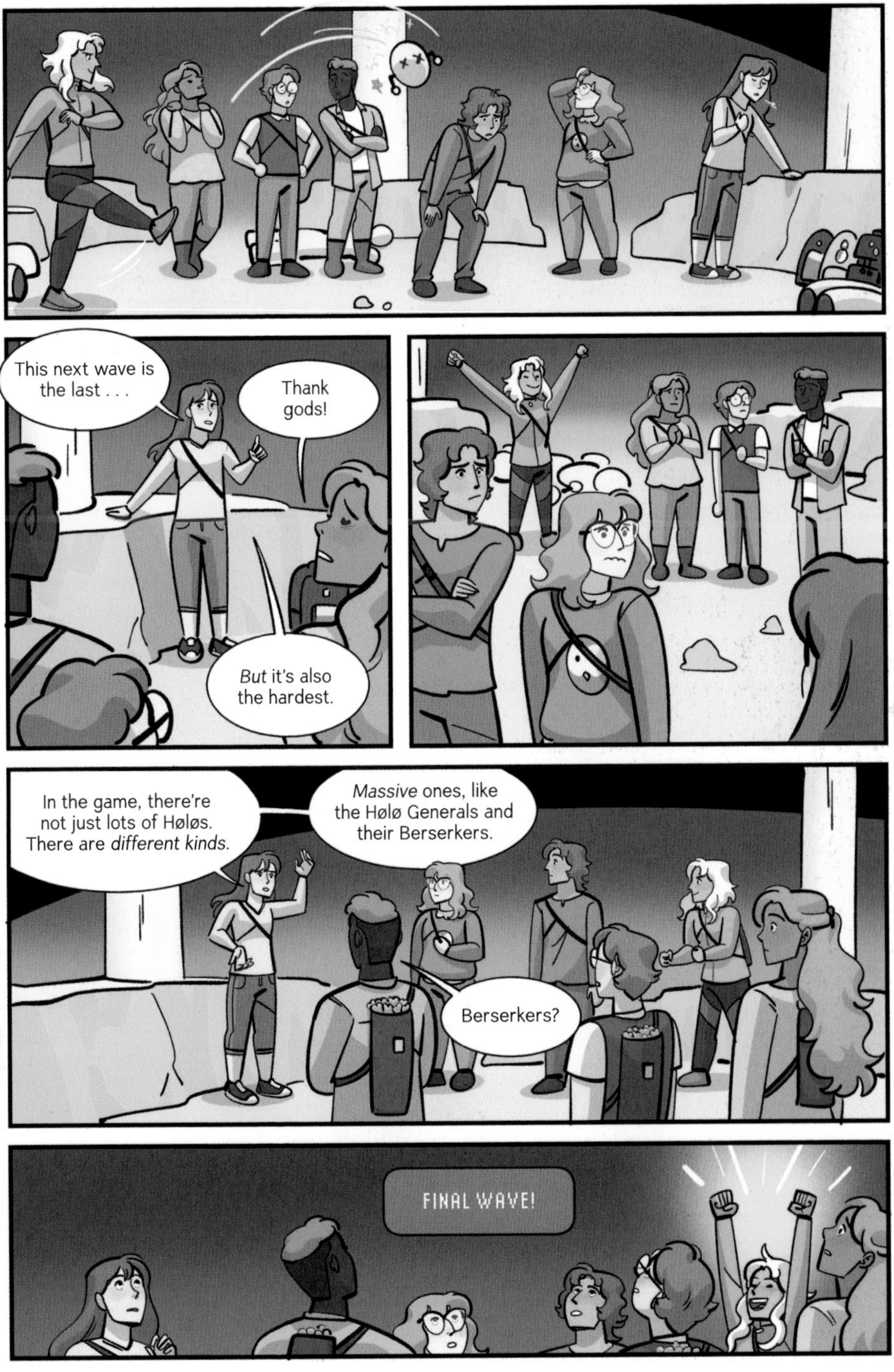
This next wave is the last . . .
Thank gods!
But it's also the hardest.
In the game, there're not just lots of Høløs. There are different kinds.
Massive ones, like the Hølø Generals and their Berserkers.
Berserkers?
FINAL WAVE!

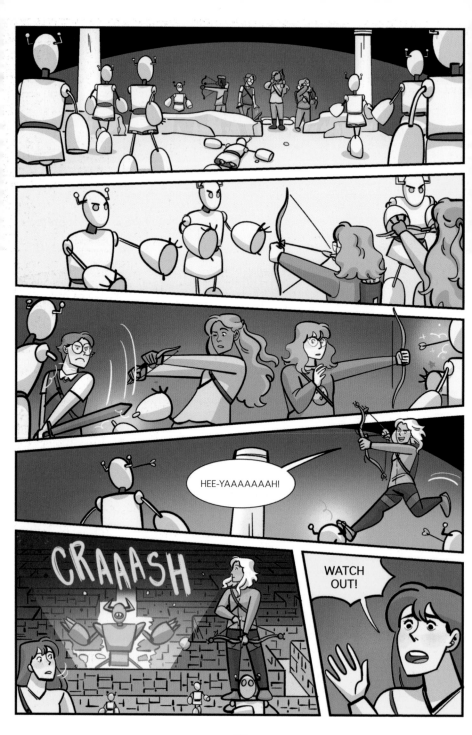

HEE-YAAAAAAAH!

CRAAASH

WATCH OUT!

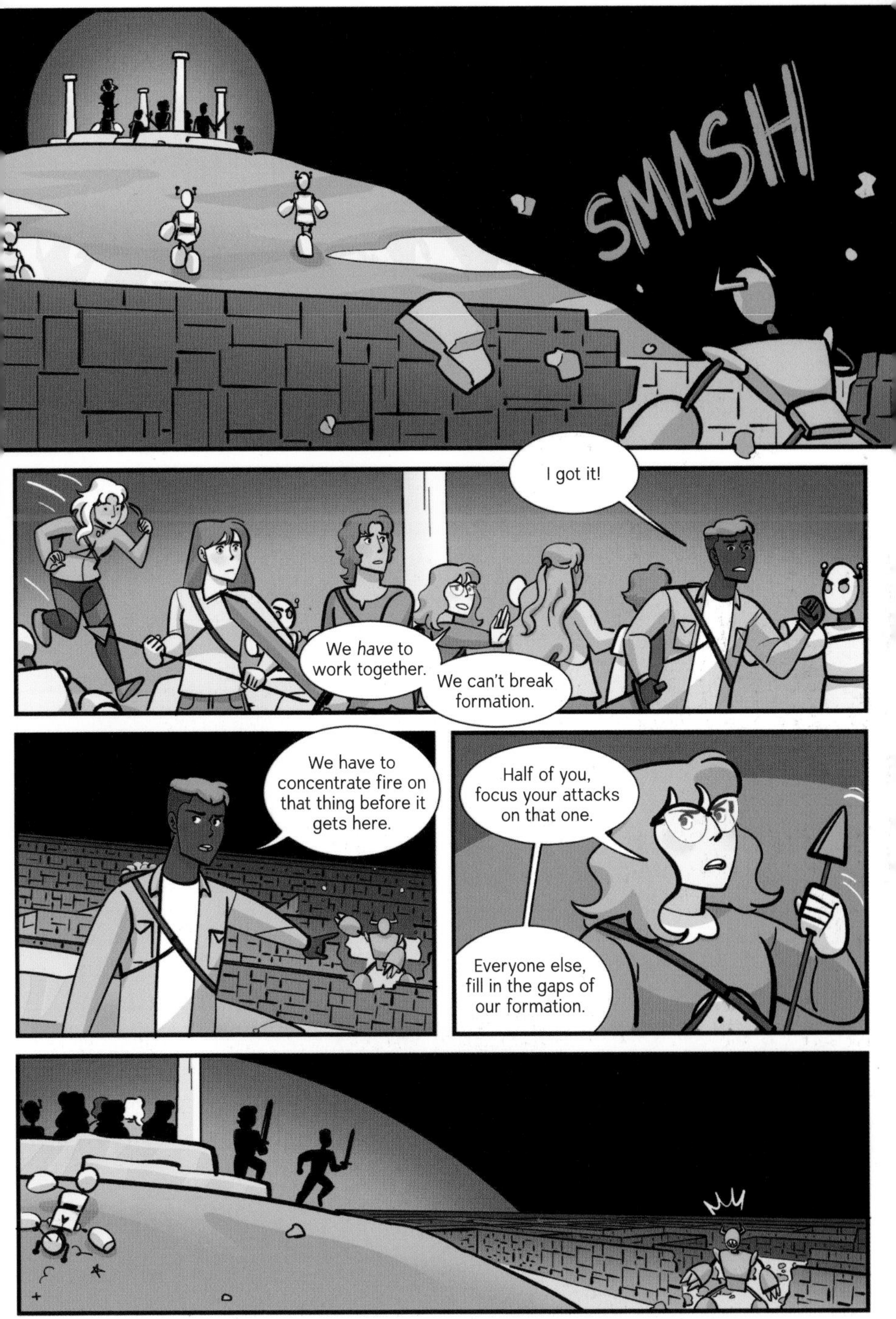
SMASH
I got it!
We *have* to work together.
We can't break formation.
We have to concentrate fire on that thing before it gets here.
Half of you, focus your attacks on that one.
Everyone else, fill in the gaps of our formation.

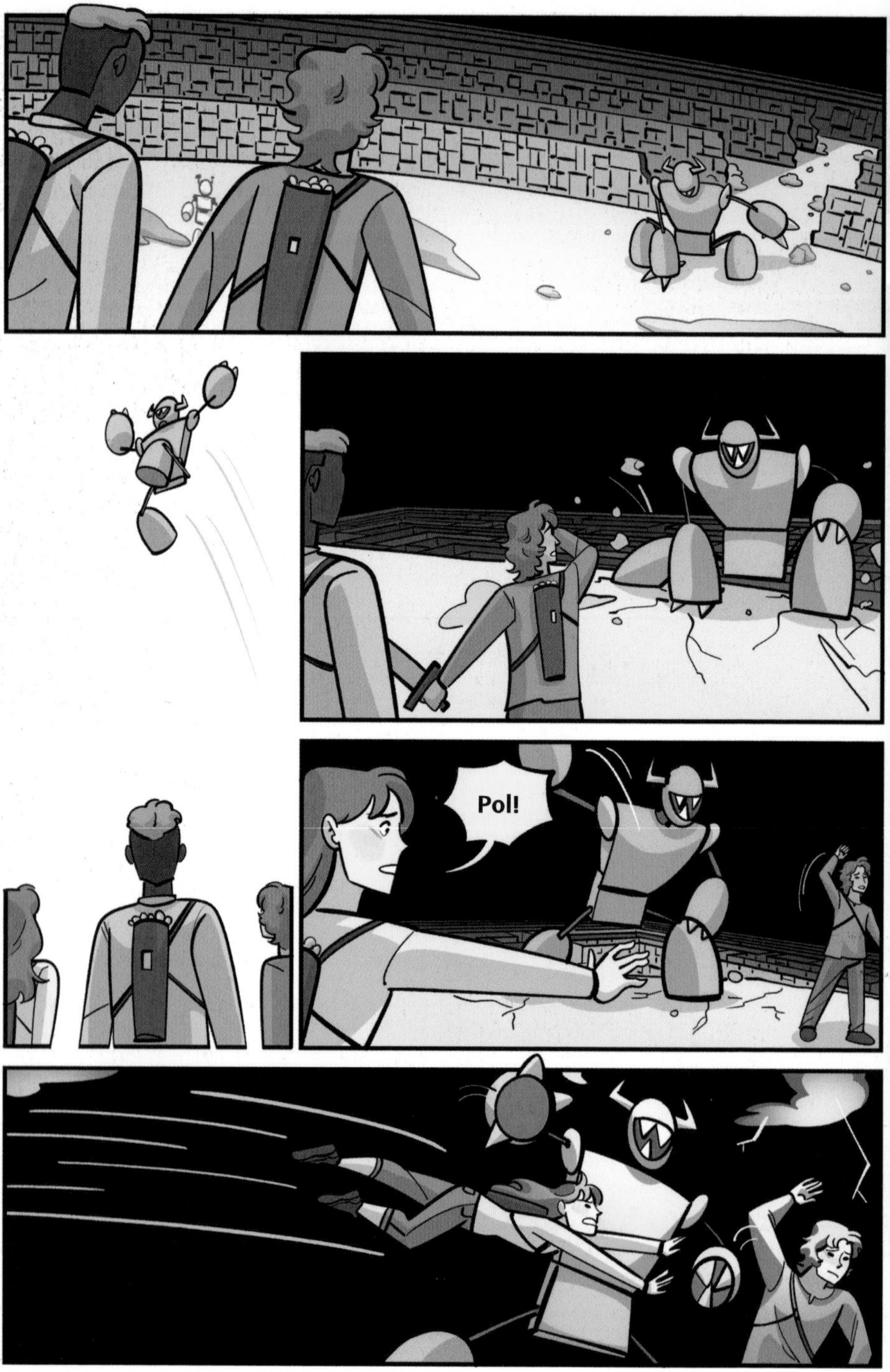
Pol!

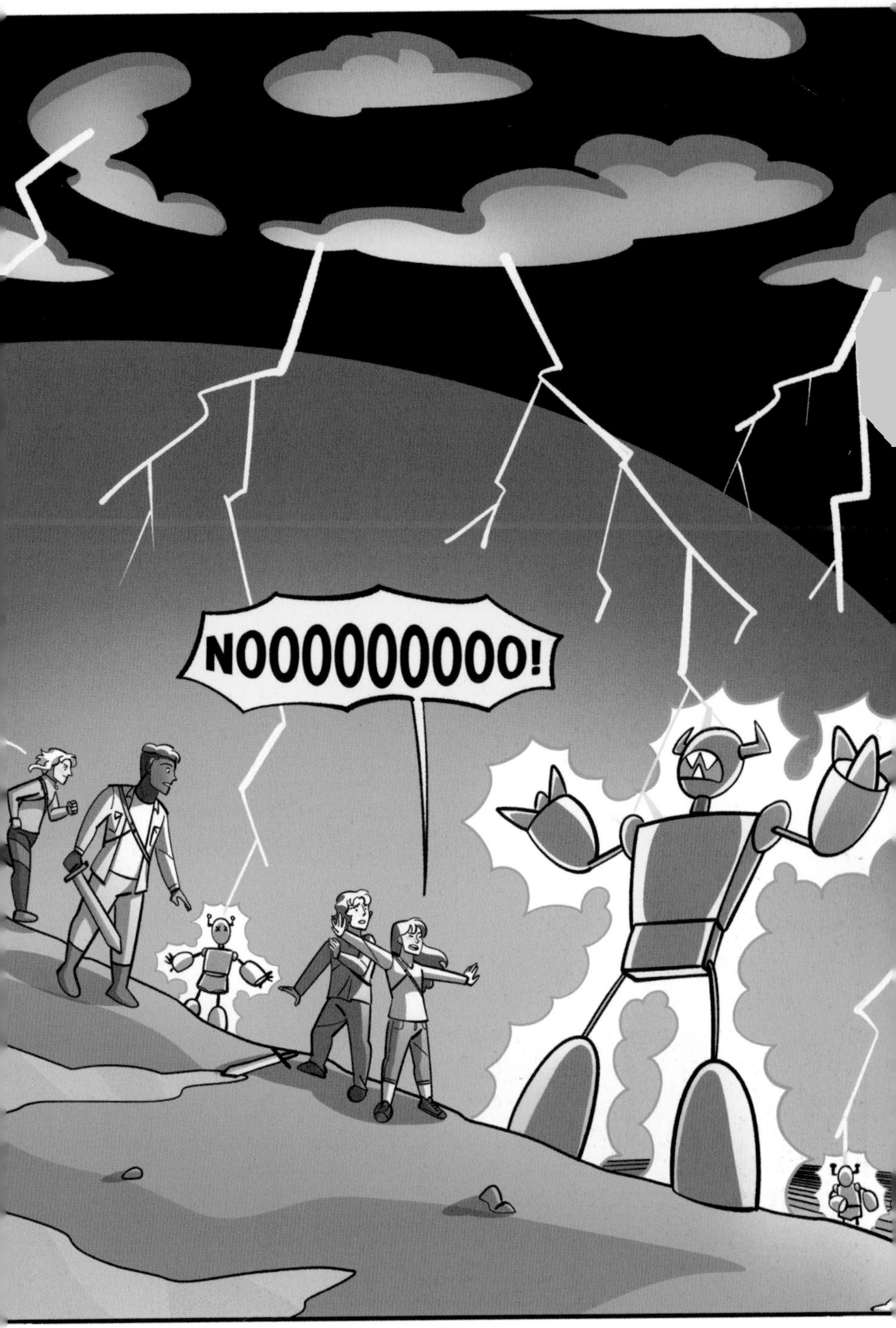
NOOOOOOOOO!

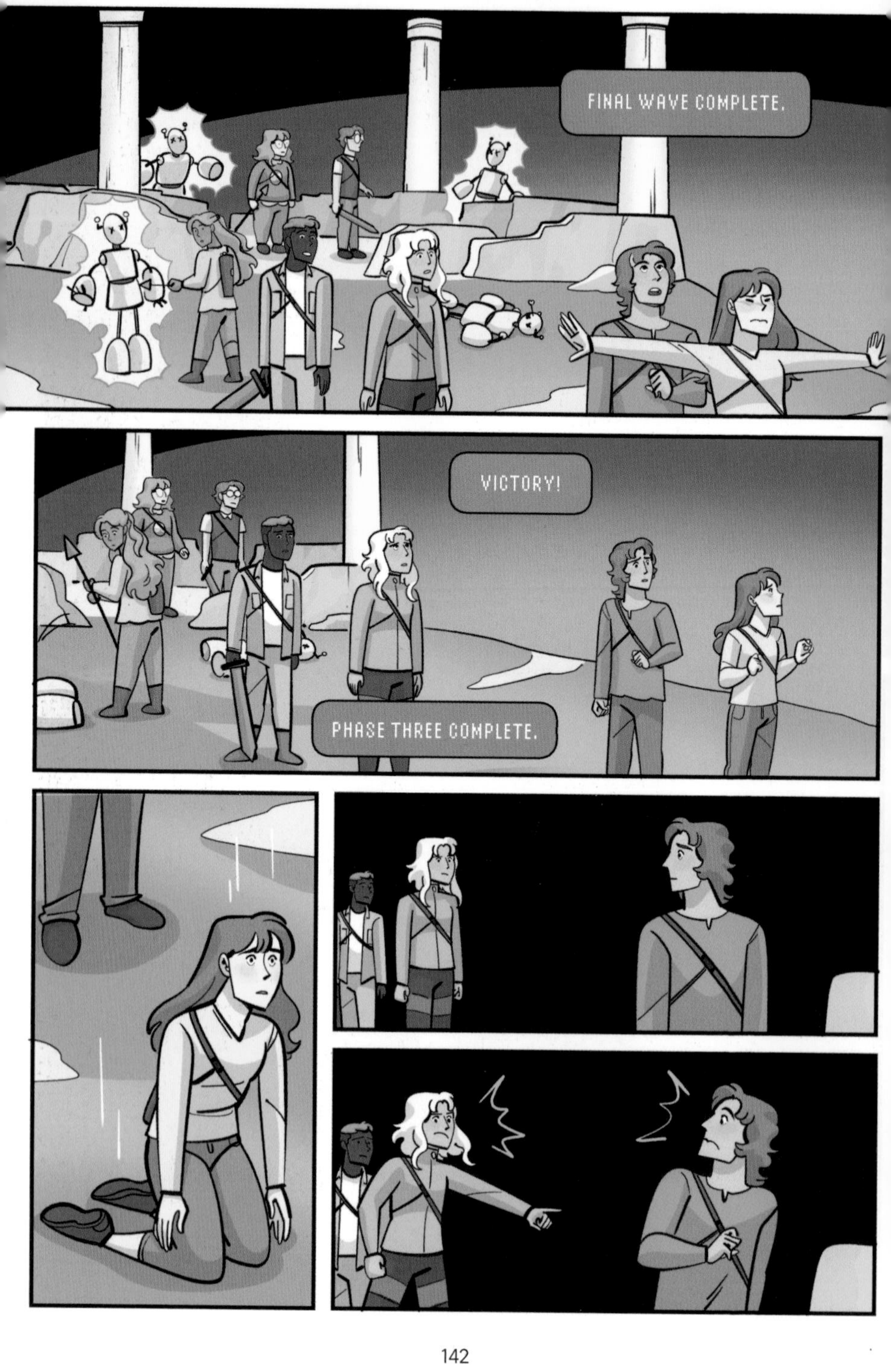
FINAL WAVE COMPLETE.
VICTORY!
PHASE THREE COMPLETE.

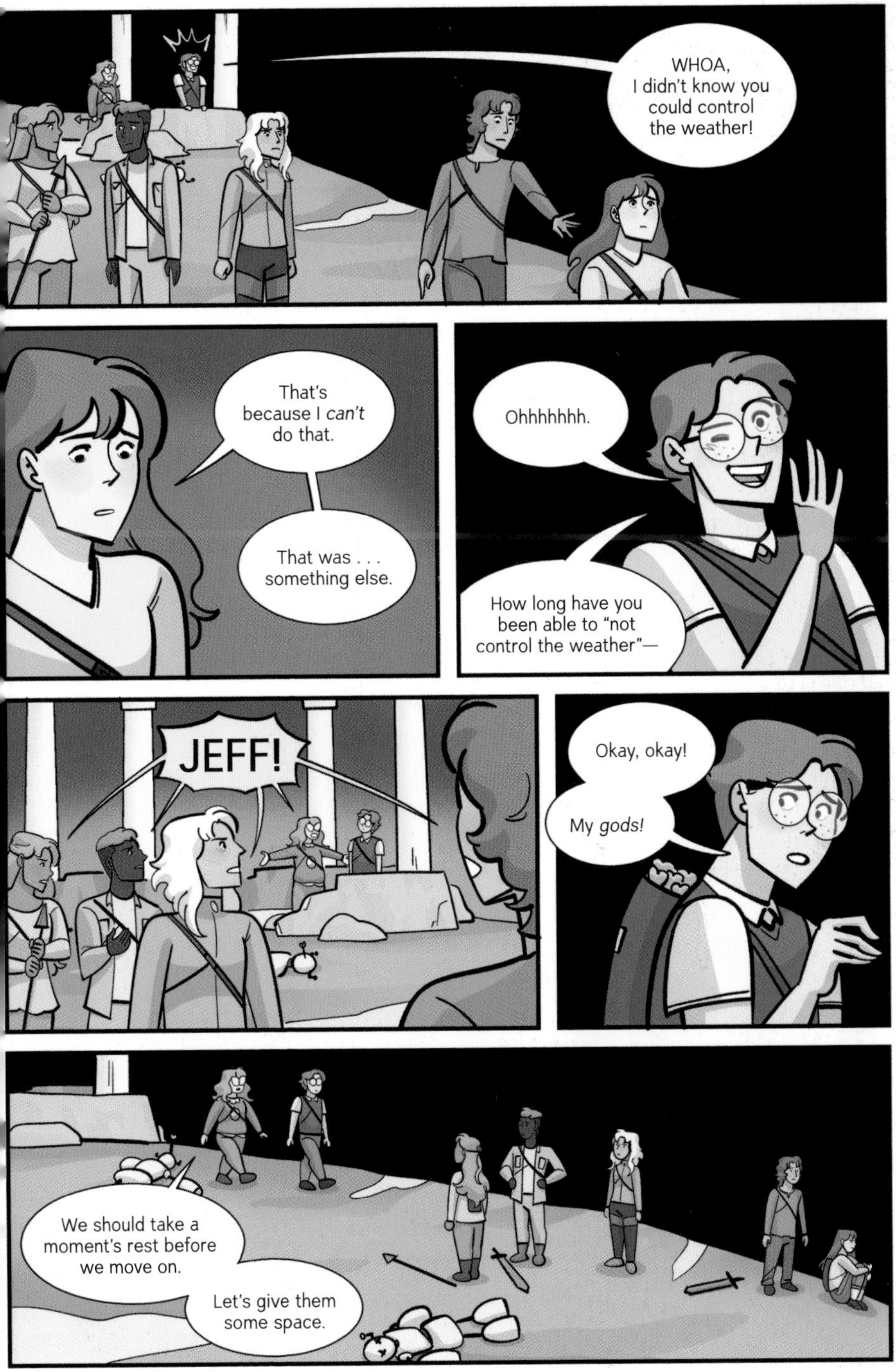
WHOA, I didn't know you could control the weather!
That's because I *can't* do that.
That was . . . something else.
Ohhhhhhh.
How long have you been able to "not control the weather"—
JEFF!
Okay, okay!
My *gods!*
We should take a moment's rest before we move on.
Let's give them some space.

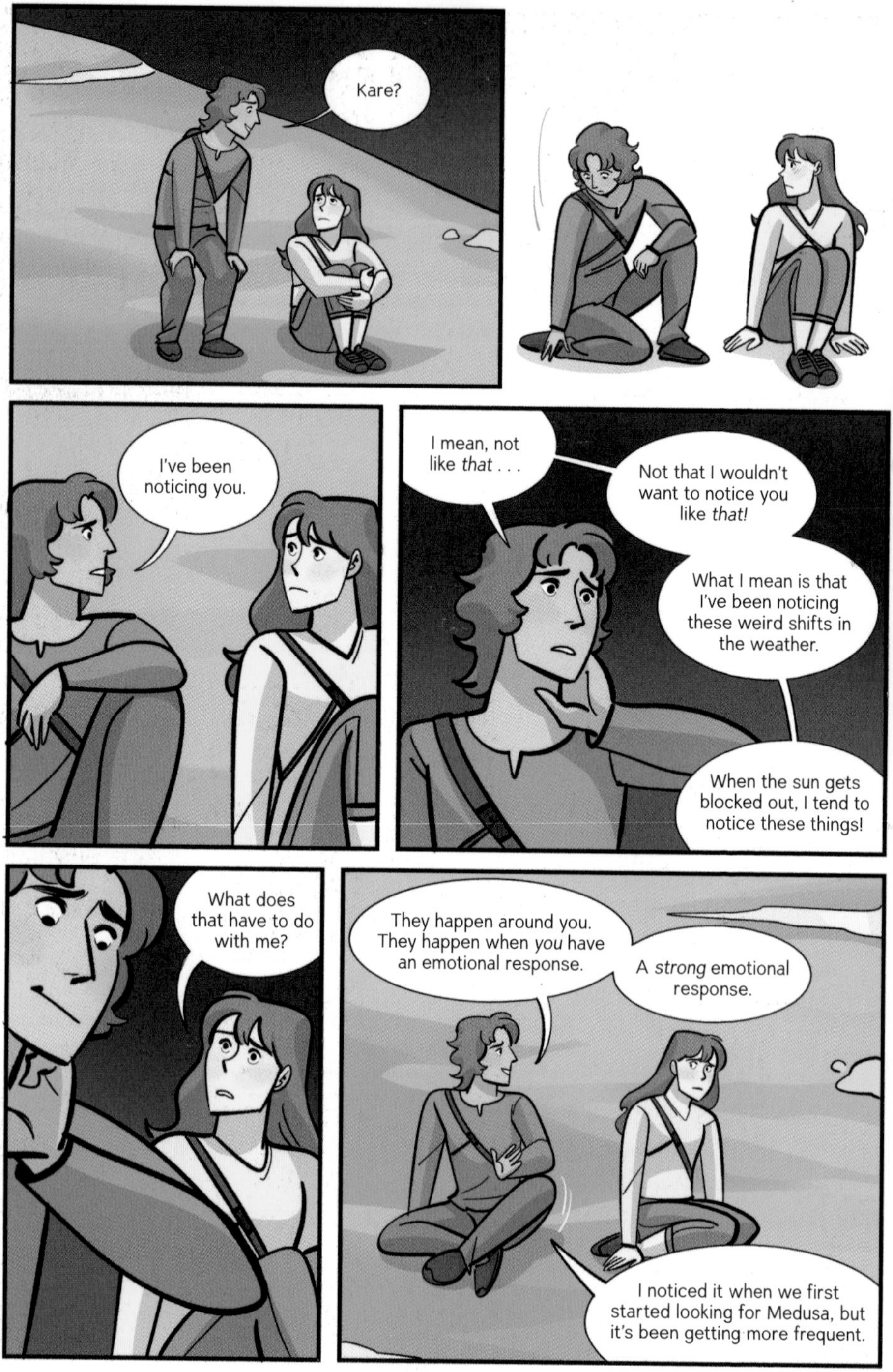
Kare?
I've been noticing you.
I mean, not like *that* . . .
Not that I wouldn't want to notice you like *that!*
What I mean is that I've been noticing these weird shifts in the weather.
When the sun gets blocked out, I tend to notice these things!
What does that have to do with me?
They happen around you. They happen when *you* have an emotional response.
A *strong* emotional response.
I noticed it when we first started looking for Medusa, but it's been getting more frequent.

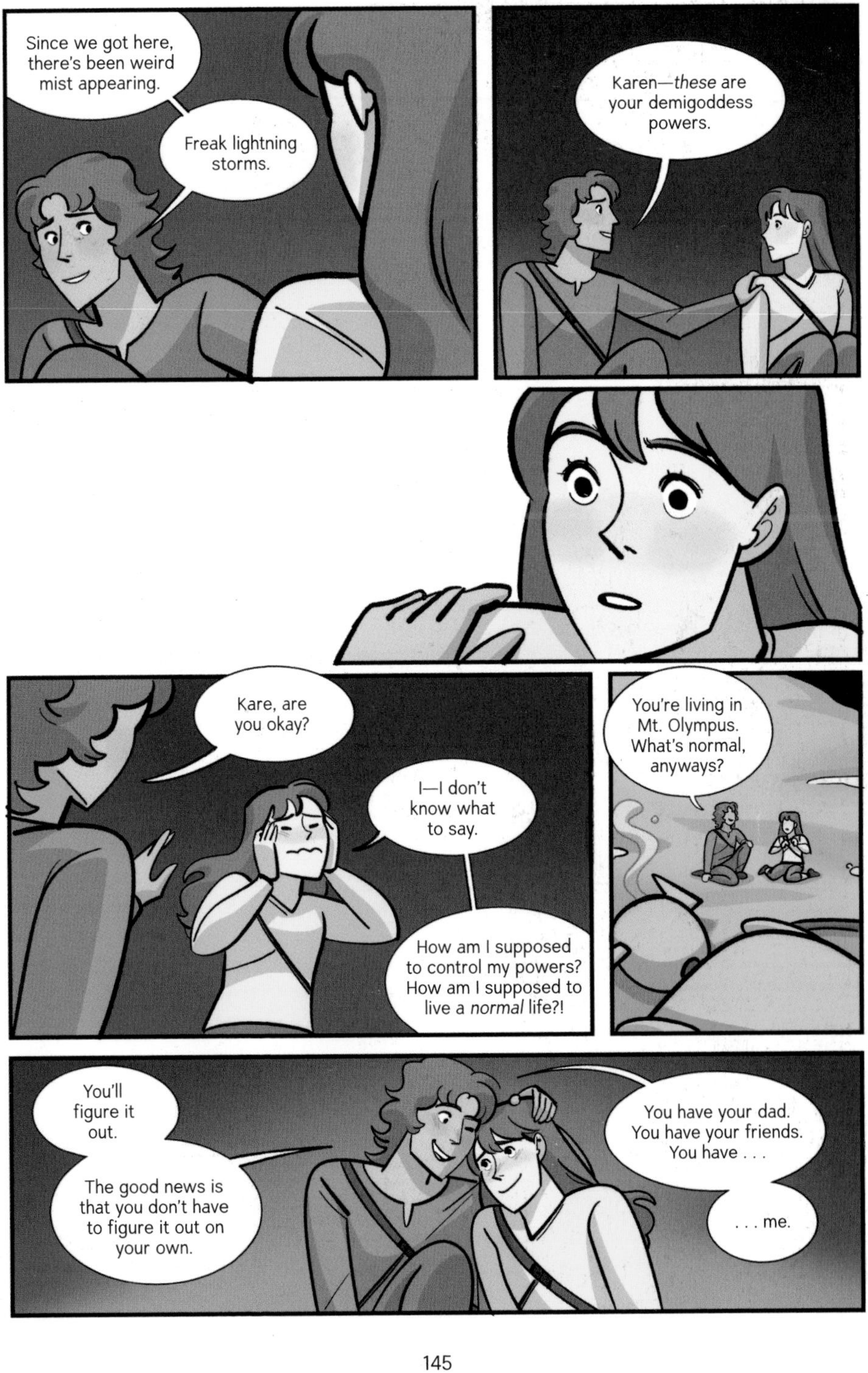
Since we got here, there's been weird mist appearing.
Freak lightning storms.
Karen—*these* are your demigoddess powers.
Kare, are you okay?
I—I don't know what to say.
How am I supposed to control my powers? How am I supposed to live a *normal* life?!
You're living in Mt. Olympus. What's normal, anyways?
You'll figure it out.
The good news is that you don't have to figure it out on your own.
You have your dad. You have your friends. You have . . .
. . . me.

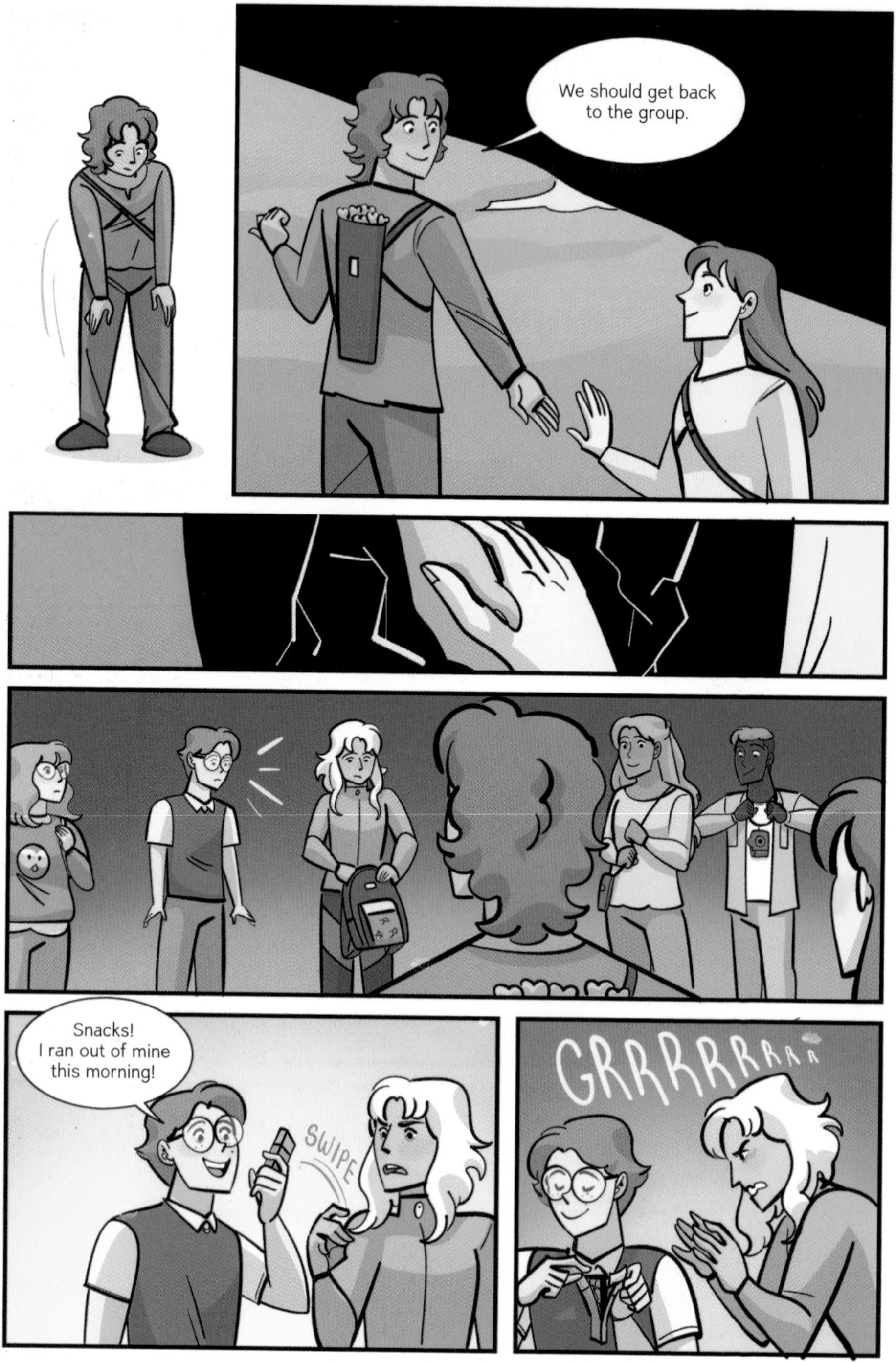
We should get back to the group.
Snacks! I ran out of mine this morning!
SWIPE
GRRRRRRRR

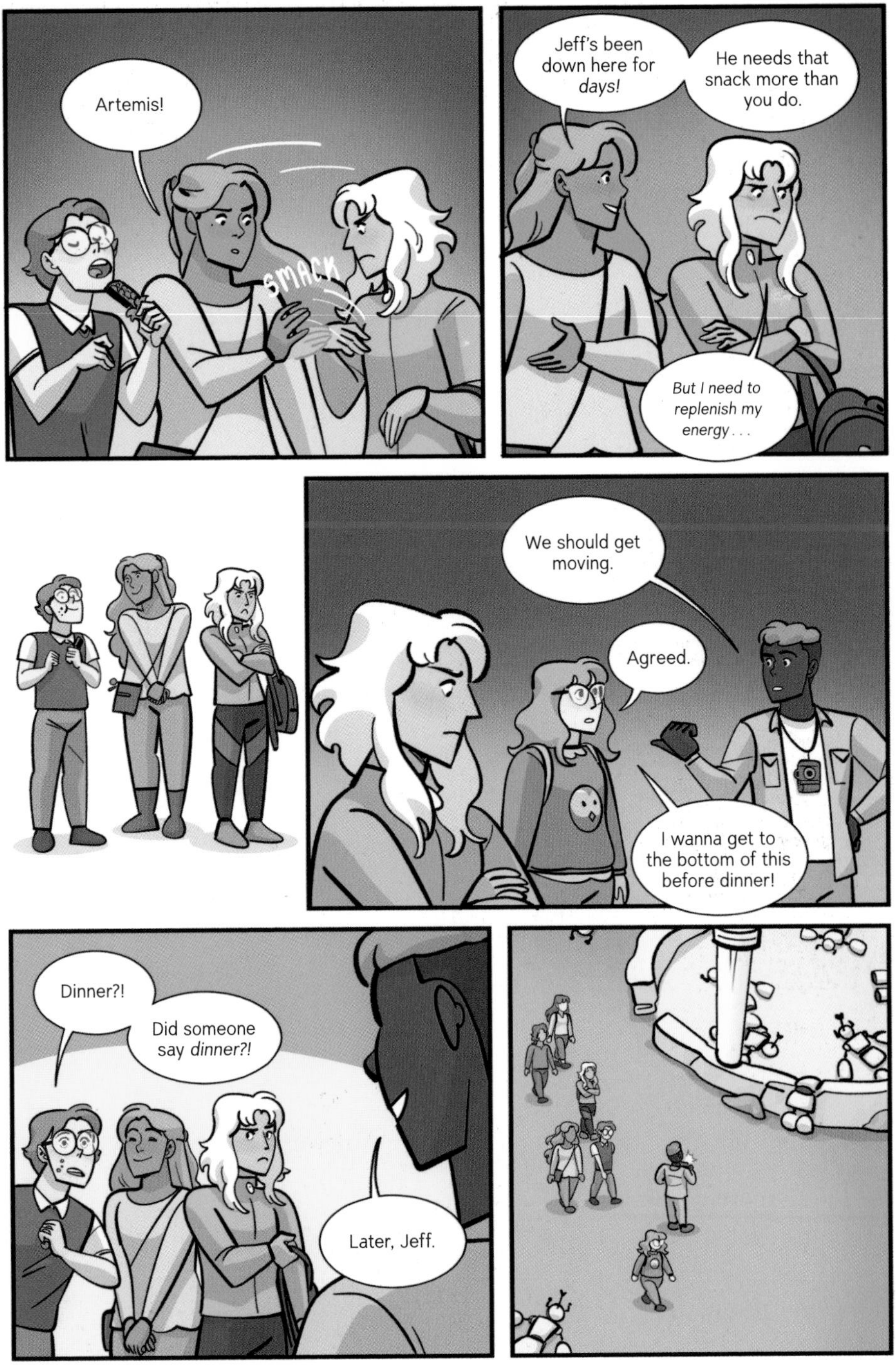
Artemis!
SMACK
Jeff's been down here for *days!*
He needs that snack more than you do.
But I need to replenish my energy . . .
We should get moving.
Agreed.
I wanna get to the bottom of this before dinner!
Dinner?!
Did someone say *dinner?!*
Later, Jeff.

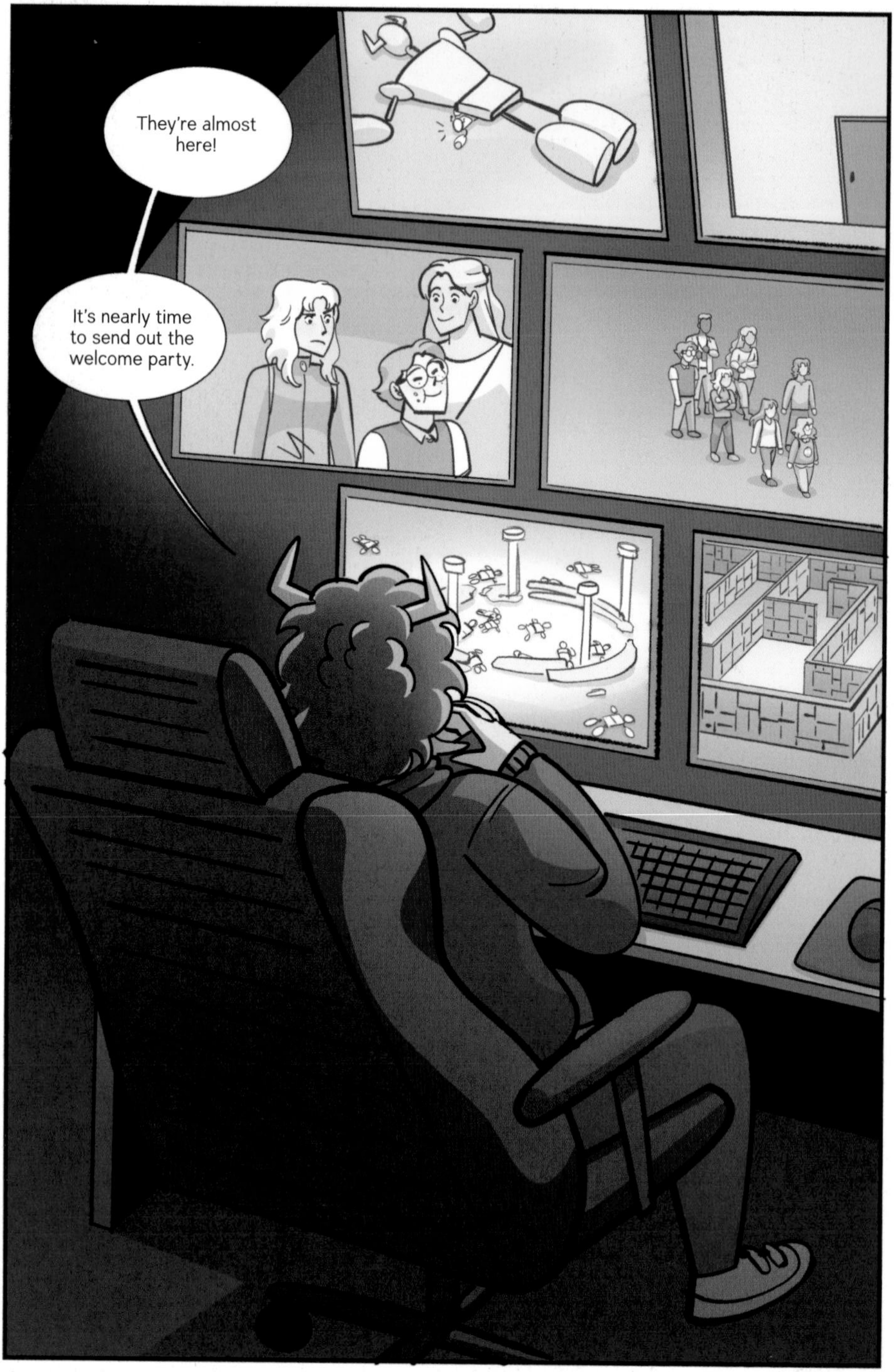
They're almost here!
It's nearly time to send out the welcome party.

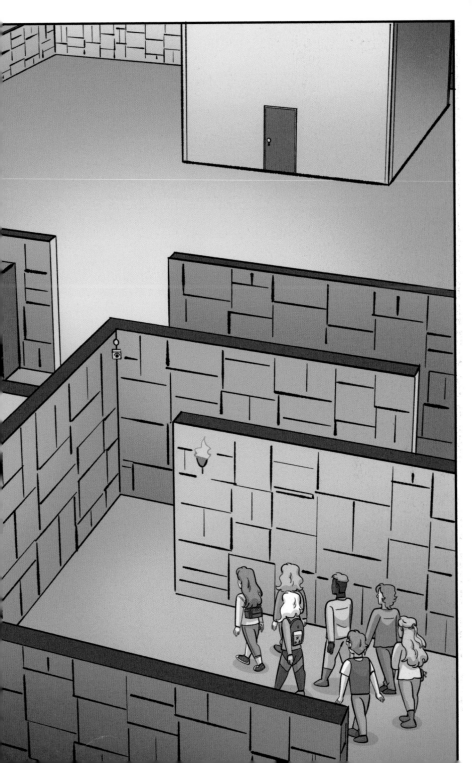

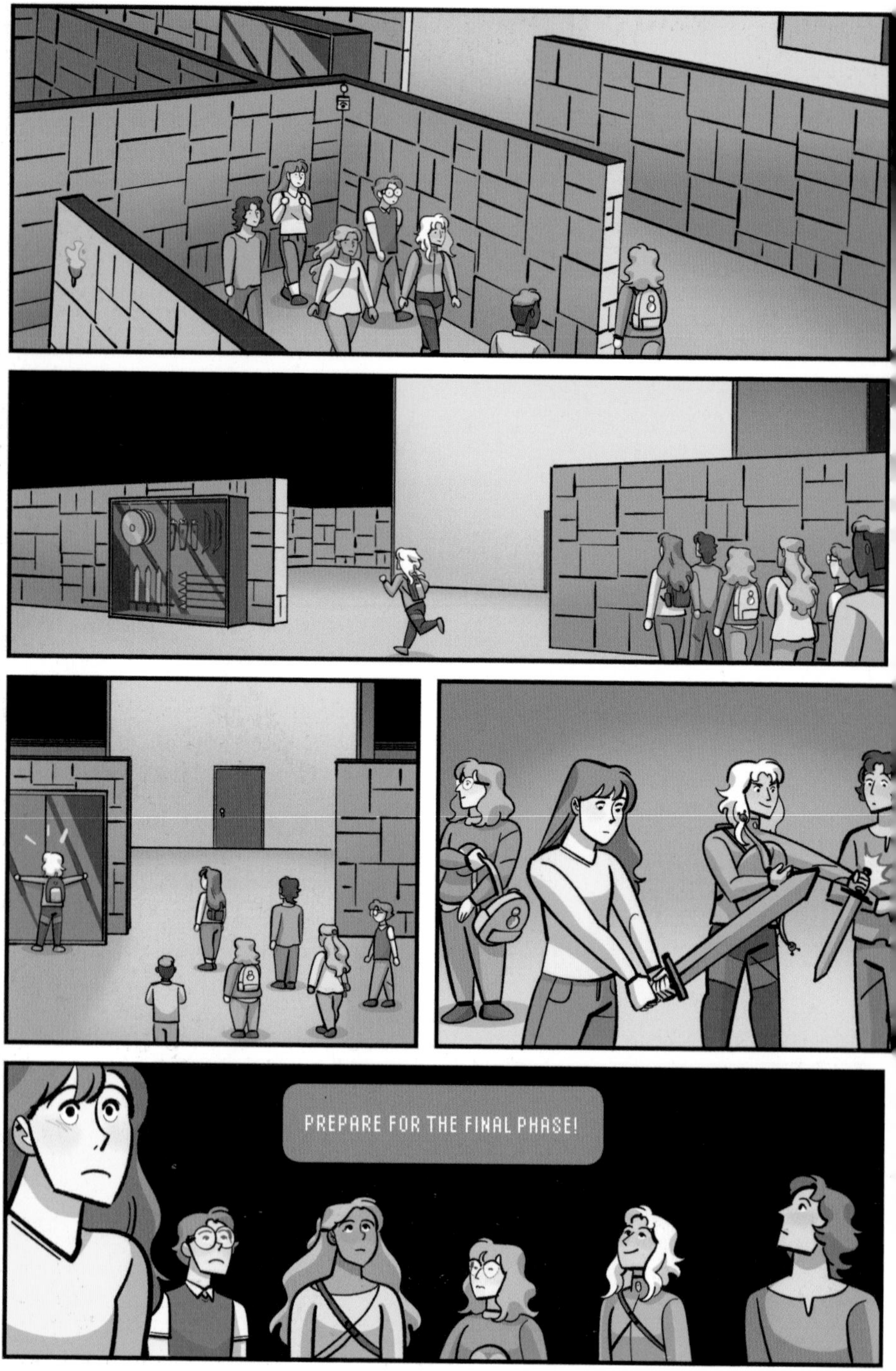
PREPARE FOR THE FINAL PHASE!

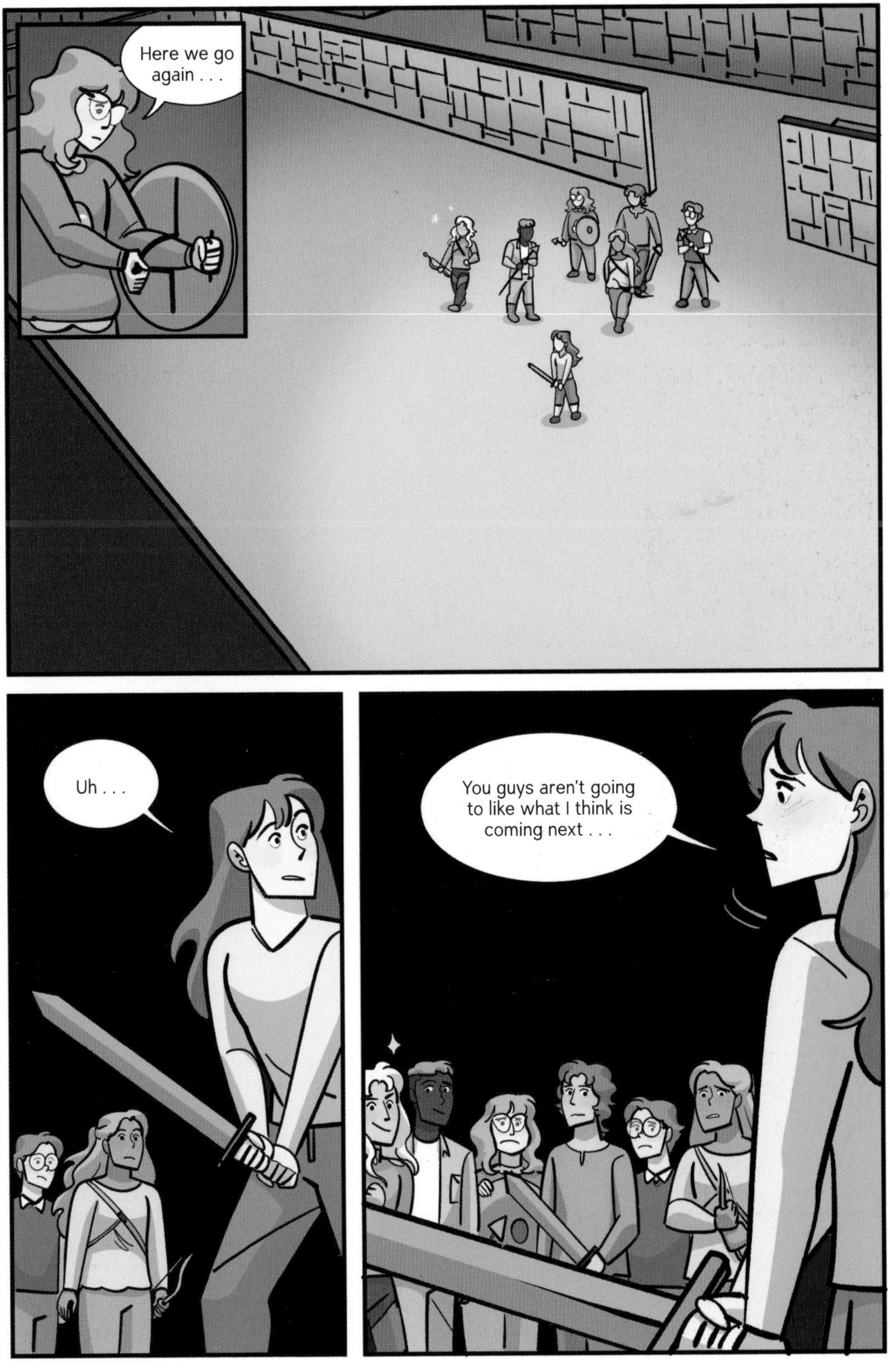
Here we go again . . .
Uh . . .
You guys aren't going to like what I think is coming next . . .

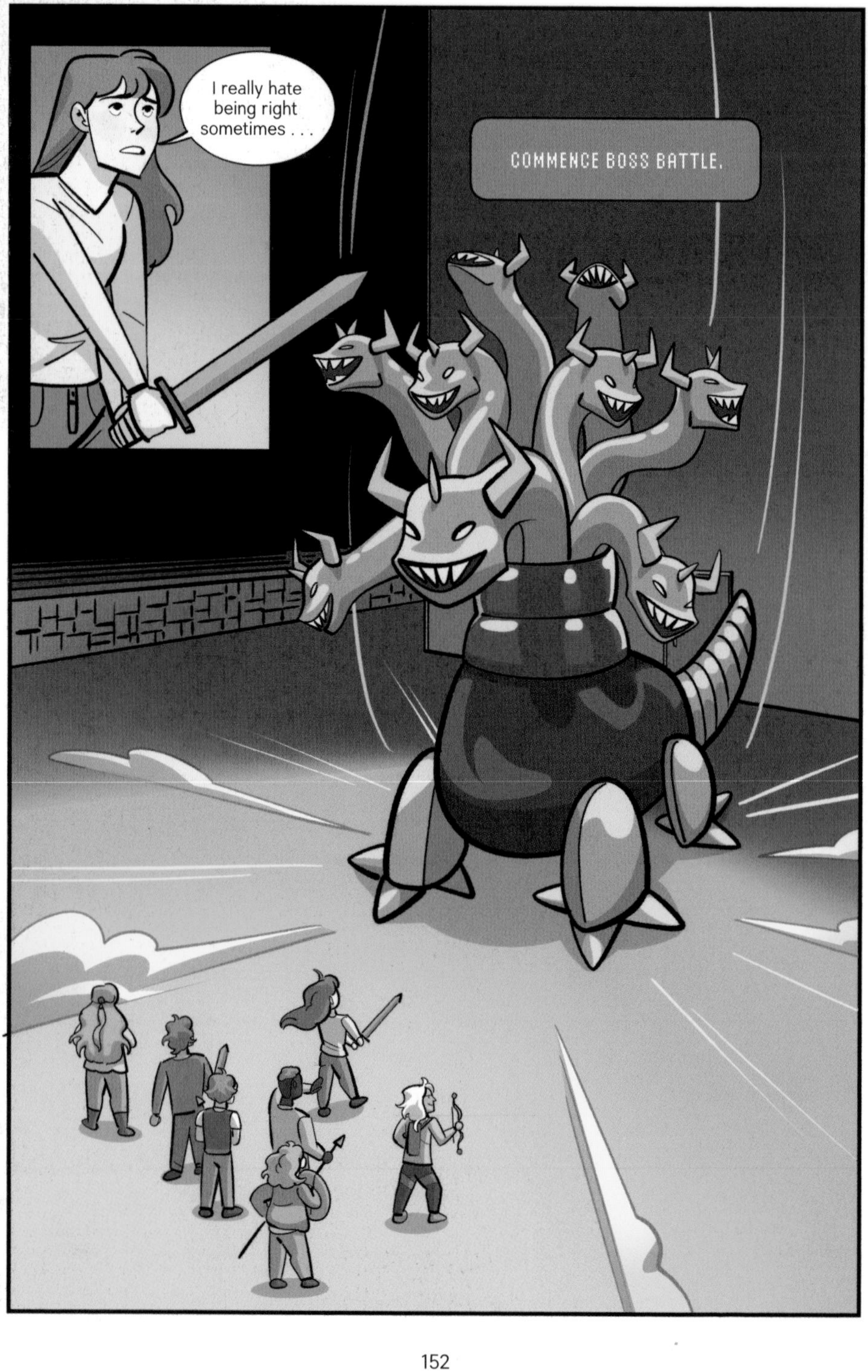
I really hate being right sometimes . . .
COMMENCE BOSS BATTLE.

What do we do?!

Uhhh . . .

Well . . .

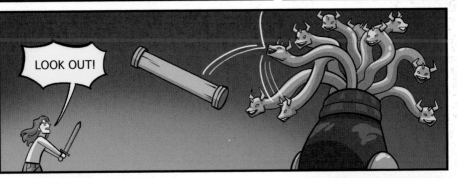

LOOK OUT!

RO

AAAR

What's the plan, Karen?

We're an easy target all together, so staying in smaller groups is our best option.

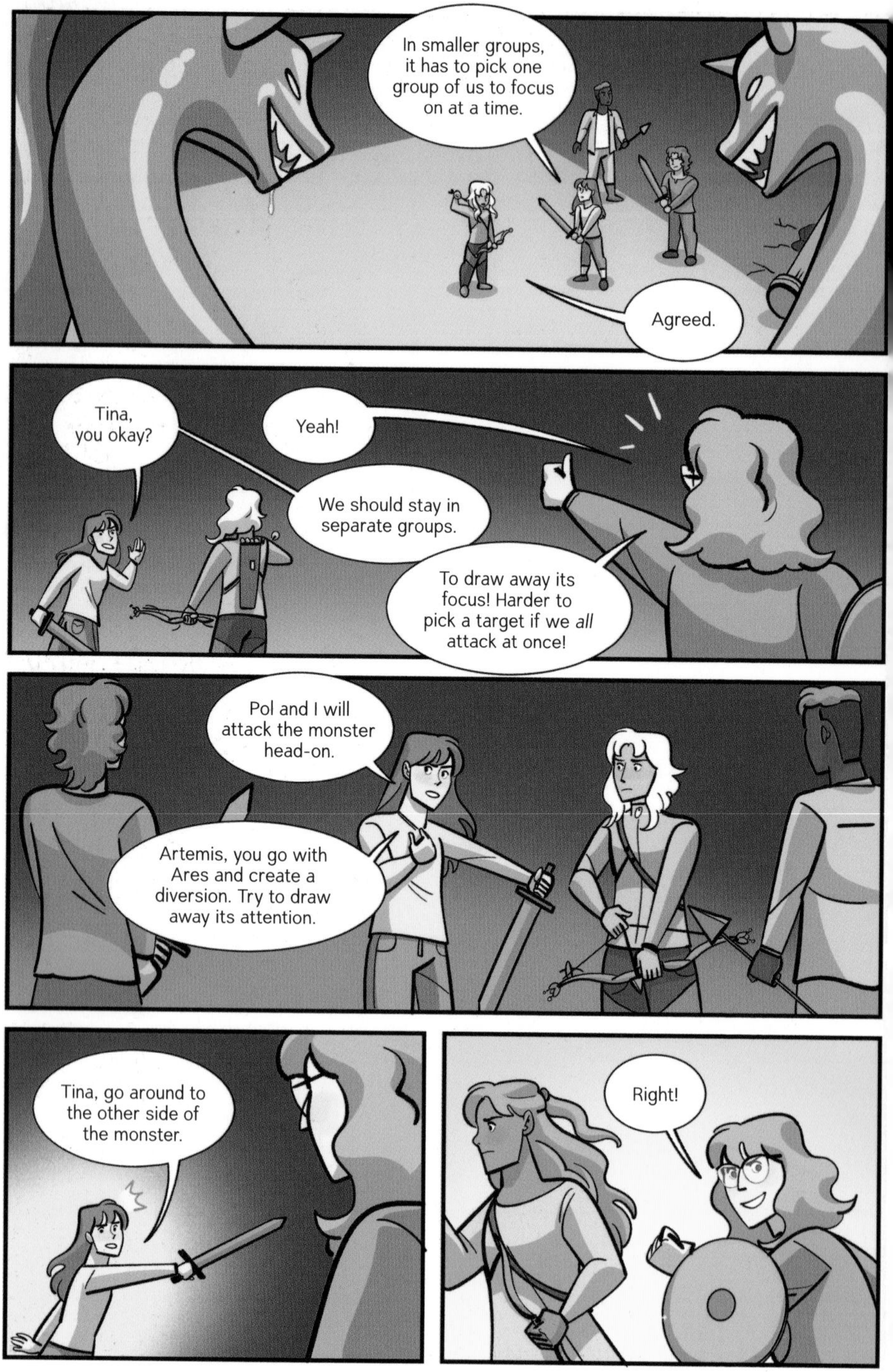
In smaller groups, it has to pick one group of us to focus on at a time.
Agreed.
Tina, you okay?
Yeah!
We should stay in separate groups.
To draw away its focus! Harder to pick a target if we *all* attack at once!
Pol and I will attack the monster head-on.
Artemis, you go with Ares and create a diversion. Try to draw away its attention.
Tina, go around to the other side of the monster.
Right!

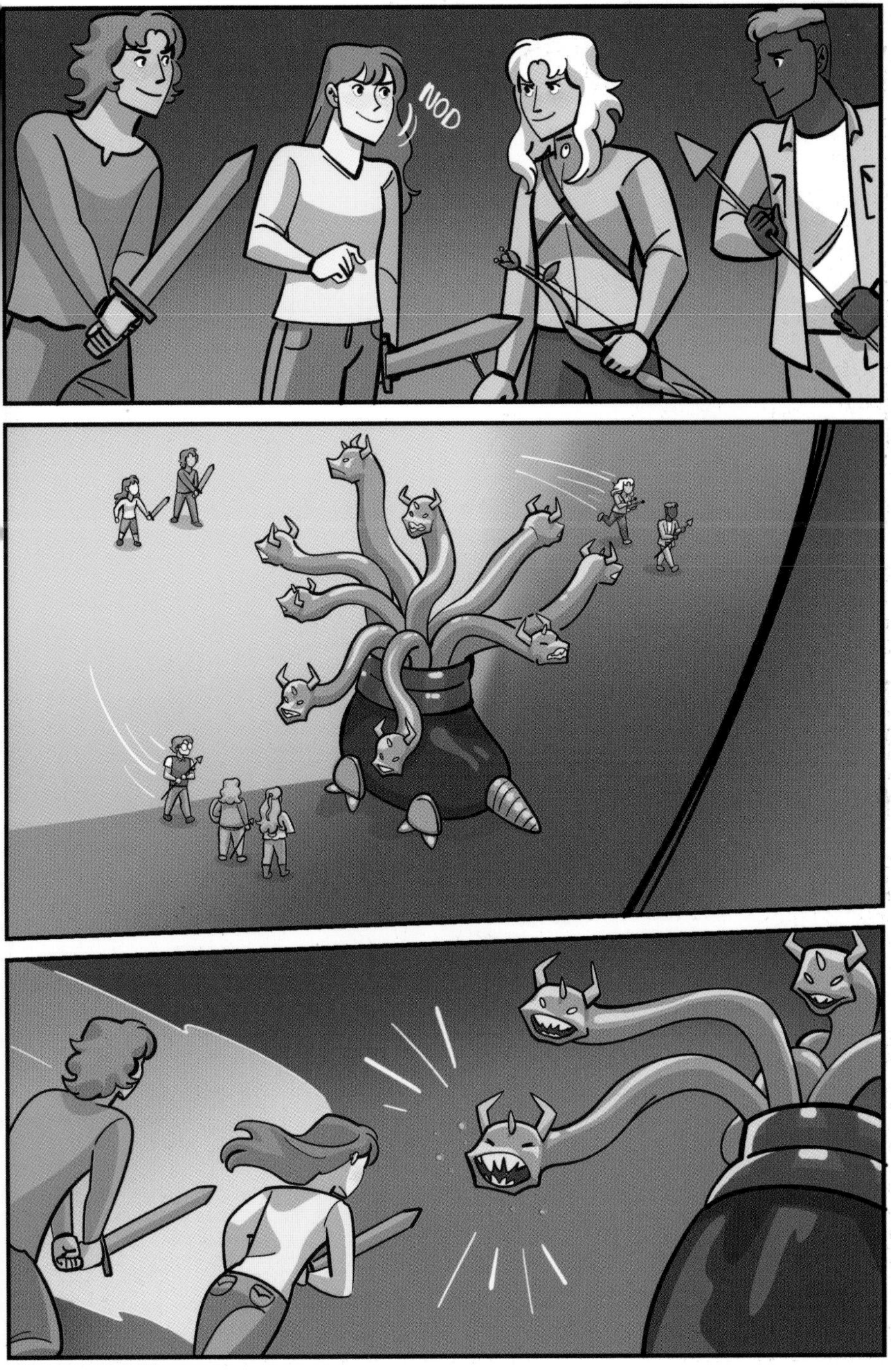
NOD

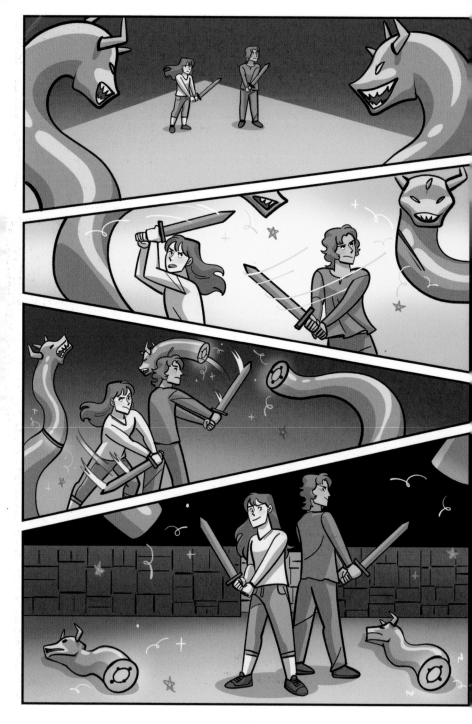

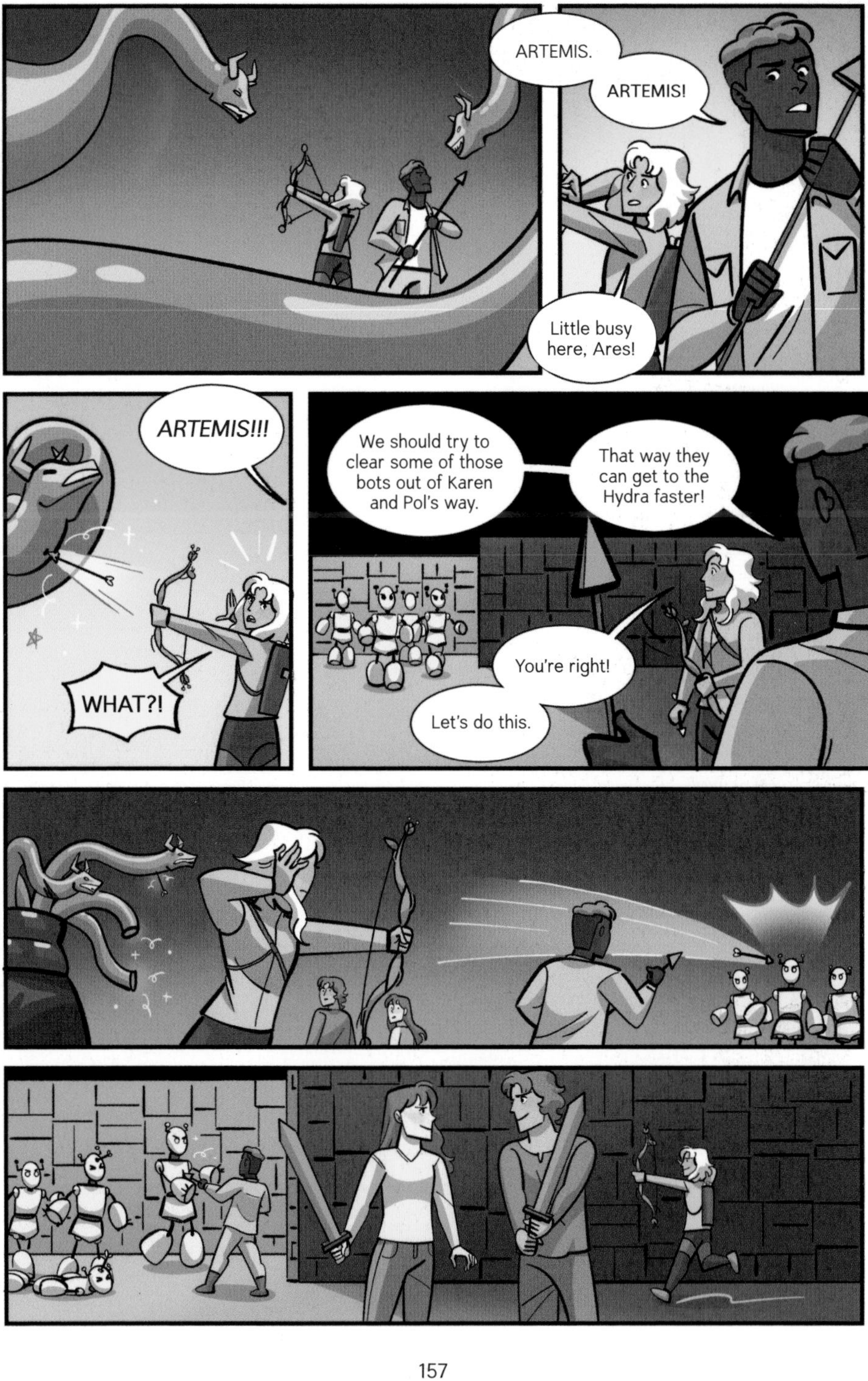
ARTEMIS.
ARTEMIS!
Little busy here, Ares!
ARTEMIS!!!
WHAT?!
We should try to clear some of those bots out of Karen and Pol's way.
That way they can get to the Hydra faster!
You're right!
Let's do this.

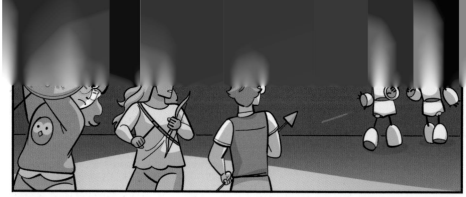

What's the plan?!

To not get hit!

That's a good plan!

We divide and conquer each side—there's no way the Hydra can do anything but focus on one side or the other.

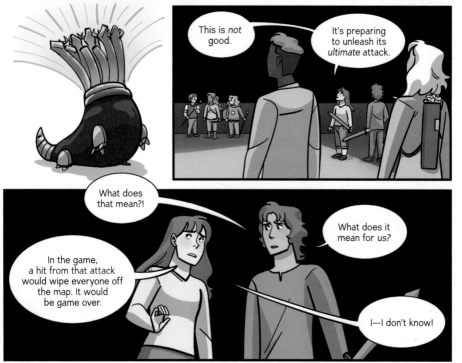

This is *not* good.

It's preparing to unleash its *ultimate* attack.

What does that mean?!

What does it mean for *us?*

In the game, a hit from that attack would wipe everyone off the map. It would be game over.

I—I don't know!

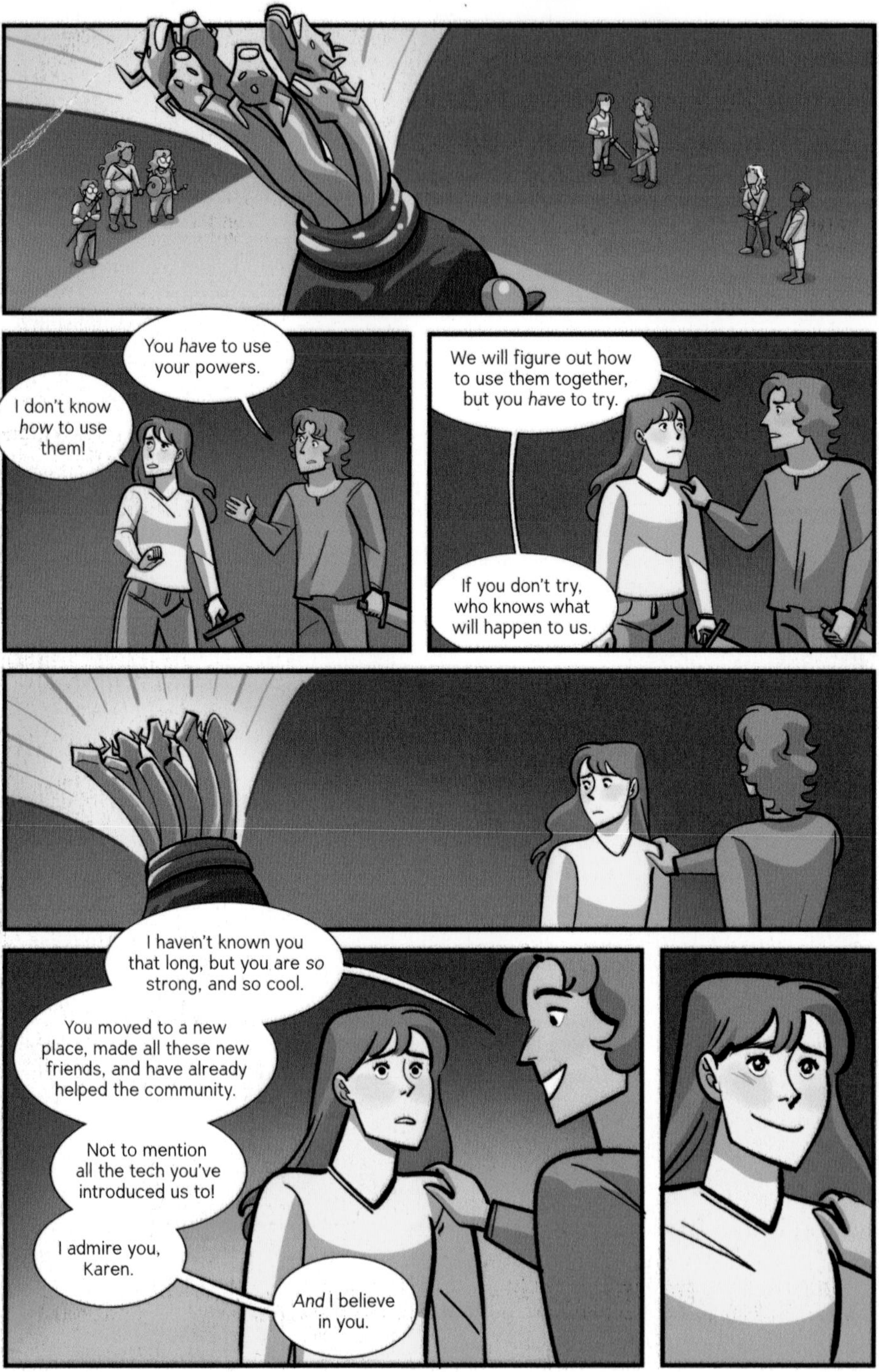
You *have* to use your powers.
I don't know *how* to use them!
We will figure out how to use them together, but you *have* to try.
If you don't try, who knows what will happen to us.
I haven't known you that long, but you are *so* strong, and so cool.
You moved to a new place, made all these new friends, and have already helped the community.
Not to mention all the tech you've introduced us to!
I admire you, Karen.
And I believe in you.

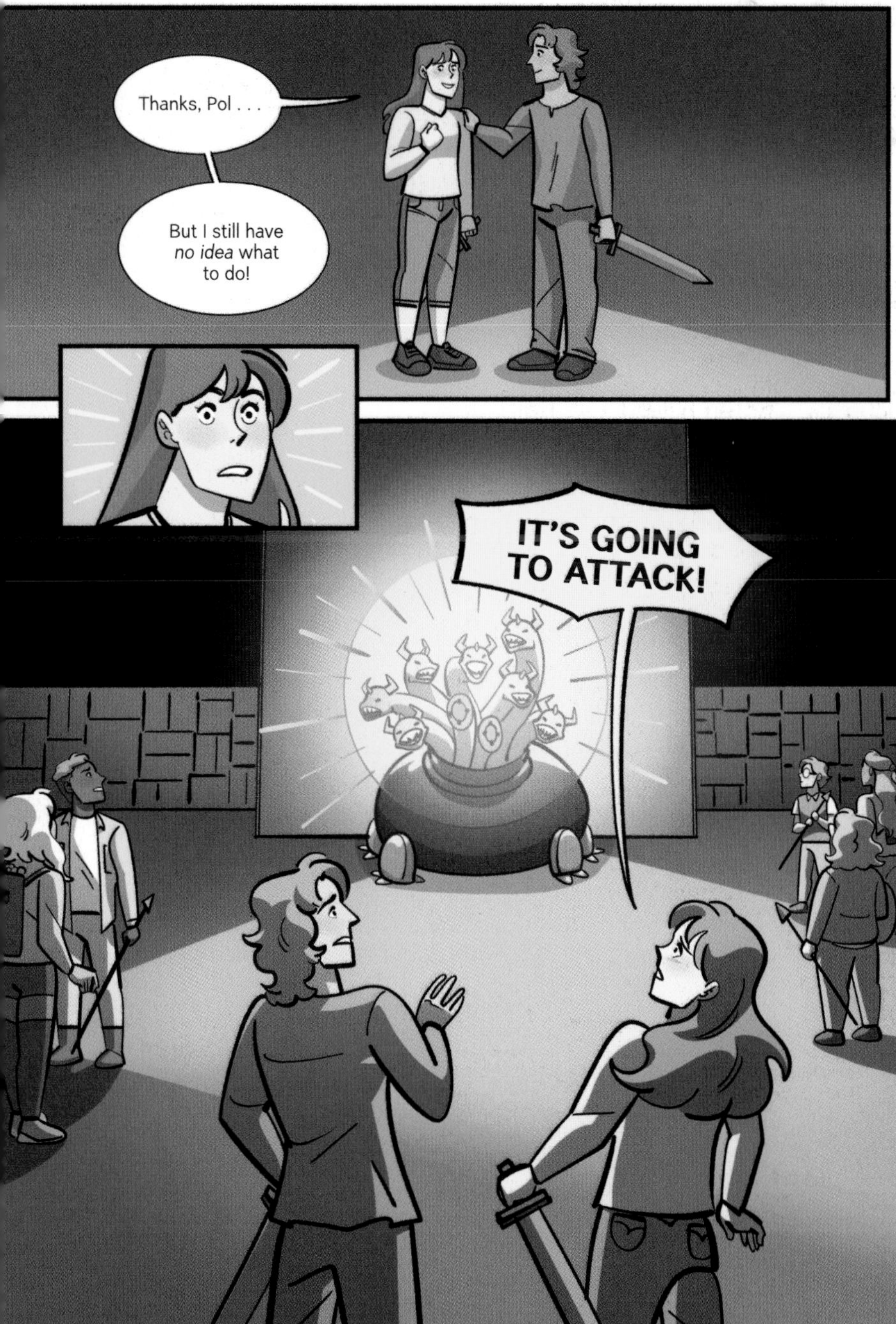
Thanks, Pol . . .
But I still have *no idea* what to do!
IT'S GOING TO ATTACK!

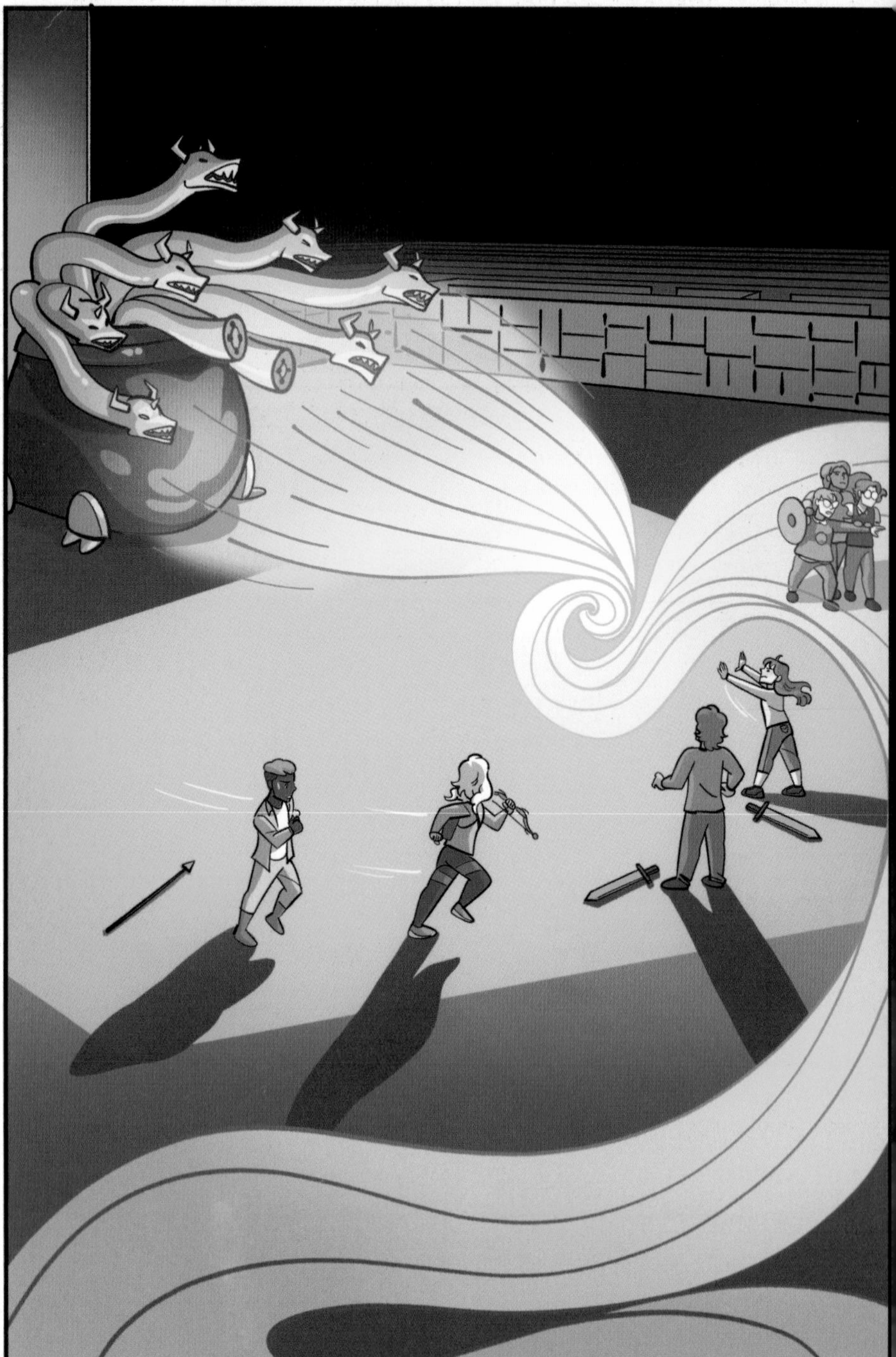

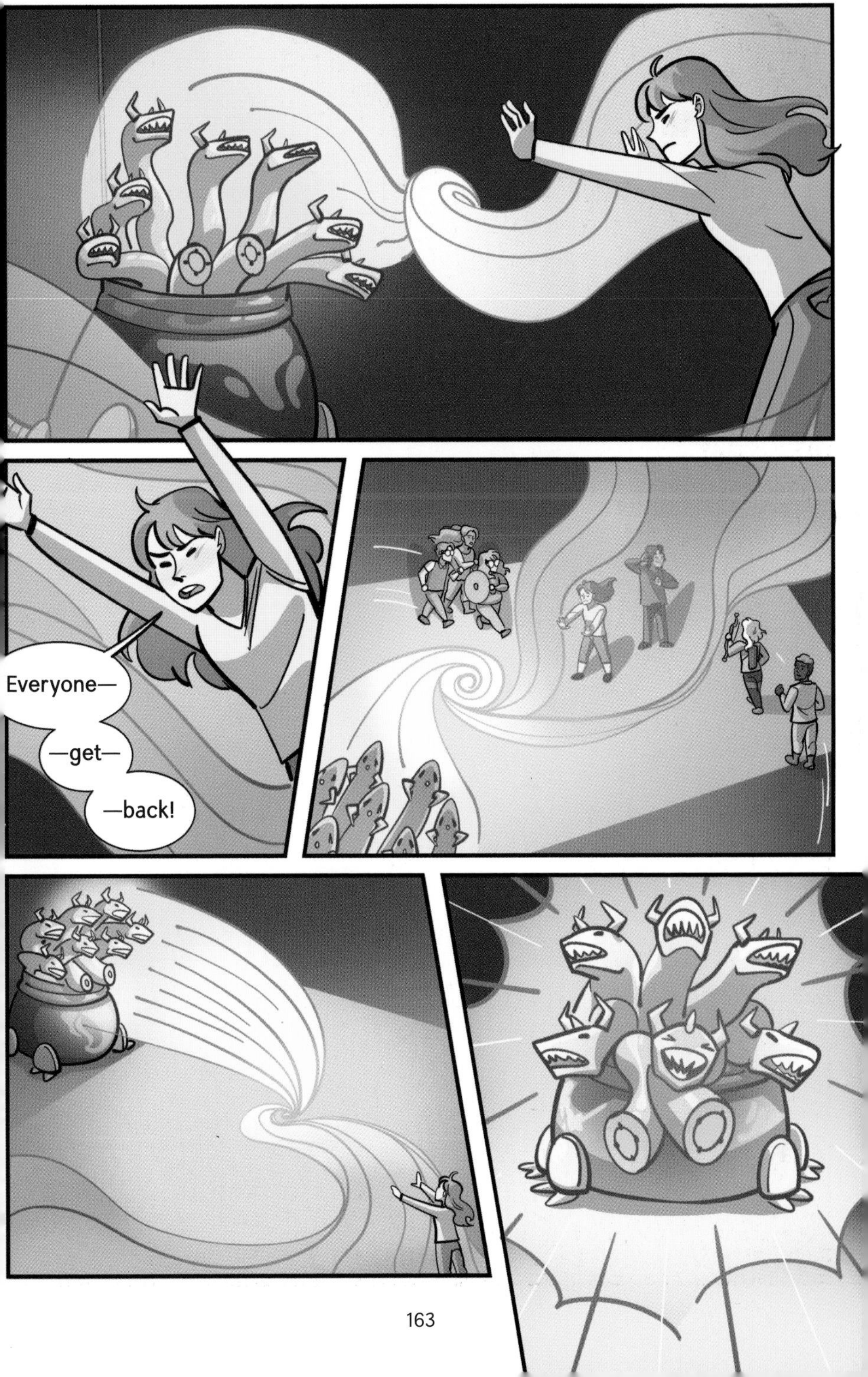
Everyone—
—get—
—back!

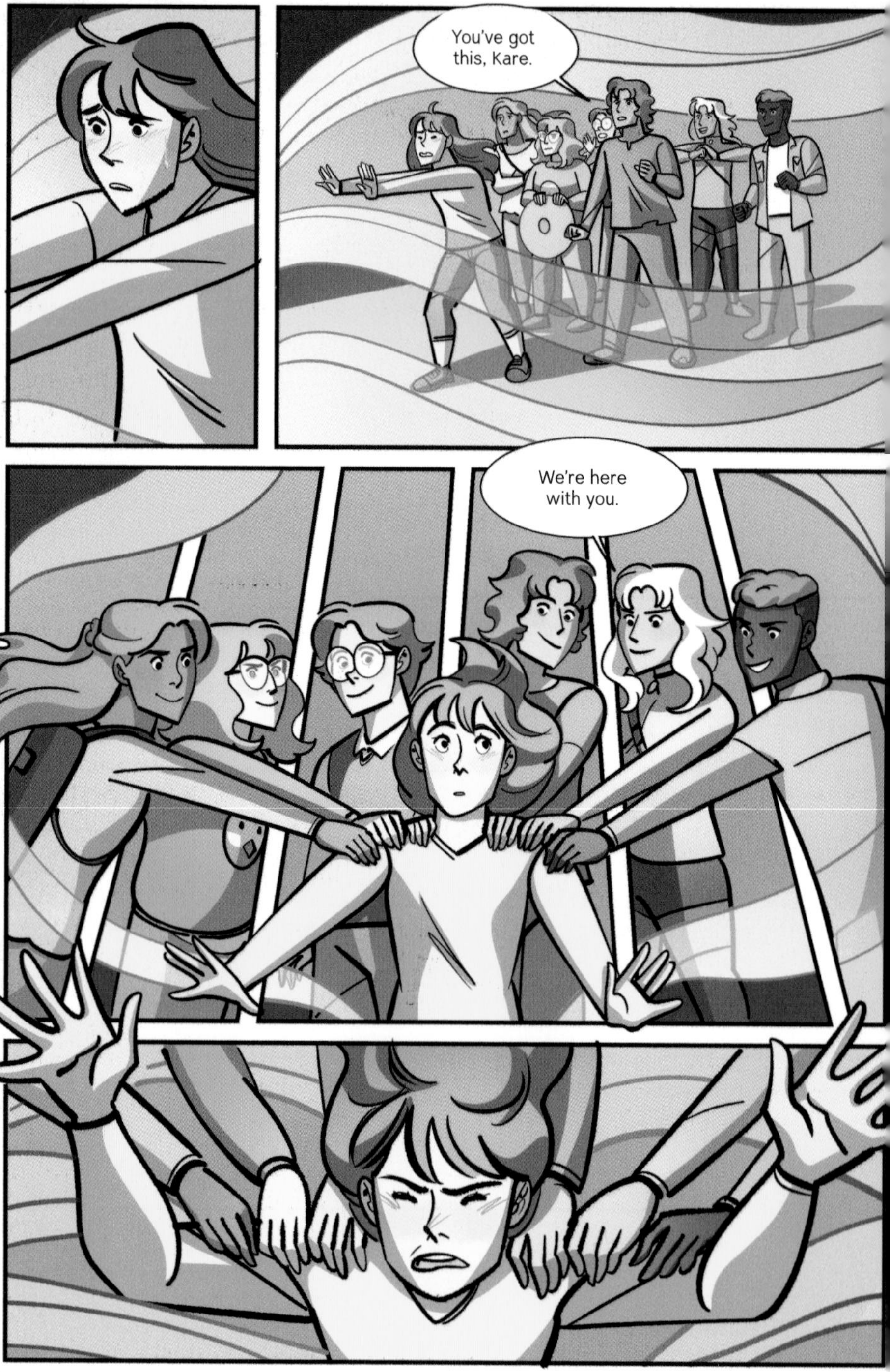
You've got this, Kare.
We're here with you.

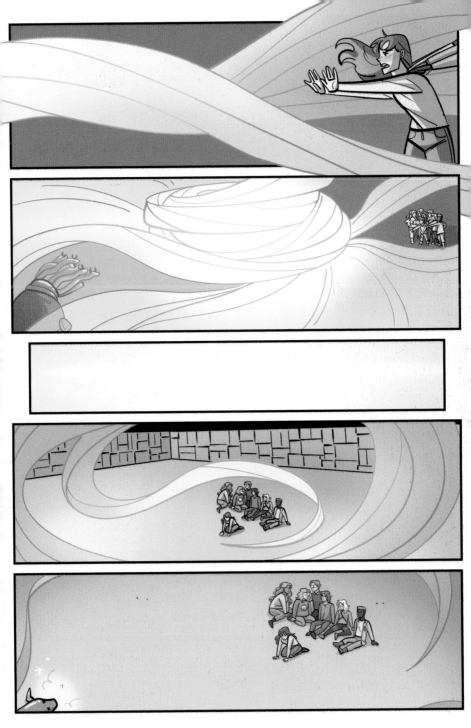

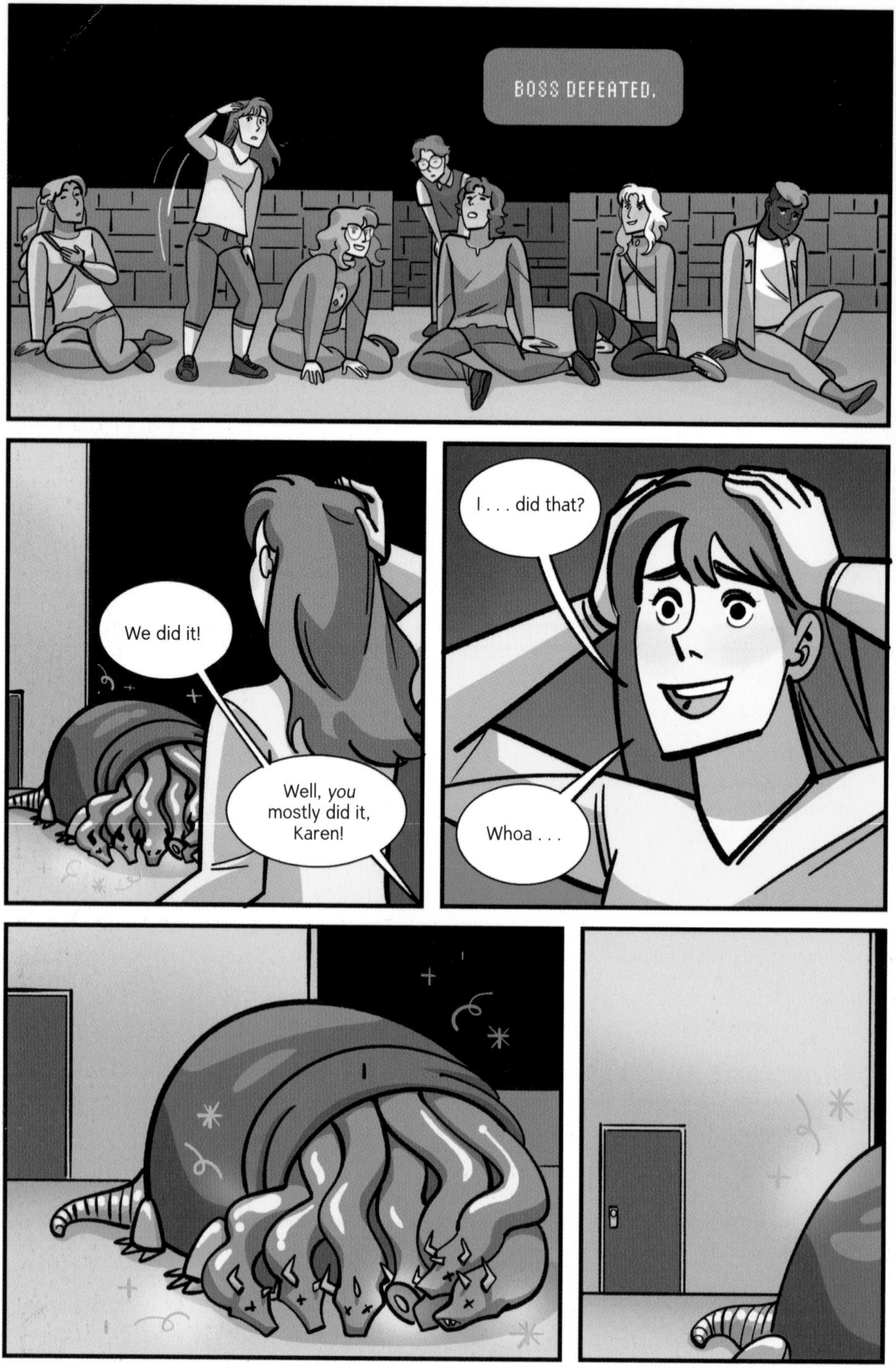
BOSS DEFEATED.
We did it!
Well, *you* mostly did it, Karen!
I . . . did that?
Whoa . . .

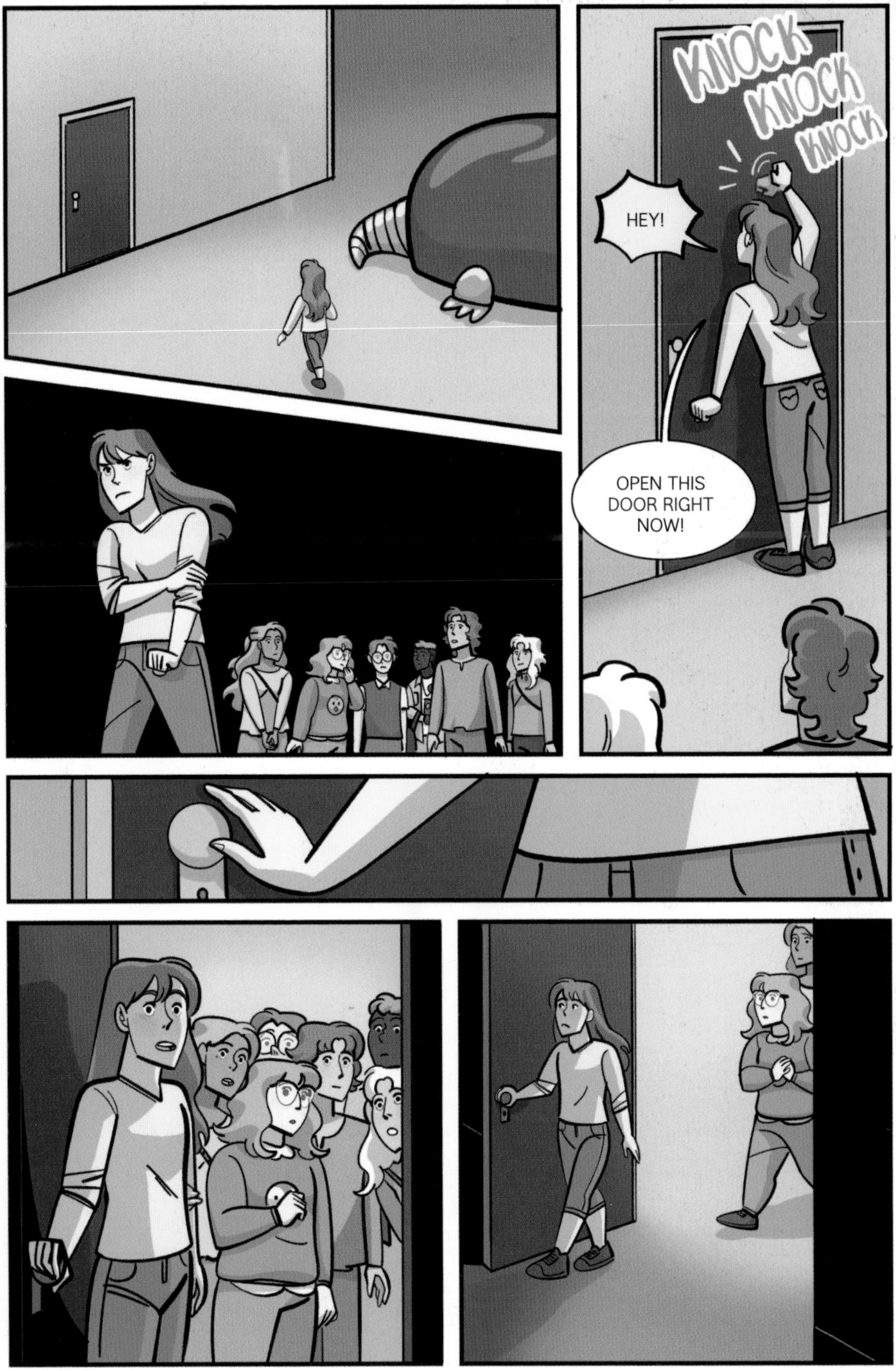
KNOCK
KNOCK
KNOCK
HEY!
OPEN THIS DOOR RIGHT NOW!

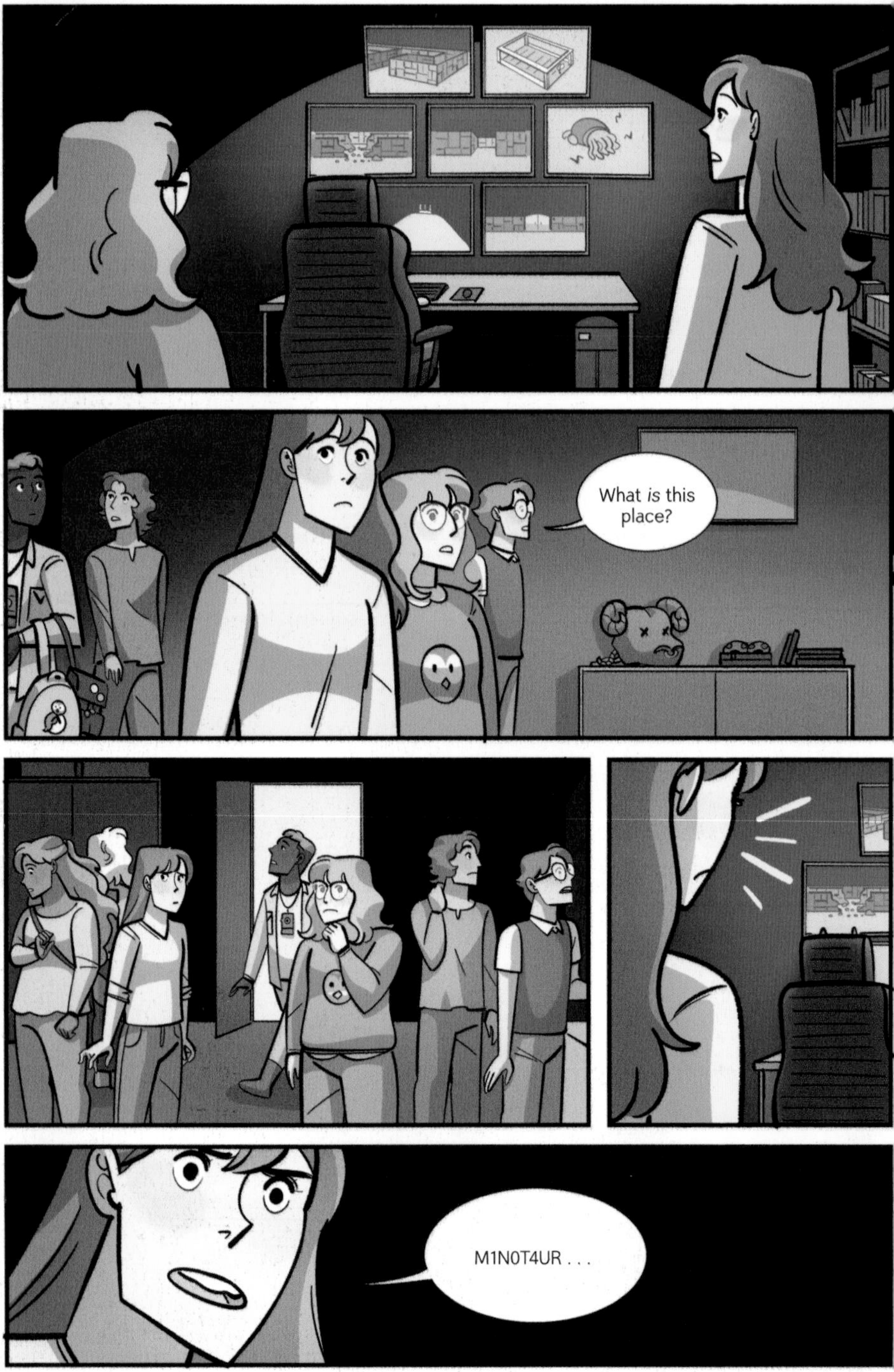
What *is* this place?
M1N0T4UR . . .

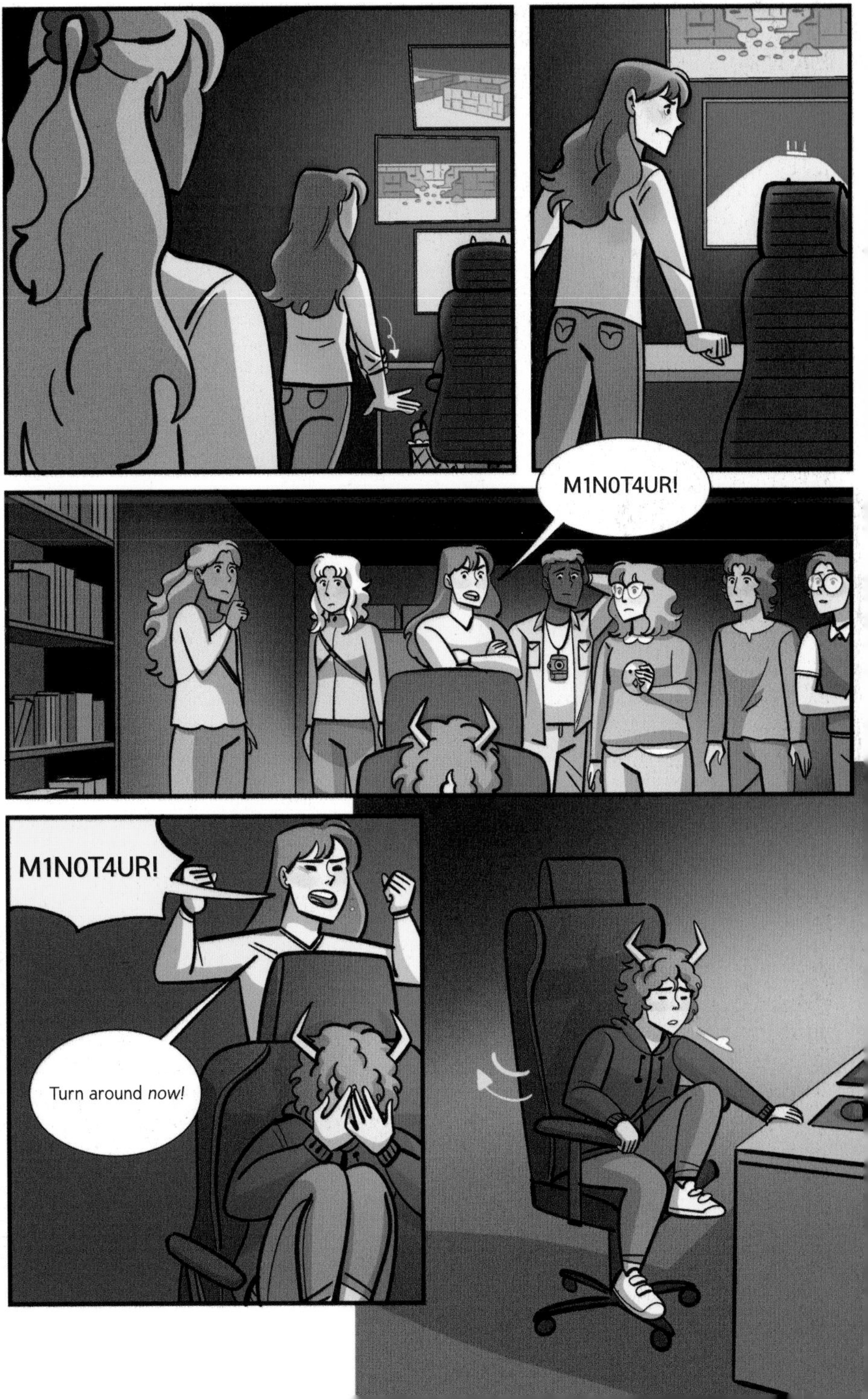
M1N0T4UR!
M1N0T4UR!
Turn around now!

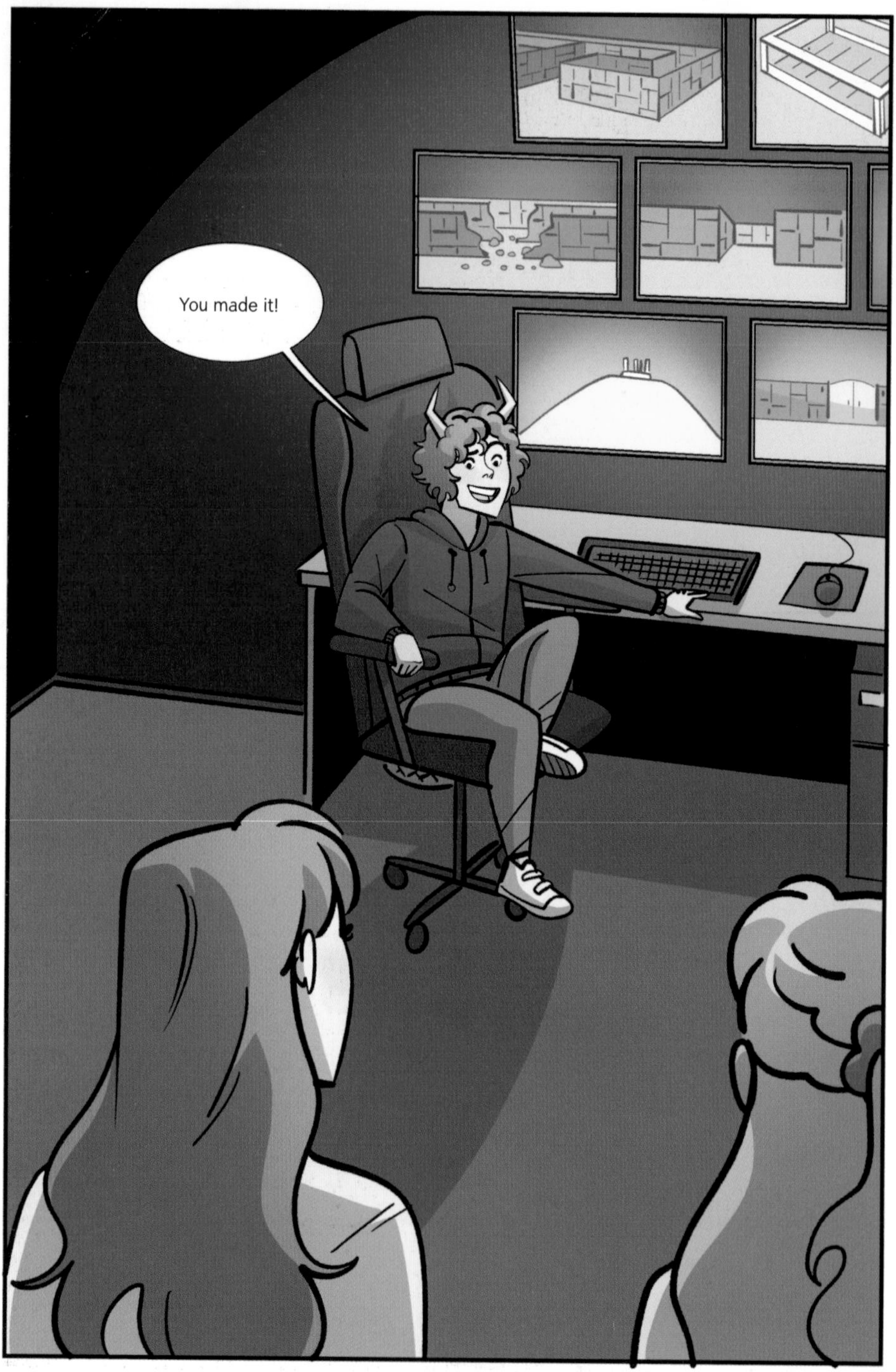
You made it!

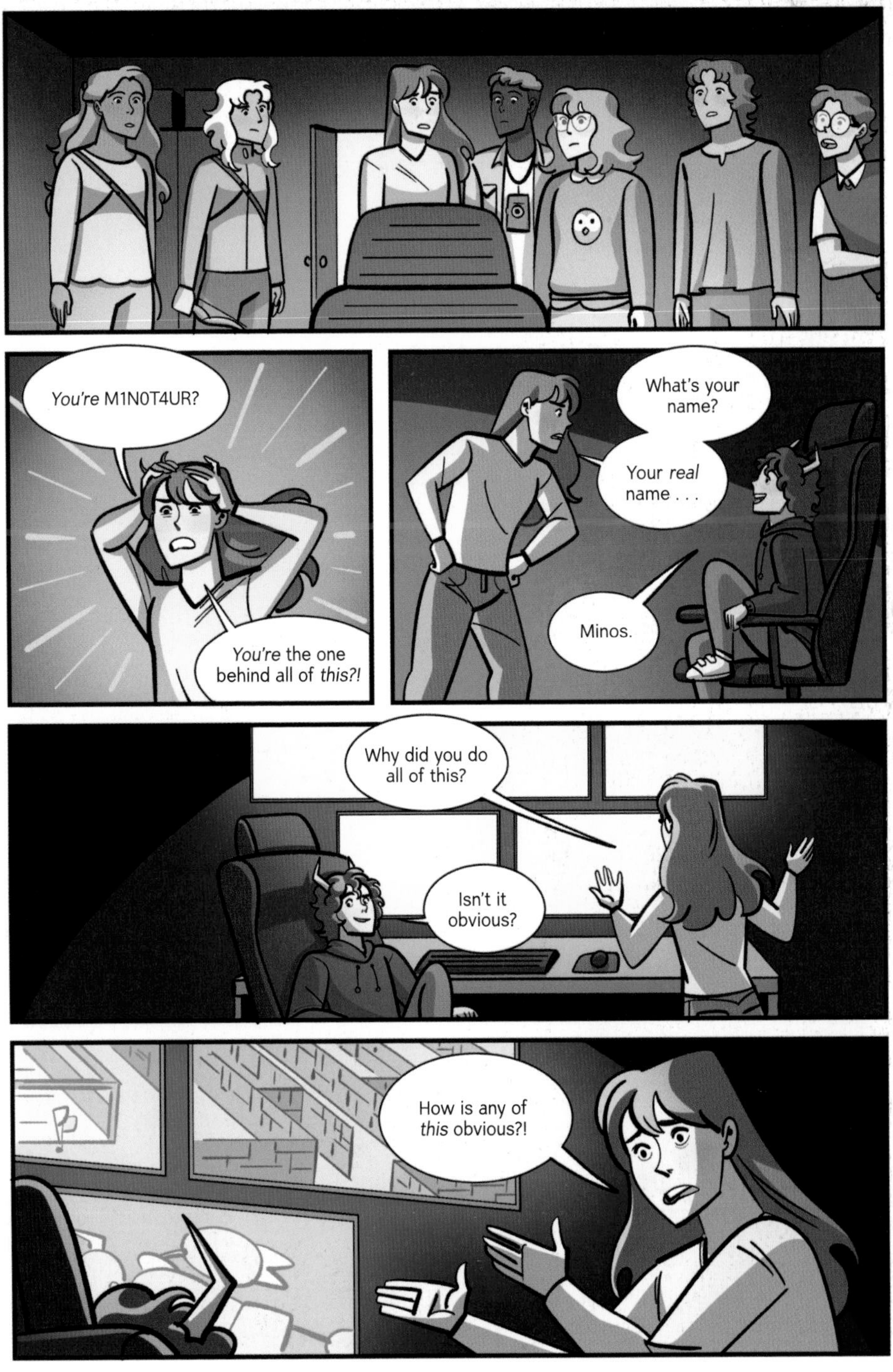
You're M1N0T4UR?
You're the one behind all of *this?!*
What's your name?
Your *real* name . . .
Minos.
Why did you do all of this?
Isn't it obvious?
How is any of *this* obvious?!

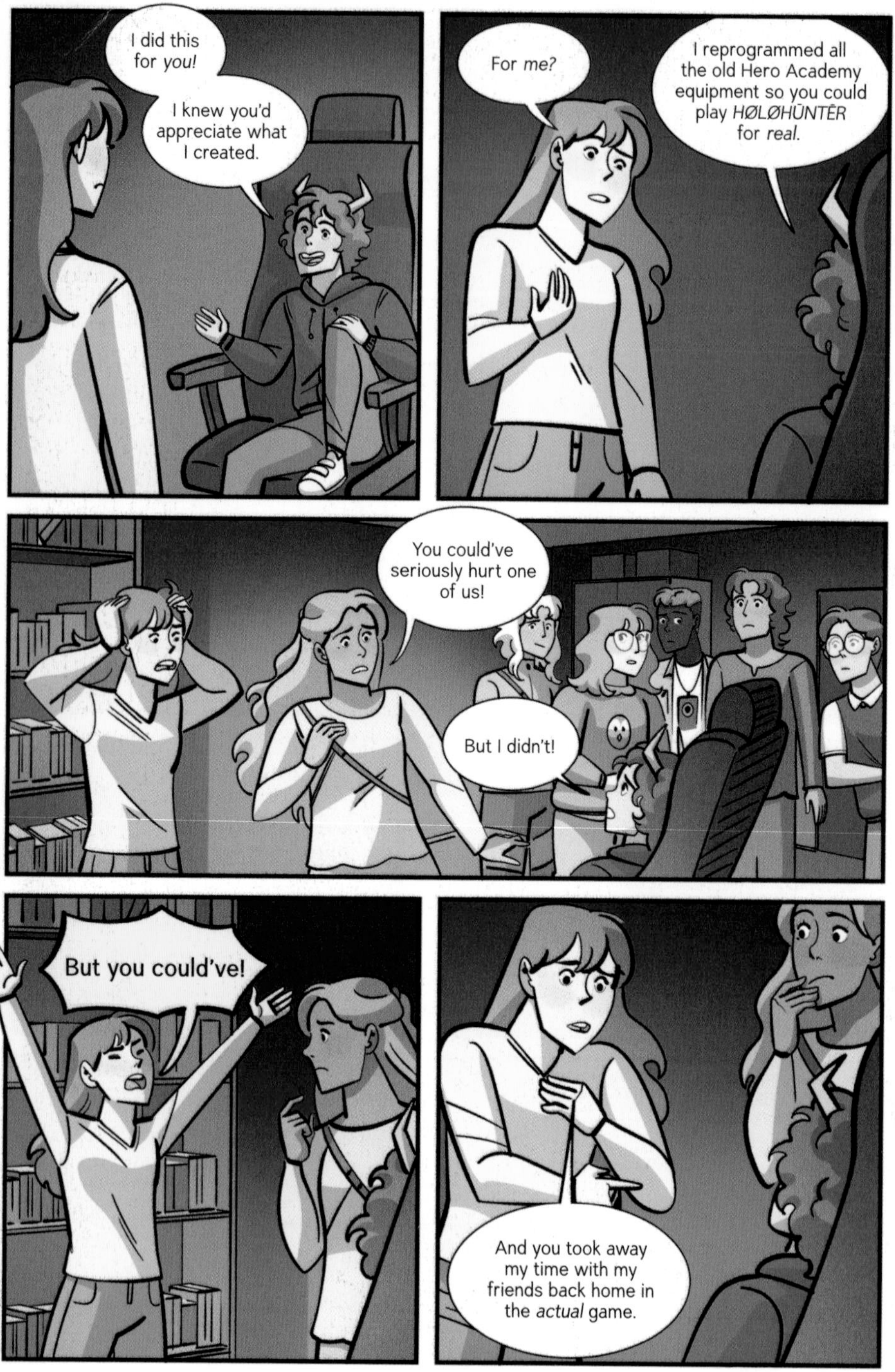
I did this for *you!*
I knew you'd appreciate what I created.
For *me?*
I reprogrammed all the old Hero Academy equipment so you could play *HØLØHŪNTĒR* for *real*.
You could've seriously hurt one of us!
But I didn't!
But you could've!
And you took away my time with my friends back home in the *actual* game.

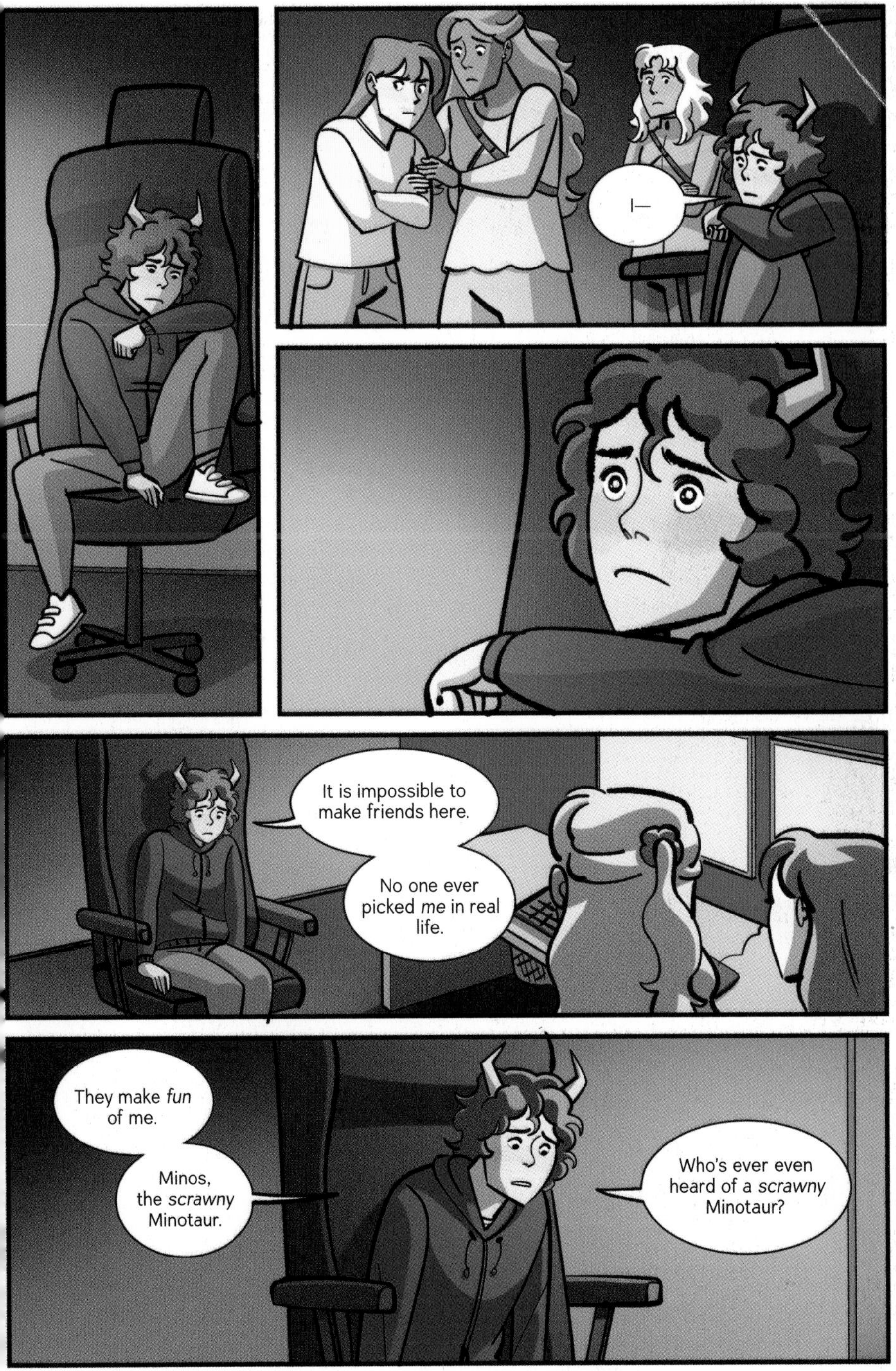
I—
It is impossible to make friends here.
No one ever picked *me* in real life.
They make *fun* of me.
Minos, the *scrawny* Minotaur.
Who's ever even heard of a *scrawny* Minotaur?

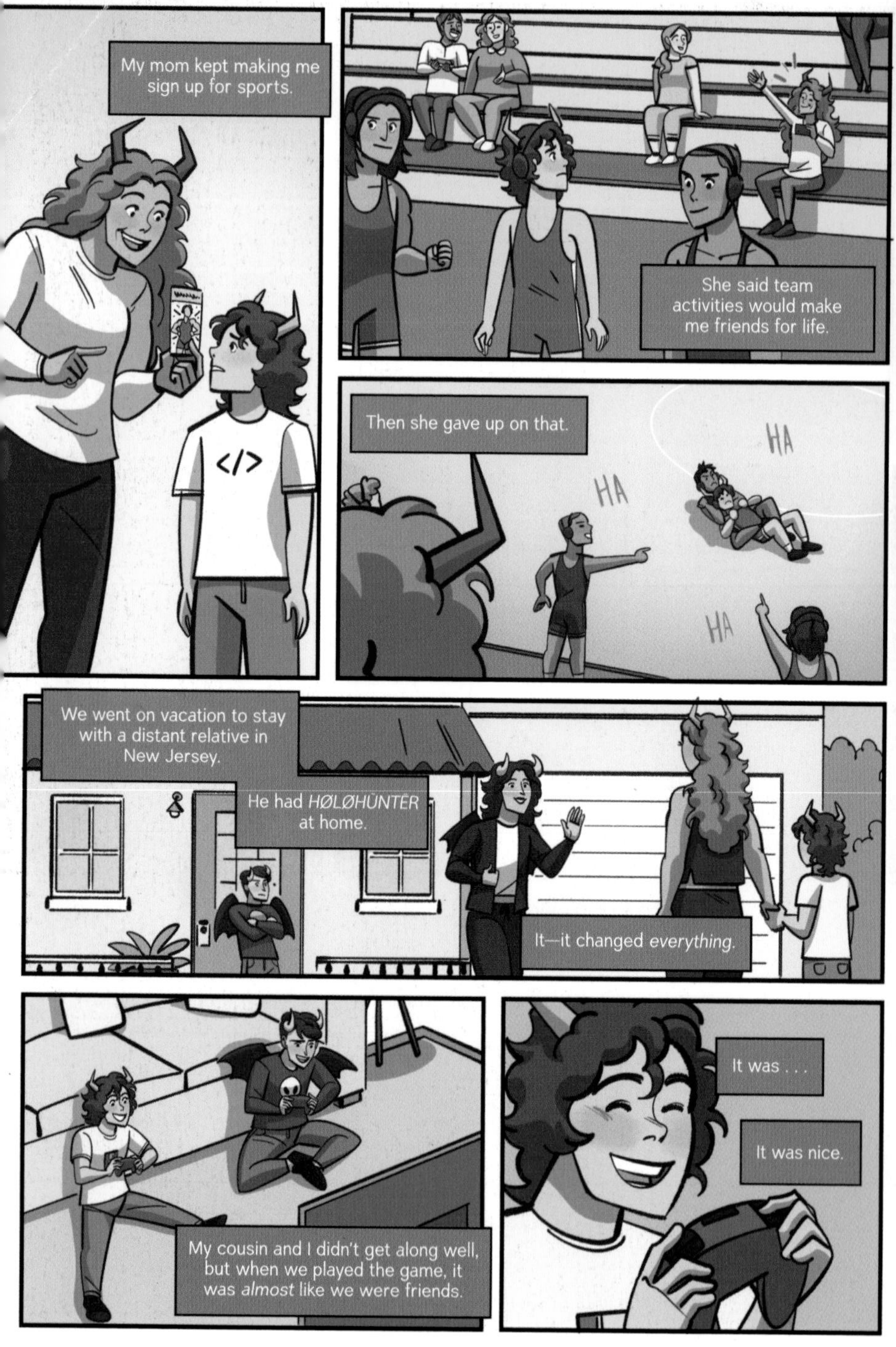
My mom kept making me sign up for sports.
</>
She said team activities would make me friends for life.
Then she gave up on that.
HA
HA
HA
We went on vacation to stay with a distant relative in New Jersey.
He had *HØLØHUNTER* at home.
It—it changed *everything*.
My cousin and I didn't get along well, but when we played the game, it was *almost* like we were friends.
It was . . .
It was nice.

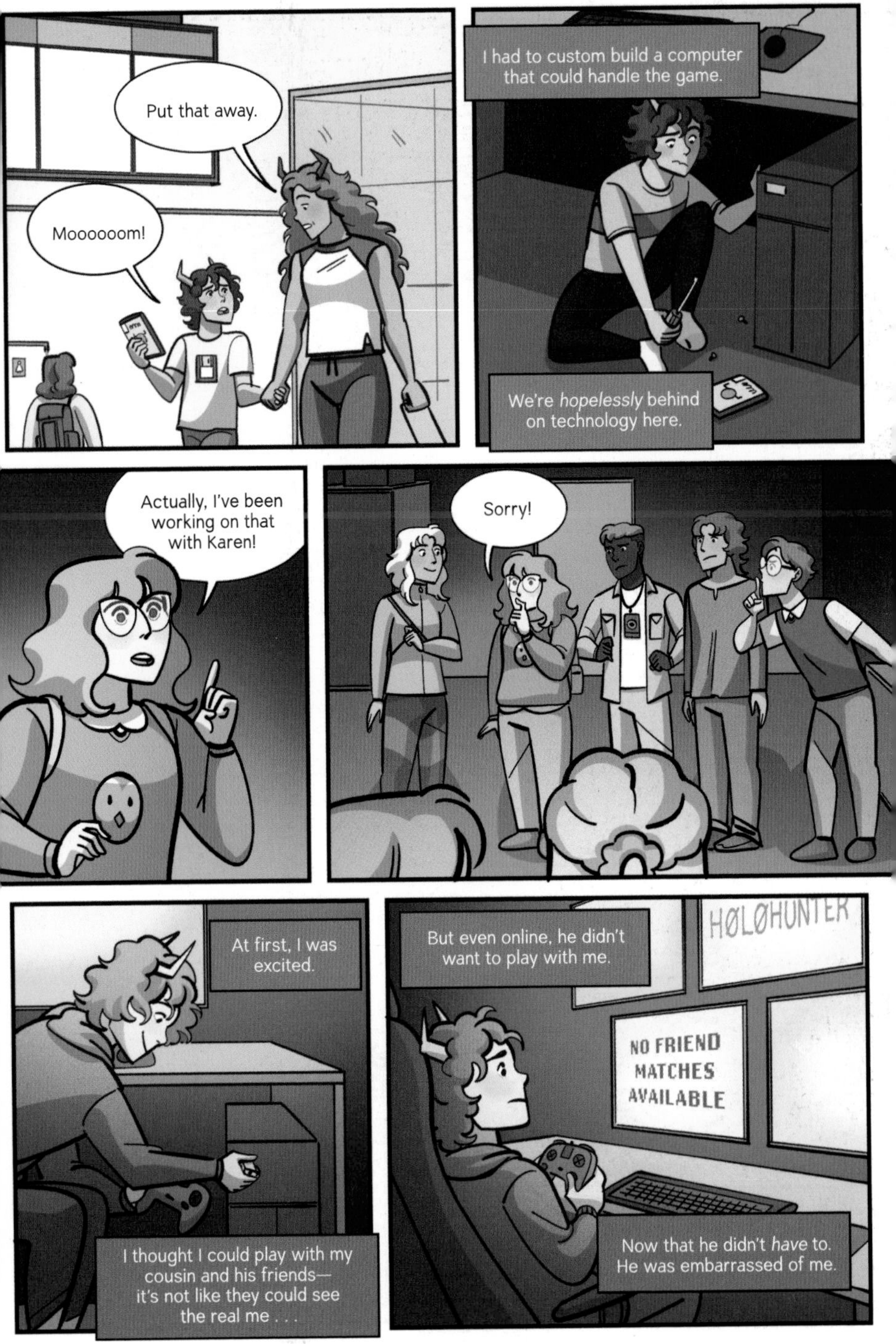
Mooooom!
Put that away.
I had to custom build a computer that could handle the game.
We're *hopelessly* behind on technology here.
Actually, I've been working on that with Karen!
Sorry!
At first, I was excited.
I thought I could play with my cousin and his friends— it's not like they could see the real me . . .
But even online, he didn't want to play with me.
HØLØHUNTER
NO FRIEND MATCHES AVAILABLE
Now that he didn't *have* to. He was embarrassed of me.

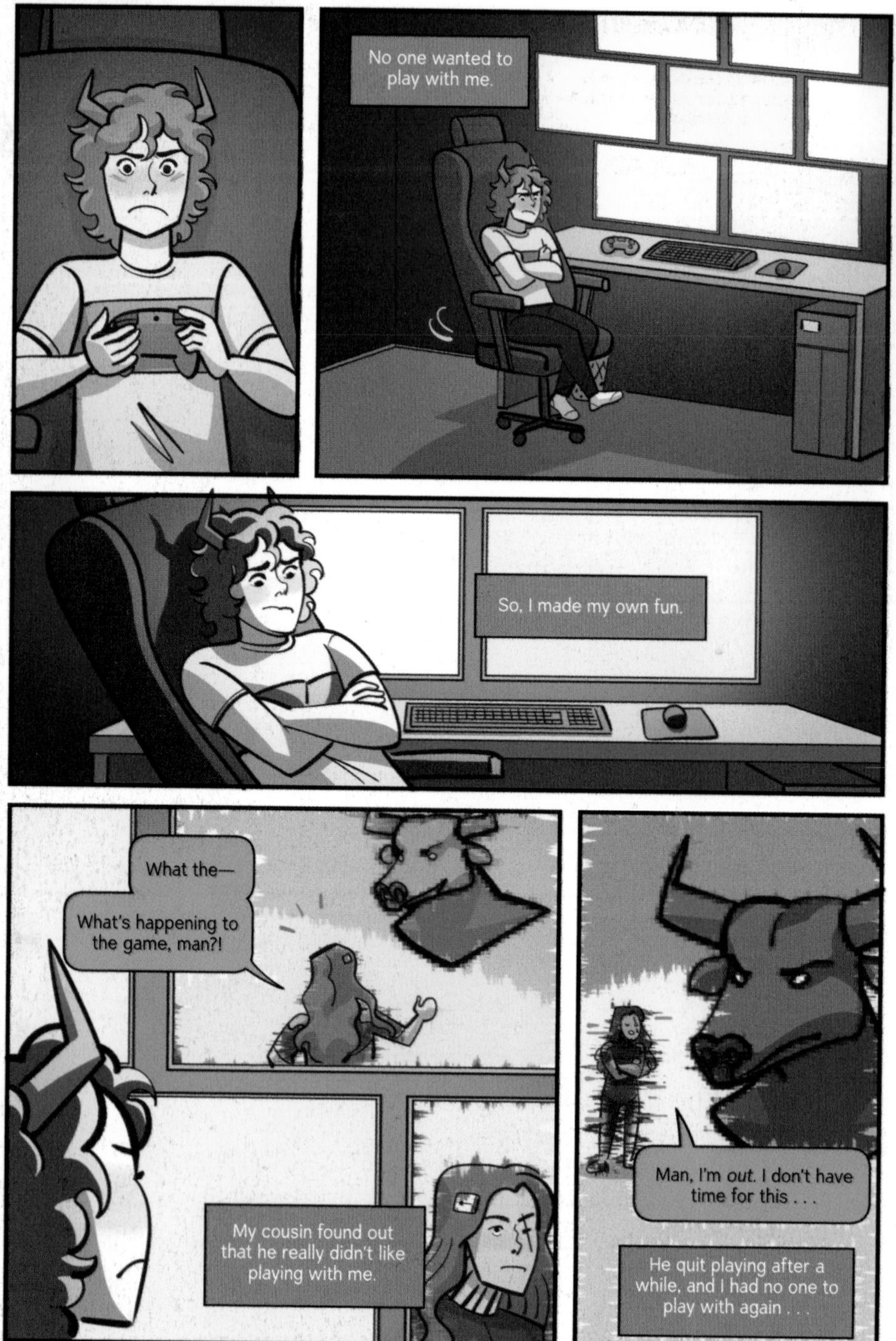
No one wanted to play with me.
So, I made my own fun.
What the—
What's happening to the game, man?!
My cousin found out that he really didn't like playing with me.
Man, I'm *out*. I don't have time for this . . .
He quit playing after a while, and I had no one to play with again . . .

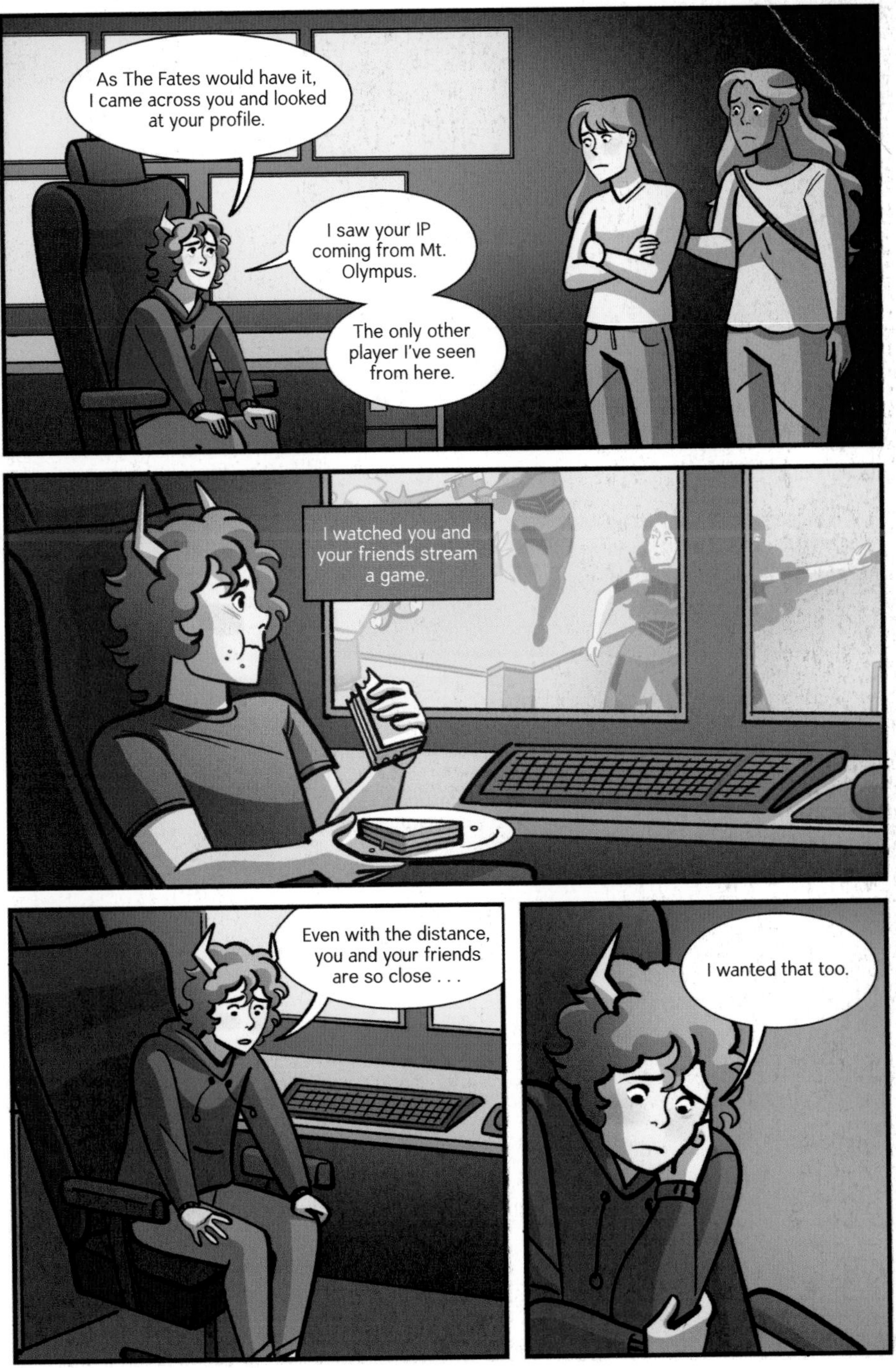
As The Fates would have it, I came across you and looked at your profile.
I saw your IP coming from Mt. Olympus.
The only other player I've seen from here.
I watched you and your friends stream a game.
Even with the distance, you and your friends are so close . . .
I wanted that too.

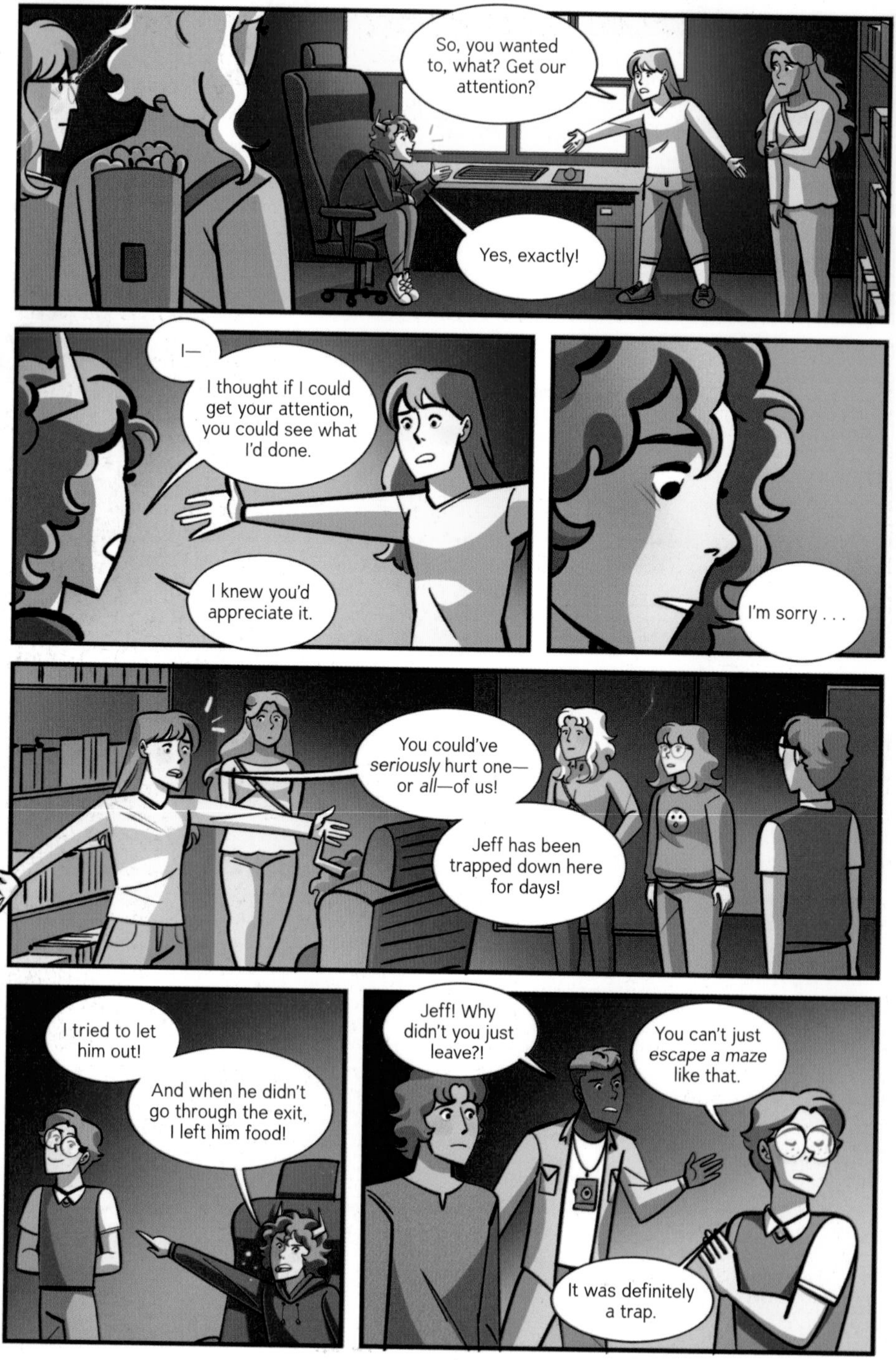

So, you wanted to, what? Get our attention?
Yes, exactly!
I—
I thought if I could get your attention, you could see what I'd done.
I knew you'd appreciate it.
I'm sorry . . .
You could've *seriously* hurt one— or *all*—of us!
Jeff has been trapped down here for days!
I tried to let him out!
And when he didn't go through the exit, I left him food!
Jeff! Why didn't you just leave?!
You can't just *escape a maze* like that.
It was definitely a trap.

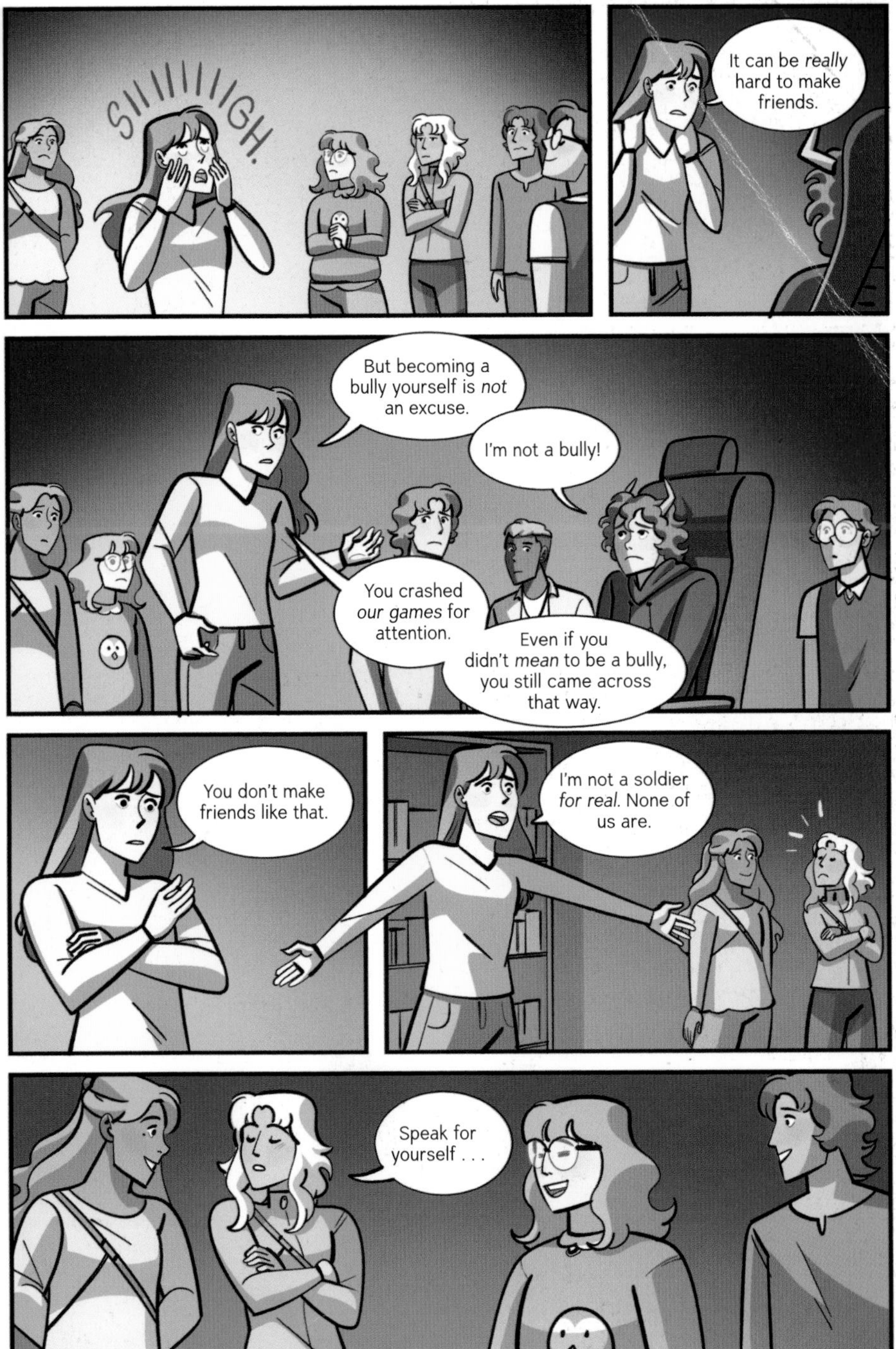
SIIIIIIGH.
It can be *really* hard to make friends.
But becoming a bully yourself is *not* an excuse.
I'm not a bully!
You crashed *our games* for attention.
Even if you didn't *mean* to be a bully, you still came across that way.
You don't make friends like that.
I'm not a soldier *for real.* None of us are.
Speak for yourself . . .

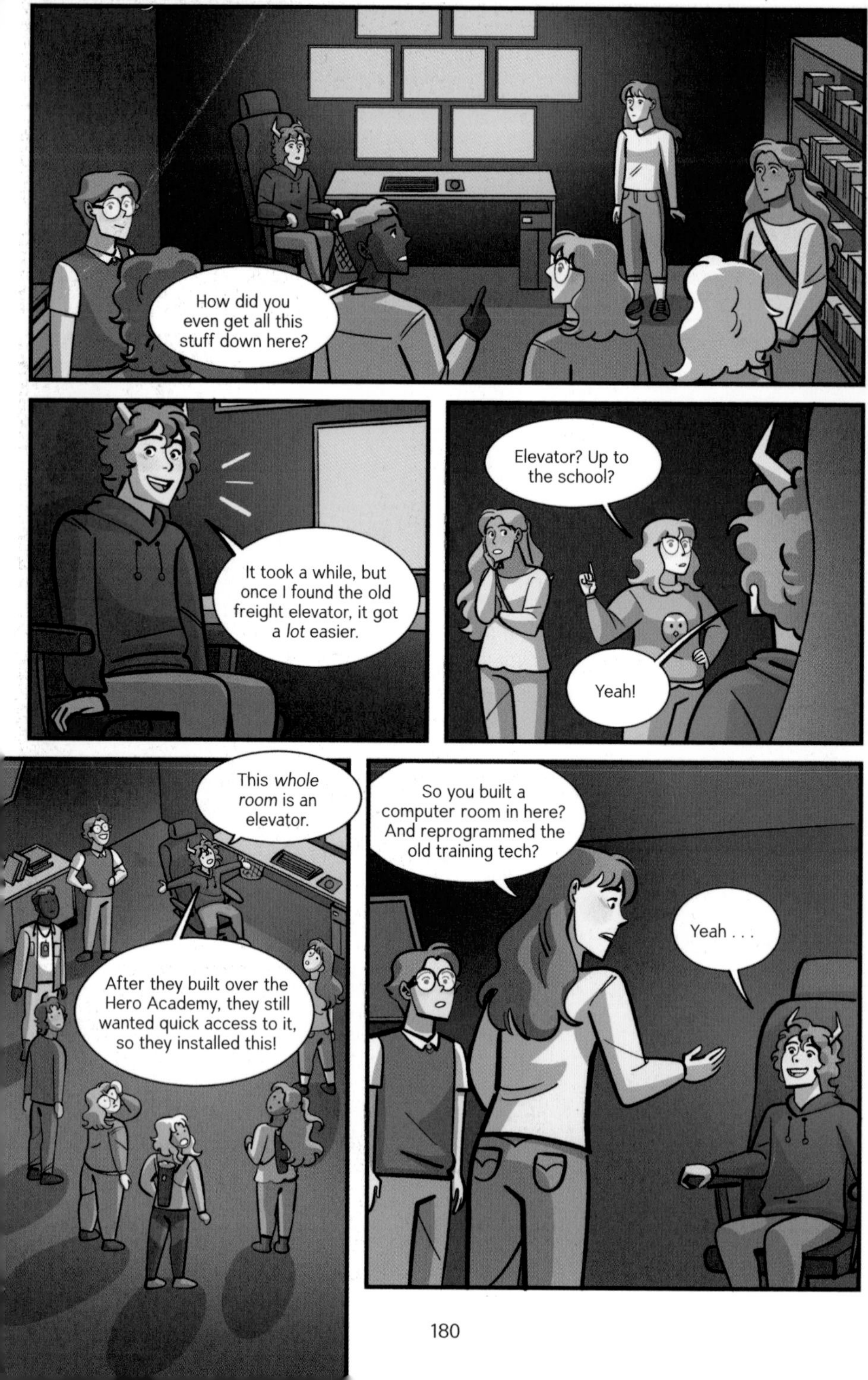
How did you even get all this stuff down here?
It took a while, but once I found the old freight elevator, it got a *lot* easier.
Elevator? Up to the school?
Yeah!
This *whole room* is an elevator.
After they built over the Hero Academy, they still wanted quick access to it, so they installed this!
So you built a computer room in here? And reprogrammed the old training tech?
Yeah . . .

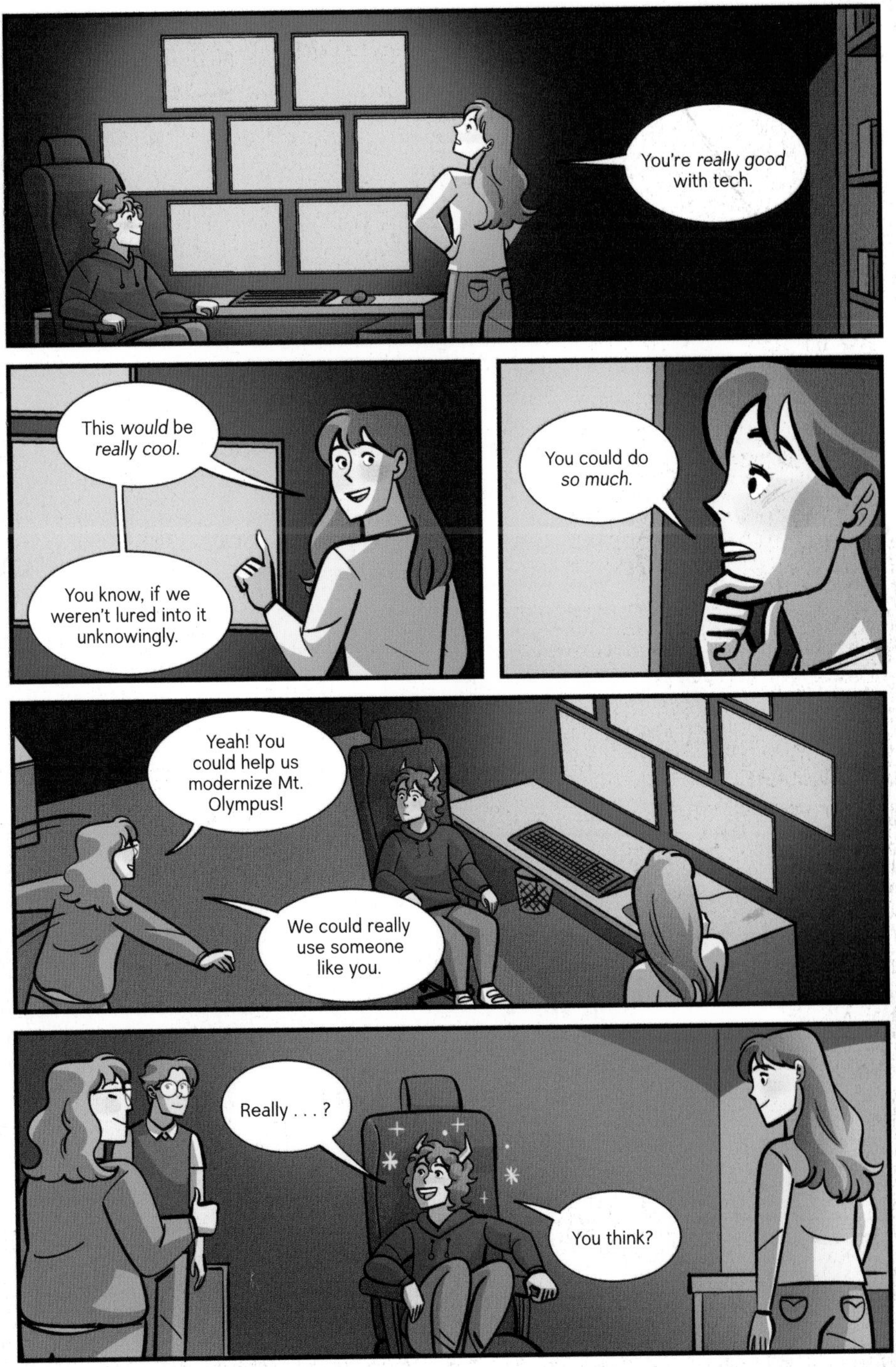
You're *really good* with tech.
This *would* be *really cool.*
You know, if we weren't lured into it unknowingly.
You could do *so much.*
Yeah! You could help us modernize Mt. Olympus!
We could really use someone like you.
Really . . . ?
You think?

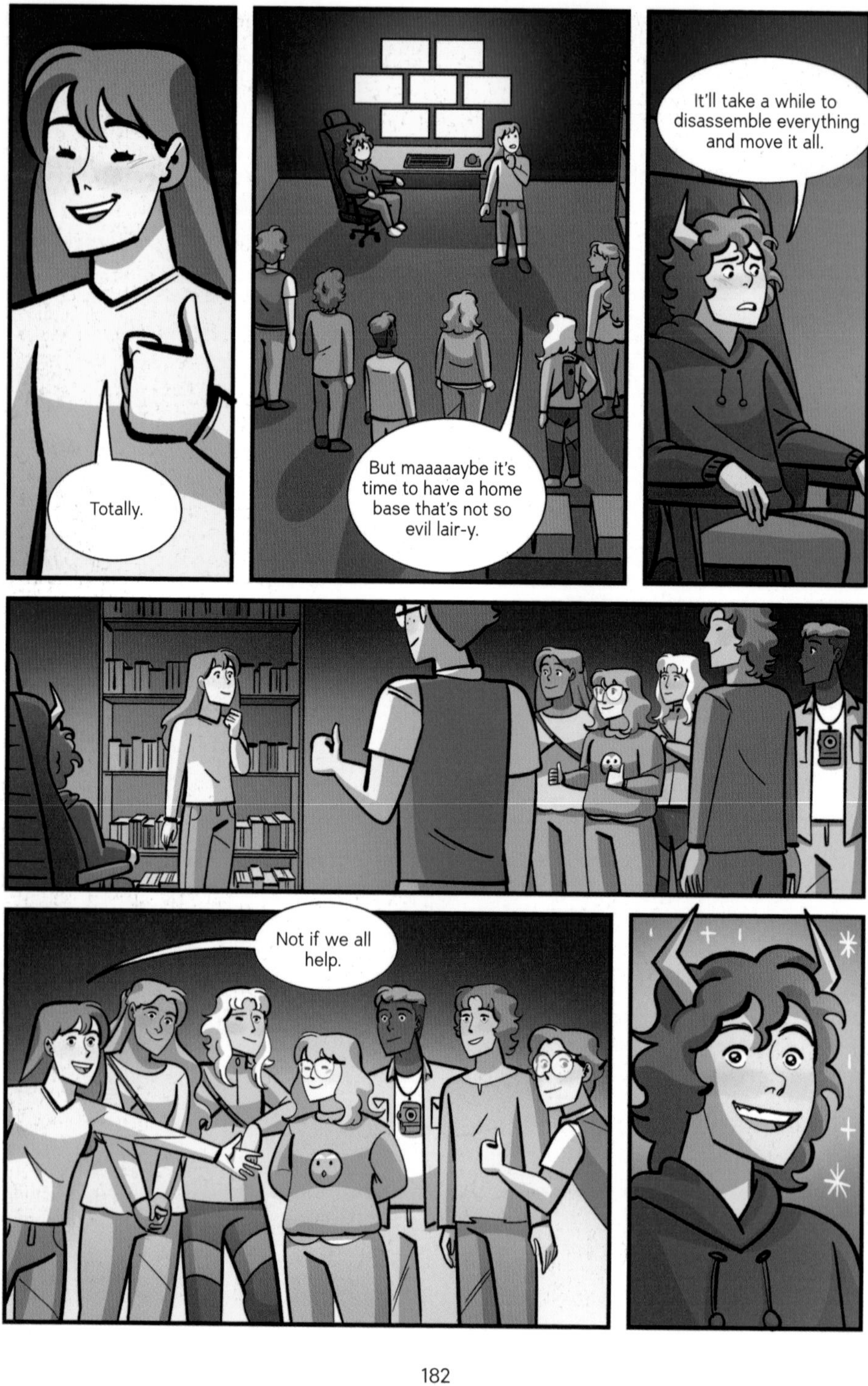
Totally.
But maaaaaybe it's time to have a home base that's not so evil lair-y.
It'll take a while to disassemble everything and move it all.
Not if we all help.

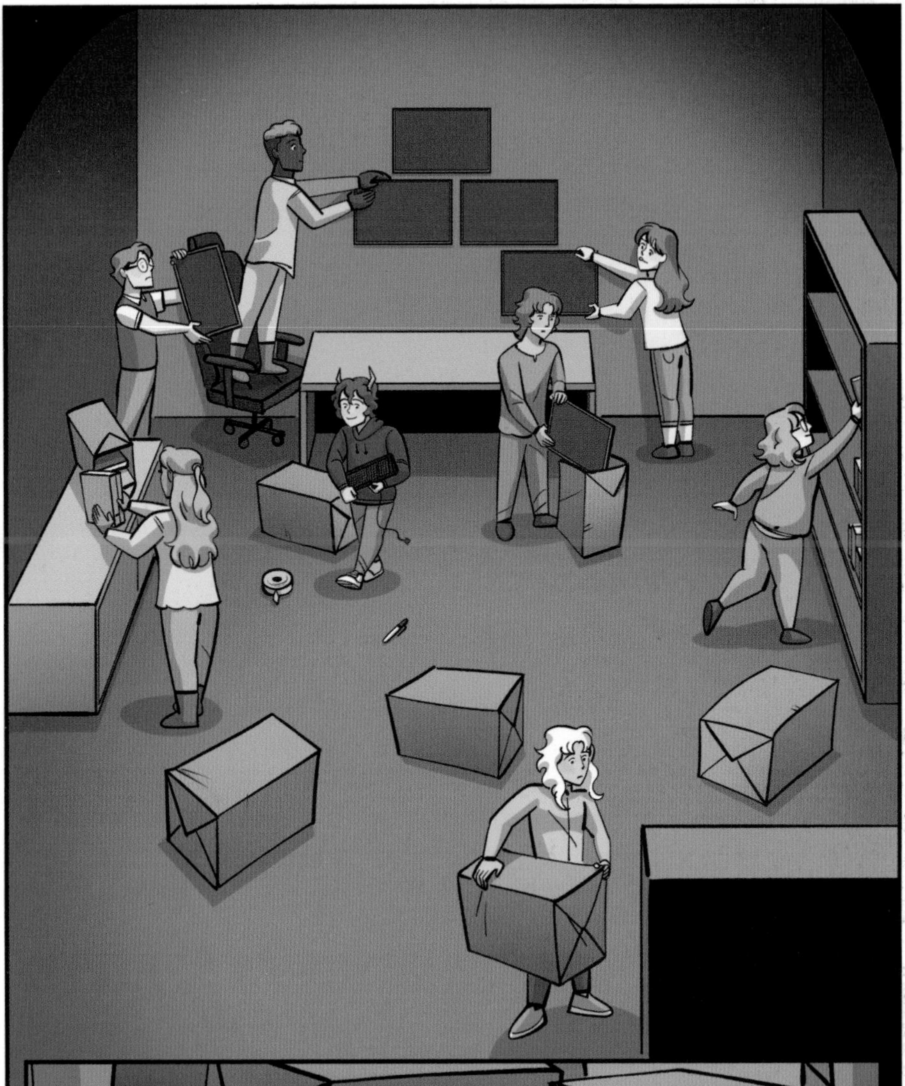

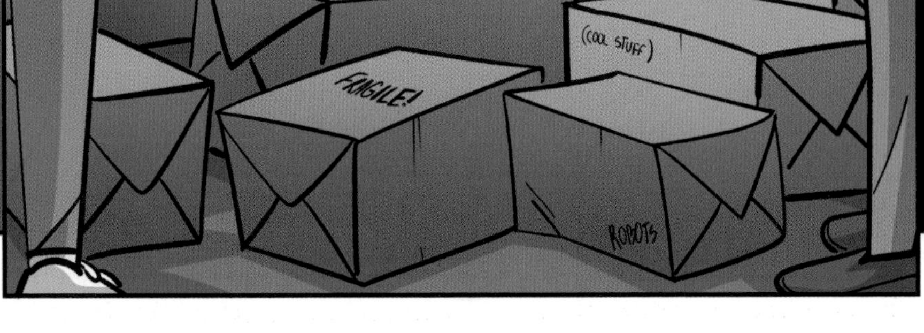
(COOL STUFF)
FRAGILE!
ROBOTS

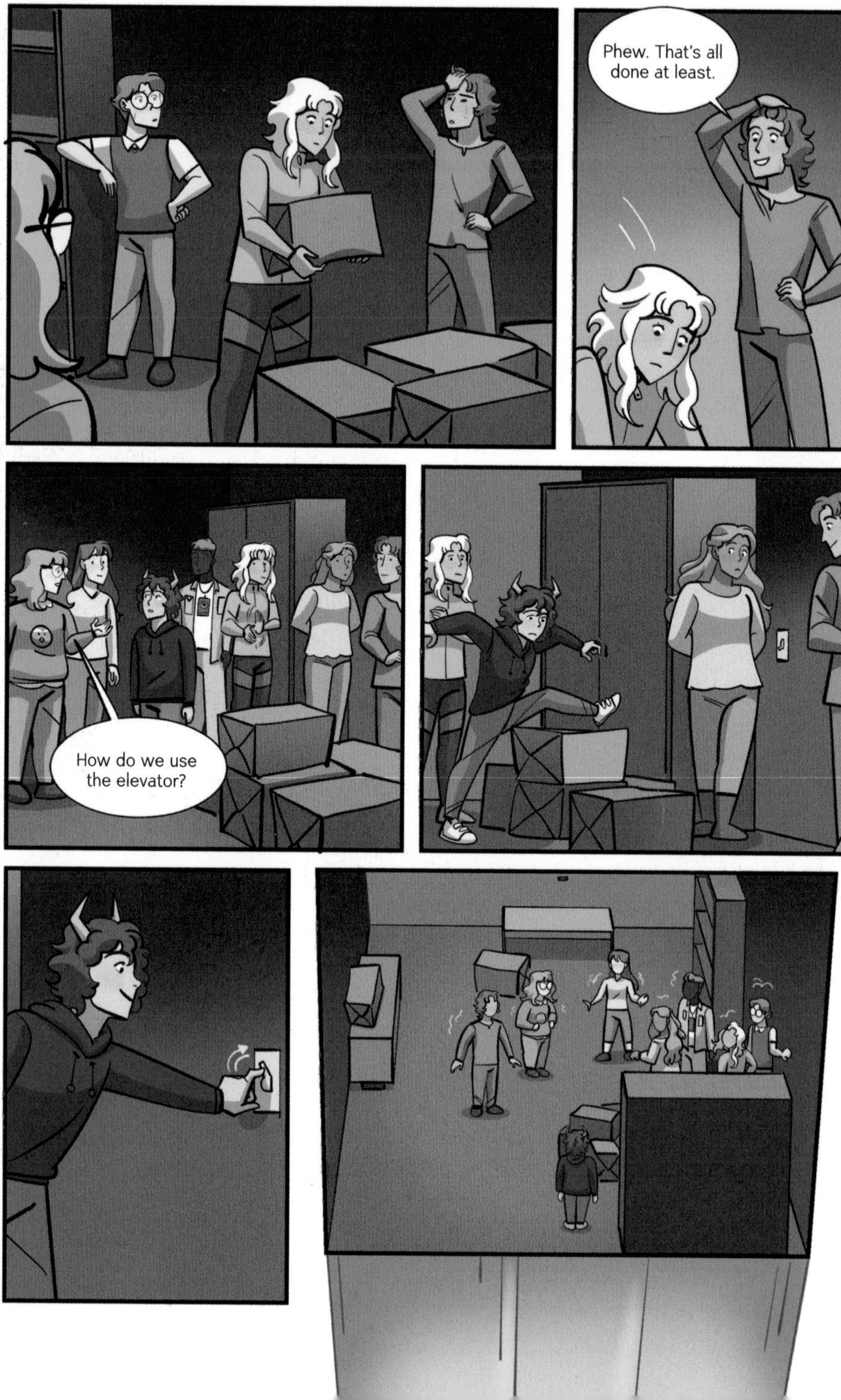
Phew. That's all done at least.
How do we use the elevator?

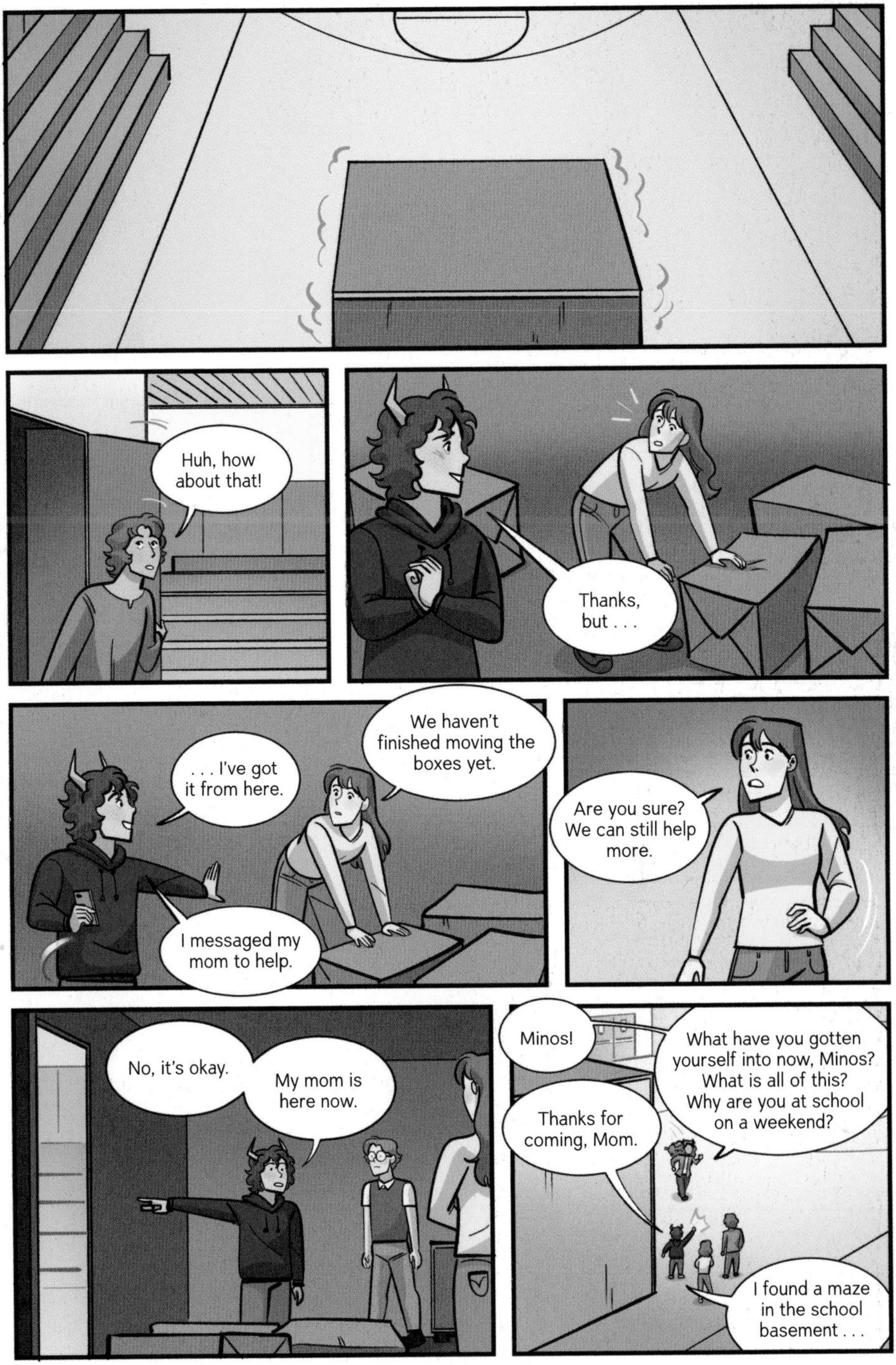
Huh, how about that!
Thanks, but . . .
. . . I've got it from here.
We haven't finished moving the boxes yet.
I messaged my mom to help.
Are you sure? We can still help more.
No, it's okay.
My mom is here now.
Minos!
What have you gotten yourself into now, Minos? What is all of this? Why are you at school on a weekend?
Thanks for coming, Mom.
I found a maze in the school basement . . .

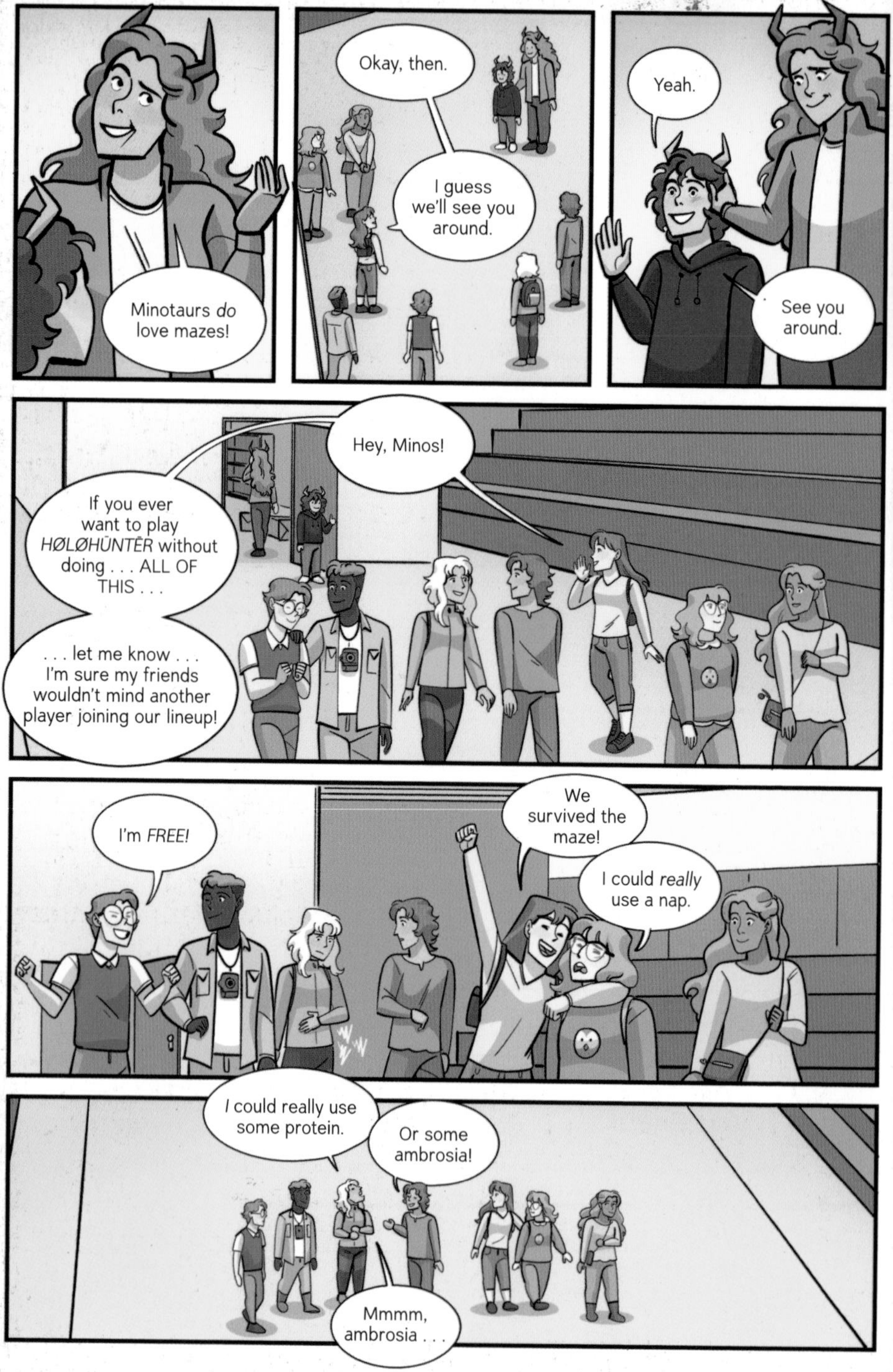
Minotaurs *do* love mazes!
Okay, then.
I guess we'll see you around.
Yeah.
See you around.
Hey, Minos!
If you ever want to play *HØLØHÜNTËR* without doing . . . ALL OF THIS . . .
. . . let me know . . . I'm sure my friends wouldn't mind another player joining our lineup!
I'm *FREE!*
We survived the maze!
I could *really* use a nap.
I could really use some protein.
Or some ambrosia!
Mmmm, ambrosia . . .

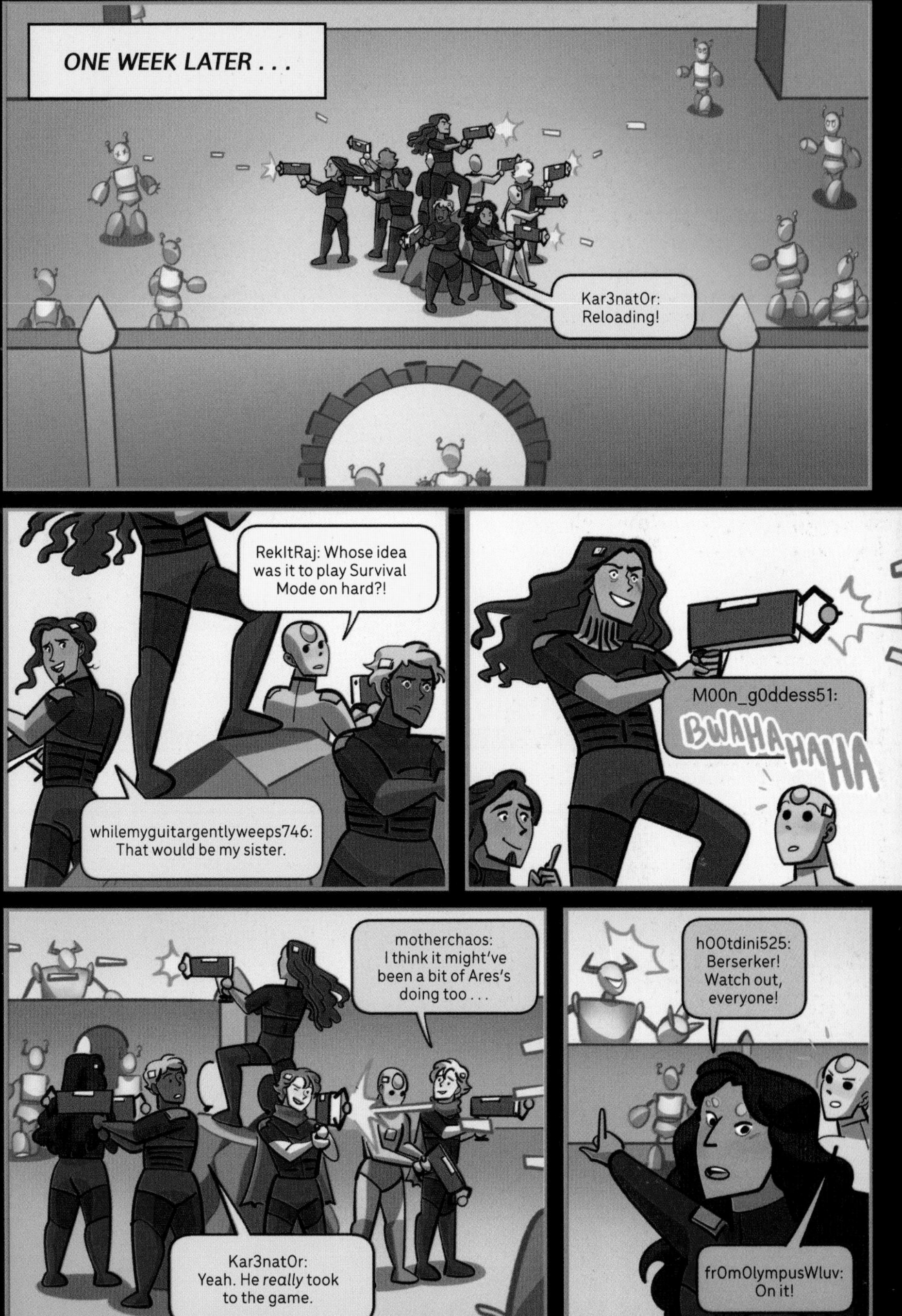
ONE WEEK LATER . . .
Kar3natOr: Reloading!
RekItRaj: Whose idea was it to play Survival Mode on hard?!
whilemyguitargentlyweeps746: That would be my sister.
M00n_g0ddess51: BWAHAHAHAHA
motherchaos: I think it might've been a bit of Ares's doing too . . .
Kar3natOr: Yeah. He *really* took to the game.
h00tdini525: Berserker! Watch out, everyone!
fr0mOlympusWluv: On it!

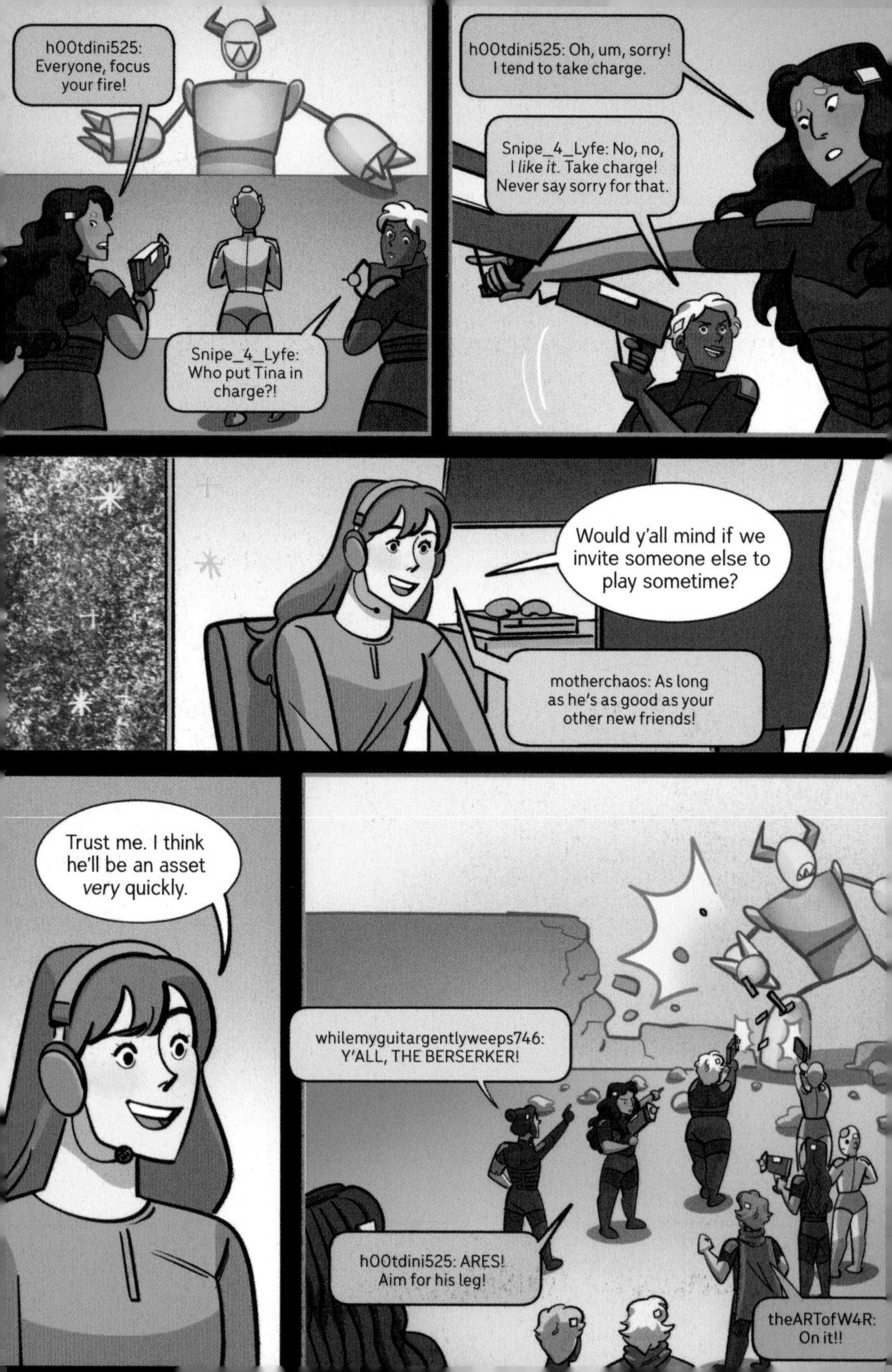
h00tdini525: Everyone, focus your fire!
Snipe_4_Lyfe: Who put Tina in charge?!
h00tdini525: Oh, um, sorry! I tend to take charge.
Snipe_4_Lyfe: No, no, I *like it*. Take charge! Never say sorry for that.
Would y'all mind if we invite someone else to play sometime?
motherchaos: As long as he's as good as your other new friends!
Trust me. I think he'll be an asset *very* quickly.
whilemyguitargentlyweeps746: Y'ALL, THE BERSERKER!
h00tdini525: ARES! Aim for his leg!
theARTofW4R: On it!!

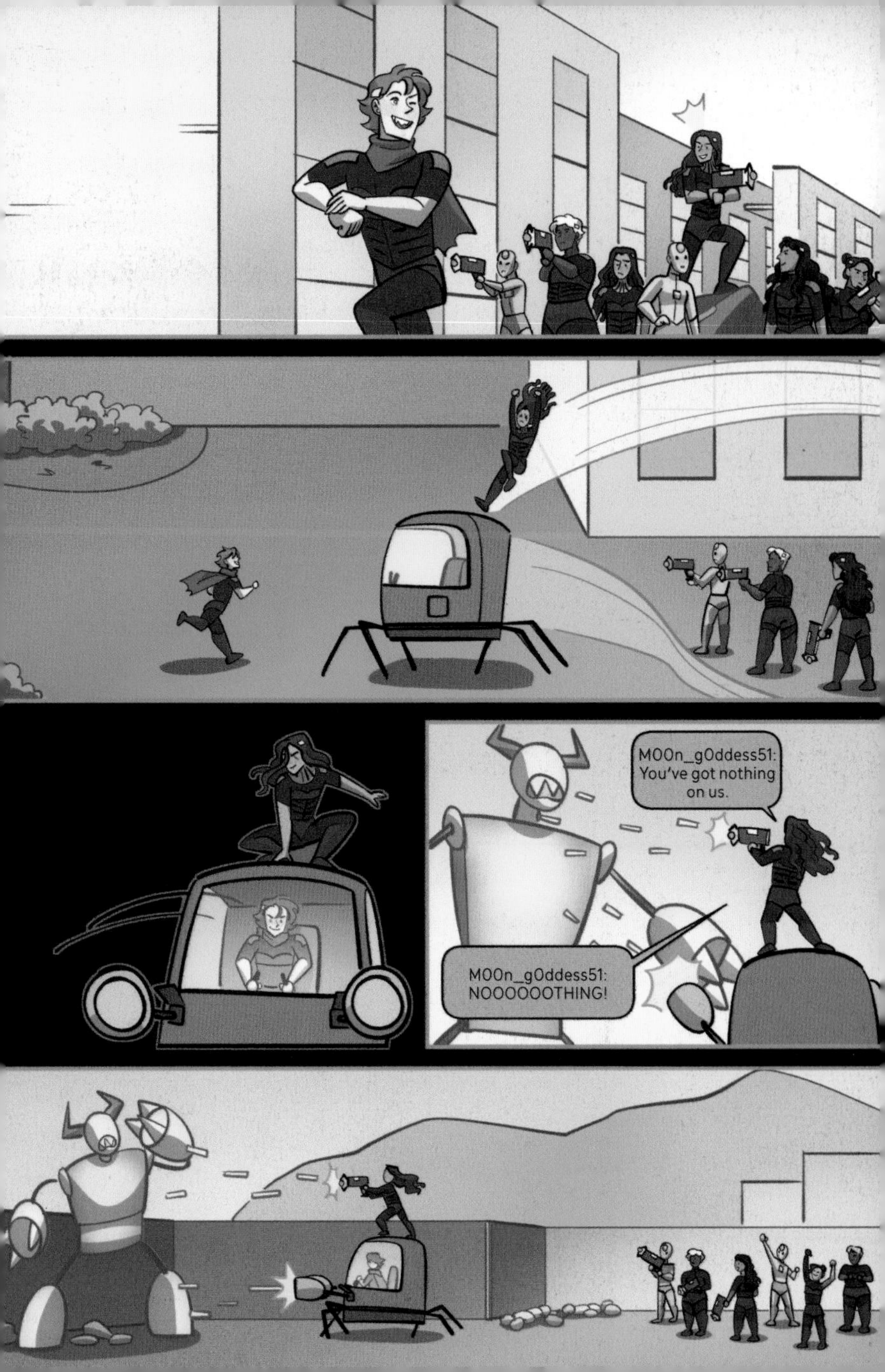
M0On_g0ddess51: You've got nothing on us.
M0On_g0ddess51: NOOOOOOTHING!

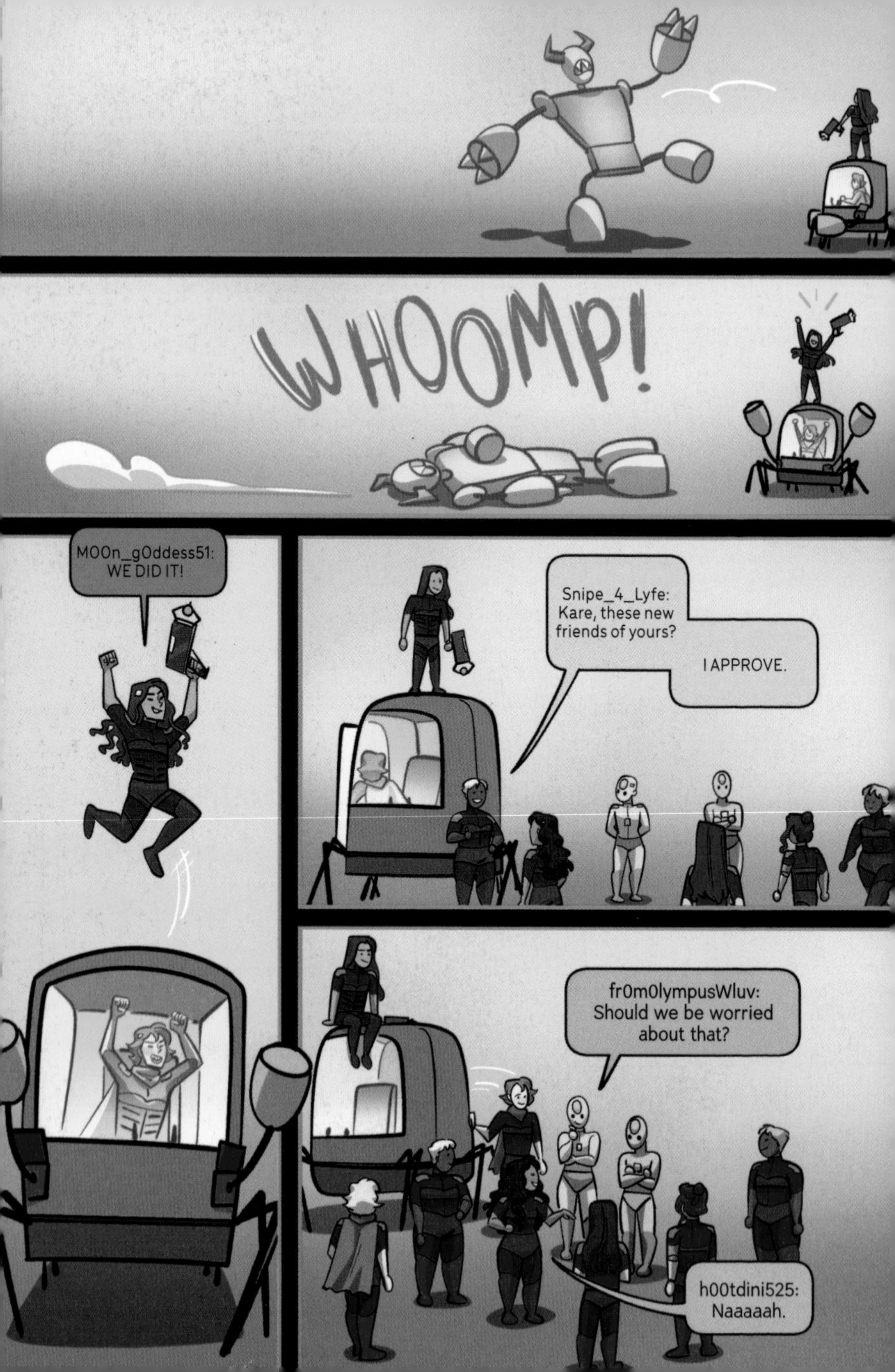
WHOOMP!
M0On_g0ddess51: WE DID IT!
Snipe_4_Lyfe: Kare, these new friends of yours?
I APPROVE.
fr0m0lympusWluv: Should we be worried about that?
h0Otdini525: Naaaaah.

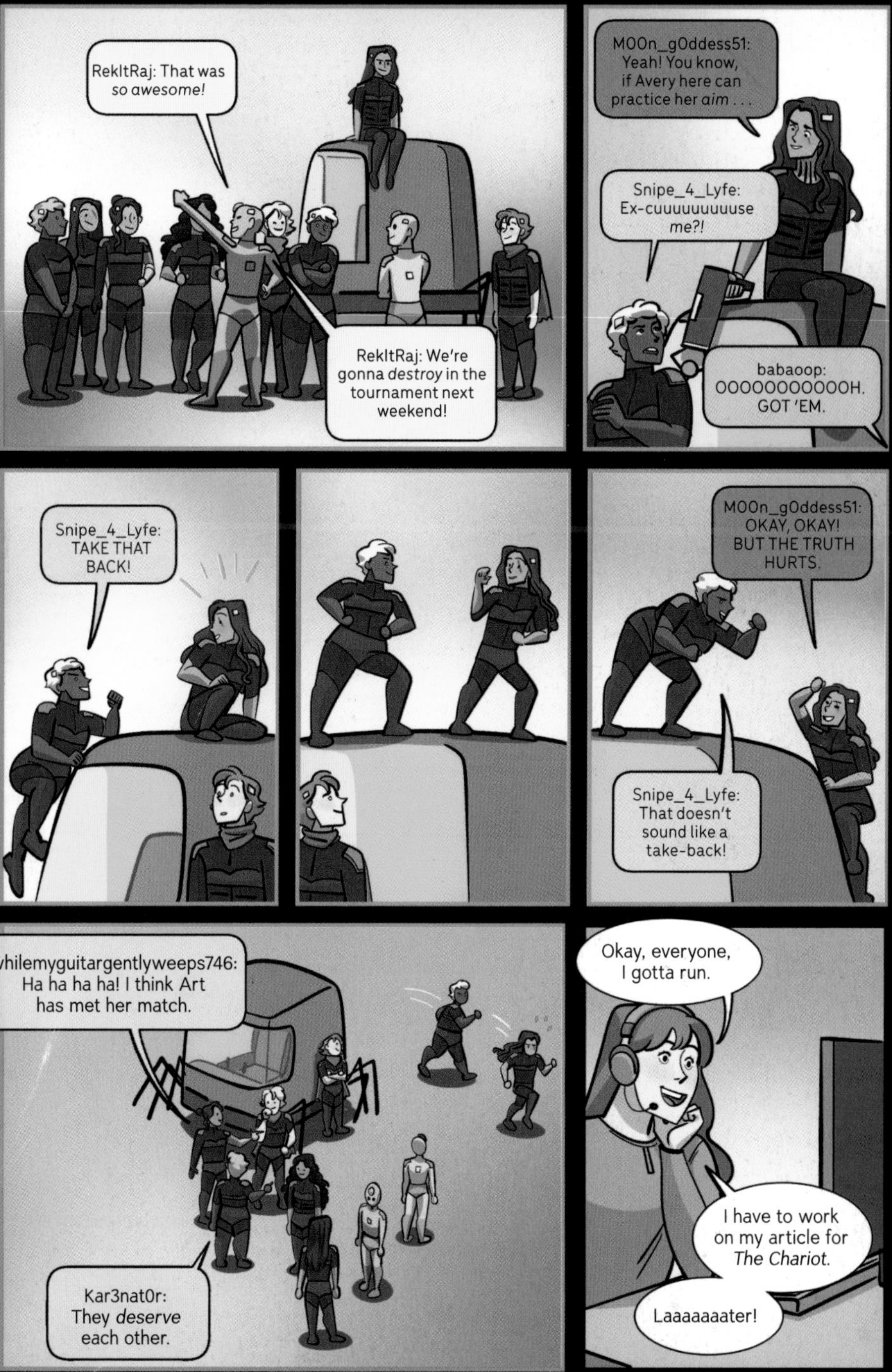
RekltRaj: That was *so awesome!*
RekltRaj: We're gonna *destroy* in the tournament next weekend!
M0On_g0ddess51: Yeah! You know, if Avery here can practice her *aim* . . .
Snipe_4_Lyfe: Ex-cuuuuuuuuuse *me?!*
babaoop: OOOOOOOOOOOH. GOT 'EM.
Snipe_4_Lyfe: TAKE THAT BACK!
M0On_g0ddess51: OKAY, OKAY! BUT THE TRUTH HURTS.
Snipe_4_Lyfe: That doesn't sound like a take-back!
hilemyguitargentlyweeps746: Ha ha ha ha! I think Art has met her match.
Kar3nat0r: They *deserve* each other.
Okay, everyone, I gotta run.
I have to work on my article for *The Chariot*.
Laaaaaaater!

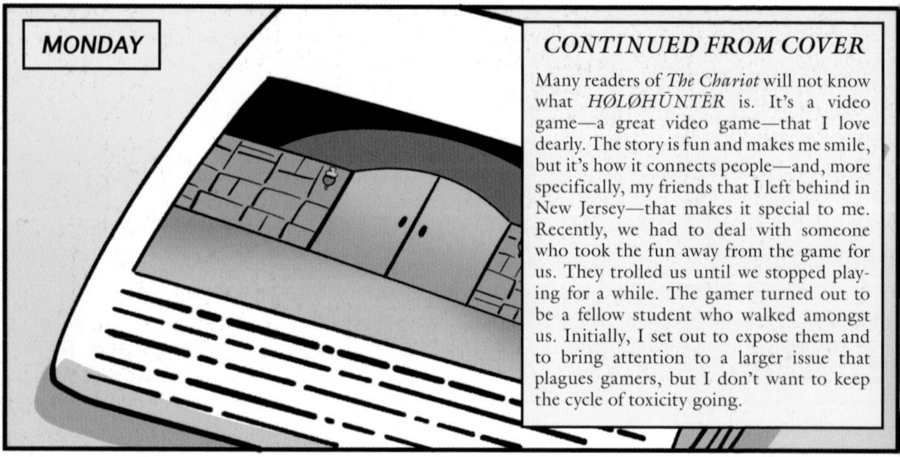
MONDAY
CONTINUED FROM COVER
Many readers of *The Chariot* will not know what *HØLØHŪNTĒR* is. It's a video game—a great video game—that I love dearly. The story is fun and makes me smile, but it's how it connects people—and, more specifically, my friends that I left behind in New Jersey—that makes it special to me. Recently, we had to deal with someone who took the fun away from the game for us. They trolled us until we stopped playing for a while. The gamer turned out to be a fellow student who walked amongst us. Initially, I set out to expose them and to bring attention to a larger issue that plagues gamers, but I don't want to keep the cycle of toxicity going.

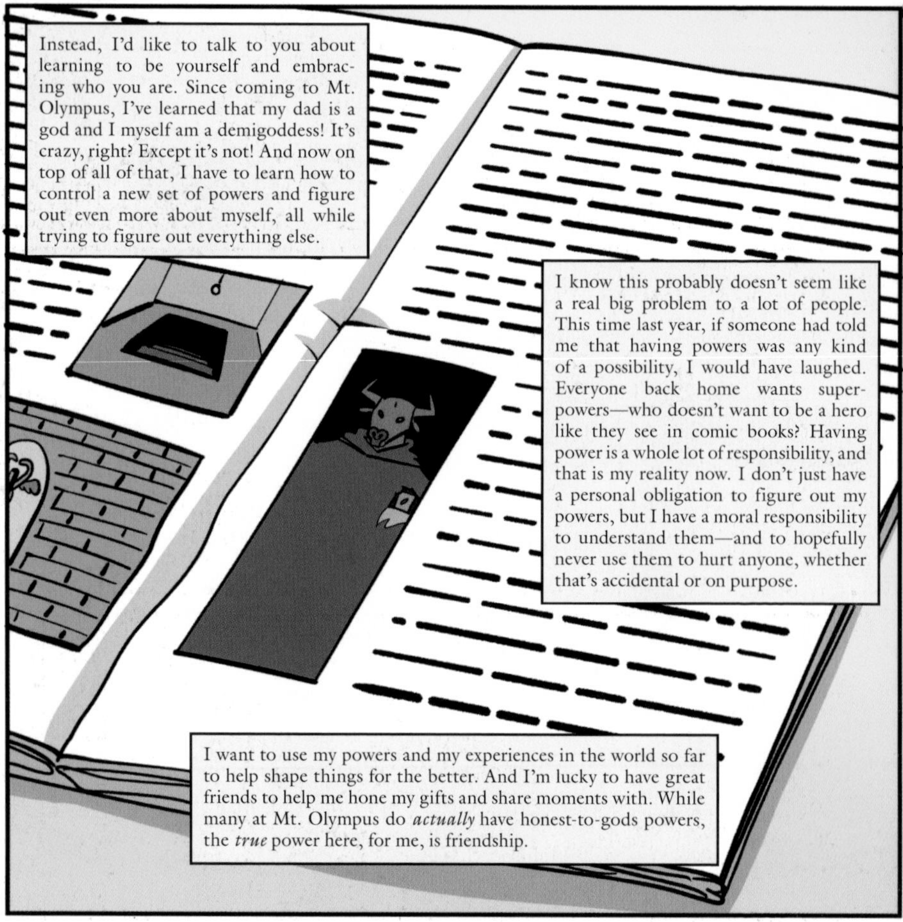
Instead, I'd like to talk to you about learning to be yourself and embracing who you are. Since coming to Mt. Olympus, I've learned that my dad is a god and I myself am a demigoddess! It's crazy, right? Except it's not! And now on top of all of that, I have to learn how to control a new set of powers and figure out even more about myself, all while trying to figure out everything else.
I know this probably doesn't seem like a real big problem to a lot of people. This time last year, if someone had told me that having powers was any kind of a possibility, I would have laughed. Everyone back home wants superpowers—who doesn't want to be a hero like they see in comic books? Having power is a whole lot of responsibility, and that is my reality now. I don't just have a personal obligation to figure out my powers, but I have a moral responsibility to understand them—and to hopefully never use them to hurt anyone, whether that's accidental or on purpose.
I want to use my powers and my experiences in the world so far to help shape things for the better. And I'm lucky to have great friends to help me hone my gifts and share moments with. While many at Mt. Olympus do *actually* have honest-to-gods powers, the *true* power here, for me, is friendship.

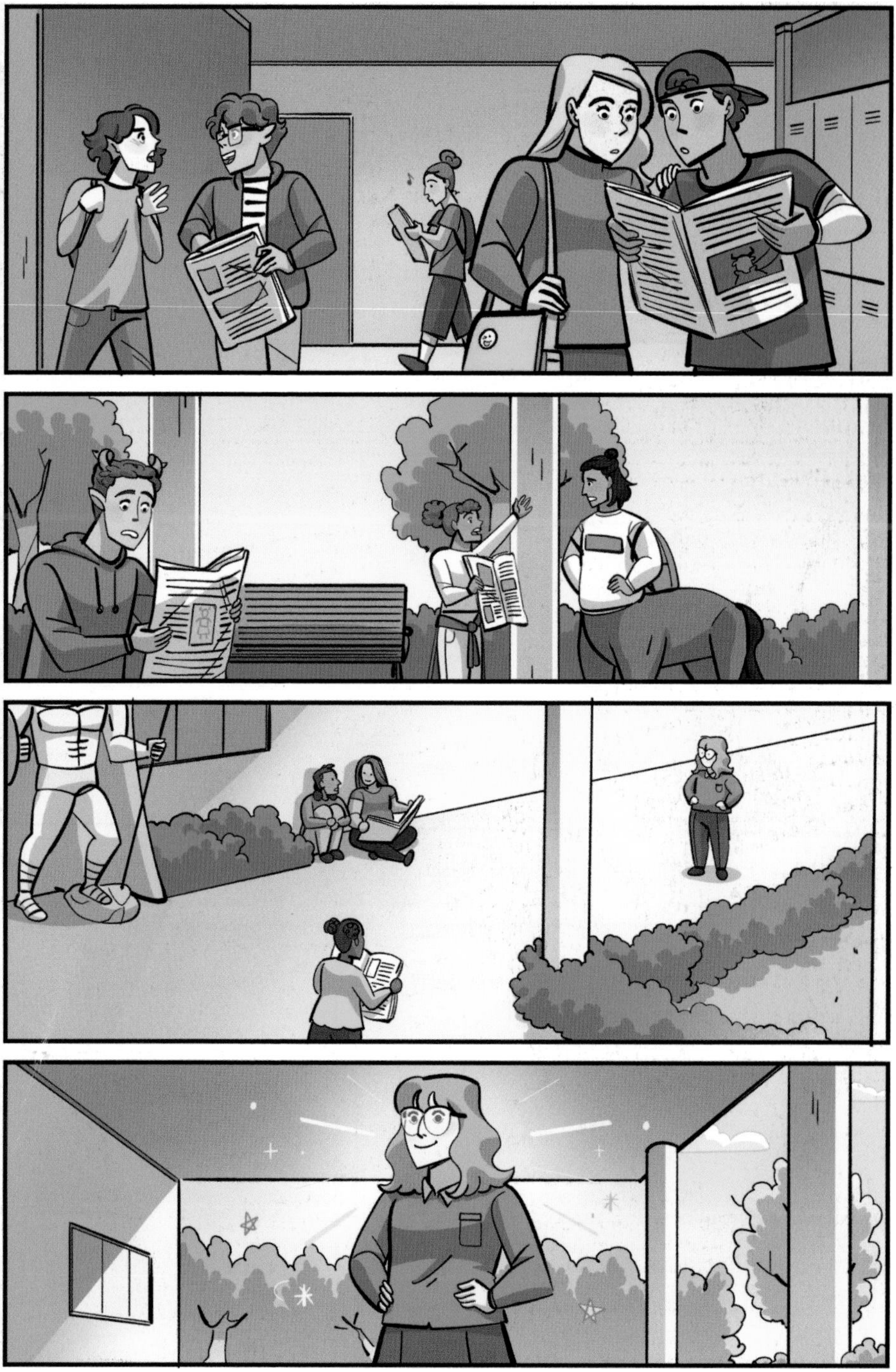

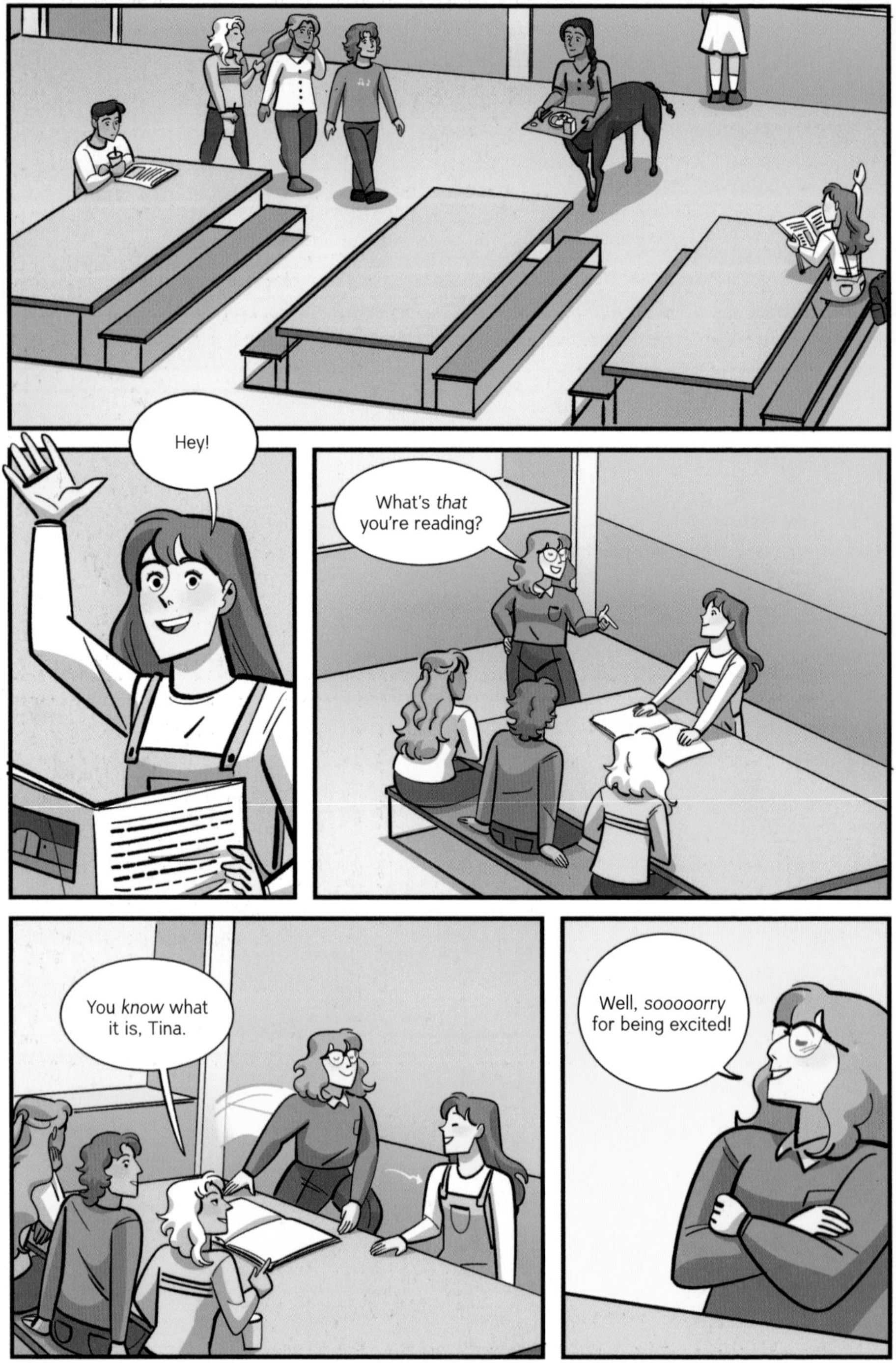
Hey!
What's *that* you're reading?
You *know* what it is, Tina.
Well, *sooooorry* for being excited!

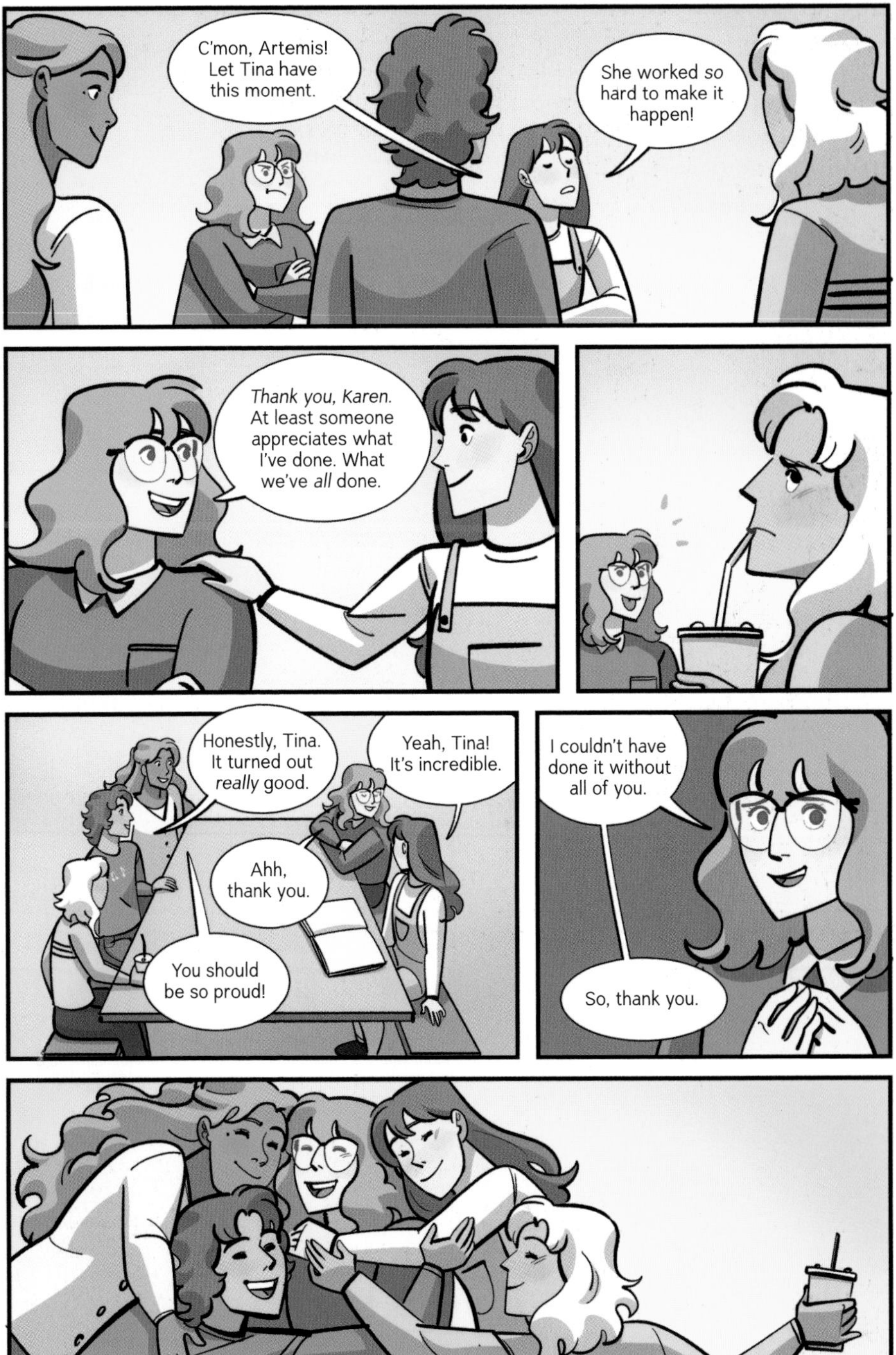
C'mon, Artemis! Let Tina have this moment.
She worked *so* hard to make it happen!
Thank you, Karen. At least someone appreciates what I've done. What we've *all* done.
Honestly, Tina. It turned out *really* good.
Yeah, Tina! It's incredible.
Ahh, thank you.
You should be so proud!
I couldn't have done it without all of you.
So, thank you.

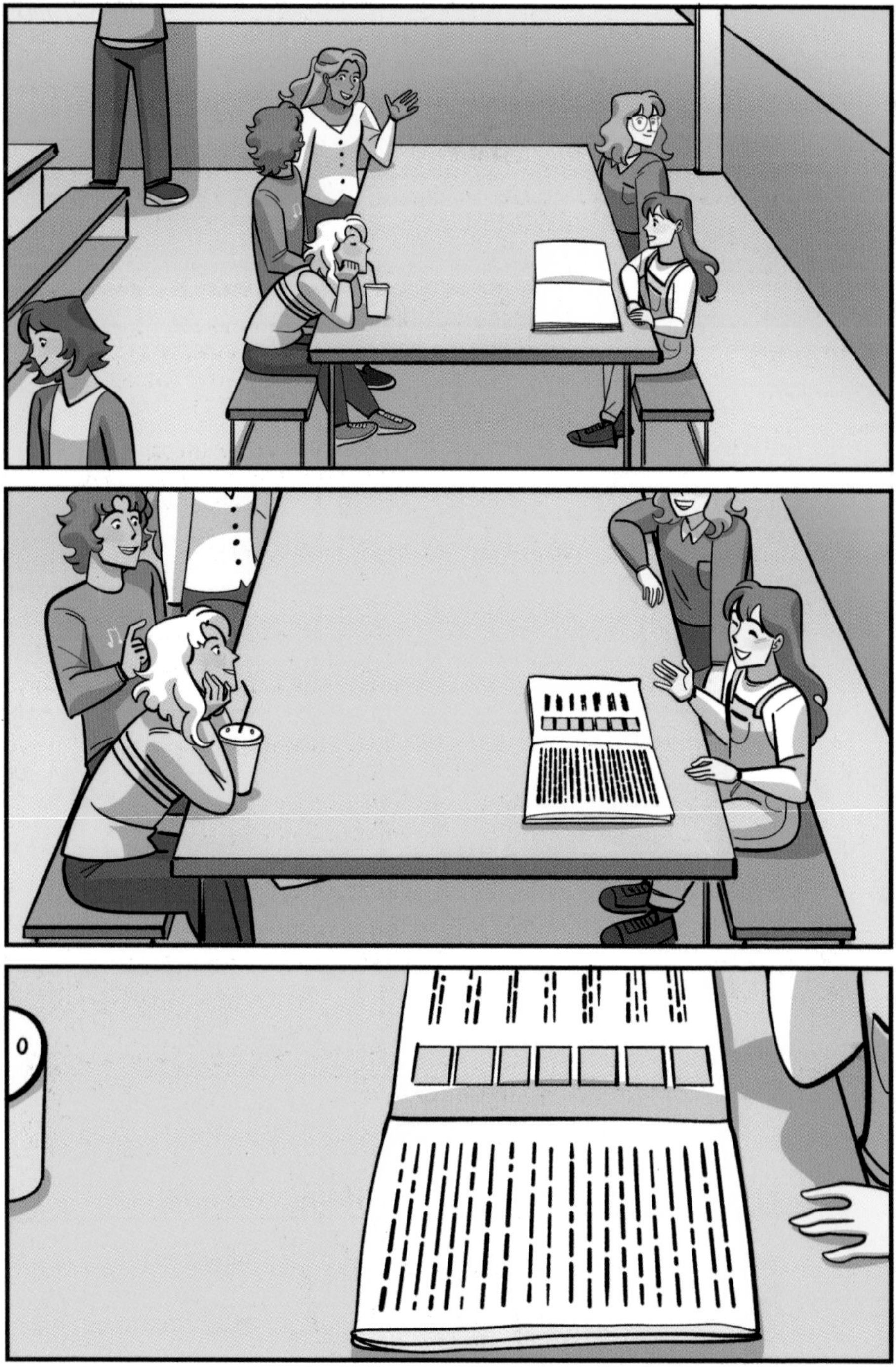

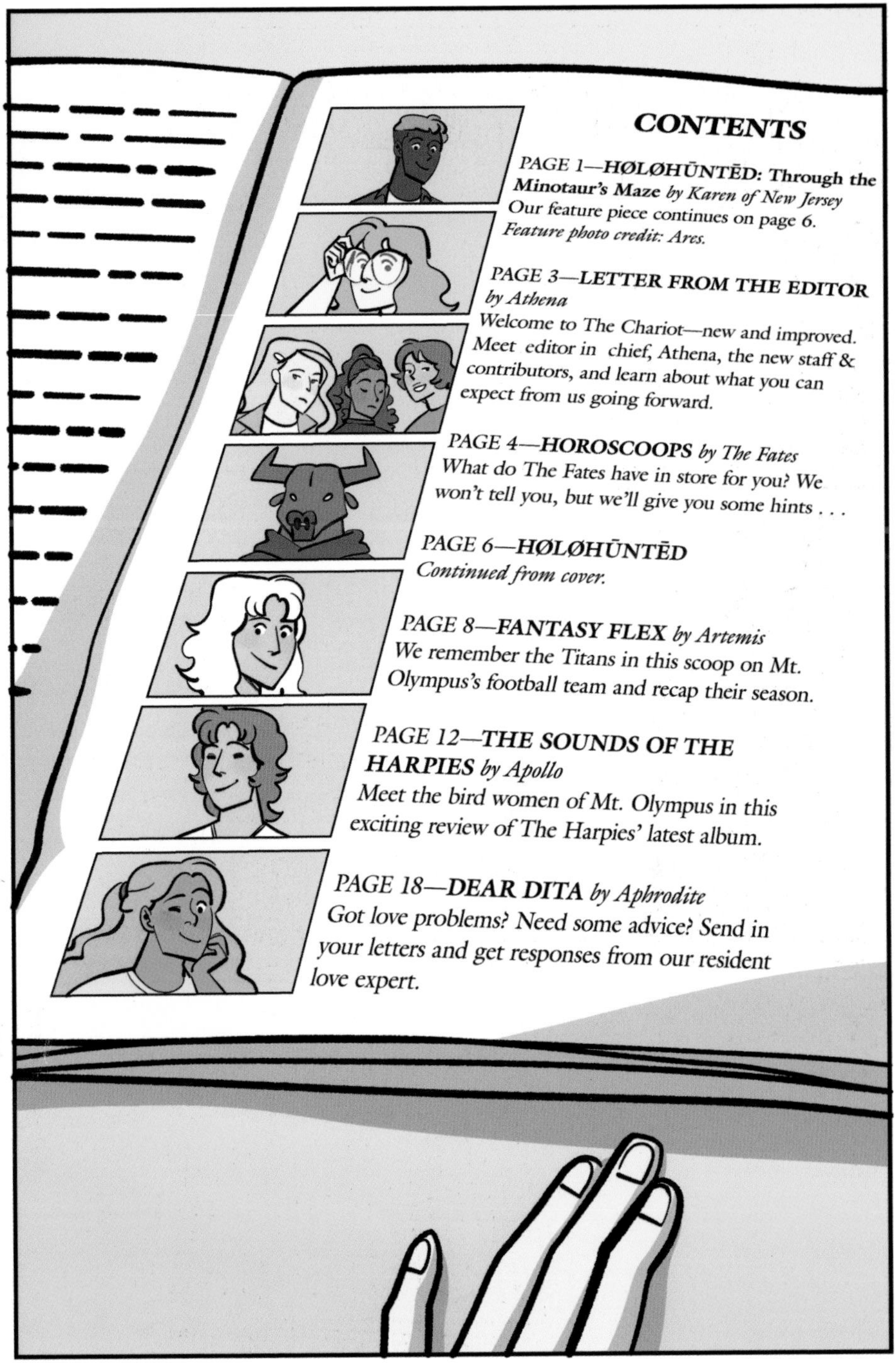
CONTENTS
PAGE 1—HØLØHŪNTĒD: Through the Minotaur's Maze by Karen of New Jersey
Our feature piece continues on page 6.
Feature photo credit: Ares.
PAGE 3—LETTER FROM THE EDITOR by Athena
Welcome to The Chariot—new and improved. Meet editor in chief, Athena, the new staff & contributors, and learn about what you can expect from us going forward.
PAGE 4—HOROSCOOPS by The Fates
What do The Fates have in store for you? We won't tell you, but we'll give you some hints . . .
PAGE 6—HØLØHŪNTĒD
Continued from cover.
PAGE 8—FANTASY FLEX by Artemis
We remember the Titans in this scoop on Mt. Olympus's football team and recap their season.
PAGE 12—THE SOUNDS OF THE HARPIES by Apollo
Meet the bird women of Mt. Olympus in this exciting review of The Harpies' latest album.
PAGE 18—DEAR DITA by Aphrodite
Got love problems? Need some advice? Send in your letters and get responses from our resident love expert.

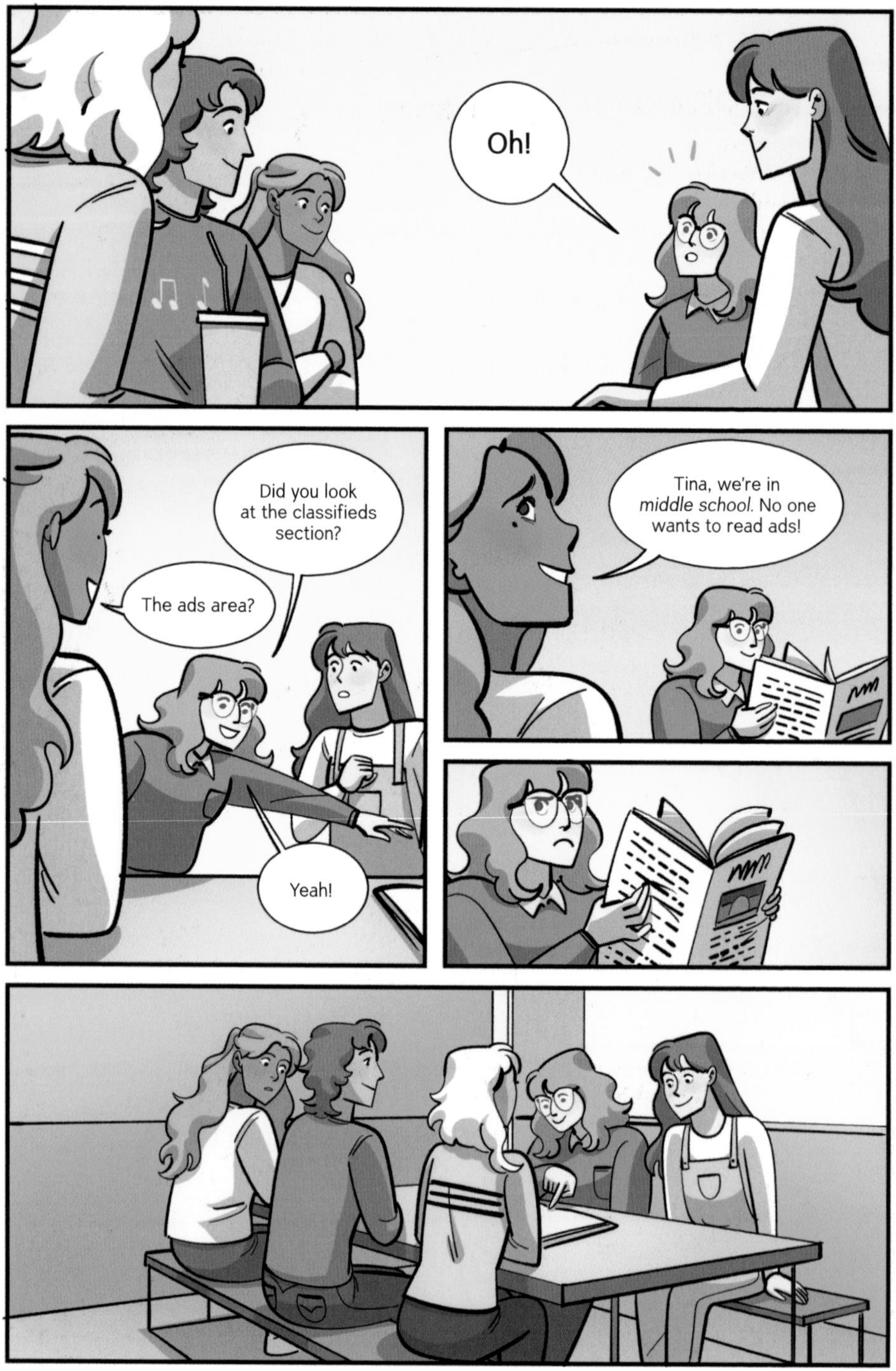
Oh!
Did you look at the classifieds section?
The ads area?
Yeah!
Tina, we're in *middle school*. No one wants to read ads!

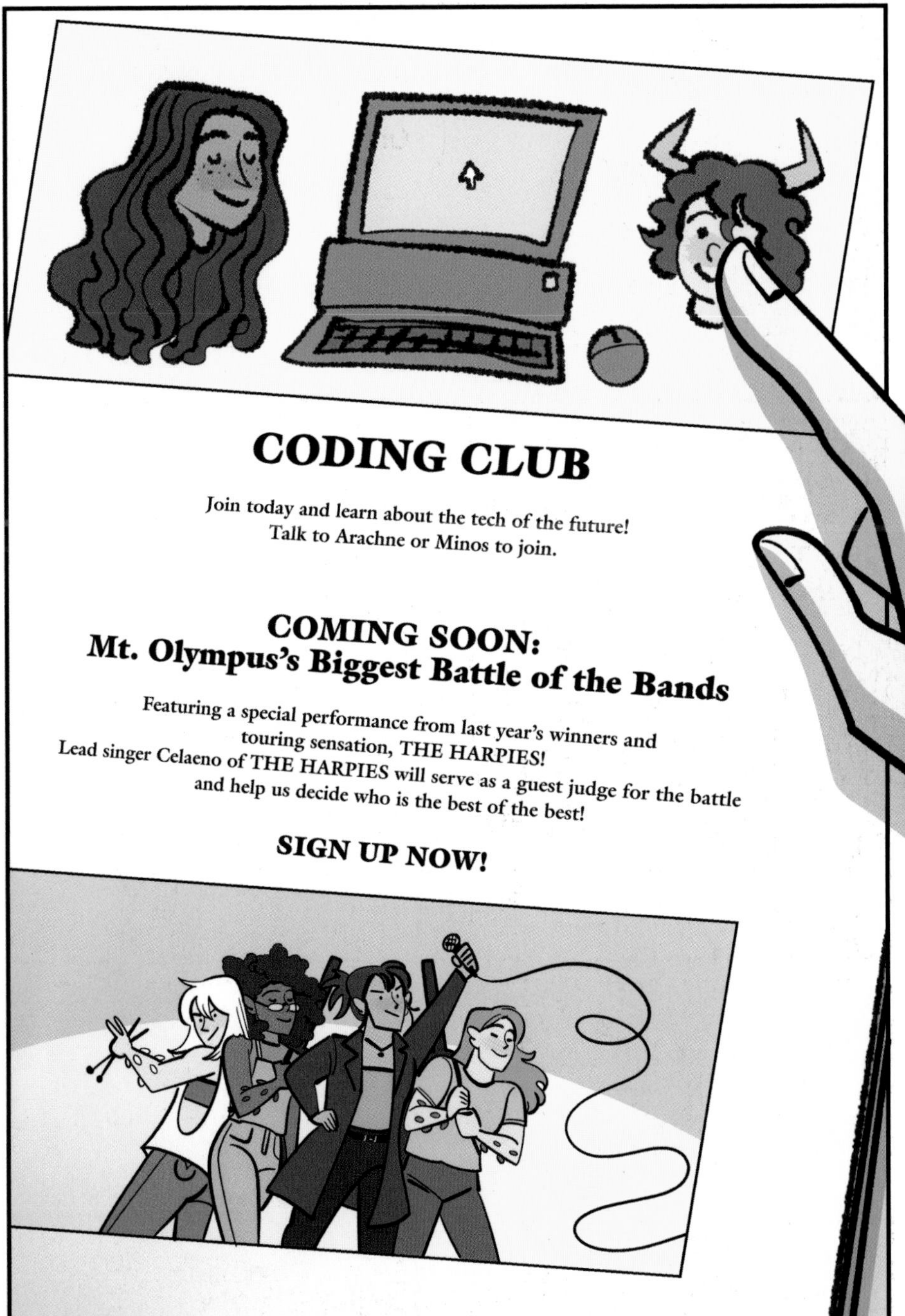
CODING CLUB
Join today and learn about the tech of the future!
Talk to Arachne or Minos to join.
COMING SOON:
Mt. Olympus's Biggest Battle of the Bands
Featuring a special performance from last year's winners and touring sensation, THE HARPIES!
Lead singer Celaeno of THE HARPIES will serve as a guest judge for the battle and help us decide who is the best of the best!
SIGN UP NOW!

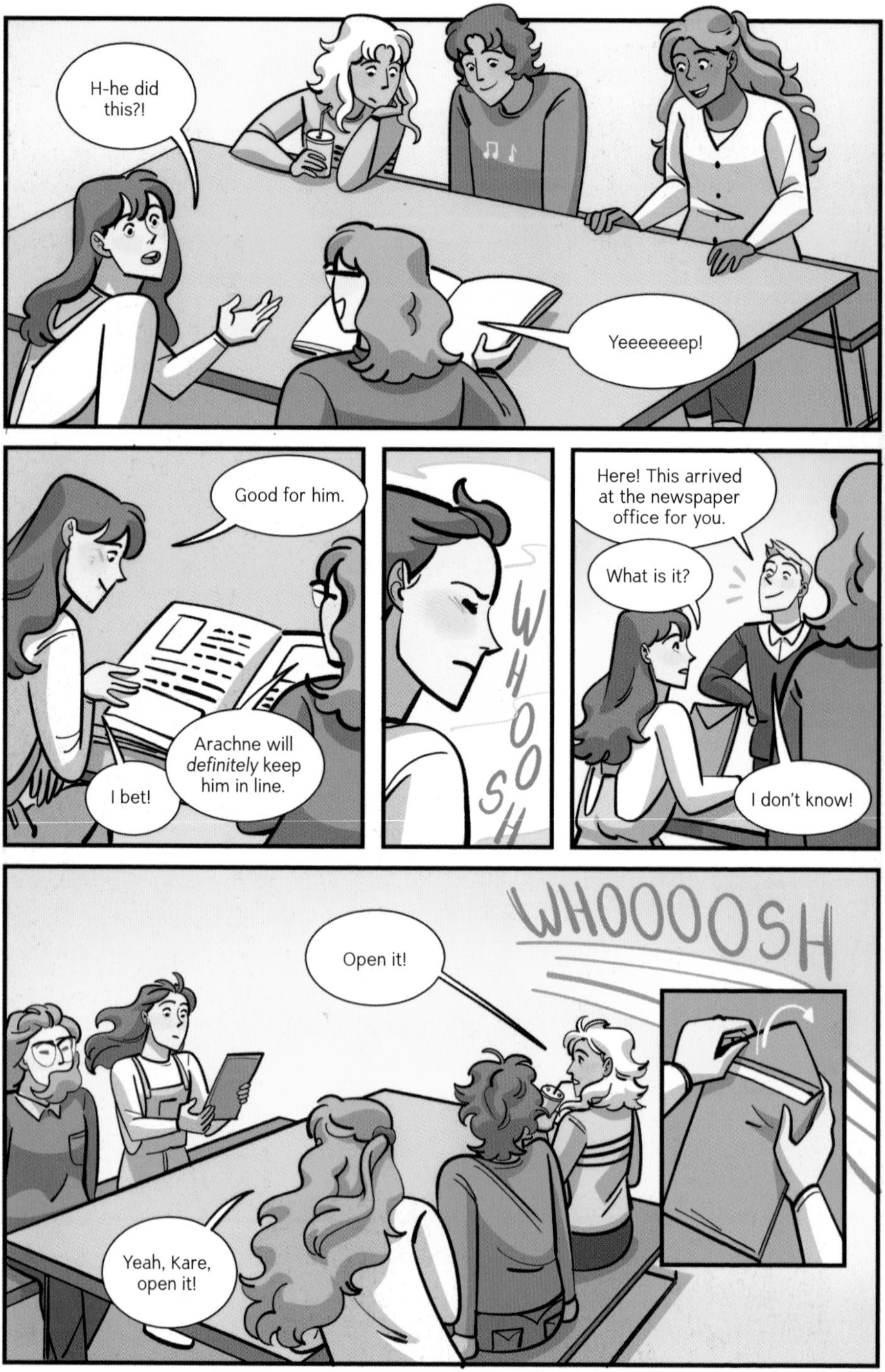
H-he did this?!
Yeeeeeeep!
Good for him.
I bet!
Arachne will *definitely* keep him in line.
WHOOOSH
Here! This arrived at the newspaper office for you.
What is it?
I don't know!
WHOOOOSH
Open it!
Yeah, Kare, open it!

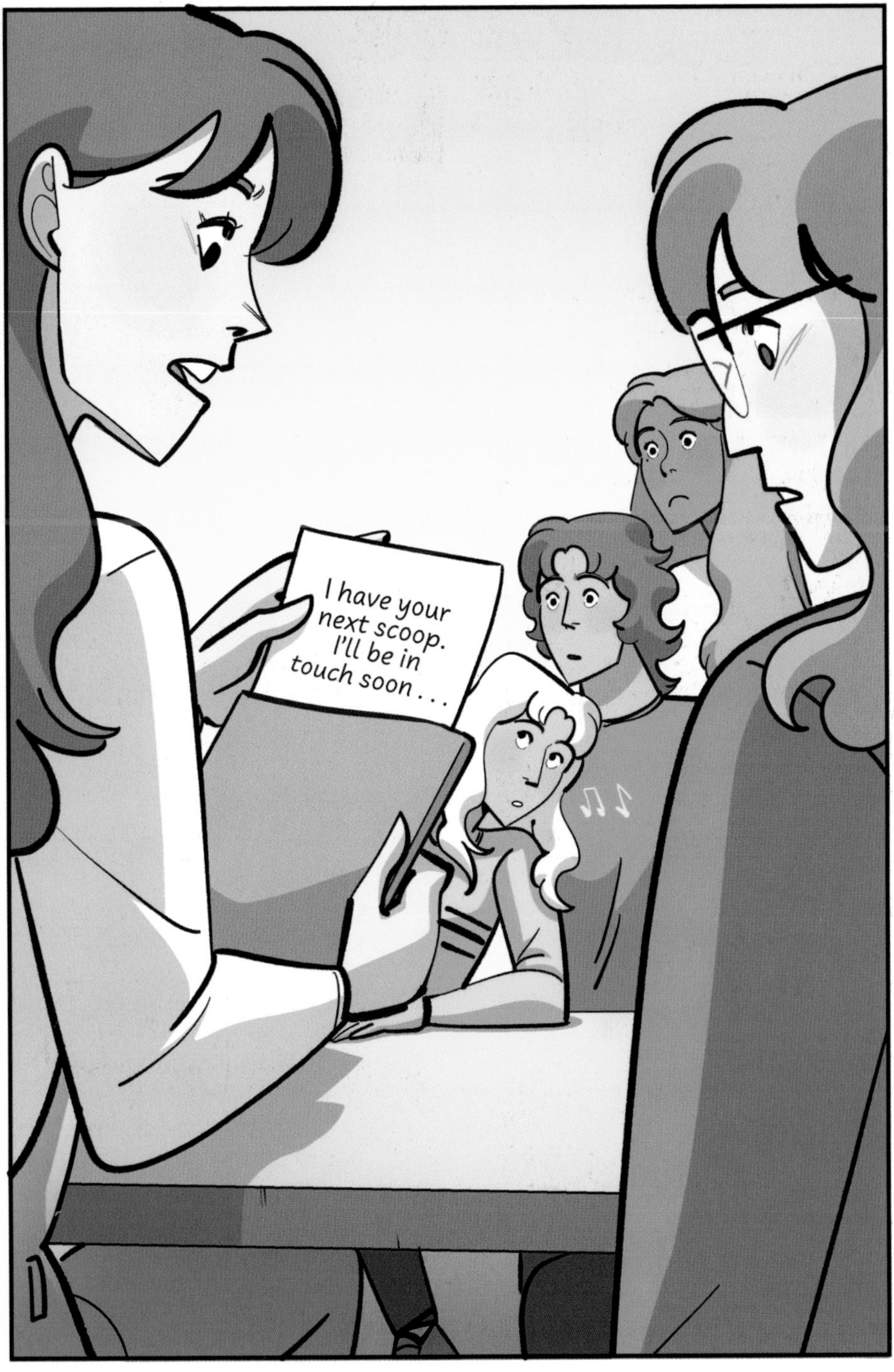
I have your next scoop. I'll be in touch soon . . .

KAREN'S MYTHOLOGY NOTES!!!

Ares seems all tough on the outside, but he's actually a big softy? He REALLY cares about Jeff and making sure he's safe. I get a good vibe from him... ♡

ARES

Ares is the god of war. This god has a love of violence and the battlefield. Ares is the oldest son of Zeus and Hera, and has two sisters, Hebe, the goddess of youth, and Eileithyia, the goddess of childbirth. Ares is known for fighting and having a bad temper. Even though many gods disliked him, he was loved by women. He fell in love with Aphrodite while she was married to her husband, Hephaestus. Ares is known for his war gear, including his helmet, spear, and Greek armor. He has been known to battle many different gods and demigods. Hercules was one of those gods. Hercules managed to hurt Ares in a fight even though Athena, the goddess of war, protected him.

At first, I was like, ? ? is that a spider girl? ? ? But then I was all like, GO SPIDER GIRL!!! She's just...so cool?

ARACHNE

Born in the village of Hypaepa, Arachne is the daughter of a wool dyer. Arachne has an incredible ability for spinning and weaving. She was known throughout her town for it and boasted frequently about her skills without giving credit to Athena, also the goddess of handicrafts and the arts. In retaliation, Athena decided to disguise herself as an old woman and challenge the girl to a spinning and weaving competition. Once Arachne accepted, Athena unveiled herself to be a goddess. Despite this, Arachne still made the finest tapestry anyone—mortal or god—had ever seen. Athena was so angry at the girl that she hit her over the head, which led to her death. However, something happened afterwards—Arachne turned into a spider! Now she can use her skill as she pleases for all time.

MINOS (THE MINOTAUR)

Asterion, more commonly known as the Minotaur, is a half-man, half-bull creature born of Queen Pasiphae and a white bull. King Minos, Pasiphae's husband, was told by the god Poseidon to kill the bull because Poseidon believed he could make anyone do anything for him. However, King Minos couldn't bring himself to harm it. As punishment, Poseidon cursed Pasiphae to fall in love with the bull. When the Minotaur was born, King Minos locked him away in a labyrinth on the advice of an oracle from Delphi, a sanctuary built to honor the god Apollo. The maze structure was built in Knossos and designed by Daedalus, a craftsman. After King Minos's son was killed in battle by Athenians, Athens sent fourteen youths to the Minotaur every nine years as a sacrifice, as the youths couldn't escape the labyrinth and were devoured. Theseus, a young hero from Athens, volunteered and successfully went through the labyrinth with the help of Ariadne, King Minos's daughter. When he found the Minotaur, they engaged in a heavy battle before the Minotaur was ultimately destroyed.

> Wow, that sounds terriBULL... Minos had a LOT going on in his life...past life? I'm glad he doesn't eat people anymore. 😋
>
> Baby steps!

JEFF

Jeff is a happy-go-lucky student at Mt. Olympus Junior High. He's not in any history books (yet), but he doesn't let that ever get to him. He knows his worth and he strives to be kind and friendly to everyone around him. Besides, who needs a lasting legacy when you have *pancakes*?! Jeff's stepsibling is Ares, and they have a special brotherly bond. Jeff has no powers . . . that he knows of. Unless the Power of Pancakes counts (and he would say that it does).

> I like snacks as much as the next person, but Jeff REALLY likes them. And pancakes? Don't get him started! Can you be addicted to pancakes?

BIBLIOGRAPHY

- Giesecke, Annette. *Classical Mythology A to Z: An Encyclopedia of Gods & Goddesses, Heroes & Heroines, Nymphs, Spirits, Monsters, and Places.* New York: Black Dog & Leventhal, 2020.
- Hamilton, Edith. *Mythology: Timeless Tales of Gods and Heroes.* New York: Black Dog & Leventhal, 2011.
- Kershaw, Stephen, and Victoria Topping. *Mythologica.* Minneapolis: Wide Eyed Editions, 2019.

QUIZ: WHICH CHARACTER FROM *HØLØHŪNTĒR* ARE YOU?

1) WHAT DO MOST PEOPLE CONSIDER YOUR BEST TRAIT?
   A. Your protective nature
   B. Your caring side
   C. Your violent side
   D. You can find anything in seconds
   E. You get back up after being knocked down
   F. Your kindness

2) QUICK! THE HØLØS ARE ATTACKING! WHAT'S YOUR FIRST ACTION?!
   A. Pick up a weapon and lead the charge
   B. Help the captain as their backup
   C. BLAST THEIR ROBO BUTTS BACK TO WHEREVER THEY CAME FROM
   D. Find out where these Høløs are coming from
   E. Get a blaster and start firing away
   F. Try not to hurt anyone TOO badly

3) WHAT DO YOU WANT TO BE WHEN YOU GROW UP?
   A. A leader
   B. You don't remember
   C. An artist
   D. A musician
   E. An athlete
   F. A writer

4) WHAT'S YOUR FAVORITE LEVEL IN *HØLØHŪNTĒR*?
   A. Capture the Flag
   B. Deathmatch
   C. ALL OF THEM
   D. Elimination
   E. Survival
   F. Escort

5) THE HØLØS HAVE CAPTURED YOU. THERE'S NO WAY TO ESCAPE! WHAT DO YOU DO?

   A. Come up with a course of action with your team
   B. Figure out any riddles or puzzles the Høløs may have
   C. INSULT THEM: "SILLY ROBO JERKS. LET US GO!!!"
   D. Calculate how much time the team has until the Høløs fry you
   E. Try to pick the locks of your chains
   F. Get scared, maybe cry a bit (MAYBE)

6) YOU'RE A NATIONAL HERO FOR DEFEATING THE HØLØS! HOW DO YOU CELEBRATE?

   A. Eat MASSIVE amounts of cake
   B. Sit down with a good book
   C. Go out on the town! THE NIGHT IS YOUNG!
   D. Update your systems
   E. Join the night out on the town
   F. Call your parents and let them know you're okay!

RESULTS

Mostly As—You are MAJOR HERNANDEZ
You're a natural-born leader! Major Hernandez is the top-ranking officer in Squadron 1.002. You're a person who wants everyone you care about to be okay, but you won't stand for nonsense either! You're supportive but have strong boundaries.

Mostly Bs—You are CAPTAIN LISBETH WELSH
You're a caring person, but you aren't afraid to kick butt when you need to. Captain Lisbeth Welsh lost her memory, but found a place alongside her fellow Hunters. You're usually down for a quiet night rather than a loud one, and you know a good book when you read one.

Mostly Cs—You are CAPTAIN HACKLER
You are the LIFE of the party! Captain Hackler is bloodthirsty, carefree, and a criminal. However, that won't stop people from loving you. You're 100% the wildest person imaginable, and you are the funniest person in any room.

Mostly Ds—You are FIRST LIEUTENANT IVAD (INTER-VERSATILE ARTIFICIAL DROID)

You're the smartest person anyone knows! First Lieutenant IVAD is an artificial droid, yet has the biggest heart. You enjoy research and also music (of all genres). You're fiercely independent, but you love working as a team and sharing your knowledge with everyone.

Mostly Es—You are FIRST LIEUTENANT HOLLI AITCH

You're super chill and not afraid of hard work! Holli Aitch used to be the golden child of the Hunters, but after seeing her squadron get destroyed by Høløs, she struggled to continue as team leader, paralyzed by the fear of being responsible for her team's safety. You work hard to make sure everyone's okay. Don't forget to take time out for yourself.

Mostly Fs—You are SECOND LIEUTENANT AYALA WEST

You're the newbie! You're kind, ambitious, and happy to be learning all you can to figure out who YOU are. Ayala West has seen the destruction that Høløs have wreaked on her planet, and she wants revenge! However, you're still a little scared about fighting; but if someone hurts you (or your loved ones), you'll make them PAY!!!!